The Butterfly's Secret, Book 2 of
The Butterfly Series © Josephine DeFalco 2025
All rights reserved.

Cover Design by Amy Albright

Flint Hills Publishing

Topeka, Kansas
Tucson, Arizona
www.flinthillspublishing.com

Printed in the U.S.A.

Paperback Book: 978-1-953583-96-3
Electronic Book 978-1-953583-97-0

The Butterfly's Secret

Book 2
of the
Butterfly Series

Josephine DeFalco

Flint Hills Publishing

DEDICATION

The Butterfly Series is dedicated to the Appalachian families who sacrificed their homes, livelihood, and heritage for the construction of the Blue Ridge Parkway. You gave your all so that others could know the beauty of the mountains you called home.

.

Chapter 1

Time

Time holds a lofty position. We usually run out of it, but when we have too much, it clings to our hands like biscuit dough. Sometimes, we want time to stand still or pass quickly and it will do none of that. It marks the generations and moves forward with its own agenda, never apologizing for its reign over our mortality.

🦋 🦋 🦋

Almost fifteen years had passed since Papaw's farm was the place I called home. I took ownership of the biggest remaining bedroom upstairs and made it mine. It overlooked the front lawn where I viewed the comings and goings, tractors rumbling by on their way to a nearby field and storm clouds pushing in. I pulled back Mamaw's faded curtains and watched the postman place the day's mail in her extended hand. Their chatter filled the air while a distant motor or engine whined as it worked. The wind picked up the chickens' cheerful cackles, and the two pigs snorted for joy when Papaw's farm hand, Archie, stopped by with a bucket of garden leftovers. These were the sounds I missed when Mama pulled me off the farm to grow up in New Jersey. This was home.

I released the curtain and sat on the edge of the sagging bed, watching them flutter with the breeze. The thin cotton fabric was marked with a print pattern from my childhood. My feelings were mixed about replacing them, knowing part of me wanted to keep to the past as if I'd never left the farm, and part of me wanted a fresh beginning.

🦋 🦋 🦋

John and I picked up dating where we left off five years earlier. By our country standards, we were getting on in age, nearing the end of our twenties. It was almost as if we'd never been apart and fell right back into being a couple.

"Let's go back to that Italian restaurant, the one where your mother had her rehearsal dinner," he suggested.

"Oh, you mean DeMarco's Italian Garden."

"Isn't that the only Italian place in town?"

He was right. There wasn't much to pick from in Mountain Grove. Years ago, Mr. and Mrs. DeMarco passed the management onto cousin Giuseppe. I heard the food was still good and it would be nice to see the old place again. As I expected, John ordered the same plate of meatballs and spaghetti he ordered five years earlier. Once that boy latched onto something, there was no letting go, not unlike our relationship. This time he threw in a bottle of wine and an appetizer of clam-stuffed mushrooms he knew I adored. It was almost too perfect until the waiter informed John he had a phone call.

When he returned, he frowned apologetically. "I'm sorry, Leandra. That was one of the hired hands on the evening shift. Our prize bull is sick and needs help. I may have to call a vet in and cut our date short."

I couldn't believe it. The night was turning out to be a repeat of our first failed date so many years before. We drove to his farm in near silence, but he was noticeably fidgety. This man had a strange relationship with his cattle. Maybe he was calculating his losses if that bull up and died. I had heard men could die if their testicles got twisted. Could be that might happen to a bull. When we got there, he opened the truck door and led me by the hand to the barn.

"Well, at least we're not delivering a calf like our previous failed date," I said. "But if this involves your bull's privates in any way, you'll get no help from me."

He said nothing to defend his position.

The barn door stood open with a faint light penetrating the night. I rounded the corner to see a small table with two chairs. The table, draped with a checkered cloth, displayed a glowing kerosene lantern and two champagne glasses. Next to the glasses rested a milk bucket filled with ice and an uncorked bottle. A straw bale was nearby, also draped with a checkered cloth.

He sat me down on the bale.

"Where's the bull?" I asked. My heart beat so fast I could hardly speak.

He reached for a small box hiding on the seat of his chair. John dropped to one knee and took both my hands in his. "It won't be a glamorous life," he said in his own country boy way. "But you know I love you with all my heart. I'll be good to you, Leandra, and we'll make a good life. Will you be this farmer's wife?"

I said the stupidest thing in my entire life. "There's no bull?"

"No bull," he replied. "Just my loving heart." And with that, I began crying and blubbering. Somewhere in there I said yes. He slipped a gold band on my left hand with the largest diamond I ever saw sitting right on top. It looked to be over half a carat with two small rubies on either side.

"It was Grandma's," he said with pride. "I know you didn't know her, but she had a happy marriage and wanted my bride to have her ring for good luck. Mom's been saving it all this time. Let's open the champagne. Oh, and Mrs. DeMarco snuck a couple of pastries in my truck when you weren't looking. She says they are supposed to look like butterflies and called them, well, I can't remember, something in Italian."

I looked down at the little cakes with their creamy filling. "Farfalla," I replied, remembering when Sal and I were in high school and he bought one for me at my first Italian festival in New Jersey. All that seemed so far away now. I thought Sal would remain a part of me forever, yet already my memories of our times together were melding into a fading past. "John Tucker, you've been lying and sneaking around for weeks, haven't you? And I'm sure your parents had something to do with this."

"Mom and Dad said any woman willing to deliver a calf or help a sick bull was worth keeping." There, in the barn filled with hay, inhaling the light fragrance of manure, and in the company of a few selected heifers, we held hands and made wedding plans for our future. This would be my new life.

🦋 🦋 🦋

John and I decided on a church wedding and Mamaw couldn't have been any happier if she was a preacher with a full collection basket. Before I knew it, we were shopping for a wedding dress.

I wore a white lace dress, a haunting thought to this day. In no way was I entitled to wear white, but I convinced myself my life in Perth Amboy was a death of sorts. Something I wanted to remember and grieve, like it was a completely different Leandra, vanished and gone. The child I birthed out of wedlock two years ago and buried last spring near the butterfly bush was not forgotten, but she was a memory meant only for me.

Mama and Roger dropped in for the wedding. Like I always say, funerals are mostly what brings folks together. But I guess she would have felt guilty missing her only daughter's wedding. She put on airs like the loving mother of the bride, though she had nothing to do with the wedding plans. Since I no longer lived with them in New Jersey and wasn't tormented daily with Mama's drinking and carrying on, I could look at Mama and my stepfather with objective eyes. My hate began to wane. I chose to pity them more than anything and was grateful they joined us. I believe Mamaw called that grace.

We hosted the reception in one of the ranch outbuildings with John's steers lowing in the nearby fields. He moved the tractors and field equipment and shuffled in tables and chairs collected from neighbors. We drove away in his farm truck with strings of shoes tied behind it and, despite our Baptist upbringing, most everyone was pickled on homemade wine or spirits as they waved us goodbye. I never felt so at home.

I am ashamed to say, I was thinking of my sweet Greg on my wedding day, well aware it had been the right decision to disappear from his life. As Mamaw and Mama pinned my veil, I wondered how many babies he and his beautiful college wife were raising. I bet he ran his own law practice or worked as a partner in a big firm. I hoped he found happiness and I wasn't even a memory after what I did to him. He would never know his mama paid me to sacrifice my high school sweetheart. To her, I was trash, a bottom feeder with an alcoholic mother living next to the railroad tracks who bought her party dresses at the thrift store. Greg would never know how much I wanted to be with him. That's what pained me the most. She was sure to have made our lives a living hell if we stayed together, and I wouldn't let her do that to him. I couldn't deny I didn't love John the same way I loved Greg. But John and I would take care of each other and build a life worth living. That's what I needed most right now. I made it clear to John, marriage or not, I would continue helping Papaw and

Mamaw since the farm would be mine, or ours, someday. John, being the good man he was, thought it was a smart thing to do for the family.

I divided my time between the two farms, sometimes forgetting if I was coming or going. One Sunday night, we were watching a movie on color television, a treat I bought for Papaw since he'd been admiring the one at our farm. Color television was a new invention. Picture yourself being color blind, then getting a new television and being able to see folks in their real skin color, knowing what color lipstick the lead woman painted on, or the color tie Cary Grant was wearing. It was a big deal.

"They don't look much like proper college girls," Mamaw commented. We were watching *Where the Boys Are* with bikini-clad Connie Francis singing her way through spring break, or what they used to call Easter vacation.

Aunt Addie put in her two cents. "Shameful the way they're dressed. Why, what if I had dressed like that when I was a college student?"

I immediately had a visual nightmare of Aunt Addie wearing a swimsuit. She had started teaching school in our parts when it was still a one-room building. Fact was, I'd never seen her bare knees.

Outta nowhere, Papaw called out, "Leandra, what happened to yo' college education? Zat eva goin' to happen?"

I gagged on my popped corn. Where did that come from? I had all but given up on my dream of being a college girl. I looked at John and shrugged my shoulders. "I got a husband now, Papaw."

"What's that got to do with your schooling?" John asked. "Don't be blaming me if you don't get an education."

"You expect me to do both? How do I divide my time between school and two farms?"

"They got a fine college in Asheville," Papaw said. "Not too far to drive. You'd be following in your Aunt Addie's footsteps."

Mamaw put down her embroidery. "Newspaper says they just made that school into a four-year college, whateva that means."

"That would take a lot of time, Papaw. When would I work your books? And the bookkeeping at our farm? Do my homework? Take care of John?"

Mamaw waved her hand at me. "John's a big boy and can take care of himself. You're just makin' excuses, Leandra. Get on with it before you start havin' babies." When she said that in front of everybody, I blushed barn red, shut up, and went back to watching the movie.

Next day, the conversation started again. It appeared everyone felt obligated to nag me about driving into Asheville to visit the university. Our washing machine broke, so I drove over to Mamaw's to finish the last two loads. While the wash was running, I figured I'd return the favor.

"Mamaw, I'm going to turn the dirt in your garden so you can start some seeds. Least I can do to pay you back."

"Thank you, darlin'," came the reply. "The men are out in the barn, and they can help you find a shovel and hoe."

I found Archie standing near the tools. "Archie, is this the best shovel he's got?" I held up a rusted tool with a cracked handle bound by a rag.

"Yes, Miss Leandra. You knows he don't throw nothin' away until it's broke in two. And I hears you is goin' to college. Fine thing for you to do. You always was a smart one."

"Archie, where did you hear that? Papaw?"

I marched around to the other side of the tractor they were repairing, but he escaped my wrath by scooting under the front end. I stood there like a young rooster ready to pick a fight.

Papaw's voice spilled out from under the tractor. "Hand me that wrench by your feet." I looked down at the giant piece of shiny metal, wanting to clobber him with it. Instead, I gently place it in his calloused open hand.

"You know I was talkin' to Mamaw 'bout yo college degree."

"I bet you were," I said. "No one seems to care what I'm thinking." He ignored my comment.

"Mamaw and I want to help you get yo' degree." I was stunned into silence, truly a rare thing. "Now don't you go thinkin' that's without you owin' up something."

"Papaw, what are you up to?"

His head popped out from under the tractor. He looked up at me, flat on his back, with oil and grime all over his tan lined face and denim overalls. "You have a head for numbers, Leandra. I watch you porin' over those books we keep. That was never somethin' I could do. I didn't get past the eighth grade." His eyes were shiny and watery. "Addie did a fine job managing the books, but you go beyond that. You're always figurin' out how we can make more money with less work. Thinkin' like that could help both our farms. Get yoself a business degree. Someday this farm will be yours."

I conceded, knowing there was a big opportunity tapping me on the shoulder. It was more like a slap upside the head. The thought of going to college with a husband and two part-time jobs was already making me weary.

"Papaw, I gave up on my dream a long time ago. Here you come along messin' with my mind. But, just to make you happy, I'll visit the university in a couple of weeks and look around."

"Don't have a couple of weeks," he piped up and rolled back under the tractor. "The fall semester starts right quick. Mamaw had them mail us a book of classes. Have her show it to you before you leave."

I shook my head. "Papaw, you haven't changed a bit. Always bossin' someone around."

I got down on my hands and knees, crammed my head under the tractor and gave him a kiss on the cheek. I would turn that garden dirt before I saw that catalog, or Mamaw's garden would never get done. Shovel after shovel, I pictured myself walking from class to class, books in my arms, while all around me the trees turned gold and red. I would ask my teachers thoughtful questions, maybe make new friends. Finally, I would be a college co-ed.

🦋 🦋 🦋

In late August 1963, I started my fall semester. I drove into Asheville for freshman orientation. We were a gaggle of twenty wide-eyed scholars—me, nearly the oldest—trying to follow our campus maps while a more experienced student, her mouth going a hundred miles an hour, herded us from one building to the next. I needed to buy new sneakers and learn how to sprint, or I would never make it on time from one class to another.

At one point during our tour, our heads turned toward a larger group of students, all yelling and screaming and carrying signs. They sat in a tight circle while a Negro woman spoke into a megaphone.

A girl standing next to me, looking almost as country as me, waved and interrupted our speaker. "What is that? What are they doing?"

"Oh, it's just a protest," the student leader said with a dismissive tone. Like we saw those every day. But the girl persisted.

"What are they protesting?"

The leader seemed perturbed. "I understand it's about colored rights," she replied. "Part of college life is learning to challenge society and redefine mores."

The girl whispered in my ear, "What's a more-aye?"

We started walking again, trying to keep up with our leader.

"Don't know," I panted. "Guess we're supposed to learn that in college."

My attention wandered from the tour back to the prior week when Mamaw had waved a newspaper in my face. "Look at this, I just don't know what is goin' on." The paper reported police were beating Negros with billy clubs for unlawful assembly. Mamaw's voice was shrill. "How can they beat another human being like that? This isn't what Jesus wants, nobody wants this. Lord only knows what really happened."

Mamaw took the paper and crammed it in the trash bin like she never hoped to see that kind of pain again. It riled her, just like everyone else in the world.

At the time, I'd thought maybe heated temperatures flared tempers at home and at school. But that first day on a college campus, I reconsidered. The demonstration I witnessed pitched me head-first into life in the big city.

I wasn't sure why people were fussing. I mean, Archie was a Negro, and we didn't treat him differently from any other person workin' on Papaw's farm. But I got to thinking maybe it was because he treated himself differently, because other folks had been mean to him. He never took meals with us, saying he preferred to eat by himself. He wouldn't dream of using our inside toilets, and always made water out back behind an abandoned shed until Papaw got fed up and built him his own outhouse. I never really thought about it until the day I watched the protesters. I realized these college folks made a good point. College wasn't about getting an education. We were learning to get along in the world.

Before our meeting day finished, our leader reminded us anything that could go wrong would do just that while we were working on our degree. It would all get in our way, but we shouldn't give up. We were told to keep pushing until a diploma was in our hand. Sure enough, she was right and as usual, life got in my way.

🦋 🦋 🦋

It wasn't but a couple of months into college when I came home from school and heard the phone ringing as soon as I stepped out of the old Pontiac. "You gonna get that?" I called out to anyone who would listen, but no one answered.

I left my books and purse in the sedan and raced inside to grab the phone.

"Leandra, thank God." Mamaw was nearly breathless on the other end. "It's Addie. Get here quick." I hadn't heard that kind of panic in Mamaw's voice since Mama went into labor. It took a lot to rattle Mamaw.

I dashed back to the car, whipped it around, and was lucky enough to see one of the hired hands walking toward the hay shed.

"A.J.," I shouted, "tell John there's an emergency at Papaw's and I'm runnin' over there."

He nodded to acknowledge.

Addie had weakened over the years. Her mind was sharp as ever, but her little body had slowed down. I threw open the front door and caught sight of her cane at the bottom of the stairs. My eyes moved up about halfway and there was Mamaw, cradling Addie in her arms. My aunt looked like a child's rag doll in a cotton dress carelessly discarded on the steps.

"Stay with her." She handed me a bloody dishtowel. "Hold pressure on that head cut. I called an ambulance. I'm gonna go out front and wave them down."

"Papaw?" I asked.

"In town. He needed supplies. He doesn't even know."

We switched positions and I slid underneath Addie, taking on the hard edges of the stairs. I heard her groan. Under the circumstances, that was a good sign.

"I will try to reposition you but stop me if it hurts too much. You hear me?"

I got an indignant, "I hear ya."

I wanted to laugh at her cranky attitude.

While I comforted her, she told me in an ever-weakening voice that death was coming, and she had a few things to say. She reminded me how proud I made her as her niece and promised me I would do great things with my life. We cried together telling each other what amazing women we were, until the ambulance arrived.

We both knew we would not speak again in this lifetime.

Addie died peacefully at the hospital with me and Mamaw each holding a hand. The doctor said there was a bleed inside her head and not much we could do about it at her age.

Adeline Barker left this world the same way she lived her life: confident, understanding the importance of family and education, and certain where life would take her. She saw the big picture right to the end and expected me to do the same.

We buried Addie next to my troubled little brother Raymond in the afternoon shadow of the butterfly bush. Mamaw said someone had to keep an eye on that boy and Addie was just the one to do it.

Chapter 2

Family

*T*he *old timers say when an elder dies, a new baby is born into the family to take that person's place. I remember when Daddy passed, Mama found out she was expecting my brother, Ray. I imagine someday, a little one will come into this family to replace my body and soul. I think it would be fun to meet that new young'un, before I leave, just to know who was filling my shoes.*

🦋 🦋 🦋

Naturally, when I suspected I was carrying new life, it came as no surprise with Aunt Addie's passing within the same year. I didn't want any fussing just because I was pregnant, so I kept my secret to myself. But, when I flew out of bed one morning and emptied my insides in the toilet, John had a good notion what was happening.

He was sitting straight up in bed when I came out of the bathroom. "Leandra, my heifers don't get sick in the morning when they get pregnant, but I hear women do. Am I going to be a daddy?"

"Probably," I said, wiping my face with a cold washcloth and catching my breath, "because I'm gonna be a mama."

There was a long pause as it sunk in. Then in a heartbeat he was across the bed and staring into my face with those beautiful blue eyes I hoped our baby would have.

"Do I have to do anything?" he asked. "You gonna be all right?"

"I'm fine," I replied, "and I'm sure you've already done what you were supposed to do to get me in this situation. But maybe you can go start breakfast and the coffee. I don't feel much like cooking."

He turned to leave the room, but I stopped him. "John, this stays between us, you understand? Otherwise, everyone will be carryin' on like I'm made of bone china."

Of course, nothing ever slipped past Mamaw. That same week, I wrapped up Papaw's bookkeeping for the month and ran out the door for my afternoon classes. My morning sickness was short-lived, and I was eating like I couldn't fill up. There were days I felt life wearing on me, but with college courses and keeping up with the farms, no one could judge me for turning in early now and then. I raced out the door, headed for the school with a slice of fresh bread slathered in Mamaw's strawberry jam, juggling a glass of milk, books, and my notebook.

"I am gonna be so late!" I roared as I gathered up my energy to move faster.

Mamaw pushed back the screen door, clearing a path for me.

Just as I passed her sweet mouth, she asked, "You plannin' to take off a semesta for yo' baby?"

My glass of milk slipped from my hand. Mamaw's eyes trailed to the shattered glass and wasted milk on the back steps. "Wait, honey, I'll get you anotha one." She hurried back in the house and returned with a thermos. "Drink it all," she told me. "You will need it to keep up your strength."

She kissed me on the forehead and walked back in the kitchen, wearing a smirk on her face. She knew she pulled a fast one, and I left shaking my head. As if I thought I could hide my baby from Mamaw.

By the time I returned from my classes, everyone on both farms knew a baby was joining the family. Seeing how John was over the moon about bein' a daddy, I was proud of him for keeping our secret. For each Old Archie shook my hand and told me he had a reason to keep on livin' and "couldn't wait until a new chil' was toddlin' around the orchard, eatin' apple worms just like Raymond used to do."

I shuddered, recalling that memory.

Mamaw had already volunteered to watch the baby while I was in school.

"Mamaw, you sure you can manage a baby while I'm in class? It's been a few years since we raised Raymond."

"Without Addie to look after—well, I'm replacin' one with anotha. Won't be a problem at all. Besides, a little one will be more entertaining than Addie ever was."

"Addie had her moments," I said. "She was sarcastic for sure. There are times I miss her sassy mouth."

"I do too," Mamaw said. Her voice sounded longing. "She was a good companion all these years, me sweeping in and stealin' her brotha. She pulled her weight and protected this family somethin' fierce. You're a lot like her, you know. I'm sure she's up there in Heaven, pushing you along."

"Hope so," I said. "It will be hard to return to school after this baby."

"We'll figure it out as we go," Mamaw replied.

My sweet Ana in New York, the kind woman who took me in when I was alone and pregnant, would have said the same thing. I realized then, my mama wasn't the best example of womanhood, but time blessed me with many strong women in my life, and I could pass my strength on to those who followed.

❄ ❄ ❄

I expected my first visit to the doctor to be routine. Old Doc Sylvan was a fixture in these hills for as long as I could remember and was almost as old as the Smokey Mountains. He delivered me and Ray, and now he was working on my family. I cringed while he poked and prodded. He finished my exam and straightened the sheet covering me.

He looked straight in my face and asked, "Leandra, this isn't your first child, is it?"

It never occurred to me he could discover such a thing.

"No, sir," I replied, and in the same breath added, "Please don't tell anyone. It would destroy John's and my marriage."

"I suspected no one knew," he replied. "You're not the first woman to be in that kind of predicament."

"It was in New Jersey," I explained. "Her father didn't want us, so he shipped me to a maternity home in upper New York state and that's where I delivered her."

"You put her up for adoption?"

I went through the whole story with him about Ana, William, and baby Autumn. Just telling my story made me realize how strong I became. No one ever wants to be abandoned, then lose their own child to sickness, lose another loved one, and have to bear that weight alone. But I had done it and with little help from anyone else. I finished my tale. "I didn't think anyone could tell I had a baby."

"Well, it's not like someone goes looking around your womb every day. A doctor is the only one capable of determining."

I had another worry preying on my mind. "Well, while we're talking about this, does a woman always bleed when she loses her virginity?"

"Most do, some don't," he answered.

"I didn't with John and John didn't ask, so we left it at that. Doctor Sylvan, do you have to write in my chart about my other baby? I'd like this to be a fresh start."

"Leandra, I'm retiring in a couple of years. Closing up shop." I watched him put his doctor tools in the sterilizer and tidy up. "I know things about this town no one else should ever know and don't need to know. True, it's not being honest, and I could get into trouble." He took a deep breath and lifted the blinds to gaze out the window like he was looking back a hundred years. "In the past, I have asked myself, if someone found out about this, would it hurt my patient more by revealing the truth? If the answer was yes, then it was forgotten. Does that ease your mind?"

🦋 🦋 🦋

It's amazing how simple life can be when family is standing on your side. John's sister, Amy, threw me a baby shower and invited most of Mountain Grove. John's family was a beloved anchor in the town and as the family farm grew, John and his father hired more and more local folks. Papaw's farm was small potatoes compared to John's, so that made me something of a celebrity in our parts.

I sailed through my pregnancy, and dang if that baby didn't time his arrival date right after final exams. I took the summer and following semester off from college. When I started back, little Donny Tucker was almost eight months old. I limited my classes to two to three days a week, running my hairless Kewpie Doll baby over to Great-Mamaw, or leaving him with John's mama, Ruby. Ruby's chosen grandmother name, pronounced "Me-me," nearly became the first word Donny uttered. Both Mamaw and Meme delighted Donny, feeding him every time his little mouth popped open. Sometimes he'd get passed off to a grandpa, Archie, and any other one of John's hired hands not presently messin' with a cow.

If you were standing there with empty arms, Donny would happily join you.

My mama didn't have any kind of endearing name to share with her grandson. She said she didn't have the time, energy, or money to visit for his birth, his welcome to the church, or his birthdays.

"Are you sure, Mama? Maybe you can catch a Greyhound down here just for a short visit."

"Oh, Leandra, I can't leave Roger to fend by himself." Her voice sounded tired and uninterested.

"I'd like Donny to get to know his other grandma."

She laughed. "My goodness, 'grandma' sounds so old! I'll talk to Roger and let you know."

I never got a response to that phone call. For all I cared, I wanted Roger to keep his distance in case he planned to put any sick ideas in my boy's head. But I hoped Donny would renew Mama's soul.

Instead, for each birthday, Donny got a card in the mail signed, Grandma Lillian, with a five-dollar bill taped inside. Each year I sent a picture. It reminded me so much of my limited relationship with Atlanta Grandma, my maternal grandmother. Shoot, grandma's boyfriend Horace meant more to me than Atlanta Grandma ever did. Guess you get back what you invest in. I planned on a huge investment with Donny.

🦋 🦋 🦋

I was nearing my last semester to complete my bachelor's degree in general business. Six long years had passed. I was sitting on a bench with my friend, Maryanne, talking about our graduation. Blooming flowers and budding trees surrounded us, everything tinged in a fresh shade of green. For the first time in forever, I felt at peace.

"We've been through a lot, you know." I pulled my meatloaf sandwich from my paper sack. "I was two months into my first semester when President Kennedy was shot. Made me so sick to my stomach I had to go home and skip the rest of my classes."

"And that Summer of Love in San Francisco. You remember that?" she asked. "The newspapers couldn't get enough of it. While all the hippies were having sex with each other, all the Negros were burnin' down the cities. Talk about a heated summer!" She lowered her voice like she was telling a secret. "You know it started when they killed that Negro Martin Luther. He was always causing trouble for white people." She shook her head. "I was so scared something would happen at our college that summer. I almost dropped out."

"My family said the same," I replied. "They didn't want me on campus when the race riots started. That was shameful. They didn't have to kill Dr. King. And you can't say Negro anymore. They want to be called Black."

"They will always be Negros to me." Maryanne's voice was emphatic. "That's how I was raised."

She took a bite out of her white bread sandwich not even knowing what she said. It was Maryanne's brand of logic that caused the fighting and agitation. There was no give and take. Most everyone in the South was rooted in the ground like Daddy's hickory tree.

She changed the subject. "I'm so scared my little brother will be drafted. I told that boy he has to go to college, or they will pluck him out of North Carolina and dump him in Vietnam. You see those protesters out on the football field today? Good thing my parents have the money to put him through college. He wasn't the brightest light, you know."

I recalled the fear Mamaw, Papaw, and John had carried at that time. They never knew I had been caught in an antiwar demonstration and thrown to the ground, the Rights and the Wrongs battling each other. I remember lookin' up after they slammed my face into the dirt and grass, feet stompin' around me, then someone yanked me by the arm to drag me out of the way. Served me right for sticking my nose into what wasn't my business. And me being pregnant and all. But something inside told me it was important enough to pay attention.

The man who saved me was wearing a khaki-colored jacket and a button that said, *"End the War."* I looked into his face and tears poured from his eyes. I couldn't imagine what he had seen. Then he disappeared. Good thing the newspapers didn't catch wind of what was going on or Asheville would have been another statistic. I reckon there were a lot of those events going on around the country.

"You got a picture of him?" I asked. "Your little brother?"

She removed a photograph from her wallet. "This was his senior picture," she said. "Isn't he a cutie?"

I leaned over to look at the picture. "Sure is." I didn't tell her I had been a big sister once. All the pain flooded back and caught in my chest. I had to take a deep breath to keep from tearing up. It would always hurt, but seeing his young face caught me off guard. Her brother was the same age as Raymond when he died. Sometimes I forgot I was an only child, like I could pick up the phone and call him. I didn't want to think about it and moved on before my eyes started filling.

"What are you planning to do with your degree?" I asked. "You going to get a job?"

"I doubt it. I'm just doing this because I got married before I finished my degree and my family always wanted me to go to college. I'll probably start having babies as soon as I get out of here. I mean, my family expects that, just like they expected me to graduate college."

Hearing Maryanne talk made me think maybe I was different. I kept waiting for my moment, when I would get to do something wonderful with my life. I called it my God Moment, my personal miracle when the divine intervened. But, so far, nothing had happened. It was plain ol' Leandra, going through the motions of everyday life.

🦋 🦋 🦋

I earned As in my accounting classes, business law, and marketing. Agricultural economics was my downfall. The teacher, a gruff old pig farmer who taught classes two days a week, didn't like teaching women. He always picked on me, and my mouth got me into trouble now and again. Even for all his trouble, he could only knock me down a notch and I walked away with a B. My reward for years of hard work meant I could choose several electives to round out my education.

Other than the war, the race riots, and the senseless murders, I got caught up in President Johnson's War on Poverty and his ideas about healthcare for everyone. College immersed me in the make-believe world of education and theory. Yet, despite President Johnson's good intentions to heal the country, I saw the real world from a country woman's perspective. Mamaw and Ruby regularly packed up hot meals for helpless old people and provided care for children and families when neighbors took sick. Papaw still drove his tractor down the road to help a farmer with broken equipment and no money for repairs. We Appalachians remained a proud people, and taking care of our own kind was central to our values. Like Papaw reminded me, I needed to do it better. How I would do that remained a mystery to me.

John was sitting at the dinner table, finishing the last of his coffee, thumbing through my college catalog. "See anything that would help me?" I asked. "I need to decide about those electives and get registered for school."

"Some home economic classes might be useful."

"You're kidding. I know how to cook and clean," I replied, drying the last dish.

"Leandra, it's more than that. Look at some of these classes." I finished wiping my hands and looked over his shoulder where he was pointing at the book. "See, they have health classes, child development, why not some of these? Shoot, a nurse teaches a couple of these classes."

He was right. Every one of those classes would be useful for my family and community. I studied on it, and the next morning, made my choices. My last semester electives would be comprised of health and child development classes. Despite various aspects of my life trying to interfere, my degree was almost a reality.

By the time I was ready to receive my diploma, Donny was wandering around the farms like he owned them, which someday I hoped he would. Now it was my job as his mother to protect them and his rightful inheritance. I was making damn sure no government agency would wander in and take our farms like they had with the Appalachian folks living near the Blue Ridge Parkway. That still chapped my ass from when I first found out as a kid that eminent domain was actually legalized theft.

On the day I graduated college, my family and community surrounded me. The air was soft and warm, and happy excited voices and faces full of smiles filled the campus. To this day, if I am invited to a graduation, I consider my attendance as important as any wedding or funeral. It is a rebirth, a door that opens.

Mama wasn't there to see me get my diploma. I didn't even get one of her five-dollar cards or a phone call. She didn't value education and thought expanding my world was frivolous. The rest of my family didn't think like her. Fighting off tears, I marched forward, recalling how far I had come since my last graduation. Mamaw and Papaw cried for me, while John and his parents and most of John's extended family passed Donny back and forth, trying to keep him from following me to the stage. It was my perfect day.

※ ※ ※

I woke the next morning, thinking, *Now what?* John and I wanted more babies, so I had a growing family to consider.

Papaw set up a desk and office for me in one of the smaller bedrooms and said, "Since I have a business manager now, I had to make it official."

John did the same, but it was more of a corner than an office, and everyone from the farm hands to John's sister and her kids, came traipsing through on a regular basis.

Life moved along fine until I went into town to get Donny new shoes. That boy grew like we poured fertilizer in his bath water. We were leaving Kole's Shoes, and that's when I saw her sitting on a bench on the shaded side of Main Street.

At first, I just kept walking like folks usually do. It's so easy to close your eyes to suffering. I looked up and down the sidewalks on Main where the red brick buildings were lined up like soldiers. American flags were waving in the breeze from every store front, but there wasn't a soul in sight. It was July 3rd, hot and steamy. Everyone was making plans for July 4th parades, fireworks, and barbeques, and folks were having a tough time figuring out how to stay cool. Her face was red and sweat marked her clothes. She looked to be under twenty and could hardly hold her head up. Health classes or not, living in North Carolina taught me to come in out of the heat. A small suitcase and paper sack sat on the ground next to the bench. I could see there was no place to call home.

I approached her. "Honey, you need some water? How long you been sitting out here?"

"I would like water." A heavy sigh escaped her. "I been gettin' water from the park across the street, but I got chased out today."

"When's the last time you ate?" She stood and revealed a small, protruding abdomen. "You're pregnant," I blurted.

"I'll move along," she replied.

Like an unwanted dog, I had no doubt she had been shooed away before.

Harvey popped his head outta his barbershop door. "Everything okay, Leandra?"

"Harvey, we could sure use some cold water," I answered. "And could we get some cool, wet towels?"

Through the years and my marriage to John, I became a name in the community and someone Harvey trusted. "Y'all come inside. I even have a lollipop for little Donny."

Donny got a haircut while I draped cool towels on the girl's neck and pulse points. She rotated a cool towel over her face like she was near to melting. My heart told me where this was going and there was no choice. All kinds of bells and sirens were going off in my head, not to mention God's grace pushing me to take this child home.

Late on introductions, I spoke up. "What's your name, honey?" I touched my hand to my heart. "My name is Leandra. Harvey's our town barber and that towhead in the chair is my baby, Donny."

I saw a faint smile. "Crystal," she replied.

"Crystal, soon as Harvey is done wrangling Donny, why don't you come home with me? You need a place to stay? We can get you something to eat." She had no strength to argue. The whole way home, I thanked Jesus I was never in her position. I was so blessed that Ana and William took me in when I was pregnant. Now I had the opportunity to help someone like me.

We were short of bedrooms in my farmhouse, so I took her home to Mamaw. I knew there'd be a nook or cranny where they could put her, and I was at Papaw's farm most every day. I walked her into the kitchen where Mamaw was putting up the first batch of summer tomatoes. Mamaw just fell into step. Her kindness made my heart swell with pride. I wanted to be a grandmother like her.

"Sit down, child." She pulled out a kitchen chair, studying her face. "You look worn down in this heat."

"Mamaw, this is Crystal. Can you get her a glass of sweet tea while I whip up something for her to eat?"

We started fussing over her like it was second nature. And that's how it all started.

Chapter 3

Crystal Clear

Over the course of my many years I have heard tell there is something called serendipity. The way it works is everything falls into place just like it was planned that way. Sometimes, you don't even know there is a plan. But because everything was meant to be, and the good Lord blessed it so, then the struggle is over, and everything unfolds in perfect timing. As it happened, when Crystal came into my life, it was serendipity.

🦋 🦋 🦋

I returned to our farm in time to prepare a light dinner, handing over Crystal's care to Mamaw. "What'd ya do today?" John asked. "Anything interesting happen? I see Donny got a haircut."

"Yes, he did," I replied, smiling at Donny. "I also bought him some new shoes."

Donny walked over to his daddy, banging on his leg. "Daddy, we made a new friend today. Mama found her and took her home." I think I stopped breathing for a few seconds.

John didn't make the connection. "That's nice, son." He proceeded to wash the day's dirt off his hands and face in the kitchen sink. "Got the steer back from the processor today."

I took an easy breath.

"A couple of the boys restocked the freezer, and I sent each one home with a pack of meat. Left some ribs out to barbeque on the 4th."

He rattled around in the kitchen drawer until he found a church-key can opener. There was a click and whoosh, and he slugged down a big gulp of the cold beer. A long pause followed. "Wait, what did Donny just say?"

John could be slow on the uptake, one of the things about him I found annoying. This time I was grateful. Even for me, it was a fool thing to do.

His eyes darted upstairs. "Leandra…"

"Ahh, don't worry. I left her with Mamaw."

He just stared at me. "Need a shower," he said, still clinging to his beer. "We'll talk over dinner."

At least he didn't jump to conclusions.

John returned to the kitchen table and didn't waste any time digging in, both with his dinner plate and about Crystal.

"So how did this all start?" He shoveled into his mouth a big spoonful of rice and chicken.

"She was hot, Daddy." I smiled at Donny and let him fill in the blanks. "She's got a baby inside her just like Aunt Amy. And she was thirsty."

I figured Donny had done enough damage. All I got from John were two raised eyebrows and one of his famous stern looks.

"Is all this true, Leandra?"

"Donny's a bright boy, John. He's got the story straight. I couldn't leave her there. You know what this Carolina heat can do to a body. Harvey and I got her cooled down. She had nowhere to go. She would have ended up in a hospital."

"Maybe that would have been the best thing."

I handed Donny a piece of buttered bread. "You know hospitals are for sick people. She's pregnant, not sick."

Dead silence. I could tell he wasn't happy with me. In my head, all kinds of potential feedback swirled around. "Look, let's get through the 4th. I'll take her to see Doc Sylvan. I bet he won't charge her. Then we'll figure it out from there."

"You must think you're Florence Nightingale since I recommended you take those health classes. Bringing home every stray. If I could kick my own ass, I would."

That was the end of dinner.

🦋 🦋 🦋

While we were gathered for July 4th, I made my offer to Crystal. We were watching Donny and his cousin Waylen playing in the sprinklers.

"Crystal, how would you feel about seein' my baby doctor, Doc Sylvan." I watched her face to see how she reacted.

Her eyebrows knit together.

I went on. "He's taken care of this town forever."

"I can't pay for no doctor," she replied.

28

"Doc probably wouldn't charge you for a quick visit. Even talking to him would help."

"Guess it wouldn't hurt," she conceded. "He delivered Donny?"

"Sure did. He even made it on time." That got her to smiling. I was one step further ahead.

Doc was still working part time, yet insisted he wasn't taking on new patients. I hoped he would make an exception since he had delivered babies in our family for two generations. We sat in his waiting room, Crystal looking like a scared rabbit, ready to bolt. Doc strolled in, wearing his usual white coat, vest, and tie, drying his hands on a paper towel. The office still smelled of leather and wood paneling, and musty old medical books, outdated like him. He was surprised to see me.

"Well, Leandra, you have a friend. I don't usually do group visits."

"Cut it out, Doc. This isn't for me." I explained Crystal's situation.

She sat there quietly, awaiting her fate.

"You know I'm retired," he stated, and sat down next to Crystal.

"No, you're not. You're working part-time."

"And I'm supposed to stop deliverin' babies. I need some sleep after forty years."

Crystal finally spoke up in a soft voice. "Maybe one more?"

He rubbed his hands over his face and inhaled deeply through his nose. He looked at me and I smiled back at his kind face. "Let's start with an exam. We'll know where to go from there."

According to Doc, the baby was underweight. I thought she was around twenty weeks, halfway there, but by her dates, she was two months from delivery. Times had changed, and it was common practice for the medical world to recommend a higher weight gain, so the babies started stronger and fought off sickness. Other than her little belly, Crystal was skin and bones. It was easy to see she needed food therapy with Mamaw and Ruby. They'd fatten her up like a Christmas goose.

I had learned from Crystal she was what I called a throw-away child. She came from a big family in the Tennessee Appalachian hills. Her little town was on the border of Virginia and Tennessee.

"We live on the outskirts of town. Daddy is a strict Methodist," she had said. "Mama made me tell him I was pregnant and the first thing he did was throw me out of the house. 'Two less mouths to feed,' he said." She stopped to stir another spoonful of honey into her tea. "The baby's daddy is a boy from town. We went to high school together and we reconnected at the diner where I was working." She looked down at her belly. "Guess we reconnected a little too much."

"So, he knows about the baby?"

"Sure, he does. But there ain't nothin' he can do about it. He's got no way to support us. No reason to marry. I left knowin' I was on my own."

Mamaw said she could room at the farm until she delivered. That gave us a few months to determine how to get Crystal on her feet. She planned to give up the baby for adoption. I knew how this game was played and wondered if God sent this child to me because he knew I was an experienced unwed mother. Trouble was, Doc Sylvan was my only resource, so I went back to his office to pester him.

"You trying to kill me, Leandra? Seems like you spend all your spare time on my doorstep."

"She needs our help. Just point me in the right direction, Doc. You have no idea how many women are faced with this situation."

"Oh yes I do," he said. "This whole office knows. You can't save them all."

"I'm not trying to, but one at a time would be nice."

The office door opened, and Geraldine Pitterly walked in holding up her husband. She could barely support him, and I ran to his other side to lend a hand. For all their lives, the Pitterlys and generations before them lived up in the hills. We rarely saw them in town. Most of their kin got pushed out of the hills when the Blue Ridge Parkway came through, took the land, and kicked the country folks to the city curb. Most of those families had lived there so long, they didn't have legal papers to claim the land. It sickened me when I saw those folks struggling to survive while the Blue Ridge Parkway entertained tourists and made money off their rightful land.

The Pitterlys were two of the lucky ones allowed to keep their home. Their plot of land would not interfere with President Roosevelt's plan to preserve the land for visitors, animals, and trees. Seems he had more consideration for the critters than Appalachian folks. Word was, they almost lost what remained of their farm and, around twenty years back, Marvin took a job working at the Sellms factory. Sellms moved into the area after World War II and produced a variety of chemicals for cars.

Several small towns fed the employee population, and that was welcomed work after the GIs came home.

Back then, some of us young'uns figured out Sellms spelled smells if you scrambled the letters. And, boy, did that factory smell. Get within two miles of the place and you could hardly breathe, what with smokestacks going day and night. I was grateful we lived upwind and miles way.

"He cain't eat nothin,'" she stated. "Awful belly pain."

At Doc's direction, we walked Marvin into the exam room so he could lie down. Doc didn't bother to shut the door so, from the front desk, I heard everything. Doc and Geraldine got Marvin's overalls down, while Doc started firing off the doctor questions and pushing things around.

"His liver's swollen, I can feel the edge of it."

I assume he kept poking because the next thing I heard was Marvin cursing and yelling. Doc did the same.

"Why the hell didn't you come in her sooner, Marv? How long you had this pain?"

"Got no money for doctorin' or hospitals," Geraldine answered for him. "Don't trust 'em neither. We been using a poultice of lard and turpentine, but it don't seem ta be pullin' out the poison anymore."

Doc called out from the room. "Leandra, nurse is out today. Call for an ambulance. Then call Mission Hospital and tell them Marv is coming in."

I did as I was told. I could see our conversation about Crystal was going to take a back seat. Doc got him packaged up, and I watched the ambulance drive away. What a shame these mountain folks didn't get the help they needed. Although Asheville had fine hospitals, the general belief of these old Scotch-Irish families was you didn't come back from a hospital. Maybe if they had some sense to get the help they needed before it was too late, the doctors and nurses could do their jobs and provide healing.

Papaw's farm was a little out of my way, but I stopped to drop Crystal off before I went home. I found Mamaw in the parlor with both feet propped up, having a glass of lemonade while she watched *The Price is Right*. Crystal joined her like she'd lived there all her life. Our little mama already looked better, more vibrant, and I marveled at what a little love and attention could do for a body.

🦋 🦋 🦋

Two weeks passed before I tried to pick up with Doc Sylvan and talk him into taking care of Crystal. Right quick, he redirected my query.

"Say, Leandra, how would you like to help me while my nurse is takin' care of her mama? I understand you took some nursing classes in college."

"First of all, they were not nursing classes, Doc. They were health classes. Second, I already have two jobs, bookkeepin' for the farms and taking care of my family."

"You could work a few hours into your day. It sure would help out when things get busy this fall."

"Would you help me take care of Crystal? See her through this?"

"You're talking about bartering one good deed for another." He rubbed his chin. "I could do that."

"You got a deal," I said. "And I'm bringing Crystal with me. It will keep her busy and she can learn something."

Volunteering at the clinic was a real eye-opener, and I mean that in every sense of the word. The first patient who walked through the door had a chunk of wood lodged in his eye. It made my stomach turn. Crystal was a natural and walked the man into the exam room while I took down his history from his co-worker. Doc did his best but decided to send him out for more specialized care.

"Crystal and I have been planning to visit the maternity ward, so we can take him."

Doc seemed pleased we were making ourselves useful. While we were checking him in at the hospital desk, we ran into Mrs. Pitterly. It had been about three weeks since they had walked into Doc's office.

"Mrs. Pitterly?" She turned to look at me. Her face was pale except for her red eyes. I spoke my truth. "Ma'am, you look like you need to sit down."

"Been sittin' forever, chil'. Doin' nothin', and tired as a worn pair of boots."

"How's the mister?"

"He's dyin'. Full of the cancer."

I spoke up for the two of us. "We're so sorry. How can we help?"

"I ain't accustomed to asking for help, but I have chores back at the farm. All we got is a few chickens and a garden. I don't want to leave him so close to his time. He says he sees family in his dreams waitin' on him. I hope some of our young'uns get here in time to say their goodbyes."

"Don't you worry. I'll call Mamaw to send Papaw and Archie over there to check up on things. Won't take but a couple of hours."

"I'd be grateful," she replied. Her voice rattled. "He's been a good man. Never once slapped or yelled at me or the children. Worked hard all his life. He don't deserve to die alone."

After calling Mamaw, Crystal and I resumed our search for the maternity ward, outwardly saddened by what we heard. "Cancer." I could hardly speak the word. It was a death sentence. "I didn't think he was so far gone."

"Well, if he's like the Appalachian people I knew in Tennessee, they're fighters. Won't give in or give up. So many chew or smoke the tobacco they grow. I'm sure that doesn't help them stay well."

"My Papaw needs to quit growing that stuff," I said. "It pays more than the other crops, but it can't be good for anyone. He's gonna fight me. He always called his little tobacco crop his Christmas money. It sells right before Christmas so he can buy presents. Awww, look at those babies!"

I was pleasantly distracted from death by a row of newborn babies, some crying, some sleeping, some daydreaming. The nurse looked up from her rocking and feeding, and smiled. We peeked in one of the empty maternity rooms. They looked cold and sterile, but I guess cleanliness was a good thing if you were in the hospital.

"It's not exactly home," I told Crystal, "but it will get the job done."

"How will I pay for this?" she asked.

"You know, it's been my experience that answers can come out of nowhere. Let's not worry about anything else today."

🦋 🦋 🦋

One by one, the mountain folks came to us, meaning me, Papaw's farm, or Doc's doorstep. We never knew for sure where they came from or how they found us. Almost always, they said it was by word of mouth. Someone told them there was this kind family just outside of town, known to help the down and out. Sometimes they'd be sittin' under a shade tree when I got to Papaw's farm. Other times a soft, tired, knock would come to the door. Now and again, I'd find them in the kitchen with Mamaw and she'd be serving a stranger coffee, a sandwich, or even a hot meal. It was just her way. Then it was off to Doc Sylvan.

"Leandra…"

"I know, I know, I'm ruining your retirement, Doc." I interrupted his never-ending rant. "Help me fix this and I'll get out of your hair. These are the Mr. and Mrs. Pitterlys, the Crystals, always left behind, the old and the young and the poor. There's so much to go around. We just have to figure out how to put the pieces together and make one hand pay off the other."

I collected some more air.

"Doc, look at how it worked out for Crystal and Mrs. Pitterly. Crystal is living with Mrs. Pitterly, so an old woman gets the help she needs. Crystal has a roof over her head. That gives Geraldine Pitterly time to figure out what to do after her mister died. And Crystal can deliver a healthy baby, make herself useful, and get on her feet."

Our fight was cut short by the nurse reminding Doc he had another patient waiting.

"There, you see?" he asked. "I have to treat my regulars and sell my office and practice. This crusade you're on isn't helping matters. Why don't you go pick on someone younger than me?" He nudged me out of his office and walked into the exam room, trying his best to ignore me.

I knew both of us were trying, but it wasn't enough, and certainly not the answer to the problem. By the time the vomiting, diarrhea, coughing, fever, rectal boils, abuse, bites, pregnancies, cancer, and chest pain got to the door, most times the affliction was blown out of proportion. Folks needed a safe place to get treatment before the sickness could get an upper hand. My poor brother Ray's mind was so twisted with drugs and alcohol and he had no way to get help. He would still be with me if only I had helped him sooner.

Just about then, I had one of my brainstorms. It was crystal clear, like looking into one of those gypsy balls. John called my brainstorms "tornadoes" because he said they always stirred something up. With all my whining and Doc's complaining, it gave me an idea. Tomorrow I was going into town to start putting those puzzle pieces together.

Chapter 4

Chrysalis

John and I never did have any more children. We sure tried, but it just didn't happen. Our son Donny was a special gift and went on to have four young'uns of his own. It's his daughter, Andrea, who is helping me out now. Funny how things go 'round and 'round. I like to think, if I couldn't give birth to another child, I gave birth to a dream and healed my mountains at the same time.

🦋 🦋 🦋

In the morning, I fluttered around the kitchen like a little butterfly, prepared to be gone most of the day with my son and my big ideas.

"You got that look in your eye, Leandra." John was watching me run around the kitchen trying to wipe the milk mustache off Donny's face, while I poured him the last cup of coffee. "What are you up to today? You know I need those bills paid or the creditors are coming to look for us."

"You're worrying yourself for nothing," I replied. "Your bills will be stamped and ready to hand to the postman tomorrow morning. I'm visiting folks in town, and I plan on bargaining with Papaw after that. It all gets done, doesn't it?"

"Yes, you never let me down, but I want to know what's going on in your pretty little head."

"Trust me, you don't want to know. You'll just worry."

He was heading out to the barn and put on his cap. "Too late for that. Just keep us out of the poor house."

I pulled him back and reached my arms around his neck. He smelled soapy, his only cologne. Sometimes I wished he were a little more sophisticated like Greg, who always wore a nice fragrance that stirred my desires. I gave John a friendly bite on the neck and a long kiss, finally reaching up to stroke his clean-shaved face. "You're so good to me, sweetheart."

"Yeah, well, you can show me your appreciation tonight. You're so dang busy I can't remember the last time we were both awake and in bed at the same time."

That situation was not likely to get better any time soon with what was coming. I would have to carve out some time for him in the weeks and months ahead.

🦋 🦋 🦋

My goal for the day was to go begging to every religious institution in town. I was tired of the Baptists judging the Methodists, or Evangelicals hating the Catholics. More so, I wanted them all to put their differences aside and collectively put their Christian mouths together for a united purpose. I might as well ask Jesus himself to coordinate this event because I was going to need a miracle to pull it off.

As it had been for the last three decades, Vernetta greeted us when we walked in the church office. Vernetta was so old it was unclear when and where she got her beginning. She was as much a fixture of the church as the white steeple on top, chugging around the office putting papers in their place, and answering the phone in case of any religious emergencies. She saw me come in holding my folder with the official plans for my project.

"Well, Mrs. Tucker, how are you and Donny today?"

My Carolina came out. "Fine and dandy, Miss Vernetta. How is your arthritis?" She held up a gnarly hand and examined it.

"Pain's not too bad today. I can bear my pain as Jesus did his." That more than answered my question, so I moved on. I was fairly sure Vernetta needed to move on too, as she surpassed the limits of employment.

"Is the preacher around?"

"He's workin' his farm today, but Preacher Dave is here. Somethin' ailing you?"

"In a way," I said. "I need to talk to a God-fearing man who can give me hope. Preacher Dave will do fine."

Preacher Dave was what we called a traveling preacher, coming through to stay a spell and then move on to a new church. He had a calling like Papaw did in his younger days. The only difference was Dave didn't have a family tying him down. Who knew how long he would stay or go?

But, without doubt, he possessed the holy spirit and the fever to save humanity. He might be a perfect target for my mission.

Preacher Dave walked into the room. For some reason he reminded me of a praying mantis, no pun intended. He was tall and lean, with a long face and a patchy brown beard. His hair was always three kinds of crazy, sticking out everywhere, but he'd plaster it down with Brylcreem hair tonic for Sunday meetings. His voice was so deep it would boom through church, and you were sure you'd be going to hell if you didn't measure up to his standards. Then there was his gentle side.

"Mrs. Tucker, so good to see you. Please have a seat."

He motioned for me to sit on the sagging couch while he pulled up a wooden chair. Vernetta left a tray with two cups of coffee and what appeared to be her stale snickerdoodles on the table between us.

Vernetta extended her hand to Donny. "Donny, why don't you come with Aunt Vernetta, and we'll see what we can do to keep you occupied."

Preacher Dave leaned forward in his chair and studied my face. "What's troubling you, Mrs. Tucker?"

"Please, Preacher, call me Leandra. If we're going to be working together, I have to put the formalities aside."

A worried look crossed his face while I stirred my sugared coffee.

"We're gonna be workin' togetha?" He shifted his weight and crossed his lanky legs.

"I'm hoping," I replied. "Preacher, we have a problem in this town, and I may have a solution. But that's not gonna happen unless this whole town comes together."

I stopped being mysterious and relayed what had happened at Doc Sylvan's office. I told him patients were flocking in while Doc was trying to get out. I presented my theory about preventing health issues from getting worse by treating folks early and keeping them out of the hospitals.

"Once Doc leaves, that's it. We are on our own. Our community is hurtin' and I mean that literally."

"I admire your desire to heal, Leandra, but I'm not a medical man. Where would we start? What do you desire from me?"

"You have a role of great importance, Preacher Dave. You can make a big impact on our flock." I was appealing to his drive to shepherd those needing faith. "We need a plan and money. If the faith community comes together for this cause, why this project could sustain itself and heal our people."

I showed him my plan to get the Methodists, Lutherans, Baptists and hell, even the Catholics, to commit to projects that would support the new health center. I told him if I could get the land and materials donated, these farm folks could raise a building. Then, Doc could help me connect with the students at the hospital and university to practice their skills with us.

"So, you would like me to present this to the congregation?"

"Of course, you need to run it by the other preacher first. Then we can figure out how to get the church family involved. It's somethin' that would benefit our whole community."

I was working so hard to sell my idea that my upper lip started to sweat. He wasn't far behind.

"Preacher Dave, I'm going to leave you a copy of my plan. I'm sure you have other things to do today besides talk to me."

He glanced at my official folder. "That is a pile of papers, Leandra. Why that's as big as Mountain Grove's phonebook."

"Yes, sir. I plan to visit every single Christian church I can today. When I get done with them, I figure I'll see if there are any other religions that might want to do the right thing." I leaned in close. "We all belong to God, Preacher."

I smiled as sweet as any Southern woman could, turned away and opened the office door to find Donny and Vernetta coloring a picture of Jesus.

"Let's go, Donny. Get your picture and thank Miss Vernetta." I waved at Preacher Dave. "See y'all at services on Sunday. Looking forward to workin' with you."

I shot out of there like a cottontail dodging a hawk.

I had a lofty expectation of how much visiting I would accomplish that day with a three year old in tow. By late afternoon, both of us were cranky. I visited with the Methodists and Nazarenes but had to schedule an appointment with the Catholic priest, as he was off blessing someone with last rites. Catholics did a lot of blessings while the Baptists did a lot of Bible studying. I was just focused on praying that everyone's heart was in the right place.

"Donny. I'm gonna stop at Dixie's Café and get a bag of fried chicken. Mama's too tired to cook tonight, sound good?"

All I got from Donny was a nod.

When I walked in the door it was past five o'clock, and John was already home. "I see you remembered where you live," he said in welcome. He eyed my bag from Dixie's. "Zat dinner?"

"I'll be about thirty minutes. Just enough time for you to clean up." I handed him Donny. "He could use some scrubbing too. I'll whip up some potatoes, open a can of green beans, and be ready for both of you." I knew what was coming so this would give me time to prepare for the cross examination.

John returned without a word, put Donny in his booster seat, and found his seat at the table. I had laid a copy of my clinic plan next to his place setting. I also sat and, while I was spooning out potatoes, he picked it up, read the cover page, and laid it back down. He looked up at me. "You gonna tell me what this is before I read it in the papers?"

I heaved a great sigh. "You should be happy I'm trying to help this community."

"I wish you'd spend more time helpin' this family."

I had a choice of getting mad or getting pouty. I chose the latter and lowered my voice to the same frequency as an angel. "Ida thought you'd be proud of me puttin' my college degree to work. If I pull this off, I *will* be helping this family and so many others." I dropped my head for effect and pushed my food around my plate.

Donny jumped in. "Mommy's sad, Daddy." He was always a sensitive child.

"This is going to take years, Leandra. Do you know that? I don't want any legal implications for this farm. Dad still owns the farm, but Jake and I are supposed to buy him out one o' these days. How am I going to do that if someone sues us 'cause some medical student cuts the wrong thing, or worse yet, kills someone?"

"No one's cuttin' off body parts or killin' patients. It's a clinic and we're not planning on major surgery. Can't you keep an open mind and an open heart?"

He studied me. "I *am* proud of you. And you're teaching Donny good things about takin' care of our own. But all your little projects. Lee, what are you looking for?"

That hit me hard. I wasn't sure what hole I was trying to fill. As messed up as my school-age years were, there was no telling what I was chasing. I wasn't much for therapy or counseling, but once that clinic was running, maybe I could let one of those students practice on my psyche.

"Can't we just be?" he continued.

"I'll make it work. I promised."

"You'd better. I'm gettin' damn sick and tired of being married and not having a wife."

He wiped Donny's face and hands and left the room to watch television. Donny ran after him, clearly seeing he was as upset as I was pretending to be.

🦋 🦋 🦋

But John was right and gave me cause for thought. From the get-go I was afraid I would take advantage of his good nature. My old boss, Matt, broke me. My high school sweetheart, Greg, crushed me. Mama disappointed me. Mama's so-called husband—well, I just plain wanted to strangle him. Daddy left me. And I failed my brother, Ray. I wasn't sure I could give my love fully to anyone. Love rewarded me with pain. John became my safe bet when I said, "I do."

After cleaning the kitchen, I sheepishly joined the boys in the parlor. I had written my clinic plan, but I needed a marriage plan. I was determined to make sure I was home, makin' a home, before John came in at night. I was big enough to admit I was neglecting my family and, if I wanted to be the grandmother my mamaw was, things needed to settle down. But, at the same time, it irked me women were forced to make these choices. It didn't seem to matter if you earned an education and wanted to do something with it. Somehow, women always ended up in the kitchen or the bedroom. Miss an appointment in either location and you were in hot water.

🦋 🦋 🦋

Moving forward, I made sure to be one step ahead of John, or at least make it look that way. I was up early making breakfast, not that I had slept the night before. Dawn was coming earlier and earlier, which meant longer workdays on the farm. He seemed a little startled to find me scrambling eggs.

"Early morning?" he asked. He filled his mug with coffee, thumbing through the newspaper for the stock reports.

"Have to look at Papaw's books today. He's worried about his taxes."

"I am too." He habitually reminded me about his needs like I was some kind of little kid and couldn't figure these things out for myself.

"You're next in line, toward the end of the week."

"You working on your clinic?"

I wanted to put his mind at ease. "Doubt I'll have time." What he didn't know was, after I looked at Papaw's books, and after Papaw was good and tired, I was going to hit him up for a clinic donation. "I want to be home by three or four to get dinner started."

"I'm not sure when I'll be in," John said. "Dad, Jake, and I have an appointment at the bank in town."

This time I asked the question. "Is there something I should know?"

"Naw, just a formality. Sometimes we need to increase or decrease our loan if the ends don't meet. They know we're good for it."

"Are we ever going to be our own bank?" I asked. "I hate depending on them."

"Probably after someone dies and we inherit the farms. My sister, Amy, will still own a third of the ranch. But, if you sold Papaw's farm, we could have enough banked to run this operation."

I turned to face him, just short of being astonished. "I'll never sell that farm while I'm alive." I waved my spatula like the American flag. "It's over a hundred years old. I walked away from it once, I won't do that again."

"We're worrying over something that's irrelevant. Both those ol' boys aren't going anywhere."

"I'll have your dinner waiting," I replied like a good wife.

Figures. The day I cook, he shows up late.

🦋 🦋 🦋

Donny squealed with joy when he caught sight of his grandparents. He plowed into Papaw with such force Papaw nearly buckled his knees. Mamaw knew we were coming, so she was collecting ingredients to bake cookies. I watched them walk out to the chicken coop to gather the day's eggs and reminded myself to thank God that night for having them in my life.

Papaw always exaggerated about the state of his bookkeeping, mostly because he didn't understand it. Within two hours I was done. I had on a pair of tattered, denim overalls, so rather than stay in the kitchen, I wandered out to the tobacco field in my work clothes where Papaw and Archie were weeding seedlings. Each year there was a period of time where the weeds could take over a field. If you timed it right, the crop would succeed with the tobacco eventually growing tall enough to deprive the weeds of sunlight. If you missed that window, you battled the entire season.

Walking between the rows reminded me of my last childhood summer before I started grade school. I was six, maybe seven years old and so excited to get out of that field and away from those sticky plants. There was nothing I liked about it, from the back-breaking planting to the bugs, sweat, and harvest. For the last ten years, Papaw chose to spray the tobacco with bug poison to keep the giant leaves looking pretty. Pretty plants got more money. On a good year with a high yield, he could net five to six-thousand dollars.

"Papaw, when you comin' in? Y'all look bushed."

"I am bushed, child. We won't finish today." He tried to straighten his spine. Archie did the same. "We need some fancy equipment to do the work for us."

"Hardly worth it," I replied. "Why don't you plant alfalfa or rent it out to someone?"

"You're forgettin' this is my Christmas money. Makes me feel like Santy Claus. And renting the land won't get me nothin'."

"I've told you, the money and labor you put into this crop, plus the misery, doesn't equate to a Christmas bonus."

Archie gave a giggle. "Heh-heh, Miss Leandra, you knows you can't talk reason to this man."

"Wastin' my breath, huh, Archie? Fine, you wallow in these poisonous plants and DDT, or whatever it is you kill these bugs with, and see if I give a care."

"I see old age hasn't mellowed you out none."

"I could say the same. And I'm not old. I'm just hittin' my stride."

Mamaw and Donny had cookies and lemonade waiting in the kitchen when we came in from the field. I was ready to target Papaw.

"Mamaw, I'm gonna set Donny up in the parlor to watch cartoons. I want to have a talk with the both of you. I have a favor to ask."

They eyeballed each other with a look that said, *We could be headed for trouble*. I knew that look and I was prepared. I didn't waste any time jumping in with both feet, seeing how I had to get back to my farm and start supper.

"I hate talkin' about this stuff," I started, "but this is important to me. I'm just gonna come out and say it." I paused again and swallowed hard. "When something happens to the two of you, I imagine the farm comes down to me, is that correct?"

Papaw spoke up. "Leandra, if this is about that durn tobacco again…"

"No, Papaw, nothing to do with that. I just need to clarify, the farm comes to me, it's my inheritance, correct?"

"Yes, but I ain't plannin' on joining Aunt Addie any time soon."

Mamaw said nothing, just lovingly patted his hand and smiled.

"Dang it, Papaw, answer the question!"

"Yes, the farm will be yours after Mamaw and I are gone. And, by the way, I want to rest right up there between your daddy's hickory tree and Mamaw."

"I assumed as much," I replied. "What if I told you I wanted to borrow an acre right now?"

"Fer what? You gonna plant?"

"Sorta." I took another deep breath. "I want to plant a health clinic there. Just one little acre off the front of the property."

"You gonna run this here clinic?"

Mamaw stayed silent, soaking it all in.

"I'll have a hand in it. But I'm planning to get medical students from the hospitals. It'll be a free clinic. We'll barter for our needs and so will the patients. The churches in town will help." I threw my plan down in front of him. "Take a look-see. Get back to me." I called for Donny. "Gotta go make supper for my family, Papaw. Good food is good medicine."

Mamaw walked us to the car. Donny gave her a big hug and a wet cookie kiss.

She stood to face me. "Leandra, honey, don't you fret none about your clinic. You are a blessed child of God, and you'll get your acre of land." She planted a kiss on my cheek and nuzzled up to my ear. "He'd better say yes, or he'll be cookin' his own suppers the rest of his life."

🦋 🦋 🦋

I stood off to the sidewalk outside church waiting for the congregation's reaction to Preacher Dave's commentary on my clinic.

I'd decided to name the clinic Chrysalis Clinic, meaning a safe place or a place of rest where you could change into something better. What it really referred to was a butterfly pupa, hard-shelled and protective. But I used my imagination and a play on words and came up with Chrysalis.

I had a few handouts for the church folks, explaining the clinic details. When I pulled the papers out of my purse, John started putting two and two together and grabbed little Donny's hand.

"Leandra, I'm not hangin' around here all morning. I'll take Donny home. Find yourself a way to get back home."

I was a little taken back, but I didn't blame him. He walked away, stopping at the social table for coffee and a treat for Donny. I eyed him. What a good-looking man. I should be taking advantage of that more often. I was just so damn tired by the end of the day.

Doc Sylvan distracted me from my woes. "So, this is your big idea," he chided. "A free clinic. How soon are you going to drag me into it?"

"Right away. I need your connections at the hospitals and schools, so we can get someone to practice on these folks." I handed him a paper. "This is how you'll retire. You attract some Doc Wannabes to Mountain Grove, sell your practice, and you're out the door."

"I hope it's that simple, Leandra. And you must have found a money tree back in those woods, otherwise I would wonder how you're going to pay for all this."

"I'm workin' on that. I'll be taking donations anywhere I can and begging all over town. Papaw's gonna give me an acre off the front of his property. Least, that's what Mamaw says. I looked all over town for something to rent, but they were too small, too big, or too expensive. Papaw's land, my land, is free."

Our conversation was interrupted by a couple with two small children. "Let us know how we can help," the woman offered.

"I'm a carpenter," the man said. "Can do a little plumbing too."

"Write your name and number on the back of this." I handed him a flyer and pencil. I wasn't about to let him get away. "Thank you, sir. I'll be callin' you."

Doc started in on me again. "You know this is years and years from completion. I hope I live long enough to see you open the front door."

"I got to start somewhere. For now, I just need to get a building put up. Next week I'll scatter out some collection jars in town. We can put one in your office. Doc, you can put in the first dollar."

Doc shook his head and started to walk away. "I should have pushed you back in when I saw you comin' into this world," he complained. "My life would have been a whole lot easier."

"You don't mean that, Doc," I shouted after him. "I know you love me!"

He waved me away and kept walking. I was sure he was going to angst on our conversation the rest of the day.

Chapter 5

Sometimes You Win

W hat is it that makes us do the things we do? Sometimes I look back on all the time I spent flitting around from one thing or another. Now and then I succeeded. Like when I raised a good son and took care of an old woman and mother-to-be. Sometimes I failed. But let's not talk about that now.

❧ ❧ ❧

My response from the congregation had been less than stellar. I went back to the town printer. Mr. Blackwell was fussing at one of his printing machines, cussing and kicking the inanimate object. He stopped his abuse when he saw me. I told him about my latest idea to get the town on board with the clinic.

"You say you need a half-page for these here jars, to collect donations. And a full-page flyer to let folks know about your town meeting. Have you considered talking to one o'the reporters at the *Mountain Grove Press*?"

"That's a great idea. For once we'll have something interesting to read in the paper."

"Well, I'll get started on this later today. Stop back day after tomorrow."

"Thanks, Mr. Blackwell. You're doing so much to help." He laid my work aside with the rest of his printing projects.

"Paper and ink costs pennies. You know, Leandra, my Uncle Joe died at home 'cause he didn't have the money to get the help you're offerin' for free at this clinic. If someone like you had been around, maybe he'd still be alive today."

"In these parts, I think all of us have had someone like that in our lives. There's gonna be a lot of panic when the town realizes Doc Sylvan is taking retirement seriously."

"Well then, let's fix this."

"Yes, sir," I replied, and marched out the door to plan for our town meeting.

🦋 🦋 🦋

Doc Sylvan wasn't too happy when I told him he was speaking at the town meeting. But I reminded him it was a step toward his retirement and getting me off his back. We sat next to each other while we waited to speak. We were last on the agenda.

Usually, a good turnout for our monthly town meeting meant there were at least a dozen residents warming the seats. But tonight, the room was packed because farmers were fighting over an issue about their trucks tearing up the county roads. Everyone wanted to voice their own opinion and put in their two cents.

Doc leaned over to whisper in my ear. "If I speak, all I'm going to do is inflict fear on the town."

"Not at all. When they hear you, they'll recognize the importance of this project."

"Well, what are you expecting me to say?"

"When I introduce you, come to the podium and back up everything I've said. It's that simple. You know my agenda."

"Yes, I do. You're like a broken record."

The town hall was actually an old whitewashed one-room schoolhouse, but still served the community well. While Aunt Addie's one-room schoolhouse grew and grew, this one never got past the four walls. The chairman sat up front with his gavel and kept control of the conversation or righteous tempers, as the case may be.

There was a small kitchen with a refrigerator that used to hold the children's sack lunches. Now, it contained a large plastic water pitcher and, just before the meeting, the secretary would remove it to the side table with a stack of paper cups. Mamaw did her part and made six dozen cookies for me to put out with the water. She knew how important this meeting was to my project. I heard the chairman call my name.

"It's showtime," I said to Doc Sylvan, and motioned for him to join me.

Before I could even open my mouth, a voice called out from the back. "These your Mamaw's cookies, Leandra?" The whole room started laughing.

"Yes, they are, Steven. But remember you're a diabetic, so not more than one."

He shouted back. "I think you're takin' this health clinic thing too seriously."

Doc couldn't stand it. "No, she isn't, Steve. Your sugar's been out of control for years."

That comment shut Steve up in a hurry.

Doc nudged me away from the podium. "We all need to take this seriously 'cause I'm headin' outta here."

The room grew deathly quiet. My insides were dancing a jig. I knew Doc would come through for me. He tried his darndest to be mean, but he had a big heart.

Doc kept going. He told everyone how he was retiring, and nothing was going to stop him. But that would leave the town high and dry if they didn't attract some new health care providers. Not only that, but he chided how half the people walking into his office waited too long to get help, making their situation a lot worse.

"Leandra here has seen a problem and she's tryin' to fix it. Her grandpa is willing to donate an acre of land. Now it's up to us to get this clinic built and staffed."

One of the farmers spoke. "That's gonna take money. Some of us are barely holding on."

"If you can't donate money, donate time," I answered. "We can have fundraisers, and when the money is collected we'll have a barn-raising. It's not going to happen overnight, but I know this is something we can do."

"Can I say something?" I looked up and saw Crystal standing. I hadn't expected her to be here, but she must have driven Mrs. Pitterly in for the meeting. Her belly stuck out a foot past her feet and she looked like she was ready to deliver the baby during the meeting.

"Go right ahead, Crystal."

"I know I'm new to this community. Maybe I don't have a right to speak about what Leandra and Doctor Sylvan are proposing for our community. But any day now I'm bringing a new baby into this town and

I know this much. If Leandra hadn't picked me up off the street, I don't know what would have happened to me and this baby. Maybe I would've ended up in a hospital. Maybe I would've lost my baby. And I know if Mr. Pitterly had had the medical help he needed, maybe Mrs. Pitterly wouldn't be alone now. We all need to do our part."

She took her seat again and I saw Mrs. Pitterly pat Crystal's knee. I hadn't asked or expected Crystal to speak. I wasn't sure Doc was going to come through, but he did.

Another man stood up.

"My son's a draftsman," he began. "I'm pretty sure he could draw something for you and get this going. If you get some plans, then we'll know what funds we need to raise."

"Once we get the plans," Doc said, "we can run it by the medical students. It should be a good lesson for them to design their own clinic."

My heart pumped faster and faster. I had a shot at making this happen. "I'm going to leave out a sign-up sheet. Anyone interested in helping, put your name and number on this sheet of paper and I'll get back to you."

The chairman concluded the meeting. I watched the town hall empty. That meeting had been a huge stepping-off point for me. I collected my papers and my plan, which never made it out of the folder. My presentation ran itself.

"The ball's in your court, Doc. We need to visit Asheville, so schedule some appointments for us to meet with the health community in the big city."

"My wife's gonna shoot me, being out so late. You know, she had set her hopes on a cruise to Alaska next year."

"Play your cards right, Doc, and you can sign up for that cruise sooner than you think. Heck, I'll throw you a bon voyage party before you leave."

"I'd like that, Leandra. I'm holdin' you to that one."

Call me crazy, but I was sure I heard some excitement in his voice. It was a nice change from his sarcasm.

🦋 🦋 🦋

John was still awake when I returned home. He got up and lowered the volume on the TV. "How'd it go?"

"Just about perfect." I wasn't going to say much. I knew every time I talked about my big dreams it was like sticking a knife in his side.

"How's Donny?'

"We read a book before bed, and he went right out. He asked for Mama a couple of times. You'd better stop in and check on him."

"You're not coming to bed?" I looked at the mantle clock and it was ten minutes to ten.

"I have some reading to finish."

That was all he said to me. I was whipped and needed sleep. Guess John had better things to do than join me in bed.

The following week, Doc Sylvan and I were on our way to Asheville to visit some hospitals. Asheville had more than its share of hospitals and sanitoriums. Sometime around the 1900s, it was decided that Asheville air was suited to healing folks with tuberculosis, so sanitoriums, and then hospitals, popped up everywhere. We had a couple of great psychiatric hospitals too, making Asheville a great place to fish for medical students and nurses in training.

St. Joseph Hospital and Mission Hospital were two of the oldest establishments in town, constructed during the tuberculosis era. Doc had a lot of connections so, mostly, it was him presenting my case to his old cronies and medical folks he'd known most his life. In the 1970s, health care was going through some real changes. There was a powerful shortage of care providers. Male doctors were starting to realize half the student population was female: intelligent, creative, and trustworthy with patient care. Still, it was a hard pill for most medical men to swallow and female doctors were a rare species. My hope was that these female doctors would open their hearts to the needs of our mountain folks.

Dr. Peter Carrington, medical director of the hospital, sat behind an enormous wooden desk that filled half his office. He was overweight and smoked a lot, by the looks of the full ashtray on his desk. There was a pile of charts sitting next to the ashtray, so I knew our time was limited. I held my tongue and let him speak first while he flipped through my business plan that Doc had mailed him the week before our meeting.

"So, Mrs. Tucker, you're prepared to donate the land, raise the funds, put up the building, manage the building, get the support of the community, and coordinate patient care?" I detected a snark in his voice.

"No, Dr. Carrington, I don't see myself coordinating patient care. From what I've learned, there are women training at community colleges right here in Asheville to become medical secretaries. Chrysalis Center would be just the place to gain experience working with your doctors and nurses."

I saw him raise an eyebrow and chuckle. He was casting doubt and that got me riled. Doc saw it too, glanced my way, and wedged into the conversation before I could open my big mouth.

"Don't doubt her, Pete," Doc said. "I've known her all her life, brought her into this world, and I don't think she'd back down from a copperhead if it blocked her path."

I turned toward Doc. "What we need is a board. A collection of interested folks who can help us develop ideas and make decisions."

Dr. Carrington answered. "All right, I have rounds in another ten minutes. I'll talk to my colleagues at our next gathering and run it by some of our instructors. Maybe discuss it with some of the residents and the nursing supervisor. Do you mind if I make copies of your business proposal?"

"No sir, this is a big opportunity for your students and a lifeline for our community. We have a lot of work ahead of us, but we also have a lot of untapped resources. If you have any questions, don't hesitate to call me or Dr. Sylvan, and we would be happy to attend one of your meetings and answer questions."

Dr. Carrington turned to Doc. "I see what you mean about that copperhead."

🦋 🦋 🦋

Word got around the medical community in Asheville that some woman from the hills wanted to start a free clinic. Rotations in a public health clinic would allow new doctors and student nurses to get out of the classrooms and experience life firsthand. Our little town was less than an hour from the city, making it an appealing location for staff and students in Asheville. While Doc sourced our staffing needs, I stirred up more excitement in town. It was time to call the newspaper.

I arranged to meet the reporter/photographer from the *Mountain Grove Press* on the acre of land Papaw promised me. The property was right off the southeast corner of our land and a short distance from the county road leading to Main Street. The crystal-clear day and smiling sun convinced me I picked the right spot for the clinic. There would be some clearing required, but we could start now, dragging the tractor around to level the land. There were a few stubborn rocks to remove and baby trees to uproot before they became a bigger problem.

I heard a car door slam and turned to see a man standing there. He grabbed the camera hanging around his neck and started snapping photos. I didn't recognize him, so he must have been a new reporter.

He walked toward me. "Mrs. Tucker, nice to meet you." He held out his hand and displayed a smile that would have melted a frozen pond. What was a male model doing writing for our little newspaper? "This is an impressive thing you're doing for the town."

I shook off his compliment. "And you are?"

"Sean Finnigan. And, no, I'm not from Ireland. My great grandfather was and grew up around here. My parents raised me in Raleigh. Guess that means I have roots in North Carolina. I had some silly notion to take a job here and find out what life is like in a small town."

"My roots go back to the Civil War, Sean." I went through the whole history of the Barker family and how my Great Papaw Jonas had made the land his. Generation after generation, and it was the same for dozens of families clinging to their farms and the hills that surrounded them. "The Blue Ridge Parkway evicted a lot of families that called these mountains home. If the government didn't take all of their land, it certainly split up families when they got relocated. Without their kin and neighbors to help out, where do folks turn?"

I explained how isolation and poverty were the enemies of health and people suffered in silence until it was too late.

"Doc Sylvan was all we had and going to a doctor cost money. These people don't want to be beholdin' to anyone. I plan to set up a barter system so folks can help one another by donating time, labor, or the products of their land to keep the clinic running. When you give to these people, they give right back."

"How did the government get away with stealing their land? How is that legal?"

"I wondered that too. When I was a young'un and the Parkway was being built, I saw all the abandoned farms along the roadside. Eminent domain gave the government the right to take their land for what the law deemed good for the country as a whole. Some of these farmers were the first settlers in these hills. They figured it was their right to live there if their family had worked the land for a hundred years. Their mistake was they never got a written deed to the land. That made it easy for the government to take it from them."

That young man was almost in tears when I finished.

🦋 🦋 🦋

Within a week the editor made Chrysalis Clinic front page news and carried it onto page five. We only had eight pages in the whole newspaper, counting the advertising. Like I said, there wasn't much going on in Mountain Grove. As it was, the paper arrived the day before I was planning to catch up on Papaw's bookkeeping. When I walked into the kitchen, Papaw was quick to speak up in his usual smart-mouth way.

"Well, we have a celebrity in the family." The newspaper was displayed in front of him while he sat at the kitchen table lacing his boots.

"Cut it out," I said. "I just started babbling and that's what came of it."

"You made us look like good Christian people," Mamaw added, and kissed me on the cheek while she handed me a breakfast plate.

Papaw stood up and grabbed his jacket from the wall hook. I felt his big, warm hand wrap around my shoulder. "I'm proud of you, Leandra." His nostrils flared and I saw tears in his eyes. "You did good. Made us proud of who we are."

He turned and walked out the door. Papaw wasn't one to easily hand out praise. I had waited all my life to hear that kind of respect. The fact that it came from my Papaw was just sausage gravy on my biscuit.

Chapter 6

The Good and the Bad

Broken hearts are a curse of humanity. I can't understand why we have to hurt just to figure out how much we love someone. And it goes both ways. Even when you have to walk away from someone you love, it still hurts. Your anger may be raging and leave you wanting to rip his or her heart out of their chest, but you'll still find a corner to curl up in and wish you could stop breathing. Mercy. We've all been there.

🦋 🦋 🦋

When the Sacred Heart Catholic Church called the following week, I hoped the newspaper story had opened their sacred heart and maybe their collection jar. Turns out my prayers were answered. Father Cunningham wasn't available to visit with me when I was on my pilgrimage, but God is a mystery. Here was Father Cunningham informing me I was blessed with a building for the clinic.

I could hardly contain my excitement. "You mean we can use it right now? It's just sittin' there empty?"

"We haven't used it for several years. It's actually an annex to our parish hall so we use the bigger room for social gatherings. There's a lot of interest in sprucing it up and making it useful again. We have a few six-foot tables stored in there and you can use those if you wish."

"How about Dr. Sylvan and I visit on Friday? I have a volunteer carpenter that may be able to help."

"Of course. Let's say 10 a.m., after morning mass."

When he said that I had a flashback to my poor brother Ray, complaining he was forced to go to church every Wednesday morning before school. I clearly remember it was a Wednesday evening when he busted those colored windows in the church. A lot of good church did his troubled soul.

"I'll see who I can round up to join me. Thank you, Father. Your parish might make this miracle happen a lot faster." I love the way kindness brings people together. I was already starting to have a very different opinion of Catholics and needed to move past my narrowmindedness.

🦋 🦋 🦋

Come Friday morning, Doc and that carpenter feller from church, Rolland Minter, stood alongside me outside the annex. The summer heat ramped up and sweat collected on my back. Father Cunnigham approached us, nearly sprinting. Instead of his church gown he wore a casual black-on-black pant outfit with his little white collar. He was a younger man than I expected with thick brown hair, a cherubic face, and a smile that glowed like heaven's door.

"Morning, morning!" he called out, chipper as a robin in early summer. He fiddled with a ring of keys, some of which looked like they had opened the first church on the continent. "I believe this is the one." He smiled at me. "I cheated," he confessed. "I had one of the staff mark it for me with her nail polish. I've never even been in here."

The wooden door groaned when he pushed it open. All the men held back, using their southern manners to wait for me to enter first. But I had my reservations. Neglected buildings had a way of becoming home to any wayward critter. I had no intention of getting mauled by an angry racoon residing in the annex, whether it was God's house or not. I peeked in and spied spider webs, mice droppings, and layers of dust, but no raccoon.

Father Cunningham swatted the cobwebs hanging in the corner of the window. "The women's Solidarity Club volunteered to clean for you. I'm told the refrigerator in the corner works, or it did several years ago. There's a bathroom to the left. Water hasn't been on in some time." He drifted away with Rolland to inspect the bathroom. Doc Sylvan hadn't uttered a word. When they got a safe distance away, I spoke up.

"Well? Will it work?"

He sighed and his gaze moved around the room. "It could work as a temporary site until you get your building up and running. I'm not sure what services we could offer, maybe have a room for screenings, another one for routine illness or injuries. Section off a space for the waiting room." He paused to sneeze out a snootful of dust and find his handkerchief. "I bet they would let you borrow some folding chairs. Have you heard from Dr. Carrington?"

"No, I figured he would call you first, seein' how you're buddies."

Rolland and Father Cunningham returned to our huddle. "I think we're going to need to update some of the electrical wiring," Rolland said, transferring grime from his hands to his jeans. "Won't know about the plumbing until the water gets turned on." He looked directly at me. "We gonna need a use permit for this here clinic?"

I had no idea what he was talking about, but I wasn't about to give up now. "We'll find out," I answered.

The general in me took over and I started spewing orders.

"Father, I can't thank you enough for your kindness and support. This will be perfect, but I think we need to do more homework. Doc, you talk to Dr. Carrington and whoever else will be staffing the clinic. We also need to know what kind of equipment they might need installed. Rolland, talk to some of your connections and see if we will need a permit or town council approval. I'm heading off to the library to do some more research on this whole process and any legal necessities." I turned to look at the priest. "Father, what color do you want to paint the walls? Oh, and since you folks are so good at blessing people and things, we're gonna need one for the ribbon cutting ceremony."

Father Cunningham gave me another angelic smile and a pat on the back. I'm pretty sure in Catholic that translated to, "No problem."

🦋 🦋 🦋

Seeing as how the Catholics came through for the town, I set out to challenge the other churches. I was returning from the Piggly Wiggly when I made a sharp right and found my way to my church. Short of Rolland and his family volunteering to help, the Baptists hadn't done a dern thing. As luck would have it, both Preacher Dave and Preacher Caleb were there. I told them what the Catholics had offered and asked what our church was going to contribute.

Preacher Caleb wasn't going to take that sitting down. He jumped up out of his seat like an armadillo in a headlight. "You are absolutely right, Leandra." He pointed a calloused finger in my direction. "It is our duty to

God to take care of the less fortunate and I can't see how we can let the Catholics do all the work. Preacher Dave, how 'bout we run up to Willow River Baptist Church and see if we can't coordinate a fundraiser? I bet our women folk could come up with something delicious, fun, or useful. The preacher up there is a childhood friend o' mine. You up for a drive? I am surely up for a challenge!"

🦋 🦋 🦋

After that, we were off and running. The semester was underway at the nursing school, so we'd need to wait another four or five months to get a new batch of senior nurses to assess the patients. That would give the teachers plenty of time to get the paperwork untangled from the nursing school red tape. First year nursing students would be hands-off, utilized for intake and patient medical history. Largely, it involved working off of a form, but I was told just getting the new nursing students comfortable talking about personal information was an education in itself. Who would ever want to ask someone's granny about her private parts?

The turnover in student nurses would allow time to build out the annex and collect furnishings for the patients and staff.

🦋 🦋 🦋

"Doc, Doc!" I shouted as I burst through Doc's front door, scaring him within an inch of a stroke. "You're never gonna believe this."

Doc walked out from the back, still clinging to a patient's chart.

"Leandra! What's all the screamin'? Quit scaring the patients and my new nurse. What do you mean bustin' in here like a bull?"

"Sorry, Eloise," I apologized to his nurse, who was wide-eyed and a little pale. I whipped around to face Doc. "Dr. Carrington talked to the hospital board, and they not only voted to rotate their medical students through the clinic, but he convinced them to donate old equipment he claimed was sitting in the basement collecting dust." My hands were flapping around like a barn full of swallows and I was nearly jumping up and down. "He said 'it was just taking up space.' And lickety-split, we were gifted three examination tables. He told me there are a few cracks in the vinyl, but we can cover that with duct tape and a nicely placed sheet. A lot of places are using rolled paper to cover the bed, and afterwards they pitch it in the trash. Whatever it is, we'll make do."

"Are you done?" he asked.

"Yes, sir." I caught my breath.

"Good. Now get out of my office and we'll talk later."

But I was too excited. I grabbed him by the shoulders and gave him a big kiss on the cheek. Both his patients, then Eloise started laughing.

The last thing I heard as I ran out was, "Dang it! Leandra! You nearly knocked an old man off his feet. Then where would you be?"

He was what I called cute-grumpy.

🦋 🦋 🦋

It was only one in the afternoon, but I was floating through the day. Four months had passed and in another 30, maybe 45 days, we might open. I had to remind myself this was the easy part. Trying to manage a clinic was going to be a serious commitment. It was time to set up a board for Chrysalis Clinic. Figuring I would have to collect volunteers initially, I wandered back into town to find Mr. Blackwell, the printer. I thought he was a kind-hearted man with a need to make things right about his uncle dying from medical neglect. That's when I saw a sight that turned my stomach.

There, plain as day, stood John and Donny, outside the back door to the bank. I casually turned my head in their direction while waiting at the stoplight. My window was down, and in another second I was going to shout out a friendly hello to them. But next thing I knew, I saw Mary Jean, the bank teller divorcée standing in the doorway, sweet as you please. While Donny pulled on his hand, clearly wanting to leave, John leaned in toward that red brick building, grinning, and laughing like a trained monkey I'd seen on TV's *Wild Kingdom*. My chest imploded when Mary Jean sidled up to him like they were best friends. All kinds of sirens went off in my head while a red flag waved overhead.

They were having an affair.

A shrieking car horn brought me back. My stomach felt like I had swallowed a bag full of lead fishing weights. I proceeded through the green light and pulled over at the next block. My hands shook with the rest of me, and I let go of the wheel, turning off the ignition. John was cheating on me and it was all my fault.

Time raced backward through my mind: days, weeks, months. How long had this been going on? Were there signs I missed or ignored? Then, my counter-thinking kicked in. What if this was nothing and I was reading into what I saw? John knew practically everyone in town. It's possible they were having an innocent conversation. If only I could get out of my head the way he had snubbed Donny's attention in exchange for Mary Jean's.

Mr. Blackwell and my new medical board would have to wait. Once I settled down, I headed back home.

I hightailed it to the bathroom and brought up vomit from my toes. Mostly it was bile as I had neglected to eat the entire day. The kitchen clock read four. I had nothing prepared for dinner, the kitchen was filled with dirty dishes and cluttered counters. Even the cat looked neglected. I reached for the phone and dialed Mamaw's number. I needed to remind John why he was still my husband.

"Mamaw? Can you two babysit Donny for a few hours tonight?"

"We'd love to have Donny visit." There was a long pause. "You okay, Leandra?"

Damn that woman was part bloodhound.

"Yes, of course. Just feel like John and I could use a nice dinner with someone else doing the cooking and dishes. Like a date night. I'm gonna hop in the shower and surprise him when he gets home. I'll stop by around six."

"Sure thing, darlin'. We'll see y'all soon."

I flew upstairs like a teenage girl on her first date with a new boyfriend. While I showered, shaved, and primped, I tried to invent a logical reason that made sense of what I saw. I knew he had been working with the bank for several weeks to reevaluate his farm loan. Maybe I needed to ask his daddy a little more about what was really going on.

When 7:15 rolled across the clock's face and there was no sign of John, I started upstairs to get undressed. I felt like a cheap whore sitting there, waiting for a man to show up and enjoy my company. What did I expect? I hadn't been spending any time at home. I wondered if my two men were having dinner with Mary Jean. If he did, it was a small town and tongues would be wagging before tomorrow.

I heard Donny before I saw him. His sweet voice called for me, and his methodic footsteps clomped up the stairs in an irregular rhythm. At some point John came up behind him and carried him to the landing at the top. When they found me, I had kicked off my heels and was putting my jewelry away.

"You smell good," John commented. "What you all dressed up for? You have something goin' with the girls?"

The phone screamed in my ear. Why did it sound so loud? Oh, my goodness, Mamaw! In one short reach, John picked up the extension.

"Tonight? I don't know anything about it. Hold on a minute." John looked at me. "Were we goin' out tonight? Mamaw said she was babysitting. Dang, did I forget something?"

I grabbed the phone from his hand and heard Mamaw's voice. He smelled like a rosebud, not a farmer. "Leandra?"

"Sorry, Mamaw. It didn't work out and I forgot to call."

"You sure everything is fine?"

"Yes, ma'am. I'm just a little disappointed."

"Well, we are too. Maybe Donny can come by for a visit tomorrow."

I hung up the phone and John was still staring at me. I gave him a half-hearted smile and tried to pretend I wasn't hurting. "I wanted to surprise you. Make it a date night. The Elks have their prime rib dinner on Saturdays. That's all."

"I would have liked that. But don't you remember? Donny, tell Mama what you did today."

"Tractors. We saw big tractors and I got to sit in them. And I milked a pig."

I opened my mouth to say, "That's nice, honey," but got wondering how Donny could milk a pig.

John corrected him. "That was a goat, Donny. You milked a goat."

Donny nodded in agreement.

"Leandra, don't you remember I told you I was going to that Future Farmer's event at the fairgrounds? They had a fundraiser our farm sponsored. We furnished the steer they cooked to raise money for their national trip. They had a big ol' tractor display and Donny got to crawl all over them. And that barbeque was good."

"I'm so sorry, John, I plain forgot. I know you have your community projects too. Maybe I should spend more time paying attention to what you're doing." I shrugged my shoulders, trying to pretend it was no big deal that my plans fell through. "I'm glad y'all had a good time."

"You could have come with us, but you had that meeting with the Catholics."

At that point I clamped down on my lips not to ask about seeing him at the bank. I wasn't ready to hear what he had to say.

"I know." I cut him short. I was a fool and wanted to exit the room. "I need to use the bathroom and get undressed. Would you unzip my dress?"

I turned my back to him. His hands were warm on the back of my neck. He pulled my hair to the side to find the zipper. All I could think about was him doin' that to Mary Jean.

He leaned in close. "Maybe we can have our date night some other weekend. An overnight trip might be fun."

"That sounds nice, John. I'll catch up with the two of you downstairs."

It was hard to answer him or even smile. Tears bubbled to the surface, and I excused myself to quietly vomit in the upstairs bathroom for the second time. I needed a cup of peppermint tea and some soda crackers.

Chapter 7

The Hand You Are Dealt

Today is one of those no-account days when I am forced to plan my life around my many doctor appointments. Fortunately, I have a lifetime membership to the free Chrysalis Clinic. On those days, I set up a game of solitaire in my parlor to fill in the hours, while I wait for them to work me into their schedule. This is the only time I play cards.

I can't figure out why I choose to do this. Some smarty-pants say solitaire is a form of addiction or believe it quiets the boredom and loneliness. Maybe it's how an old woman makes certain her mind still works and prays her body will follow suit. Secretly, I know as long as I can play solitaire, I will cheat death.

To this day, every time I lay out those cards, I hear Mamaw's voice, "It's the hand you're dealt."

🦋 🦋 🦋

How was I going to tell Doc that my stomach was in knots 'cause I saw my husband with another woman? For the last seven days, I could keep precious little in my stomach. It tore up my insides. I had to fix myself before I could get my head around a failed marriage.

Doc started with his usual list of questions. "You say this has gone on for a week? Anything you ate that may have been bad? How long's it been since you tested your well water?"

"If it's our well water, why am I the only one having problems?"

"Donny and John are okay?"

"Yep. Even if my food stays down it goes right through me."

"Anything upsetting you? I know you have a lot going on with the clinic opening, but it could be you're winding yourself up like a yo-yo and tearing up your gut."

How much I wanted to open my heart and tell him what I'd seen. I knew Doc would keep my secret like so many others, but if I did tell him it would only give credence to what I believed I'd seen. I wasn't ready to accept that.

You'd have thought he was reading my mind. "You and John doin' alright?"

Oh God, had he seen John running around town with Mary Jean? I was gonna get caught in a lie. Or was he dropping a hint? No wonder I had the runs.

"We've been having words," I replied. "He thinks I spend too much time away from home. And I do."

We'd had more than words. It was a dragged-out screaming match that morning. It seemed like nothing made sense anymore. Neither one of us could do anything right in the other's eyes. We were both good people, but I wondered if we had crossed that invisible line you can never cross back over. I would find the most stupid nitpicking things to point out to him, things that never bothered me before.

"Leandra, the milk's soured again! Can you find time in your busy schedule to go shopping?"

I stood at a sink full of dirty dishes and turned to see him in front of an open refrigerator. My eyes caught sight of crumbled dirt clods scattered across my white linoleum floor.

"John, can't you just once sweep up after you track in dirt? Or better yet, is it too much trouble to kick off your boots before you come in from the cattle yard?"

He was steaming but changed the subject. "I'll be late comin' in tonight. Maybe I'll catch dinner in town, so I know the food isn't spoiled."

"I bet you enjoy stayin' in town 'til all hours of the night! I hope you have someone pretty to keep you company."

"What kinda fool comment is that? What's that supposed to mean?"

I turned to reply when a soapy platter slipped from my hand and cracked open in the sink. I stared at the broken dish. I loved that platter. Someone gave it to me for a wedding present. I grabbed the two halves from the sink and slammed them to the floor. They sprinkled the kitchen with shattered china.

"Are you crazy?" he screamed. "I might never come home if you keep this up!" He stormed out the door.

Doc listened without judgment. "You're not one to sit still, Leandra. I understand that, but John might not. Any chance you could be pregnant?"

My mouth dropped open like a trap door. Dear Lord, that's all I needed. A pregnancy with an unstable marriage. But maybe that would boot Mary Jean out of our marriage once and for all. I didn't answer.

Doc continued without my input. "I suspect you hadn't considered that possibility. Just the same, we should check. Pee in this." He handed me a cold metal pan.

I swallowed hard. I didn't need a pregnancy right now. The first one, Autumn, was definitely unwanted. I was young, unmarried, broke, and abandoned. My penance for that was losing my sweet baby before her first birthday. When Donny was on the way, I was so happy. I thought my life would always be sunshine and rainbows. But here I stood with one leg in a tornado.

He was still charting on me when I went back to the exam room. "You can get dressed now. I'll call you later today or tomorrow." Doc put his hand on my shoulder, his way of saying it was all going to be all right.

"So, I can't do anything about my guts?"

"Not until we know if you're growing a baby. In the meantime, stick with bland, light food. Nothin' spicy or greasy. We'll know soon enough. Get some rest, Leandra. You look plumb tuckered out."

I didn't want to go back home. Mamaw was watching Donny for a few hours, and I needed to clear my head. I started out of town toward the bridge that would take me across the river to Lover's Leap. *Appropriate enough*, I thought to myself. Maybe I would find some understanding there. For all my years living there, I had rarely hiked the Appalachian Trail. Today it called to me.

The air was thick and steamy from the summer heat, but cool breezes passed through the trail. Everything smelled green with crushed pieces of last fall's leaves still nestled under the pines and leafy trees. When the wind shifted in the right direction, or the forest stood still, you could hear the running waters whisper. I crossed a wooden bridge spanning a small wash, this time only hearing my footsteps echo.

Nausea rose to my tonsils and urged me to sit. I was glad I grabbed some snack crackers from the gas station before my hike. While I chewed through my crackers, my thoughts gnawed at me. I was stupid and over-emotional, picking my marriage apart with one hand, holding distrust in the other. I didn't know anything for certain and wondered, *Should I just ask?* Did I need to spy on him? Follow him around like some sick jealous wife? Us Southerners were not known for our tact and patience.

In a little over two hours, I finished my walk and circled back to the car. I decided I needed more information, and nothing could move forward in my life until I knew I had a future with John. I pulled into the driveway to Papaw's farm, packed with one car stacked behind another. I thought I recognized some of them. Who knew what Papaw had going on for this kind of crowd to gather? Around back, I saw Donny and Archie by the barn. He came running to me with melted chocolate smeared all over his face. I'm sure Archie was sharing one of his Hershey bars with him.

"Mommy, Mommy!" he shouted.

"I need a chocolate kiss," I replied and collected him in my arms. He willingly puckered up and kissed my lips with his sweetness. We were laughing when we walked through the kitchen door and into the parlor.

"Hello?" I called out.

Ten eyes were upon me. I looked at Mamaw's face. She was holding a tissue in her lap. My mother-in-law Ruby was there. Donny slipping from my grip, my life froze in time.

"Leandra." Mamaw stood and started to speak but her face crunched up and she squeezed her eyes tight, trying to hold back what had to come out. I was so afraid my skin crawled like a snake winding up my left arm. In a brief second, I scanned the room and saw Papaw standing in the corner. Who was missing from my family circle?

Mamaw glided toward me while Ruby quietly sobbed from her high-back chair. "We didn't know where to find you. Doctor Sylvan said he thought you were on your way home." It was her soft, church voice, soothing and articulate. She took my hand. I saw a thick tear fall and stain her purple apron. "There's been an accident, honey. It happened early this afternoon." I started shaking my head no before she finished. I was crying with her and I didn't know why. She bit her upper lip like she didn't want the words to come out.

"John's passed, Leandra. The tractor he was driving tipped, and he was thrown. It fell on top of him. He's with Jesus now, darlin'. It happened so quickly."

I wasn't sure how long I held my breath, but I started to grow lightheaded. Ruby's sobs were louder. Someone was shaking me.

"Leandra! Leandra?"

Someone said, "Sit her down."

The air rushed back into my lungs. "My John?" I looked at their faces, shaking my head in denial of what they said.

Papaw spoke up. "These things happen on a farm, Leandra. You know this. John was out in the pasture with his brother Jake and John Sr. His daddy said he couldn't figure what was wrong with him. All morning it was like his head wasn't screwed on straight. They were getting ready to disc the field and next thing he sees John's tractor with the bucket straight up in the air, the wheels lifted, and the tractor tipped to the side. All the rain this month saturated the ground and it gave way. The bucket pulled the tractor right over. John Sr. raced across the field, but he slipped in the mud. By the time he got to his feet and ran over there, John was already gone."

"Jake and his daddy are beyond themselves," Mamaw added. "They were right there and couldn't stop it. John's sister, Amy, is taking care of them."

I managed to get a few more words out. "Where is he? What have they done with my husband?"

"He's over at Nelson's mortuary." Ruby wiped her nose. "The sheriff ruled it an accident. Maybe tomorrow, the next day, we can go over and make arrangements."

Pain washed over me like a dam had burst. I hadn't considered what Ruby was feeling. Her son. Her youngest son. I knew her pain. I had been there myself. But no one else knew about that hole in my heart.

I stood up, nearly falling into Mamaw's glass antique chest. "I have to go home and feed the cat." I couldn't seem to get my balance, like I was standing in a rowboat.

"No, you don't," Papaw said. "It's not your job to worry about the cat." His dry chapped farm hand grabbed my arm. He was still strong as an old bull, and he steadied me. "Let's get you upstairs and into bed. Mamaw will bring you some hot tea. You hungry? Mamaw has a pot of beans and warm cornbread on the back of the stove."

My stomach turned upside down. I sat on the bed, unsure if it could support me. I was unsure of everything.

"Make sure Donny gets something to eat." I turned toward him. "It's a good thing that Donny won't remember his daddy, right, Papaw?" Tears poured down my cheeks and I ignored them. "I mean it won't be like me, just getting to know my daddy and he got killed in the war. I was older. I knew him. Donny's just a baby, so he won't know the difference." I couldn't control my thinking. "Where will I bury John, Papaw? Should he rest by the butterfly bush with me? Should he be with his family?"

With a gentle move, Papaw put his index finger over my mouth. "I'm sorry, Leandra, but you're talkin' about things we don't need to worry about tonight. You need rest. Tomorrow will make better sense to all of us."

🦋 🦋 🦋

There was no sleep that night. Guilt ran through my veins like battery acid. John's daddy said he wasn't acting right, like his mind wasn't there. I knew where John's head was when that tractor rolled onto him. I was certain of his last thoughts. We were in a rage when he stormed out of the house. All day, he must have choked on our hurtful words until his last thoughts ended on our ugliness. Could his soul hear me now? Did he know what a terrible person I was, and the past I had laid behind me?

I drifted downstairs and ended up in the parlor. The shadowy room, now empty, stared back at me. I thought of the people who filled it a few hours earlier when they told me my husband was dead. I pictured them like ghosts still sitting there. I pictured John sitting with them.

When I pulled open the squeaky front door, the outside air rushed past me. I recalled that day John drove to the farm for our "church date." He stole my heart that summer. Where was the silver butterfly necklace he gave me? I should have never taken it off. How could he leave me now?

I stepped off the front porch stairs into the wet grass and darkness. My sleeping gown was thin, and the cold ground chilled my soul. I checked the sky to make sure the stars were still hanging above. In answer, a bright star arched across the night sky. How I wanted to run and never look back! But no matter where I ran, my damned life followed me. I crumpled to the ground, wishing I could sink into the soft dirt where a good part of my family was buried.

"No, no, no!" I pounded my fists, crushing the grass until it covered my hands with green ooze. My voice elevated and filled the empty night. I didn't know if I was cursing the farm, or God, or my very existence. "Not again! You think you can keep taking? My father? My child? My brother? My husband? Take me! I'm tired," I sobbed. "Take me."

I don't know how long I screamed at the black earth or when Mamaw and Papaw surrounded me, lifting me from the muck. I saw Donny standing in the doorway, frightened, unsure of what he had witnessed. I wanted to comfort him, yet I didn't have anything left to give.

"I'll stay with her, Zachary. Get me a couple towels so we can dry her and take Donny back inside. He doesn't need to see his mama like this. No one's taking your child, Leandra, see? Donny is right there. And you're right. You have had more than your share of loss. Let's make this the last."

We sat on the porch swing, me tightly bound in a plaid woolen blanket, while Mamaw rubbed my hands and legs dry.

"Look there, it's starting to dawn." Mamaw pointed to the east horizon, already promising another day. Shades of orange and pink intensified as the colors squeezed through light fog.

"I don't want to see another day, Mamaw. It will only bring more pain."

"Don't take life for granted, Leandra. You, above all, should see how precious it is." She wrapped her arm around me and pulled me in tight. "Don't you think John would be here in a heartbeat if he got a second chance? He loved life, his farm, you, and Donny."

"I'm not sure he loved me."

She reared back and looked me in the face, not uttering a sound.

"We were fighting that morning." I started crying again. "Oh, Mamaw, he wasn't paying attention to his work 'cause we were fighting. I killed him!"

"Hear me good, Leandra. You did *not* kill John. If he's listening now, he's pitchin' a fit for you sayin' that. It was an accident. It's not the devil, it's not God, it's not you. It's the cards we're dealt. You understand?"

I told her I understood, but certain things you can't let go.

I wiped my nose on my gown sleeve.

She muscled me out of the swing and led me back upstairs to my room. After digging in the dresser drawer, she threw a dry gown my way. "Get back to bed. No sense in you stayin' up but I should probably go put on the coffee and start some grits."

"What makes you think I can sleep?"

"Wait. I got a little something to calm you. C'mon now," she ordered. "Get changed and under the covers. I'll be right back."

She disappeared down the hall and returned to hand me a white pill. I stared at it for a moment until I realized what I was seeing. *God in Heaven,* I thought, *I'm just like my mama.* I remembered how they drugged her after Daddy died. And her carrying Raymond inside of her. It was the alcohol and drugs that made him a dull child.

"No thank you." I handed it back. "I'll just try to rest on my own."

"Suit yourself. Get some sleep."

I looked at the alarm clock sitting on the nightstand. In about five hours, Doc Sylvan would call about my pregnancy test.

Chapter 8

Community and Kin

So many hardships have shaped my life. I wonder, how did I get through those times and keep my sanity? How did I find the will to keep going? Part of it was the good people holding me up. I won't ever forget that. In times since then I have made sure I am there to help others as best I can. It's The Golden Rule we need to remember each and every day.

🦋 🦋 🦋

The devil caught up with me. My jealousy stole my husband. Then Doc advised me I had another child on the way. If anyone had asked me then what was in my heart, I'm not sure I could have answered with any degree of certainty. My feelings were as jumbled and scattered as a broken strand of beads.

I grieved for a man I loved, having had a hand in contributing to his death. I carried his child, who would never know his or her father. I walked down that same road with my first baby, Autumn. All I could do now was put one foot in front of the other and pray to keep walking upright.

Ruby, Mamaw, and I clustered in a room filled with caskets. About ten feet away, Mr. Nelson Sr. described the virtues of each box. My eyes skimmed the cotton-candy colored satin lining each casket. One death leads to another, and I thought of little Autumn and my brother, Ray. Both their deaths were different, long done, but somehow it all came forward again. I took a deep sigh and leaned over to whisper to Mamaw.

"It's a damn box," I whispered. "It's going in the ground. John wouldn't care about any of this."

Ruby latched on to the conversation. "I agree. I think the services and celebration would be more important to John."

"Then I'm stopping him here and now. Mr. Nelson?" I waved at him, halting his recital. I stepped through the grove of caskets to a simple pine box with white satin. "This will do fine," I said, running my hand over the polished, light wood. That simple action connected me to the reality that John was gone. I saw him in the casket, holding a small black Bible. He was too beautiful and young to be buried. The broken ribs and spine, punctured lungs, crushed heart, and fractured pelvis would not be seen inside his best suit. His face would be at peace, not like the anguish in his final seconds of life.

My knees weakened and I collapsed on the floor.

Mamaw and Ruby rushed to my side, giving directions to Mr. Nelson. He was no spring chicken, but he managed to pick me up and usher me into a chair.

"Should we get a doctor? Call for help?" he asked.

"No, all the help she needs is right here," Mamaw replied. "Ruby, drive the car around. Mr. Nelson, we can probably take care of the rest of this later or on the phone. She needs to rest."

The nervous man nodded in agreement. I guess the dead were a lot less trouble than the living.

I despised being fragile and weak. Death brought interruptions and hurt. On top of that, I was dealing with the new life growing inside me. I swore Doc to secrecy and told him I would tell the family about the baby when the time was right. Back at the farm, I refused to lie down. There was too much to do.

"I got the rest of my life to catch up on my sleep. We have to finish planning John's memorial, so save your breath and quit coddlin' me."

So, there I sat in the parlor, with four old people planning the funeral for my young husband. It went on for two days with Donny's Aunt Amy getting him out from underfoot. Pastor Dave dropped in and reassured us he would have a fine send-off for John. God sends out his angels in a variety of forms, and casseroles started coming in until the refrigerator and freezer were jam-packed. Even Vernetta, the church lady, dropped by with one of her lemon loaf cakes.

Unlike my mama before me, I refused the temptation of drowning my pain in drugs or booze. The day before the funeral, keys in hand, Papaw advised me he was picking up Mama from the bus station. I could swear the devil was poking at me with every pitchfork he possessed. With Mama, I learned to expect the unexpected. Until that time, I never considered she would come to stand by my side.

"I don't believe it," I replied. "You mean Roger sprung for a bus ticket?"

"I can't address that," Papaw said in his noncommittal way. "But, Leandra, let's give her the benefit of the doubt. People can change."

"Papaw, you're gettin' soft in your old age. My wounds from Ray are still fresh. It's hard for me to trust her. What if she embarrasses me and gets drunk at the funeral?"

He started in with religion. "Forgive us our debts as we also forgive our debtors."

I shook my head. "I can't. I just can't." I walked out of the room.

The funeral was one day away. Thinking about all the trouble Mama could cause, I pushed my way out the back screen door and climbed the hill to my special tree. The challenge was greater than in the time when I was a young'un, but I managed to dodge every last cow patty and watched the cows scatter like they did when I was a kid. I worried I couldn't find my tree, but sure enough, there it stood in a cluster of wild woods. In the middle sat my old wooden crate. Papaw's rusty hammer was still hiding underneath it, but the tarp that sheltered my hideaway had long since blown to pieces. I plopped down on the crate and looked around from my vantage point. Life had been simple when I was a young girl but, even at that time, I was hiding from my father's recent death. Was it easier back then? I examined my heart and, no, the same hollow feeling echoed inside me. I was a shell and half of me was missing. No one could hear my cries and screams, so for the next hour I cursed God, my life, my future and past, the land, anything I could think of to let the world know how it hurt me. The trees listened with sympathy. It wasn't fair for one person to stew in this much pain.

🦋 🦋 🦋

I have always been grateful we cannot stop time. If I could, this would have been one of those opportunities and I would have grabbed it like a life preserver. I was not ready to say goodbye to John. But the day came as planned and I dressed in black head to toe. I wanted my grief to show.

In paying respects to the Tucker family, town folks packed the church. There was no need for police escorts because everyone was at the funeral and nearly every business was shut down.

"Zachary," Mamaw directed, "the parking lot's almost full. Pull up here and let us out."

We got out of the car and I paused to look up at the white church steeple. "Mama, do you know this is where he took me for our first date? And now here I am for our final goodbye."

Mama just smiled. She knew I was babbling and half out of my mind. We were early, but folks were already collecting, and I felt their eyes turn toward me. I was too shaky to stand and make conversation, so Mamaw and Mama held me up like two pillars and walked me to the front of the church. The Tucker family sat across the aisle. I couldn't sit down until I hugged each one of them. I had to. I needed their strength.

Pastor Dave's booming voice was gentle this time. He explained that John's short time with us was his special gift. We needed to appreciate how he touched our lives with his generous nature and helping hands. While I wiped the tears from my swollen face, all I could feel was cheated. My life kept getting busted into pieces and cast away like broken limestone, brittle and filled with things that had long since died. I would remember my life with my husband, and my life afterward without him. These lives could not be compared, just recognized for what they were.

It's always the music that gets to me. Once the organist plays "Rock of Ages," "Amazing Grace," or "Abide with Me," and the voices meld together like honey and butter on toast, I can never hold it together. That was true that day too, but I sure hope someone plays those songs at my funeral. It's like the angels themselves were singing John home. I've heard tell that our spirits show up at our own funerals. I tried to picture John sitting next to me, patting me on the shoulder to calm me down like he always did.

John's casket was carried to the mortuary limousine by men he had known all his life. Winding like a serpent, the line of cars followed and made their way from the church to the family plot. The butterfly bush, stationed like a sentry, let all mourners pass. Filled with purple and some pink, spiked blooms, I imagined what that graceful bush witnessed in the hundred years it had stood over the Barkers. I glanced at Autumn's flowers, Daddy's hickory tree, Ray and Addie's headstones. The family picked a site near the back of the hill. I hadn't had time to clear a trail to the spot where John would rest, but we made sure I would have a place next to him. I thought of generations to come who would stand over us and say, "Why, those are Tuckers, not Barkers. What are they doing here?" I made a mental note that my headstone would be titled Leandra Barker Tucker, so folks would understand our connection to the land.

I was flanked on each side by family. Even though they seated me, my knees still shook. Donny sat on Papaw's lap. What was my poor baby thinking? Across from the casket, I caught sight of the Tuckers. Ruby and John Sr. held onto each other as they stared at the pine box draped with white roses. I could hardly breathe watching the casket lowered into the ground. It was the Appalachian ground John had farmed all his life. It wasn't supposed to swallowed him up at the height of his life. Death never makes sense to us mortals.

🦋 🦋 🦋

I wanted the gathering to be at our home on the cattle farm. Once again, the line of cars crept through the two-lane country roads until they stopped in the same field where they had parked for our wedding a few short years before. The equipment barn was cleared of machinery, making room for our guests to gather. While the visitors collected, I wandered off to the side of the out-building where they'd stashed the crumpled tractor, the metal beast that killed my husband.

Mama found me standing there. "I see you, child." She took my hand. "I see you are a stronger woman than me. You raised yourself and you did a good job. You'll feel better once that ugly thing is moved to the scrap heap. For now, come back to the barn with me. There will be stories about John, happy stories, which will make you feel better about your loss."

We walked arm-in-arm back to the barn. Papaw was right. It was time to forgive. The years she had tormented me with her drinking and failure as a mother must be put aside. Holding onto pain never does any good.

Faces and voices blurred. People handed me food and drink. They sat me in a comfortable chair, and I was blessed with a beautiful day and kind people. Then, I looked up to see Mary Jean walking toward me. Now she wouldn't have him any more than I would. The crowd was thinning, and I hoped she would leave. Instead, she pulled up a chair and sat down next to me.

"Leandra, I'm so sorry about John." She placed her hand on top of mine. "Honey, I need to tell you something."

My heart stopped. Was she going to tell me she was in love with my husband? What gall! I was astounded and felt heat rising to my head.

Mary Jean retracted her hand, resting it in her lap. "I debated about saying anything to you. I had to ask myself, and several friends, what should I do? What would *I* want'?"

I let her carry on and tried to decide which two men would throw her off my property.

"Leandra, John had stopped by the bank several times. You know he was updating his loan arrangement with us. That's always important to these farmers with the upcoming season. Well, we got done, and he asked me how I would feel about increasing that farm loan by a couple o' thousand dollars, so he could take you to Hawaii on a second honeymoon." She pulled a tissue out of her purse and wiped her eyes, she shook her head, and turned down her mouth in a severe pout. "He was so excited. He wanted it to be perfect. I even gave him the name and number of my friend who owns a travel agency. Every time he met with her, he'd come back and tell me how his plans were going. I wanted you to know. He loved you so much, Leandra."

We were both sobbing. She pulled out another tissue for me.

"Did you know?" she asked. I couldn't speak so I shook my head, no. "He tried so hard to keep it from you, he wanted to make it a big surprise." She pulled out a business card and handed it to me. "This is her card, Lisa Davis, Getaway Travel. I don't think he had purchased the cruise tickets, but you can talk to Lisa."

"Cruise?"

"Oh, yes. He wanted to take you on one of those big ships and visit all the islands. Maybe I didn't make that clear." She stood to leave. "I didn't mean to upset you, Leandra. But Lisa and I thought you should know. I expect you'll be stopping by the bank to settle things up. I'll be available any time you need me."

She gave my hand a gentle squeeze and walked away without me saying another word.

How would God ever forgive me? How would I forgive myself? I tore into John because he was planning a special trip for me. There was no affair. I might as well have pushed the tractor over with my own two hands.

I couldn't move. It was my turn to die. I sat glued to the folding chair, completely overwhelmed. Pretty soon the women folk got me up and moved into the house.

"Leandra," Mama said, "I'm stayin' with you for the next few nights."

I looked over to Mamaw.

"You don't want to be alone now," Mamaw reminded me. "Yo mama is goin' to help with Donny. And if she has any questions, you're right there. It will be a wonderful chance for the two o' them to get to know each otha."

Forgiveness whispered to me. Mama called to Donny, and he came running, eager to play with his new grandma.

"I didn't know I had two grandmas." He handed her a flower he had pulled from the field.

"For me?" she asked, and he nodded in reply. She looked up at me. "Oh, this one's gonna be a heartbreaker."

"Do I have two Papaws too?"

"In a manner of speakin'." She smiled at me and winked. "I'll explain durin' yo' bath."

After Donny's scrubbing, I settled Mama into our guest room. "How've you been gettin' on, Mama? Is Roger treatin' you okay?"

"Well, you know, Roger does his thing and I do mine. Most the time we stay out of each other's hair. He's still helpin' with the housework. The doctor thinks I might have some problems with my liver. That's no surprise with my drinkin' and all. I can't be the drunk I used to be. Makes me sick as a dog."

I nodded sympathetically and stopped asking questions.

Exhaustion overtook me and I could hardly move. She tucked Donny into bed and went in the kitchen to make herself a sandwich from the funeral leftovers. I couldn't eat, so I walked out to the back porch that overlooked the east pasture. The cattle had bedded down for the night and the sun fell below the ridge, making a golden glow over the land. Now and then I could hear a mournful moo. Often the mama cows would cry for days when their calves were suddenly taken from them. I didn't want to share their pain and loss tonight. I couldn't see myself living here with pieces of our lives scattered everywhere I turned. Last week, we were a family and had a future. Today I buried it.

With my last ounce of energy, I climbed the stairs to the bedrooms, announcing to Mama I was taking a bath, and asked if she would keep an ear open for Donny. The steaming water fogged the mirror and blurred my image. I didn't want to look at myself anyway. How would I live with myself for the rest of my life? Out of humiliation, I vowed to never tell anyone about John's surprise trip and my jealous bones.

I climbed into the tub, immediately soothed by the warm water. I've always loved water and Hawaii would have been heavenly with John. Now he was in heaven by himself. My head fell back against the tub and the tears started again. I bit hard into my wet washcloth, sobbing, closing my eyes, and praying my agony would pass. When I finally opened my eyes, the bath water was blood red. I was losing John's baby.

I stared at the water. In a week's time, I had lost my husband, found out I was pregnant and now, lost that life too. Numb, I washed off, rinsed the tub, and watched another life drain away from me. One more secret to take to my grave.

🦋 🦋 🦋

I wanted nothing more to do with the Angus farm. They tell you not to make any big decisions when you lose someone you love. Wait a year, they say. This farm killed my husband and my baby. I had no business being here. I wanted to go home to my farm.

When someone related to you dies, there is always a lot of paperwork to shuffle. John didn't have a will. What young healthy man does? North Carolina divided John's property between me and Donny. I went to see Eugene Sutter, attorney at law. Papaw always had an intense dislike for attorneys, but in this case I had no choice. Mama had long since returned to New Jersey and I was settling into my new life. Death shouldn't be so complicated, but it certainly wasn't going to make any allowances for me.

I decided to take John Sr. and John's brother, Jake, with me to meet with Mr. Sutter. They owned most of the farm and I didn't want the family thinking I was doing anything to threaten their livelihood. Farming is edgy as it is. One year you're swimming in gravy and the next year you're eating beans.

"Mrs. Tucker," said the lawyer, "do you understand your position with your inheritance? John owned one-third of the ranch, so depending on what you decide with the family, you have several choices."

I turned to John Sr. "Do y'all know what those choices are? Do you favor one over the other?"

The Tucker family was always very polite. "We have a good idea 'bout what he's gonna say, but let's hear him out."

"Your first choice is to sell out to the Tucker family. The equipment and property would be appraised, and they would put that money into an account for you and Donny. You were renting the farmhouse, correct?"

"Yes sir, that was part of the estate. There are several more out buildings and barns, and there's one or two old farmhouses set aside for the farm hands."

"Your second choice would be to retain the property as part owner of the ranch."

"I don't know much about raisin' cattle," I replied. "What use would I be to the business?"

"You're our bookkeeper," Jake answered. "You know more than you think."

"It would be more like an investment," Sutter added. "As the farm prospered, so would your bank account."

"Any other choices?" I asked, wanting to find some arrangement that excited me.

"You could pick and choose, meaning, you could sell them all the equipment and assets and keep the real estate for yourself and Donny. That also means you own part of the responsibility of keeping up a farm."

Dejected, I replied, "I'll already be inheriting Papaw's farm. Don't know if I need two."

"Well, you think about it, look at the pros and cons. I would, however, recommend you set up a trust, so little Donny can't get his hands on his inheritance until he's jumped a few hoops. Young men have a bad habit of spending their money on wine, women, and fast cars. You need to give his brain a chance to catch up with his hormones. We can set an age where he inherits the money, or earmark it for education, health, or whatever makes sense. Don't rush this, Mrs. Tucker. These are life-changing decisions and you're still grieving. You might not be yourself for quite a while."

❀ ❀ ❀

I decided to take the attorney's advice and slow things down. I stopped making plans weeks in advance. I left one day to follow another. Making time for Donny was my most important consideration. I tried to keep both of us so busy we would fall into bed at night and not wake until the birds were singing. We spent more and more time at Papaw's. One day, we were outside near the springhouse, and I asked Donny how he would like living with Mamaw and Papaw. He was at the end of his fifth year and using his ever-expanding vocabulary.

"Well, that might be nice. Mamaw's a good cook." I smiled, thinking he had his five-year-old priorities straight. "And I like spendin' time with Papaw and Archie, but they're kinda old. Are they gonna die soon?"

That sucked the air right out of my lungs. I remembered having those same fears with Mama when Daddy was killed in the war. I got down on his eye level. He was a tangle of shaggy blond hair with a splash of freckles scattered over his face, just like his Daddy.

"Donny, none of us know when it's our time to join Jesus. Mamaw and I are healthy as we can be. We'll keep close watch on you three men."

I couldn't even bring up John's death. I knew that would come later. "Donny, this may be silly, but I have to make some decisions about the cattle farm. Do you think you would want to be a farmer and rancher like your daddy, grandpa, and uncle? In ten years or less, you could be helping out with the cattle."

"I do like all the animals on the farm, especially when I get to feed the baby cows."

"Well, the little calves are cute, but it's a lot a work to take care of all those animals. Do you remember how hard Daddy worked on the ranch?"

"Uh-huh." He nodded his head. "And sometimes it smelled bad, and the flies were icky. What else can I do when I grow up?"

Little kids can be so perceptive sometimes. To this day, he has to weigh out all his choices before deciding. Even something like choosing what brand of cookies he wanted from the Piggly Wiggly caused him, and me, horrific anxiety.

Then it came to me. I found a place to sit and pulled him up in my lap.

"Let's do this," I offered. "Let's move in with Mamaw and Papaw and keep our part of the cattle farm. In the meantime, you do your growin' up. You might decide down the road you want to be a fireman, or a doctor, or a teacher. But if you do decide to be a farmer, then you can learn from the two best farmers I know, and you'll have your farm waiting for you. That way, we don't have to rush to decide anything. We'll revisit our plan every five years or so and change it if need be."

"I like that idea!" His enthusiasm made me happy for the first time in weeks.

The cicadas were singing their summer song and the white clouds scattered across the sky were perfectly spaced as if they were lined up for a barn dance. A beautiful butterfly caught my eye. A red-spotted purple butterfly, appearing more blue than purple, landed on Donny's arm.

"Stay still," I told him, "you have a new friend." Donny could listen when he had to, only turning his head to admire the insect slowly waving its wings to warm in the sun. "You know your daddy's favorite color was blue. You think he sent you that butterfly?"

His eyes got so big it looked like they'd roll back into his head. "You think so?" he asked. "Is he around here?"

"The butterfly's right there." I pointed to the insect and it sailed away.

"I mean Daddy. Sometimes I think I see Daddy."

I had heard of young children doing that. Sometimes they see things the rest of us can't. Unlike us adults, tainted by life, its hardships and fears, children were still so close to God they could see the angels. I had no intention of beating down that gift.

I held back my tears and cleared my throat. "It's very possible, baby. He loved you so much. He hears every one of your prayers and blessings, so you talk to him any time you want."

🦋 🦋 🦋

It was the dogdays of summer when we started packing to move. I had lost sight of my dream to open a free clinic. I wasn't giving up, but I needed time. I spoke to Mr. Blackwell, and he agreed to oversee the board for me. Thankfully, with summer, I had a reprieve with the students out of school or away for summer jobs.

Sorting through Donny's baby clothes was difficult. He had outgrown them so fast they were like new, and I had doubts there would be another baby in my life. John's clothes would be the hardest to work through, his soapy smell still steeped in his dress shirts. He'd only use aftershave when we stepped out, saying it attracted biting flies. That gave me a giggle to remember his ways. Like Donny, he was sometimes there talking in my head. As I boxed his belongings, the idea came to me to save John's clothes and Donny's baby clothes for the clinic. Surely, they would be useful for many poor families. That seemed to patch some of the holes in my broken heart.

Things are only useful for a specific time. You can choose to pass them on to someone else, but they might not cherish them like you did. All we have in this life is the family we cling to and the friends we bring in close to us. The rest of it doesn't matter because we're not taking it with us.

Mamaw and I went through my meager furnishings, sorting through what could be used to update the farmhouse. Archie made use of some things. Amy was pretty particular and didn't want anything I had.

Ruby commented, "At my age, I need to be gettin' rid of stuff, not collectin' more."

My life had been parceled out and my remaining life began.

Chapter 9

An Impossible Dream

Sometime around '65 or '66, a popular song, "The Impossible Dream," told the tale of a man whose dream was to make the world a better place. Now and again, you can still hear that ballad on the radio. It reminds me of the early days when the free clinic was just a dream.

When a dream takes hold, it's hardly more than a prayer you whisper in the dark. From a dim corner, that light grows and grows, and when your dream becomes a reality, you witness the best of mankind. I saw it all and I lived it all. How blessed my life has been.

🦋 🦋 🦋

Whether it was pity or dumb luck, folks came from everywhere to help open the clinic. Since I was a new widow, I regretted starting this whole business with the clinic, but I wasn't one to leave something unfinished. Mr. Blackwell did a fine job enlisting folks for the board of directors and it was a relief to have input from others, instead of relying on my limited experience.

I called our first meeting to order. "Listen up, everyone. First off, thank you for being here." We sat around a long table in the very church annex where the clinic would operate. "Y'all know Mr. Blackwell and me. Can the rest of you introduce yourselves?"

"I'll start." A petite woman with greying blonde hair in a purple paisley dress raised her hand. "I'm a member of the Sacred Heart Sodality. My name is Eleanor Gess. We're so happy we can help with the clinic."

"Mrs. Gess and her Sacred Heart Sodality club did the scrubbing and cleaning to get this place polished," I added. "Please extend our appreciation to your group." She nodded in reply. "Mrs. Gess will also be our church representative should any issues arise."

We circled the table. Rolland introduced himself as our clinic handyman. Crystal took ownership for being lost, pregnant, and in need, and being the primary cause that initiated the clinic plan. Mr. Blackwell shared his uncle's story and how the poor man died waiting for medical attention.

And Dr. Georgia McGraw was there to hold it all together. "I'm an intern and first year resident and will represent the Asheville hospital. It won't always be me attending the meetings, but the residents will rotate on and off, schedules permitting."

"Thank you, Dr. McGraw. And we also have Dr. Sylvan on our board as a consultant. He couldn't be here tonight. If we can pull this off, the community will benefit as well as the students and residents."

I pointed to the other side of the room. "The hospital was very generous in donating equipment, so we need to decide how we want to set this up. Rolland has agreed to help us divide the space and build out the area."

"I can rustle up a few more guys to help me," he added.

I pushed on with my agenda. "Let's talk about policies and how we want to serve this community. Who should be eligible for care?"

"Anyone," Crystal said. "But everyone should be responsible for givin' back. You know, helpin' out in some way, even if it's an exchange of goods for medical care."

Mr. Blackwell spoke up. "What hours were you planning on having this clinic open? We don't know what is needed around here."

"I've been studying up on that," I replied. "We need to be available at least one night a week, when folks get done with their chores or factory jobs. Maybe Thursdays from five to nine. What do all of you think?"

Dr. McGraw scribbled in her notebook. "I'll take that back to the hospital and the staff can discuss it. Ultimately, it's the teaching staff's decision, depending on what kind of experience the students need."

"We need a locked cabinet for the supplies and medications," I replied. "I don't favor anything with glass as that can be broken into."

"Maybe instead of a locked cabinet, we have a secured closet for the supplies. You'll need a small refrigerator too. Some drugs will need to be kept cold."

"What about those tanks for people that can't breathe?" Crystal asked. "In case there was an emergency."

"Oxygen tanks," Dr. McGraw answered. "She's right. We need to keep at least one tank on hand. And I suggest every volunteer be trained in CPR. They just started mass trainings in Seattle. It could save a life."

"I'm sorry, I have no idea what you're talking about." Crystal rolled her eyes and waved her off, saying what all of us were thinking. "But if you say we need it, I'm willing to learn."

After a couple of hours, I was anxious to go home and see Donny. He was in good hands with Mamaw and there was no husband waiting for me, but I still longed to be close to him. He was an extension of his daddy and since his daddy was gone, my boy deserved more from me. I wondered if what I was feeling was some deep-rooted fear that fate would take him away.

"Crystal, can you and Mr. Blackwell design a flyer to make handouts for the opening?"

"Happy to," she replied. "I love doing that artsy stuff."

"We have made incredible progress today, everyone. I know you have your own lives to get back to, so let's adjourn. Rolland, I'll get some lumber dropped off this week for the partitions and build-out. Mrs. Gess, can you find us a small refrigerator for the medications?"

"Of course, dear. The Sodality may be a clutch of old ladies, but we're very resourceful."

🦋 🦋 🦋

Within a month, the clinic build-out was nearing completion. The last volunteer left the clinic, and I locked the door behind me. I turned to leave and took pause on the clinic steps. The summer afternoons were already cooling off as another season ended. I still had my dark days, when the notion would creep into my heart that I wanted to give up, that this clinic was too much for me.

I pondered why I had done this. Was this clinic supposed to make me happy and fill my emptiness? I was starting to believe we were never genuinely happy with who we were. Maybe we have a driving belief that a better version remains undiscovered: prettier, more accomplished, wealthier, more confident, recognized. Was it just me, or did everyone feel that way?

I took a deep breath, continued down the steps, and reminded myself a small child depended on me to raise him. Donny started kindergarten in a couple of weeks which would give Mamaw and me a chance to catch up during the day when his teacher was in charge of twenty others just like him. Oh, to have that kind of strength and energy again.

🦋 🦋 🦋

Donny and I were setting the table for Mamaw when Papaw stomped up the back steps huffing and puffing. He started a coughing fit that just didn't stop. I was no nurse, but his face took on a funny color, grey or blue like his overalls. Maybe it was the dust all over his face and neck.

"Zachary," Mamaw scolded, "get out of your filthy clothes and shower off those chemicals. You and Archie shouldn't be breathin' that stuff. Why don't you wear a bandana over your face? Don't they have masks you can use?"

"Never wore one before and not startin' now. Breathin' through those things is like tryin' to get air through a straw. And Archie didn't show up for work this afternoon. Said he was feeling poorly. But I killed me a mess o' leaf hoppers with that new pesticide."

"Between you and Archie, I don't know which o' you is fallin' apart faster. Go take a shower," she pushed. "Get that stuff off o' you. Supper's in thirty minutes. Throw those clothes directly in the washer."

He wandered past me, leaned in, and winked. Speaking loud enough for her to hear him, he said, "She still loves me."

All he got out of Mamaw's yelling was, "She still loves me?" He pushed through the swinging door and into the parlor. The wind caught a chemical odor he was carrying and threw it back at me. I wrinkled my nose. They had just banned DDT for all the harm it inflicted on wildlife, including rumors about cancer. I wouldn't have been surprised to know he was still spraying it from some old can stashed in the barn. I could still hear him coughing and hacking on the other side of the door.

I turned to Mamaw. "Am I plain ignorant, or has he always coughed like that?"

"Oh, he's always had his spells," Mamaw replied. "Only the good Lord, Archie, and maybe the cows know what he does out there every day. He had a farm rep out here a couple o'days ago, so I expect he's trying some new poison on those pesky bugs. The coughing usually wanes after a couple o' days." She stopped shucking corn to stare out the window. "Come to think of it, he does seem to be coughing more. Even at night."

Papaw and Mamaw didn't know it, but right then I made plans that the Barker family would be the first patients to get their checkups at Chrysalis Free Clinic.

🦋 🦋 🦋

When two more weeks passed, Rolland and his friends finished building the examination rooms. One of his buddies prided himself in donating a twenty-four pack of beer to counteract dehydration during construction. At least that's what they told me. Rolland wasn't much of a drinker, but his friends made up for his slack. It unnerved me. I worried about men using power tools while drinking beer, so I bartered a deal that I would bring them sandwiches and soda pops, if they would hold off on the beer until two or three. Since John's accident, I opened my eyes to the kind of trouble that can make itself known in a heartbeat. Life can take a sharp turn and I didn't want to push the odds in that direction. If the work was done in the morning, I didn't give a care if they sat around drinking and offering advice for the rest of the day. When the first one slurred his words, the party was over, and I'd send them home.

I was getting free labor, so I had to be understanding. I expect it was their way of staying away from their women folk and kids. Men think they're fooling us females, but most the time all they do is fool themselves. I told them if they didn't want to go home, they could sober up and watch while an emergency doctor from the hospital trained the first batch of us in CPR.

Turns out CPR, something called cardiopulmonary resuscitation, amounted to pushing on someone's chest while someone else blew air into their mouth. I wasn't fond of that idea, especially if it involved someone else's vomit or blood, but I guess I could cross that bridge when I had to run over it. If it were Donny, kin, or any small child, I wouldn't hesitate at all.

"When you push on someone's chest, you might hear ribs cracking," the instructor said. He was kneeling over a mannequin he called Annie, pushing hard on her rubber body. "Don't be alarmed if this happens. It's better than being dead."

I expect that made it worthwhile.

Pretty soon we had all our supplies and the only thing that stopped our doors from opening was medications from the hospital. The residents who worked on the days the clinic was open delivered the drugs to restock, accounting for the delivery with a senior nursing student. It was a good lesson for them and kept everyone honest when handling the supplies.

Crystal and Mrs. Pitterly stopped by on the same afternoon when Mrs. Gess and I were taking temperature checks on the used refrigerator she acquired. A Sodality member donated her old one to the clinic after successfully talking her husband into getting a new one that made its own ice cubes. Shoot, we didn't care about ice cubes and could surely make our own in metal trays.

Crystal took Mrs. Pitterly around, showing her the exam rooms and the donation station off the kitchen with food boxes and a rack that displayed clothes for those in need.

I asked Mrs. Pitterly what she thought. She turned around slowly.

"It looks like a rainbow," she commented. "Every wall is a different color."

"That is the handiwork of the teen groups from the Baptist and Methodist churches," I replied. "They didn't have quite enough paint of one color, so they painted a wall at a time."

"Well, it sure is purdy. If my husband had somethin' like this, mebbe he wouldn't o' waited so long to get doctorin'. It's been over a year since he passed."

I didn't know how to reply to her pain. In that awkward moment, I noticed Crystal had wandered off when she called me from across the hall.

"Leandra, how would you feel about me painting a giant butterfly on this wall?" She ran her hand across the newly painted wall, like it was a clean canvas begging for artwork.

"Can you do that?" I asked. I had seen Crystal's work and she had a talent. "It would be nice, but I'm not sure the church would let us. They might say it's too 'hippie-like.'"

"Don't you worry about them." I turned around to see Mrs. Gess standing behind me. "I'll talk to the powers that be. You go right ahead and start on your butterfly, honey."

"I'm excited!" Crystal took hold of my arm. "I'll design something right away. If the church says no, then I'll have Mr. Blackwell make copies of my design, get some crayons, and the kids can have a butterfly to color while they wait to be seen."

Part of what pulled at my heartstrings was how this town came together. Soon enough, Doc Sylvan would be vacationing with his missus. Nearly everything was done but planning the grand opening and notifying the *Mountain Grove Press*.

Chapter 10

Launch

I can still remember when the United States sent a rocket to the moon. I can't imagine how much planning and building, training, and organizing there was, leading to that moment. The excitement was palpable on those days before the launch.

I recognized that feeling as opening day approached at the clinic. We weren't headed to the moon, but without a doubt, the sky was the limit.

🦋 🦋 🦋

"I don't want to waste money buying party food and drink for a free clinic." I stood before the board on our last meeting prior to our grand opening. "It just doesn't seem right when we can use the money for healin'."

"Well, why don't we have a potluck?" Mrs. Gess suggested. "We always do that for our Sodality meetings and socials after church."

"I'll make that suggestion when I announce our open house to the newspaper," I replied. "And we can have a punch bowl, coffee, sweet tea, and unsweet tea. That should be plenty."

"How many you reckon are comin'?" Rolland asked.

"Lord, I wish I knew. We have no idea, but the more people that join our celebration, the more we help, and the more likely we get donations."

Rolland spoke again. "Will the clinic be open for patients that day?"

"No. I want this to be a celebration and recognition with all of you and Doc Sylvan standing beside me. We could have never done this without all of you. Someday, we'll build a free clinic on my land," I added. "But right now, it's more important to provide services to the community."

On those nights when I couldn't sleep, I recalled Crystal and Mrs. Pitterly and how they ended up helping each other out in hard times. An idea had come to me to pitch to the team.

"Some time back, Crystal had mentioned the need for folks to give back. Maybe patients can consider dropping something off for the donation station or giving time to help. They could share a basket of vegetables from their garden, or a chicken, so we can make a pot of soup for a hungry child. There's cleaning, answering the phones. These people are proud, and they won't take if they can't give."

Rolland agreed. "I know that's what I would want to do."

"Good, then it's settled. And I have exciting news. Doc Sylvan found a doctor to buy his practice, so as soon as he gets back from his retirement cruise, he said he would donate time." I put my finger to my mouth and made like I was zipping it shut. "I want us to surprise Doc with a plaque in recognition for over thirty-five years of caring for this community. I'm planning to shine the light on that sweet old man."

🦋 🦋 🦋

On Saturday, November 10, 1973, at two in the afternoon, I unlocked the front door and entered into the stillness of Chrysalis Free Clinic. In another hour, people would see the clinic for the first time.

In the quiet, I wandered through the space, and marveled that the clinic was finally a reality. I sure wished John had been there to see it. Crystal's butterfly mural was completed, and I smiled, recalling yesterday's conversation and her final artistic attempt when she had thrown glitter on the wet paint.

"It's beautiful, Crystal, but you'd better get that glitter off the floor before the Sodality ladies see it. They'll pitch a fit."

"It was an experiment," she replied matter of fact, admiring her work.

"Well, you should have laid down a tarp or newspaper before you took to shakin' glitter everywhere. I think there's a vacuum in the back, so see how it works. Hurry, before one o' them walks through the front door and sees your sparkles, and we have to treat them for high blood pressure."

Our little Chrysalis Clinic was on its way—butterfly, glitter, and all.

Chapter 11

The Worry Seed

Do you know how a worry first takes hold of you? It starts like a tiny little seed, deep inside your heart. Pretty soon, little white, hairy roots sprout, looking for someplace to wander. Then a tiny stem erupts and starts making itself known. As that seed grows and grows, its demands grow too. Pretty soon it becomes your entire focus.

At some point in time, you need to determine if that seed is good or bad. A bad seed intertwined with something precious means you might have to sacrifice the good with the bad. All the worrying in the world won't save the good. That's when you put it in God's hands.

🦋 🦋 🦋

On the day Chrysalis Free Clinic opened for patients, I drove Papaw over there to get a checkup. His coughing had weighed on my mind since I first heard him gasping for air. A day hadn't gone by that I didn't worry about it. He couldn't even remember the last time he visited a doctor.

"Confound it, Leandra, doctors are for sick people. All I got is a cough. You're looking for trouble with a man my age."

"A cough is a symptom. It's just a checkup and it's good for the students to work with such an ornery old man."

"You know he's going to be sweet as a puppy to them," Mamaw threw in. "He's always sweet to strangers, but given the chance to battle with his family…"

"Ain't no point tryin' to win with you women. One was bad enough, now I got two, just like the old days with Addie. I suppose you made an appointment."

"Yes, sir. You got just enough time to change your clothes and shave that day-old beard." I took my hand and rubbed it over his jaw and looked back over my shoulder to Mamaw. "You too."

"I knew that was comin'," she replied.

"Think of it as a donation of your expertise for the students," I suggested. "And, while we're in town, I'll take both o' you out for lunch. The chores will be here waitin' when we get back."

✄ ✄ ✄

I think if Papaw could have turned tail and run, he would have made like a spooked heifer and bolted out of there. But there was no escaping my insistence, and I pushed him through the clinic door. Crystal had been attempting to teach Mrs. Pitterly to be a receptionist. Mrs. Pitterly wasn't much of a people person, so she moved onto the kitchen, cooking up a nice pot of beans and ham hocks as her contribution for the day.

"Come on in," Crystal offered Papaw a clipboard. "Please sign your name and phone number on our waiting list."

"You know who I am." He scowled at Crystal. "Opal, you take care of this and sign us in." He handed off the clipboard to Mamaw. Papaw always was a little uncomfortable in new situations. "Where's Doc Sylvan?"

Crystal answered, "Today, we have Dr. Bancroft from Asheville. Please take a seat and she will be right with you."

He looked at me. "She? I'm seein' a lady doctor?"

"Now Papaw, lots of women are becoming doctors. And why not? They are just as bright as any man and probably more nurturing." I knew that nurturing part wasn't true. They had to be smart and tough to get through medical school and likely had to prove themselves even more to their professors.

"One of our nurses will meet with you now." Crystal directed him to a table with two chairs hiding behind a partition. He gave Mamaw a concerned look. "Come on with me. Maybe they can work us over together."

"You'd think he was going to meet his Maker," Mamaw lamented. "I best go hold his hand."

They disappeared around the corner.

I waited for what seemed like forever. Once Papaw relaxes and gets to talking it's like trying to silence a sewing circle. But neither one was talking much when they returned to the sitting room.

"Well?" I probed. "What'd she say?" Papaw made a beeline for the front door.

"Finish yo' business," Mamaw replied, "and I'll be outside waitin' with Papaw."

"You need anotha appointment?" Crystal asked.

"I don't know," I replied. Mamaw shuffled toward the exit, pushing a handkerchief back in her handbag. "I have to find out what the doctor said. I'll call you later, Crystal."

🦋 🦋 🦋

I joined them in the sedan. "How does the diner sound?" I tried to be upbeat, but I sensed it would be a struggle. "You hungry, Papaw? Was the doctor nice?"

"Diner's fine. Think I'd enjoy one of their barbeque pork sandwiches." I saw him reach for Mamaw's shoulder from the backseat. "Course, it'll never be as good as your Mamaw's cookin'."

Then Mamaw burst out crying.

"Would someone tell me the what-for?" I wanted to curse but my timing wasn't right, and I worried Mamaw would cry again once she stopped yelling at me.

"Tell her, Opal. I can't remember half of what that lady threw at me."

Mamaw took a ragged breath and refolded her hanky. "She didn't like the way your Papaw's lungs sounded. She wants more tests."

When I heard that, my gut raced backward twenty years to the doctor's office in New York with Ana and William when they were looking for trouble with baby Amber. That was two lifetimes ago, but when they say, "more tests," it means something is gnawing at them and they're not sure what it is.

We arrived at the diner.

There wouldn't be any privacy at the diner. The waitress, Dora Gene, was all kinds of cheerful as she greeted us.

"Could you seat us at the back?" I requested.

"Sure thing," she answered. "How y'all doin' today?" She knew damn well we were not doing good, but she had a reputation for sticking her nose in the wrong places.

"Everything's simply fine, Dora Gene. Papaw's hungry as a wolf and weak with hunger, so bring us some sweet teas, would you?" While she pattered off, I returned to business. "Did the doctor say what concerned her?" I directed my question to Papaw.

"Aww, she was fussin' over my coughing and said she heard some noises in there, like the air wasn't movin' around right. Where's it supposed to go?"

"The rest of your body," I said. "Look, she needs to check this out. You breathe in all kinds of dust and chemicals and poisons on that farm. There could be stuff in there hurting you."

"I told him," Mamaw said. "For years, I told him he needed to keep covered."

"How can I work if I can't breathe?"

Mamaw lowered her voice. "Zachary, I need you next to me. I can't run the farm without you. Now you get yo'self fixed."

"I'm sure they took enough blood from me to figure out how to keep me alive and, once they do, they'll have more orders for me. Now let's just have our lunch."

We ate in relative silence. Mamaw ordered a bowl of ham and bean soup with crackers and left half of it sitting there. I hated seeing her worry like that. It was hard to imagine how it would feel knowing your spouse could be seriously ill. I didn't doubt her for a moment when she said she couldn't live without him. She commented about running the farm, but the real issue was loneliness and an empty bed after sixty years of companionship.

"Tests should be back in one or two weeks," I advised. "I'll have the receptionist keep an eye out for them."

"Can you talk to the doctor, Leandra? Maybe you'll understand better than us."

"Sure thing, Mamaw. I'll do that today."

Dr. Barrett had finished her day's charting when I returned to the clinic. Her black doctor bag was on the table, and she was stuffing her stethoscope into the bag as I opened the door. We had scheduled some time together.

"Leandra, come in." She had a warm smile and a childlike face.

"I won't keep you. I know you have a long drive home."

"I was hoping we could talk. By the look on your grandparents' faces, I don't think they comprehended a lot of what I said."

"What are you looking for? Anything specific?"

"I'd like to run it by a couple of other physicians," she started, "but I'm fairly sure we're dealing with 'farmer's lung' or something similar. I'm sure you've heard of it."

"Of course. It's serious."

"If you're implying he could die from this, yes, that's likely. He's had a long, productive life, but as the condition progresses, he'll slow down, have increased breathing problems, his energy will slump. It could happen suddenly with additional exposure to mold or dust. But it's more likely to be chronic and slowly worsen."

"What about the farm? How is he going to work the farm?"

"He shouldn't. This is the big problem. These men don't know how to not work. I had an eighty-six-year-old patient with farmer's lung and I couldn't get him off his tractor. Even after he went on oxygen, he kept right on farming. Your grandfather is going to reach a point where he can't spend the entire day in the fields or dusty barns without becoming short of breath. Because he's not getting enough oxygen, he'll tire easily. His workdays will get shorter and shorter. He may get frustrated and angry because he knows his performance doesn't match his expectations. And pneumonia is likely."

I soaked it all in, feeling it ooze into my pores like paint into dry wood.

"If you want to keep the farm going, you need to make arrangements," she continued. "What about your parents? Shouldn't they be able to work the farm? Or is that out of the question?"

"I'm the only one left. My father enlisted in World War II. He died at Market Garden. There were no other children and I'm Papaw's only grandchild. If we're saving the farm, it's all on me."

"Just keep him coming in for regular check-ups, or if anything suddenly changes. Any fevers, shortness of breath, increased fatigue, aches, and pains, could all be signs things are taking a turn."

Driving back from town, it occurred to me I finally heard the words I never wanted to hear. They were the same thoughts that crept through my mind on nights when I couldn't sleep, twisting and turning while I visualized the farm without Papaw. It was something I didn't want to acknowledge. Now it sat weighted in my lap like a fifty-pound sack of feed.

Papaw was coming up on his eighth decade. Once his sickness took hold, and it had a good start already, there could be a fast decline with Mamaw close behind. It would break her heart and she wouldn't want to have anything to do with living if he wasn't with her.

How was I going to make this land work for me? Who was going to help? This farm had been in my family for over a hundred years. It was supposed to be my daddy's, but that generation was lost to war. For certain, I faced more sleepless nights. Like my old friend Ana always said, "You need sleep. The answer will come." I hoped her Polish folk wisdom still rang true.

🦋 🦋 🦋

"It's like this," I began. "The doctor is almost positive you have farmer's lung." Papaw sipped his morning coffee, his best attempt at ignoring me. "We all know what that is."

"I don't have no farmer's lung. You're worryin' yo' Mamaw fo' nothin'."

"Papaw," I sat down at the rickety kitchen table while he buttered his day-old biscuit. "We're just waiting for the test results. And they're going to schedule you for a chest X-ray in Asheville." I turned to face Mamaw, who listened intently and said little. "I can drive you to that appointment and we should get the results pretty fast." I took a deep breath. "Then we have to decide how to keep the farm going. There'll need to be some changes."

"Over my dead body!" he bellowed.

"It could come to that!" I shouted. "Let's try and make this as difficult as possible!"

Mamaw had enough. "Stop it! I will not have this nasty bickering in my house. Not now. Not ever." She reached out and placed her veiny hand over his leathery arm. "Zachary. We know our time is coming when Leandra will need to run the farm." She turned to smile at me. "We need to be grateful to God that we have such a beautiful granddaughter. She loves our farm and is willing to take this on. If tomorrow you died on your tractor in your own field, I know you will have lived your life happy and died doing what you love. I'm okay with that. But if you want any say in how your farm will get passed down to your next kin, now is the time to start thinkin' about it." She chuckled and shook her head for emphasis. "We sho can't drive that tractor to heaven and take it with us." She was talking like she was dying with him, and I expected that was her plan. So many times, we had known elderly farm couples who died within months of each other.

I lost my spine and started crying. I hoped not to do that, thinking it would make Papaw feel like he was on the highway to meet St. Peter. "Papaw, you have always been there for me and now it's my turn to pay you back. All I'm sayin' is we need to put our heads together and figure out what we want the Barker farm to be. Someday I will turn it over to Donny. We all run out of time, Papaw. We've known that since the day of our birth."

It was important for that to sink into his thick skull for a few days. When the tests confirmed what was slowing him down, we could talk again. Maybe if he saw it in black and white he would listen to reason. I wasn't sure if that damn clinic was a blessing or a curse. But no doubt it had brought my future to light.

🦋 🦋 🦋

By the time Papaw's test results came back, we had simmered down and were behaving like loving human beings. I was trying to get into his head and feel what he must have experienced when he took over the family farm. I couldn't remember him ever speaking about it.

"Papaw, did you go through any of this when your daddy gave up farming?"

He put his newspaper aside and removed his spectacles, rubbing the bridge of his nose. "Well, the situation was a little different, Leandra. I had worked 'long side your Great Papaw all my life. I knew the farm inside and out. He wasn't really sick, at least that's what he claimed. He was just worn out. As his days got shorter, mine got longer. Me takin' over just sorta happened."

"Did you change anything?"

"Oh, I'd try out a different crop now and then, maybe grow what my neighbor had boasted about and give it a whirl. Those farm salesmen are always pushin' somethin' new to get more from the land. 'Bout the only thing I added was the tobacco. I always did good at growin' tobacco."

"Farming is changing, Papaw. I only know this 'cause I been readin' up on it. It's different on the cattle farm. People are always going to eat beef, so John Sr. and Jake have a built-in guarantee of success as long as they keep their animals healthy and growin' fast. Little farms like us are getting bought up by large corporations that own lots of equipment. And now the government is paying farmers to get rid of tobacco."

Mamaw burst through the parlor door with a mug of hot coffee and handed it to Papaw. I knew it was an excuse to get in on the conversation, and expect she was standing on the other side of the door hanging on every word being exchanged.

"Hot coffee, Zachary. It's bitin' cold tonight. Hot drink will do you good." She parked in the easy chair and looked at the two of us like we were going to present her with a golden goblet. I ignored her. I could only fight one battle at a time. I turned back to Papaw.

"Tell you what I'm gonna do. Let's sit down tomorrow and look at the numbers that will show us profit and loss for everything produced on the farm. I can start on it tonight, and tomorrow we can take a look-see and consider what we might change."

"Leandra, I have heard there are some women folk who work the farm themselves after their men can't no more. Is that something you might want to do?"

In my heart, I knew he wanted me to say yes. I had imagined what it would be like starting my day at four in the morning to take care of the animals. Then I'd have to get a young son to school, attend parent/teacher conferences, and after-school activities. Around all that, I'd be running tractors and discing the fields, cutting, and baling feed, watching the markets and the weather and such. My health and happiness wasn't even in the equation. No sir. I didn't want to walk that road.

"That's just it, Papaw. That's not the life I want." Neither one said a word. I wasn't even sure they were taking in air. "I'm Donny's only parent and I have to put him first. But that doesn't mean I'm not willing to fight tooth and nail to keep this farm in the family. I just need to figure out how, and I need both of you to help me figure that out."

🦋 🦋 🦋

Next morning, I called a family meeting. By the looks of my fancy spreadsheet and calculations, the cattle had to go. That was easier said than done 'cause my grandparents were attached to their bovines.

"Papaw, the ratio of work to what we make on these cows isn't really panning out."

"You mean we have to get rid of all of 'em?" Mamaw asked. She was the one who milked our dairy cow, Jenny, twice a day. Sometimes, Papaw would help with the evening milking, but nothing made Mamaw prouder than bringing in a fresh jar of milk from the dairy house. Years ago, Papaw built Mamaw a milking stand that was safe and easy for her to use when milking the cow. Every time they freshened that cow to breed her, we'd get buckets of milk. Mamaw always found a way to use that milk for baking, cheese, butter, and ice cream. If she couldn't use it, she'd find someone who could. She had even taken to dropping some off at the clinic every day, despite my protests that it was against the law. Back then, most folks, along with the United States government, were paranoid about getting sick from unprocessed milk, so she was always sharing her milk on the sly.

"No, Mamaw, we won't get rid of Jenny. The fact is, it would still be nice to have some animals around the farm. We could limit it to one milker, and a few chickens, maybe a couple turkeys. We can get our beef from John Sr. and Jake if we need it. By the time we pay for feed, vet bills, and vaccinations, put in our labor and lost sleep, it's not worth it for the few heads of cattle we sell each year."

Papaw wasn't saying much.

"What do you think?" I asked.

"I'd like to keep some of my animals. Won't be the same around here without my herd."

He sounded dejected. Those animals were part of our lives. It had been years since our old mule Molly died, but I still grieved for her. When I was a young girl, I'd make a special trip to the meadow, just to pet her velvet nose. Then she'd lay her muzzle against my shoulder for a neck hug, like we were long lost friends.

On the other hand, I wanted to remind him about all the times I had stepped in a warm wet cow patty or scraped it off Donny's shoe. I was fine with a reduction in manure production.

"We'll just finish with these animals and the next season we won't buy anymore. That way you won't get rid of any you, ah, know personally. Now, let's talk about the crops." I expected that to be fertile ground for me and Papaw to butt heads, so I opened the discussion carefully.

"Let's look at the spread sheet with just the crops. Without the cattle, we could rent the alfalfa field to another farmer. Or we could grow corn, keep a little for Jenny and the birds, and sell off the rest. I'm going to leave those decisions up to the two of you. We have the equipment, but we're going to need help in the summer. Plenty of farm boys looking for summer work."

"Archie stays on the payroll."

"Of course. And gets his medical care at the clinic. And Mamaw, we'll see to his final resting place, wherever he chooses."

"I will talk to him about that," Mamaw replied. "I hear tell he has a daughter somewhere."

"That still leaves us with the apple orchard and the tobacco field. That tobacco is poison, Papaw. Between the tobacco barn and the drying, the dust and mold..."

"I ain't givin' up that tobacco."

"Whoever works out there is likely to get Green Tobacco Sickness or something worse from those pesticides. You know those young boys aren't used to working tobacco fields. We could make more money not planting if the government agrees to pay us."

Mamaw looked at his face and then looked at me. "Leandra, you've lost this battle. Figure somethin' out 'cause he's keepin' that field."

"Yes'm," I replied. She was right. I wasn't going to waste my breath. Or his, which was confirmed to be in short supply.

"I saved the best part for last." I was really excited about my idea. "The orchard is established, and we've kept up with care and replanting. Papaw, you have always had some of the finest apples around. But most those little grocers in Asheville have closed or been pushed out by supermarkets."

"That's a fact," he agreed. "I just can't price my apples with those big producers."

"But city folks still like to drive to the country for a picnic and maybe apple picking in the fall. They take home pumpkins, drink hot cider, walk the orchard. Why don't we let the city folks come to us?"

"You mean like a fruit stand?" Papaw asked.

"Oh, more than that. Make the Barker Family Farm a place for families to experience nature again. Show them how a cow is milked. Demonstrate applesauce making, teach how the old spring house worked, have a picnic area for families to play. Since Mamaw always grows too many pumpkins, we can let the kids pick their very own, right off the old wooden wagon."

Almost at the same time, I saw both of them wipe their eyes. Mamaw had her hankie ready, but Papaw had to use his callous old hands. I didn't want to embarrass them, so I kept blabbering.

"We don't need that big barn without the cattle, so we could build out a section like a little store. Maybe some of the artists and craftsmen in the area want to sell their work or demonstrate on the weekends. Papaw, it would be your legacy."

His chin quivered. I saw him take a deep breath. It was a good long breath, like someone had just piped fresh air into his lungs and he was healed again. Mamaw spoke up first.

"What do you think, Zachary?"

I went on. "None of this has to be decided tonight or even next week. But consider this as our first step. Shoot, we can keep changing things around 'til the cows come home." I paused. "Or at least Jenny."

🦋🦋🦋

After that, Papaw's light shined a little brighter. He wanted to make his "petting zoo" more substantial, so I agreed to a black-faced lamb and a pink pig to add to the collection, *if* he gave up the turkeys. In turn, Mamaw and I would let him ride his tractors for as long as he wanted, assuming we invested in an enclosed cab. He had to leave the spraying to someone else and wear a bandana to cover his face when he was around the hay and stalls. I knew he wouldn't, but Mamaw, Donny, and I reserved the right to yell at him when we caught him misbehaving. I should have got it all in writing.

What is it they say about the key to happiness? Isn't it something to hope for, something to love, something to do? And with that, the Barker Family Farm was restructured for two more generations.

Chapter 12

Turning Seasons

I think it's interesting how we mark our own seasons the same as the plants, animals, trees, and such. About the time I finished the summer of my life, Papaw and Mamaw were rollin' through their winter season at full speed. The odd thing was the end of my summer season snuck up on me like a snapping turtle chasing a tadpole. We always think of turtles being slow and tadpoles being quick, but let your guard down for any reason, and before you know it, you and that tadpole are history.

🦋 🦋 🦋

Over the cold months, we set about designing our new farm. Mamaw became quite the public relations woman, telling all her lady friends about our big plans to bring the city folks to us to market our apples, pumpkins, and country ware. When Papaw and Archie were having good days, they fired up the furnace in the equipment shed, and repaired machinery for the coming growing season.

I was going through my own change of seasons. I no longer identified as a young woman while I raced toward middle age. It was about that time when I got an unexpected call from Mama.

"Well, hello, Leandra." Her voice sounded stronger than usual. The liquor always made Mama sound a little sleepy, but not today. She had a little southern twang to her words that overshadowed her New Jersey accent.

"Hey, Mama. Haven't heard from you in quite a while. Somebody die?" I knew that was mean. I was kind of hoping she was going to say Roger. What she said disappointed me.

"Mrs. Scudari died, just a couple of weeks ago."

"What? Why didn't you call me then? She was my New Jersey Mamaw. How is Mr. Scudari?"

"He seems lost. The neighbors been taking food over. He's talking about moving his sister in so they can save some money for old age." She laughed. "That man was old when we moved in."

"How'd she die?"

"She had that blood sugar disease. She wasn't a small woman so I guess her organs couldn't keep up. And then she found a lump in her breast. She was too afraid to go to the doctor and it ended up killing her. But that's not why I called."

Mama did that sort of thing. She didn't really give you a chance to move past one thing before she'd plow forward and dump something else on you. If it wasn't important to Mama, it wouldn't be important to anyone. All I could figure was something happened to Roger, or she was sick. I really didn't care what happened to Roger. A city bus could run him over in front of me and I wouldn't flinch. If she was sick, then I had a problem.

"I have an invitation here for your high school reunion."

That was a club-me-in-the-head moment. I did a quick calculation. My twenty-year reunion. How did that happen? How could I be so old?

"Well, what does it say?"

"I didn't open it."

"Mama, for pity's sake, open it and read it to me."

She wrestled with the envelope, with crinkling and ripping that went on forever. You'd have thought she was fighting a badger.

"There's a pretty picture of the high school on the front of the card and inside it reads, 'You are cordially invited to Perth Amboy High School for the twentieth reunion of the graduating class of 1954. Festivities will include…' Wow, fancy. Leandra they're hosting a picnic…"

"Mama! Just read the dang invitation." I swear, I didn't know if it was old age or liquor that gave her the attention span of a two year old.

"Okay, well there's a family picnic on Friday afternoon, then a formal dinner and dance on Saturday. Sunday, afternoon they're meetin' at Santone's for pizza and if anyone wants to visit New York, there's a side trip for that on Monday."

"When?"

"Uhm, October twelfth to the fifteenth. If you're comin', let me know. I still have the two beds in the room off the kitchen. I sleep in one of the beds now, but you can have the otha one."

I tried to picture myself there, in that same tiny room Ray and I shared as kids. Nausea crawled out my stomach and up my throat.

"Leandra? You there?" She reeled me back to the present. "You want me to send this to you?"

"No thanks, Mama. I'll let you know if I decide to go. Is that all you needed?"

"Yes. I thought you'd want to know about this. How's little Donny?"

"Gettin' tall, lookin' more and more like his daddy. You knew Papaw was sick, right?"

"Mamaw said he has a lung disease, somethin' about all the farm dirt and chemicals."

"He's doing fairly good. I keep him goin' to the clinic for check-ups. And Archie's doin' his best to keep up." I could tell she was getting bored as the conversation lagged. There wasn't much more to say.

"It's good hearin' your voice again, Leandra. Give my best to everyone."

"Yes'm, I will. Bye, Mama, and thanks for calling."

I put the phone receiver back in its cradle. What I really wanted to do was rip it out of the wall.

🦋 🦋 🦋

The idea of returning to New Jersey for my twenty-year reunion made my stomach turn like the paddles on Mamaw's old butter churn. My high school years were woven with threads of Mama's drunken binges, my brother Raymond's pain and eventual death, Roger's man-chasing, and a low-life boyfriend who abandoned me and our unborn child. My high-school boyfriend, Greg, had been my only joy, and I was robbed of that when his mama paid me to walk away from him. I still felt her distain and my shame for letting her win. Now the Thunderbird convertible she had given me, payment in lieu of her son's love, was tucked away in an old barn as invisible as the diamond wedding ring he never gave me. What if Greg and his beautiful wife showed up at the reunion? How would I feel standing there as a lonely farm widow from hick town? Mama couldn't know what hornet's nest she had wacked by telling me about the reunion. The hornets surrounded my heart, stinging again and again.

While those thoughts gnawed at my craw, I considered how it was possible I survived my childhood. While still a teen, I took on the responsibility of the entire family, thinking it was all a part of normal life. I didn't even know there was safety and security in a family. All I experienced was chaos and pain.

As the night wore on, I pulled out my yearbook, turning the brittle pages with the utmost care. I read the sweet notes of students who had long since passed from my life. My church friend, Helen, always gentle and kind, inscribed that I would be a huge success someday. Sal's note gave me a belly laugh when I read his promise to marry me if no one else made the offer. I thought about Betty's interest in older men, and her unexpected pregnancy came to mind. I had sworn that would never happen to me, but I would give anything to hold my illegitimate daughter Autumn in my arms again. Despite her untimely birth and death, if Autumn had lived, she would be almost the same age I was when I birthed her.

I read notes from Evy and Maggie teasing me about Greg and our perfect senior prom. I wondered if they married their high school sweethearts or found true love in college at a sorority dance just like my mama. I wouldn't blame them for still hating me for abandoning Greg. My chest ached with guilt and a longing for their friendship.

When I got to Greg's note, I put my hand over the written words. I knew it would leave more wounds on my heart. Carole King's song, "So Far Away," played on the local radio station. I swear, the timing couldn't have been more painful. Sometimes God has a sick sense of humor. Hot, fat, tears dripped down my cheeks.

Donny passed my bedroom door and saw me curled up on the bed holding the yearbook. "What is that book, Mommy? Is it making you sad?"

My instinctive little man. There was no use trying to hide my feelings from him.

"It's a book with pictures of all the kids I went to high school with in New Jersey, where Grandma Lillian lives." I stood to grab a tissue off the dresser. "I guess I miss them more than I thought."

"Are you in the book? Lemme see your picture!"

I pointed to my senior picture and a girl stared back at me with what I perceived to be a fake forced smile. Was I ever that young? That hopeful? I remembered the day that picture was taken. I wanted to look perfect for the yearbook photo, a sophisticated senior with the world at her feet. As I had left the house that morning, I found Mama sleeping on the sofa in her clothes with an empty glass lying on the floor. I had picked it up and sniffed it. Bourbon.

Donny pointed to my photograph. "That's you, Mommy? You were pretty. Your hair was a different color."

"It was lighter. Grandma Lillian's hair was that color too when she was young. Look, I'm over here too." I turned back several pages and showed him the photo of the student council. "I was the secretary of the group. We made decisions about the high school events and represented the students."

He pointed to the other students. "Who are these other ones?"

"This boy's the president who led the meetings, that one's the treasurer who took care of the money. This is the vice president. His name was Greg Humes. He was Mommy's good friend." I leaned in close like it was a secret. "He was my boyfriend."

His eyes lit up. "Like Daddy? Did you marry him too?"

I smiled. "No, his mama didn't like me, so that was that. I moved back to Mountain Grove and fell in love with your daddy."

He bobbed his blond shaggy head up and down in a nod, understanding every unspoken word.

"And that's why you're sad," he replied, "you miss Daddy and this guy." He pointed to Greg's youthful face.

I swallowed hard and flinched. The hornets stung again.

🦋 🦋 🦋

Eventually, I chose to put Amboy out of my mind and prepare the farm for our first fall opening. Mamaw, Papaw, and I had so many ideas swirling around our heads, it was hard to stay on task. I knew some plans wouldn't work to our satisfaction, but that was the beauty of it, being able to make it anything we wanted. The farm was alive with banging hammers and buzzing saws while the hired help built out the on-site store where we would showcase our apples, cider, and local artists. I was already feeling like the space was too small for what we needed.

One day, Mamaw promised to stitch some checkerboard curtains for the store but got sidetracked preparing dinner for Archie. We hardly saw him anymore, but when he did hitch a ride to visit Papaw, he appeared to be skin and bones and weakened to the point where he couldn't work anymore. The farm seemed incomplete without him. Rain or shine, Archie had showed up for work, keeping up step-for-step with Papaw and his list of chores. He had always lived on his own, so Mamaw expected there would be no one preparing meals for him if he felt poorly. Mamaw always took care of the needy, so she decided it was her job to feed him.

"Leandra, you and Donny run this over to Archie, so he has a hot meal for a couple o' days." She had a paper grocery sack filled with various Tupperware containers. It smelled so good my mouth watered.

"What'd you make him?" Donny asked.

"Well, what do you smell?" Mamaw teased.

"Cinnamon, bread, and gravy," Donny replied, grinning ear to ear.

"Your nose is pretty smart," Mamaw said. "We're all having beef stew, hot biscuits, and apple pie."

"Can we eat now? I wanna eat now!"

"You help your mama deliver this food and then it's your turn."

Archie's house was a ten-minute drive through the back roads, so we loaded up and made our way toward the river bottom. We turned off the pavement onto an unmarked dirt road lined with small wooden homes. Some looked abandoned, most tilted to one side or another. But, heck, nearly any farmhouse does. Children dotted the street playing kickball. As we got out of the truck with Archie's dinner, a young man in overalls and a torn grey T-shirt walked by carrying two dead rabbits by the ears. He cradled his shotgun in the other arm.

"Y'all lookin' in on Archie?"

I looked up. "Bringing him dinner. You a neighbor?" I slammed the car door.

"Down the road a ways. I hear he ain't well. Haven't seen him in a couple o' days. Usually, he comes out on his porch at night to smoke his pipe."

"I'll be sure to see to his needs. Thank you."

When Archie didn't answer the door, I lifted the latch, opened the door, and called for him.

"That you, Miss Lee?" I saw him in his bed, pushed into a corner of the room, struggling to sit up. His one room home had a kitchen in one corner and his sleeping area in the other. It was perfect for a bachelor. The cold temperature in the room alarmed me. The nights were getting chilly. He had ample blankets on the bed, but I didn't know how he was going to keep a fire going this winter. It was late afternoon, not the time a healthy man would be in bed.

"You not feelin' well, Archie?" I put the sack of food on the table. "Tell me what's goin' on."

"I am just so tired these days." He paused for a deep breath. "Seems like all I do is sleep." He shook his head like he could hardly believe it himself.

"Are you able to do your chores? Is there somethin' I can help with? Mamaw made you some dinner."

"I appreciate that, Miss Leandra. I don't have much need to eat, just don't feels like it."

"Well, I'm going to warm this stew anyway. Maybe you'd enjoy one o' Mamaw's biscuits with butter to rev up your appetite."

I had him sit forward in bed and fluffed up his pillow. Mamaw always said a tidy bed makes a sick person feel better. He had a small television on a TV table. I turned it on to make some noise and hopefully stir some interest. Was he depressed? Sometimes that caused fatigue.

"Let's get you over to the table," I suggested. "The stew is almost hot."

"I needs to make water," he replied.

The outhouse was behind the house, and I wasn't sure how stable he was. "Donny, you walk with Archie out back and make sure he's okay."

Donny's protective nature took over. "C'mon, Archie. I'll take care of you." That made Archie laugh. I hadn't heard that rich laugh in a long time. When the boys returned, the cabin had warmed up a little with the tiny gas stove. I stacked some logs next to his old wood burning heater, made from an old drum and a smokestack. At least that would make it easier if he needed to light a fire.

We sat around his table and watched him labor to eat his stew. "What else needs to be done around here?" He put down his spoon and sat back in his chair.

"Doesn't take much to keep this place goin'," he replied. "I just ain't sure how much longer I's a gonna keep goin'."

"I hear you have a daughter, Archie. Should I call her?"

"She lives quite a ways from here. I don't want to botha her."

Without thinking or asking I blurted out, "Then you're comin' home with us. We got an extra room." He started to argue with me, but I stopped him. "It's just until you get on your feet again. I'll get this kitchen cleaned up and you can tell Donny what you want to pack, and he can throw it in a pillowcase."

I concluded he was too tired to fight me. He might be a little uncomfortable in our home, but he would be safe. I'd take him to the clinic in the morning. That would take a little finesse on my part, but I could talk him into almost anything. I scurried around the kitchen while Donny took orders from Archie and packed his belongings. Donny wasn't very good at folding his clothes and mostly just shoved things in the pillowcase like it was an old duffle bag. I figured Mamaw would have an iron if we needed it later.

"C'mon, Archie." I heard Donny's encouraging words. "I'm hungry for Mamaw's biscuits and stew."

Archie laughed again in his good-natured way.

We squeezed into the truck and Mamaw met us at the back door to help Archie up the back steps.

"I brought home a new boarder," I said to her.

"I'm glad you did. These two old roosters can keep each other company." She nodded toward Papaw, sitting at the kitchen table.

Papaw perked up. "Well, doggone it, Archie, you owe me a game o' checkers. I demand a rematch tomorrow afternoon."

We walked Archie into the spare bedroom. "My, my, my, this is as fine a place I have ever laid down my head."

"Bathroom is down the hall," I told him. "Papaw's room is a shout away and so is mine. You need anything, night or day, you just call out."

"You folks been so kind to me. All my life." He shook his head. "I don't knows how to thank you."

"No thanks needed," Mamaw said. "You have always been there for us, Archie. You're family."

"Get your pajamas on and get into bed," I told him. "You must be exhausted. I'll have Papaw or Donny check in on you later. Maybe you'd like some hot milk and honey later tonight, so you think about that."

I walked downstairs on Mamaw's heels. "I don't like it," I said. "He seems to be failing so quickly."

"God knows how old he is," Mamaw replied. "Bless his soul, we're all he has."

"I couldn't leave him there, Mamaw. I knew this day was comin'. I'm glad he and Papaw have each other to ease into this season of their lives."

Chapter 13

Starts and Stops

The Barker Family Farm Festival opened a new chapter in our lives. While it was a lot of work reinventing ourselves, it became something to stir our interest. Bringing Archie back into our lives made Papaw more content as he eased into retirement. I placed a pair of weathered chairs under the oak tree and the old boys started a little routine where Papaw would putter around the yard in the morning, have lunch with Archie, and then they'd wile away the afternoon under the giant oak where they used to slaughter and hang the fall hogs. It seemed like only yesterday when all that was happening on the farm, when in reality, forty years had passed. They were younger men then, strong, and productive with the certainty of their place in life. Now their place was not necessarily where they wanted to be, but rather a place they had accepted. I have learned this comes to all of us sooner or later.

🦋 🦋 🦋

The doctor at the clinic diagnosed Archie with late-stage heart failure. His sweet old heart could hardly do its job anymore and it was only a matter of time before it gave out. I didn't tell Archie too much about his condition. His days were numbered and there was no sense worrying him. I just hoped it would be a peaceful passing. He deserved that more than anyone I knew.

When the end of August rolled around, we were almost ready to open our new business. The summer farm boys fenced in a pen for the petting animals and fashioned a couple of sitting benches so our visitors could picnic.

We got most of the cow smell out of the store, hoping the fragrance of the apples would eventually take over. Fresh straw was bound to help. I took out ads in the Knoxville and Asheville newspapers and arranged for a local reporter to interview Papaw about his boyhood farm and how he wanted to invite city folks to visit. When the story broke, Mamaw was sprinting from the kitchen to the living room all day picking up phone calls from neighbors reading about the new and improved Barker farm. Country folks are kind of funny like that. If they think someone has a leg-up, they need to make sure they're not missing out. At the end of the day Mamaw was so talked out she told Papaw, bad lungs or not, it was his turn tomorrow. She was "tired o' bein' a celebrity." I had no idea how many families we would attract to The Barker Family Farm Festival, but we hoped it would be a big showing.

🦋 🦋 🦋

Twenty-four hours before opening day, Donny and I toured the remodeled barn for one last look. The last light of the western sun spilled across the barnyard. A large overhead sign in green, red, and gold, read *"Little Red Barn"* with apples around the border. Inside, to the right, new baskets held the sweet juicy apples. Papaw would only grow heirloom apples, some dating back to the early 1800s. Most of the early apples, Lowry, Virginia Beauty, and Grimes Golden, had been collected and stored. We'd pick the late fall apples as the chill set in, but he'd always have at least one red, one yellow, and one russet per season. I took a deep breath, inhaling the fragrant blend of sweet apples and fresh straw. Our local beekeeper had lined up his jars of honey on a table next to the old dairy cooler reserved to hold icy cider. Once folks filled their paper bags with apples, they'd cross to the left and hand their treasures to Papaw. He'd weigh the apples and write it on the sack. On good days when Archie felt up to it, he would probably join us. Mamaw would collect the money. The back of the store was lined with tables and benches where the artists would display their work and greet guests. My job was to keep everyone happy. When I explained all this to Donny, he furrowed his young brow.

"What do I do?" Donny asked. "I don't have a job." I gave him a serious look. He was nearly eight years old and shooting up like a Roman candle. I swear, I could see him growing.

"This is real work," I reminded him. "If you earn wages, I expect you to do things right. It was the same with me when I was a kid."

"I will. Promise." He crossed his heart.

"Someone has to keep the petting pen clean. You have the strongest, young back. Can you keep an eye on the animals, scoop up the poop, and put down fresh straw so people don't step in it?"

He wrinkled his nose. "Is that all you got?"

Remaining businesslike, I continued the negotiations. "We want people to know we respect our animals. You might get an extra tip out of Papaw if you do a real good job." I offered him a handshake. "Is it a deal? For the next three months?"

His soft little hand slipped into mine. "I'm proud of you, Donny. You take care of these helpless animals, and you'll learn to take care of yourself. Your official title is Animal Ambassador." His eyes got wide and he ran off to tell Mamaw the good news. Dang. Now I had to make him a name badge. Probably best to make one for all of us.

🦋 🦋 🦋

I had such a time getting to sleep before opening day. Anxiety filled my room, spilling off the bed, crossing the floor and climbing up the walls. Finally, at five that morning, I couldn't stand it anymore. I staggered out of bed and wandered to the window. And, of course, the skies poured rain.

"No, no, no," I mumbled to myself and threw on my robe. Mamaw was up too, and we nearly collided in the hall.

"Did the weather girl predict this?" she asked.

"I hadn't really paid attention to the weather reports this week."

"It's early," she replied. "I'll turn on the radio and television and see what they say."

By all accounts they predicted the skies would clear in the next three hours. I just hoped those city people in Asheville and Knoxville wouldn't get discouraged with a little wet weather.

"We gotta assume we're still gettin' visitors," Papaw said. "It's business as usual."

He was right. I put on my rain slicker and mud boots and went outside to assess the damage. The biggest mud holes would need straw laid down so no one would slip in the muck. We'd need extra straw in the animal pen too, but the apples and artists would be safely tucked away in the barn. More was at stake than just selling apples. I had to assure Papaw this was going to work and convince the community this would be a fun fall event they could plan on every year. Me and my big ideas.

At ten o'clock the rain stopped. Not a car was in sight.

"Give'em time," Papaw reassured me. I didn't know who was going to be more disappointed, me or him.

"Mama, if no one shows up, do I still get paid?"

I reassured my little entrepreneur he was still earning money. The artists and crafters arrived early and patiently waited for the visitors. My Lord, I felt guilty for dragging them into this. I was in the barn trying to sweet talk them when Donny came running in all excited.

"Mama, mama, we got visitors!" I raced outside and sure enough, not one, but two cars pulled in together and unloaded a pile of kids and parents. It was a start. It was also the last time I sat down that day.

A steady stream of guests turned out, lasting through the entire weekend. I must have gone back and forth to the spring house six times restocking the baskets with fresh apples. I wasn't sure how successful the artists had been, but two asked if they could return the next weekend. Papaw busied himself planning which apples would be ripe for picking in the coming week. And Mamaw worked her pencils and scratch pad, calculating how many gallons of cider to order for the remaining weeks in the month. She had big plans for canning apple butter for next year's sales. Donny, Archie, and I were just plain tuckered out.

By the middle of October, our apple business had been in operation for over a month and we had ourselves a fine system. Archie and Papaw always gave it their best but sadly, with their sicknesses, the constant chatter with visitors left them short of breath. When afternoon approached, we'd send them inside for lunch and a midday nap. This meant Mamaw and I had to step it up to finish the day. We managed to keep going, but I had no hesitation agreeing to shut down apple season by Thanksgiving.

Toward the end of one day, I had just enough energy to fill the display one more time.

"Donny." I called him in from the animals. "Stay with Mamaw while I retrieve another load of apples and a few more pumpkins. I want to be ready for tomorrow."

I picked up my load and returned to empty my truck bed. I had my back to the crowd, but I could still hear the excited chatter and the children's laughter filling the barnyard. I glanced up to see Donny sitting on the ground holding one of our sweet hens while a little blond girl petted a chicken for the first time in her life.

I froze. You know that feeling when someone is in your space? I checked my peripheral vision and saw nothing but instead, felt someone's hot breath on my neck. My skin twitched and tingled right up the side of my head.

"Youz got any apples?" It was a whisper, a hush, but I knew that voice and whirled around.

"Sal!" I shouted and wrapped my arms around his neck "It must be nearly twenty years since I've seen you!" I stared into his big doe eyes, remembering the first time we had met in New Jersey under the bridge near the railroad tracks. I had just turned fourteen and was as country as a cornfield. "You drive here from Jersey? What are you doing here?"

The man standing next to him, hands in pocket, grinned ear to ear.

"Lennie?" I asked.

"Nah, that's my baby brotha, Artie. He's a priest. Father Artie."

I couldn't reply but my face must have shown the shock.

"My ma finally got her priest in the family," Artie chuckled.

"And Lennie? He okay?"

"Shua. He's a car salesman. Makes good money. He begged to get out from under the mob. He'd been loyal so they let him off the hook. Ha! Maybe for real! Anyway, he married this ditzy blonde and really pissed off Mom."

I looked at Artie. He shrugged his shoulders.

"I'm used to his colorful language," Artie replied. "He really can't offend me. But I pray for him anyway."

"What are you guys doing here?" I paused to direct a visitor toward the scales. "Did you ever get married?" He and Artie gave each other a sideways glance.

"Me and the wife aren't exactly seein' eye to eye. We're takin' a little break. Besides, I didn't want to stay in town for that damn Perth Amboy reunion."

"I feel the same way." I looked up to meet his eyes. "You knew my husband was killed in an accident a few years ago. Can you imagine how I would have felt explaining that to everyone?"

"Yeah, your motha told me about it. I'm sorry, Leandra. That must have been tough."

"You don't know the half of it. But you are staying a while, right? We have so much to catch up on." I grabbed his arm. "Come meet my mamaw and son, Donny."

We walked over to the scale where Mamaw was managing the last few customers of the day.

"Mamaw, this is Sal and his brother, Artie. They're going to be staying with us for a while."

Mamaw didn't miss a beat. She continued to ring up orders.

"Y'all those boys from New Jersey? Pleased to meet you." She held out her hand. "I think we have one or two bedrooms left." She looked up and smiled at the two strangers.

I was sure she'd been watching us the whole time.

"I'll only be here for the night," Artie corrected. "I'll be spending some time at Immaculate Conception in Hendersonville. That's really how this trip got started. Can you keep him out of trouble for a while?"

"Mamaw's got a pan of barbequed pork in the oven, and we'll whip up some potatoes. You need to meet the rest of my family."

That night we moved supper into the dining room. Our numbers had expanded over the last couple of weeks. If we tried to eat in Mamaw's small kitchen, I would have felt like we were a box of kittens crawling all over each other.

I introduced Sal to Papaw and Donny, but Archie was the one who caught his eye. When he followed me into the kitchen to collect the serving dishes, I knew he was up to something. I handed him a stack of dinner plates.

"Leandra, you can't tell me that old Black man is part of your family."

I tried to keep a straight face. "I don't know what you're talking about. Archie was on our homestead before I arrived. He's family."

"Okay, if you say so, but why's he livin' with you?"

I slapped a stack of napkins on top of the plates he was holding. "Look at him, Sal. A good wind would blow him over. He took care of our farm for decades, now we take care of him. It's the right thing to do. Besides, he's got no one else." I paused to stare him down. "What, you don't think we look like relations?"

Old Archie was as black as a moonless midnight. All I got back from Sal was an eye roll and a head shake. I forgot how much I missed our banter. He was probably still a skirt chaser, but it was fun having him around again.

The conversation circled the dinner table for hours, all of us telling stories about our past. Mamaw's cooking was not to be outdone by the New Jersey Italians who served piles and piles of food. After dinner and baked apples, she brought out coffee, cookies, and homemade ice cream.

"Sal, did we eva have homemade ice cream?" Artie asked in between spoonfuls. "This must be straight from Heaven."

"No," Papaw replied. "That's straight from Jenny, our milk cow."

"Wait," Sal interrupted. "You not only make your own ice cream, but you also get it from your cow?"

Donny corrected him. "No, Mr. Sal. The cow gives us the milk and cream and my mamaw makes it into ice cream. You wanna help milk her tomorrow?"

I had this vision of Sal and Artie nestled up to Jenny's warm belly, trying to figure out how milk came out of a teat.

I jumped right in. "Why Donny, that is so nice of you to offer to teach them how to milk Jenny. Let's let them sleep in until six tomorrow morning. Jenny can wait an extra hour for her milking."

Papaw spent a good deal of time telling the Donotello boys how our relatives arrived in North Carolina after the Civil War, a generation before their family crossed the ocean from Sicily. Sal and Artie shared stories about their brother Lennie and the mob, their overprotective sister, and Ray's encounter with Mother Superior when he broke her stained-glass windows. He finished by bragging on me which made Papaw glow.

He turned toward Mamaw. "She was always a good girl. She kept her nose clean and took good care of her ma. It wasn't easy."

There was a long silence. Papaw fidgeted with his placemat, then smoothed his napkin. He cleared his throat.

"You knew Raymond, did you?"

"Oh, sure, Artie here was about the same age."

"Did you know any of the boys he spent time with?"

Sal looked at Artie. "Eh, not too much."

"Our ma was pretty strict," Artie added. "She kept close tabs on us."

"That's good," Papaw said. "Keeps you outta trouble."

"Ray struggled with life, Mr. Barker. It was a difficult situation when he was moved to a new home."

"Father Artie, I blame his mother. I know I shouldn't, but she wasn't capable of keepin' an earthworm alive. And I never did take to that Roger fella. Talk about a square peg in a round hole." Papaw shook his head.

"Well, you can certainly say that about him," Sal said.

I think he had more to say on Roger's particulars, but I gave him a quick sideways kick to the shin to halt the conversation. That was more information than Mamaw and Papaw needed, and a topic I didn't want to cover in front of Father Artie and my son. As long as I was alive, that skeleton stayed in the closet.

As Donny promised, the next morning the two city boys were introduced to our unsuspecting cow. I positioned them on either side of Jenny's sweet face while she stood in her stall, chewing her morning treat. Her expression said she was bored and a little put-out, but the alfalfa calmed her while I snapped pictures with all our cameras to memorialize the event. I decided to victimize Artie first.

"Sit on this stool, Artie, right close near her belly. You can rest your head on her side." Mamaw was up front, talking sweet to Jenny, but we switched places and I let her and Donny do the teaching.

"C'mon, Father Artie. She won't bite." Donny waved Artie on.

Sal took a long hard look at the opposite end of Jenny. "What happens to Artie when she's gotta go?"

"Go where?" I teased.

"Yeah," Artie chimed in. "Won't she splatter?"

"Nah, the straw catches most of it," Papaw answered.

"Now, look here." Mamaw grabbed an old bucket, turned it over and sat herself down next to Artie. She still had pretty good balance for an old lady. "See how puffed out her teat is? We gotta get that milk out of her." She took her warm bucket of soapy water and wiped down Jenny, grunting slightly as she moved along. "We gotta get all this dirt off of her so it doesn't end up in the milk. She put down her washing bucket. Watch what I do." As she had done it time and time again, her thumb and index finger wrapped around the top of the teat. "Give a squeeze, and out comes the milk." She let go and repeated her demonstration. "Your turn. And don't go to yankin' on her. Squeeze…"

Artie looked completely intimidated. "Does it hurt?"

"Course not. 'Long as you do it right." She stood up from her bucket seat. "Sit here, Sal."

Sal shuffled into position.

"You tell 'em cows kick sideways?" Papaw asked.

Mamaw stepped back, defending her baby. "Jenny's not kickin' no one. But if you two don't hurry up and finish the job, either Jenny or I will die before you finish."

'Course Sal couldn't stand it and had to squirt Artie before it was all said and done. Jenny did her part not to splatter them and was never happier to be turned out to pasture.

Mamaw herded us back to the kitchen and laid out a breakfast feast of ham, eggs, biscuits, honey, and fresh slightly-warm milk, another first for Father Artie. He stared into the milk bottle on the table.

"Zat cream floating on top? Sal, look, that's real cream."

I caught Mamaw raising her brows and shaking her head. She had a hard time understanding how city people were so disconnected from their food.

We watched Father Artie drive off to his church visit with a bag of apples and a gallon of cider. Mamaw loved giving away food, but it was especially sweet if she could share it with religious folks.

🦋 🦋 🦋

I put my arm on Sal's shoulder. "Time to get to work, Sal." I advised him of his duties, knowing we had a full day of customers arriving in a couple of hours. "I wasn't expecting company."

Since he was acquainted with Jenny on a personal level, I had him and Donny move the animals to their petting pen. Once that was done, I put him in charge of the apple display.

"That's all I gotta do?" he asked. "Keep the apples lookin' pretty?"

"Customers like to see full baskets. There's more in the cellar and the spring house. Later this week, we'll be picking more apples. Today we have to mix socializing with work."

Sal was a natural. I looked up to see him chatting with the visitors, making up stories about the apples and why they were superior to store produce. We dressed him in a red apron to wear over his white long-sleeved shirt and blue jeans. His curly, somewhat frizzy, black hair displayed signs of grey, but I still thought of him as the same cute guy who drove me nuts during high school. I reminded myself not to start something I couldn't finish. He caught me staring at him and his ego couldn't stand it. He sashayed over to where I was standing.

"You seein' somethin' you like?"

I felt color rise to my face. "You'll never change, will you? Let's remember you're a married man."

"Yeah, we'll see about that." He sounded defeated.

"Sal. You have a second chance. I didn't. One day we were a couple, the next day I was alone."

"I know. I got two little kids, a son as good as Artie and a beautiful daughter. I want them to have the family I did. We always had each other, no matter what."

I took a deep breath. "I don't think I ever told you how your family was the only stabilizing thing in my New Jersey life. I always knew I could run to your house and someone would help me. Your mom was always in the kitchen cooking something wonderful." I smiled, recalling how I could smell her cooking before I knocked on the back door. "Even crazy Lennie was there when I needed him to keep Roger out of jail. Your family was everything my family wasn't."

"You have a good family now," he countered, "and you're the anchor."

We turned back toward the barn where Archie and Papaw were weighing apples and yucking it up with the guests.

"You're right. I had to leave to recognize how special it was here. Maybe tomorrow I can take you up the hill to the butterfly bush and you can meet the rest of the family."

"There's more family?"

"Oh yeah, lots more." Of course, I didn't tell him they were all dead. But I could still make introductions.

🦋 🦋 🦋

My two precious weeks with Sal Donotello was passing too fast. Little by little, the protective walls I built over the last twenty years crumbled. I was young again, reliving the excitement and uncertainty of youth. I found trust with the only person who knew what life looked like on our side of the track. I showed him everything important to me, even my climbing tree. Artie would return in two days and they would leave.

I missed Sal already.

We had just dropped Donny off for an afternoon with Grandma Ruby, when I got the notion to show him my treasure, stored in one of the old outbuildings on the Angus farm. I pulled opened the large sliding door to the shed and there sat my turquoise Thunderbird. I yanked off the cover.

"Remember this?" I asked.

"Holy shit! You still got this car? Why aren't you drivin' it?"

"It's a bittersweet memory. Besides, it needs work." I brushed the dust off the door handle. My hand moved over the white convertible top, cracked and brittle. I opened the door and sat in the cold driver's seat, clinging to the steering wheel like it was a ring buoy there to keep me afloat. I lifted my head.

"I never told you the full story about this car." He had climbed into the passenger side, waiting for me to unveil yet another mystery of my pathetic life.

"You got this when I was at boot camp," he started. "You said you'd saved money and wanted somethin' nice, right?"

"Not quite." I could feel my throat tighten. I stared straight ahead, watching my past unfold. "It was the price I paid for giving up Greg. His mother hated me and thought I was beneath their family. Of course, she was right. She gave me the car and two thousand dollars to promise I'd never see him again. God, Sal, how could I go to that reunion? How could I face him?"

"Wait, his motha gave you the car to stop seein' him? I knew there was somethin' fishy about you not stayin' with him. You two were the real thing. Why'd you give in to that bitch?"

"I wasn't going to win. Even if we got married, she would have made us miserable. I never stopped loving him. I stopped seeing him."

His crass Jersey voice was softened. "Jesus, Leandra. I didn't know."

"That's not all." I continued. "I had to use the cash to pay off my mother's loan sharks. But it wasn't quite enough, so my boss paid the debt, so I wouldn't need to sell the car. That meant I owed him. When he got me pregnant, he forgave the loan."

"Whoa. What the fuck? Are you kidding me?"

Sal's anger peaked.

"He sent me away to a home for pregnant girls. It was a very nice home. Remember when I moved to upstate New York? I had a baby girl."

"You give her up?"

"No. I loved my daughter and planned to raise her on my own. I named her Autumn. But she was born with a birth defect." I couldn't bring myself to tell him my baby didn't have a brain. "She died right before her sixth month."

Sal got out of the passenger side and walked over to open my car door. I could see tears in his eyes. He helped me out and held me in his arms like he was never letting go.

"Is that all?" he asked.

"No. Ray died a couple years later. We found him in an abandoned building after he ran away from home. He was still a kid, Sal. I watched my baby brother die from dirty needles and poisoned blood. Then I brought him back home to his family and the butterfly bush."

I pulled away and looked into the darkness of the outbuilding. "I don't know why I'm telling you all of this. I've never told a living soul."

"You went through hell, and I wasn't there to help you. I feel like a real shit." He cupped my face in his hands and looked deep into my eyes.

Unlike any other kiss we had shared as kids, this one was filled with passion. He pushed my body against the old car, mocking the pain it had caused. I hadn't felt like this since Greg. He must have felt it too. Were we reliving our youth? His hands tugged at my jeans as he fumbled with my button and zipper. Another second and I was going to let my guard drop, something I swore I would never do with him.

Oh, my God, what if I get pregnant again? I came to my senses.

"Wait! Stop! What are we doing? I'm not going to be the other woman!"

His voice softened as he nuzzled my neck. "No one has to know, Leandra. You know we both want this."

I caught my breath. "You're right, I do want this. But Sal, this is reckless. We're both hurting. This isn't the way to fix what's broken."

He laughed at my country wisdom and brushed my wild hair away from my face. "You always were the smart one, logical. I always took the easy way out." He pulled back, and suddenly I was uncomfortable with the intimacy. "I'll try and make it work for the kids' sake. But once the kids get out of high school if we're still miserable..."

"I'll still be here. I'll always be here."

We started to walk out of the shed when he turned back to glare at the T-bird. He stopped in his tracks. "You know what you need to do? This car hasta go. You gotta get rid of this thing and set yourself free. You could fix it and drive it, but why? It will always remind you of something painful.

Do you understand what I mean? Let me help you now."

He was absolutely right. The T-bird had sat here, year upon year, as a memorial to my pain. I held onto it to remind me of my love for Greg, but it wasn't about that at all.

"Let me get it running. We'll drive it back to Jersey. Lennie's got connections. He's always got connections. He can help me make it pretty, sell it, and all you have to do is pay for the repairs and throw him a little cash."

"What would I do with the money? It's dirty money."

"No, it isn't. You paid in blood and heartache. Put it in the bank and forget about it. Someday, you'll need the cash for something, and it will be there for you."

I shook my head. "I don't know…"

"How about this? If we're both still kickin' by our fiftieth reunion, you use the money to come back to Jersey. It will be a hell of a party. What do you say?"

Chapter 14

No Escape

The smell of my holiday turkey fills the kitchen. I open the oven door to peak at our bird now wearing a coat of crispy brown skin. A generous basting will keep him browning while I prepare the gravy and biscuits. They'll be here soon, Donny, Kathy, and all my grandkids, bringing their sides, as they call them. Thank the Lord, 'cause I can't keep up with the cooking anymore.

I close the oven door, pull off my mitts, and walk outside to the back porch, grateful for the cool air. The first snowfall is glazing the grass and fallen leaves. It triggers my memories of Papaw's turkey slaughter in late November.

I hated the turkey slaughter. With no escape, the turkeys' submission on the chopping block bothered me the most. Quietly, they waited for death. Their trails of red blood marked the white frost leading to the scalding pot. Once the birds had been plucked, they looked like dinner instead of our barn birds, and it was easier for me to accept their sad demise. I am so grateful today's holiday bird came from the Piggly Wiggly.

🦋 🦋 🦋

"Here you go, Archie. Hot apple cider." He reached for the mug with two unsteady hands. "You must be sick of this cider by now. I promise, this is the last of Mamaw's inventory from the apple barn."

"Not to worry, Miss Leandra. I eat like a king here."

With the apple barn closed for the season, Papaw claimed he made more money from his apples sales than ever expected and had a good time doing it. Now we prepared for the Christmas holiday just a couple of days away.

My greatest Christmas wish was for Papaw to give up next year's tobacco crop. But he made good money this year, and tobacco remained a sore spot between us.

Mamaw walked into the sitting room carrying a dish of cookies. "Here we go. Hot ginger snaps. Now we can decorate that tree."

It wasn't a big tree, but it fit nicely in the corner of the living room, next to the television and hi-fi. A Christmas episode of *Laverne & Shirley* blared on the television, so I did my best to ignore those silly women. But Papaw and Archie enjoyed their antics and sat there laughing while Mamaw, Donny, and I did the decorating.

Donny, holding a box of glass ornaments, walked up to Papaw. "Look Papaw, these are really old."

I shuddered in my slippers as he carried those fragile globes across the room but managed to hold my tongue while I asked baby Jesus not to let them crash to the floor.

Papaw adjusted his glasses and peered into the brittle box holding the delicate painted ornaments. "Oh, yes, I remember the day our mama brought those home to us. We looked at these shiny baubles and thought we were rich folks. Most of the time we just strung popcorn and berries and tinsel but, little by little, we collected some fine pieces. Why don't you and your mama put them up on the tree like I did with my mama?"

A horrible thought raced through my mind like a lightning bolt tearing down the branches of a pine tree. Could this be Papaw's last Christmas? Last year at this time, we didn't even know he was sick, and already a year had passed. He had gone downhill so fast. I still couldn't picture my life without Papaw. He grounded me to the farm as sure as the very soil it sat on.

Donny admired his tinsel and ornament-hanging handiwork. "Did you have a Christmas tree as pretty as this, Archie?"

"Donny, would you all believe this is the first Christmas tree decoratin' I has eva witnessed to? Why my family was too poor to buy or gift presents, much less put a tree in the house."

"Well, why didn't Santa love you?"

Oh God, I held my breath. Donny was getting to that age where rumors were flying around school that Santa didn't exist. I wasn't ready to lose my little boy. That Christmas song, "Toyland," always made me sad. Silently, I waited for Archie's answer.

"Why o' course he loved us poor children as much as he loves your freckled face! Do you know every year he talked with the church ladies around town, and they helped Santa get a present for every one of us kids?

And we had a meal on Christmas Day that filled our bellies right up to our eyes!"

He made his eyes wide, and Donny reflected the same. Archie was such a storyteller. There may have been one or two times that happened, but I guessed there weren't too many happy Christmases in his family.

"Well, in a couple 'o days, Mamaw and Mama are gonna make Christmas dinner with Papaw's turkey, gravy, cornbread dressing, and pies." Donny leaned in close to Archie. "I bet they make me set the table again." He sighed. "They always make me do that."

"You suppose that's a fair trade for all their cookin'?"

"Yeah, I guess so," he replied and went back to draping tinsel which held more importance at the moment than helping with Christmas dinner.

I breathed a sigh of relief and surmised that Donny was still my innocent child, at least for this holiday season.

🦋 🦋 🦋

Thursday was usually bookkeeping day. Christmas Eve was the day after that, so this was my last chance to finish the year-end books for the farm. I had sat at my desk for about an hour when Donny wandered in.

"Why's Mamaw standing in the hall crying? I asked her what was wrong, but all she said was, 'Go get your mother.'"

"Where is she?"

"I told you, Mama. Standing in the hall. Near Archie's room."

I glanced at the clock. It was twenty-two minutes after ten. Archie was usually done with breakfast by nine. I knew what was wrong with my mamaw.

"Go in your Mamaw's room, Donny, and get a clean handkerchief from the top drawer in the dresser while I go tend to Mamaw. You take that hanky to her."

I climbed the stairs, steadying myself with the rail. My legs were heavy and hard to move. Mamaw leaned against the hallway wall by Archie's room. Donny ran up to hand her a fresh hanky and we stood by without uttering a word, waiting for her to compose herself.

"He was late this mornin'," she began. "He would nevah miss breakfast. I thought he must be sleepin' in, you know we were up pretty late last night with that tree." She wiped her face, top to bottom. "I even

125

checked on him around nine or so. He was still in bed." She shook her head, "I should have known. I should have made sure he was breathin'."

Her sobbing started again.

I reached out to hold her while Donny looked on, still and silent as a snowy morning. I turned my mouth to her ear. "Mamaw, we gave him a good life and comfort in the end of his days. We did good. Archie was our special blessing."

"He didn't have a soul in this world, bless his heart. No one. No family, so sad, so sad…" As if convincing herself, she shook her head side to side.

"Mamaw, he had us. And he'll have us for eternity. He's gonna be with us by the butterfly bush."

"You don't think he wants to rest with his kind in the Negro cemetery, near his home?"

"Well, I asked him about it once. I always knew we'd be the ones to see him through. And he said, 'Miss Leandra, once I am dead and gone, they's nothin' there but my ol' bones. I trust you will find a good place to put me. But you know I won't be there. I be up in heaven with Jesus, havin' a good ol' time.'"

Mamaw's eyes met mine and she gave her nose a good blow. Her chin quivered and she bit her lower lip. "Leandra, that sho' does sound like Archie. We'll give him as fine a funeral as any one of us."

"Let's go in now," I said. "This day isn't turning out the way I expected, but I imagine it didn't work that way for any of us, especially Archie." I turned toward Donny, placing my hand on his shoulder, more to steady myself than him. "Donny, Mamaw and I are going in Archie's room. You wait here quietly for us, understand? Don't go running off to Papaw and telling him what happened. I'm not sure how he's gonna feel about all this."

"Will I get to say goodbye to Archie?" Tears spilled from his brown eyes and, dropping his head, he broke into sobs.

"Of course, you will, honey."

"Mama, I loved Archie."

"As it should be, baby. And I know he loved you with all his heart."

Inside the room, the air was heavy with death. But as we approached Archie, still laying on his back in bed, I had never in my life seen such a sight of pure peace. Under his chin, the sheet and blanket were neatly folded back and smoothed. His arms lay on top of the covers, resting on each side. Even his eyes were closed, and if not for the stillness of his chest I wouldn't have known his soul had passed.

"I just pray he didn't die in pain," Mamaw said. "His poor little heart."

"Look at him, Mamaw. It's almost as if he did see Jesus and decided not to come back. That is a look of contentment. Let's just shut the door behind us and go downstairs to tell Papaw. You best stay with Papaw after we share the news 'cause he could have a hard time with this."

Donny took to his room while Mamaw and I went downstairs. We found Papaw reading his morning newspaper on the front porch rocker. The south sun filled the porch with warm light. Once we sat down with him, he spoke up from behind his paper.

"Archie's hasn't joined me yet. You women comin' out here to bring bad news?"

Most people are more instinctive than they know. Those two old farmers spent a good part of their lives together. He knew Archie from his mind to his soul and body.

Papaw lowered his paper. "He wasn't himself yesterday. I couldn't put my finger on it. He had a harder time putting thoughts together. Seemed awful tired."

Mamaw seated herself in the wicker chair. "He passed in the night. I went lookin' for him this mornin' when he didn't come down for breakfast."

"We left him in bed, Papaw, if you want to say your goodbyes. I'm gonna start by going through Archie's belongings to see if there is a phone number or address for his daughter. If not, I'll go look around his house, maybe talk to some neighbor women. They'll know what to do and who to call."

"C'mon, Zachary, I'll help you upstairs to see him."

"I think I'm gonna sit here a while." Papaw turned to look toward his tobacco field across the road. He must have been looking back on better times when he and Archie worked that field together.

Mamaw and I walked inside so he could have his thinking time.

"You watch him," I cautioned. "Don't let him walk around by himself. He's likely to get weak-kneed and fall."

"I'll mind him," she replied. I started up the stairs to put together the puzzle pieces of Archie Jackson's life.

I walked into his room like it was a holy place. I wondered if old Archie was looking down on me and wondering what I was doing. My gaze turned upward and I spoke to the ceiling.

"Archie, you could make this a whole lot easier if you directed me to the right place."

Mamaw had pulled the sheet over his face. I wanted to be respectful and place this man where he needed to be.

The top drawer of the nightstand failed to turn up anything but his medications and Bible. I looked inside the Good Book, thinking he may have left something in there to discover. The bottom drawer was empty except for his pipe and tobacco. Only the closet remained. Looks like I was taking a drive to Archie's house.

Inside the closet, though, I found an envelope neatly pinned to his suit jacket lapel. I recognized it from Mamaw's stationery.

"You old devil. You knew what you wanted and how to get it."

He must have picked out one of his good days to ask Mamaw for some paper to write down his last wishes. I guess living on your own nearly all your life made a man pretty self-sufficient.

I opened up the envelope and found a note with forty dollars:

Der Miss Lee, Miss Opal, and my good frend, Zachry,

I thank you for yur kindnes so many yers. You are good peeple. This is Ester's phon numbr. 305-265-9101. Ples let my girl now I am ded and my hous is hers. I wud like to be in this sute at Wildwood Creek Baptist Church. Reverend Wiliumson and his misus can help. The mony is for the buryal. Ples tel Ester I am sory I was not a good fathr but when I thinks about her it made me smil.

Archie Jackson.

It must have taken him all day to write that note for us. Christmas was going to take a backseat to Archie's final goodbye. I raced downstairs, envelope in hand, grabbing my purse along the way. I walked out to the porch where Mamaw and Papaw were filling up on coffee.

"I found his last wishes," I said with relief. I sat down with them and read his words out loud.

"I have never felt so close to him," Mamaw replied, wiping at her eyes. "You go do what you gotta do, Leandra. We're gonna sit with Archie a spell while you talk to his neighbors and pastor."

Closure wasn't a word we used back then, but I'm pretty sure Mamaw knew what that meant. She understood the importance of their final farewell to a man who was as close as family without being a relative. Heck, he was closer than some of the family we did have.

The Baptist church Archie spoke of was at the end of the road through Archie's neighborhood. It wasn't hard to find with the traditional white steeple topping the narrow wooden building. Reverend Williamson sat in a small office near a makeshift kitchen in the back. He appeared startled to see my white face when I knocked on the door frame. I was still clutching the envelope.

"Reverend Williamson?"

He stood. "Yes, ma'am, can I help you?"

"Reverend, my name is Leandra Barker Tucker. I'm a friend of Archie Jackson."

"Oh yes, yes, Archie." At first, he was excited, but then you could see the thoughts coming together. "Oh dear, how is Archie?"

I went through my whole story and showed him Archie's note. "He said you and your wife could help us plan his service. I don't think we'll get much help from his daughter. We have a family cemetery near the farm, and we want Archie with us."

By the expression on the reverend's face, I knew I stepped on a toe or two. I continued, "Of course, I think it would be best if you contacted his daughter to see what she thinks."

"I'll get my wife on that task right now," he offered.

"And Reverend, Archie is still out at our farm. Do you know who we should call?"

"Give me your address and we'll take care of that too."

Relieved, I reached into the envelope and pulled out the two twenty-dollar bills. I handed it to him, lying just a little.

"Archie left this in the envelope with his note. He wanted the church to have it."

"Thank you, ma'am. We will see that Archie has a homegoing he would be proud of."

I returned to my own home, and no more than two hours later a large white hearse pulled into the driveway. Two men in dark suits got out, tugging on their jacket sleeves and adjusting their ties. I let Mamaw and Papaw greet them at the front door. I was spent and had nothing else to give. I was reading *The Giving Tree* to Donny, trying to move through a heartbreaking day.

Donny looked up. "They taking Archie now?"

"Yes, baby. These nice men will take him to a special place, bathe him, dress him, and get him ready for his burial."

That's when I remembered the gray-striped suit in the closet. I ran upstairs where Mamaw and Papaw were politely holding back, standing in the hall while the men readied him.

"Papaw, I need to give them Archie's suit and shirt. And do you have a tie you would like to give him to wear for his service?"

Mamaw stepped in. "I think you still have about three ties, Zachary. Maybe that tie you wore for Lillian's wedding would go nicely with his suit." They wandered down the hall to their bedroom. I peeked in Archie's room. The men had secured him to the gurney to carry him down the stairs.

"Wait!" I called out. "There's this suit he wanted to wear and my Papaw's getting a tie."

I handed the closest man the clothes and he draped them over Archie. The suit looked pretty old but would serve Archie well. "One more thing." I walked over to the nightstand. "This is his Bible, but I'm going to hold onto it in case his daughter wants it. But take this." I handed him Archie's pipe. It had the faint fragrance of cured tobacco he had planted, grown, and nurtured on our farm. "Can you put this in his hands? He always enjoyed his pipe."

"Yes, ma'am. Anything else?"

"When we walk out, I got one more thing to give you."

Papaw followed them out the front door while I ran to the springhouse. Mamaw handed them the tie she and Papaw selected. I handed them an apple from the springhouse.

"He loved these trees and took good care of them for fifty years. Can you put this in with him? No one has to see it, but I want it with him." I wiped my eyes with my sweater sleeve.

The man looked at the apple and smiled.

"I can tell you cared deeply for this man." He reached into his pocket and handed me his business card. I read *Howard Funeral Home. Arthur Howard, proprietor.* "You let me know if you think of anything else you need."

I pointed across the street to the hill where the butterfly bush stood waiting for Archie's arrival. "Behind those trees is our family plot. That's where he'll rest if there are no objections from his daughter and congregation. He'll be in good Christian company."

I turned my thoughts back to Christmas and Donny. It would be nearly a week before Archie could have his service as we had to work around the Christian holiday. I knew Archie would understand and we would have to blend in our grief sometime later. That simple man had left such a void in our lives. We took Archie's Christmas presents and set them aside. I figured I'd give them to his church and they could use them for a needy family.

🦋 🦋 🦋

During the week between Christmas and the New Year, two days were set aside to celebrate Archie's life. I found myself wishing I had spent more time with him, learning about his life and the places he'd seen. He had so much wisdom but kept most of it to himself unless someone took the time to drag it out of him.

Mamaw, Papaw, Donny, and I looked like four lightbulbs in the crowd of Archie's friends and congregation. Reverend Williamson decided to host the wake during the afternoon and into the evening to allow working folks to get home and pay their respects. We arrived early afternoon for Papaw's sake, hoping his strength would be at his best.

This was all new to me. I'm not referring to funerals, I'm referring to Black funerals. The good Lord knew I had more than my share of burials to face in my lifetime. More were coming, that was a certainty. We Southerners take death seriously and the Black community had their own traditions. As the good reverend had said, Archie was getting a fine homegoing.

"My stars," Mamaw said, "do you see all those flowers? Why that had to set these folks back a pretty penny. And they are friends, not even family." Some of the flower wreaths looked homemade. Many were plastic, being it was winter and fresh flowers would be expensive to bring in. Our family sent a lovely arrangement of pure white lilies and red roses in a tall, clear vase. Someone else had brought two red poinsettias positioned on both ends of the casket. Archie would have been embarrassed by all the attention.

But that's how it was with a homegoing. It was a big to-do. One family after another filed past Archie. Folks were dressed to the nines, all in dark colors. The women wore hats and more jewelry than Mamaw and I owned together, while the men dressed in stylish suits and ties, standing stoic and tall beside their families.

On our arrival, I couldn't bring myself to walk up to the casket. Nothing felt real to me. "Mamaw, I need to sit for a while. I'm feeling awkward."

"I understand, honey. I don't think I'm ready either."

We took seats near the front of the church facing Archie.

Papaw didn't say much. He kept staring at the casket from where we were seated, clearing his throat, and looking down at his folded hands. Now and then, he'd check in with Donny. I wasn't positive Donny should be there, but I didn't want to isolate him from death and a man he had loved since the day of his birth.

"You must be the Barker family."

I looked up to see a large woman wearing a paisley pink and navy dress. Her skin was the color of garden soil just after an afternoon shower, rich and brown, and her smile was warm. I stood to greet her, slightly distracted by the rhinestones on the hat net draped over her face.

"Yes, ma'am. I'm Leandra."

I finished introducing the rest of us.

"Well, I am Geraldine Owens. Archie was as close to a boyfriend as I eva will have." She turned around to look at him resting in the casket. "We got together after my husband Leonard died, about ten years past." She dabbed at her nose. "He talked often about your family. Archie nevah ran out of stories to tell. And I know you have had your share of sadness. You are good people to take him into your home in his final days."

She paused to take a breath and pulled a paper fan out of her handbag. I found another chair for her to sit down, worried she might collapse right in front of me. I had heard of those things happening at Black funerals where things could become highly emotional.

"Miss Owens," Mamaw began, "none of us here can remember a time when Archie wasn't a part of our life. We couldn't imagine leaving him alone."

"I understand it was his heart that failed."

"Yes, ma'am," I replied. "He just wore out. He worked alongside my Papaw five, sometimes six days a week, depending on the crops or whatever else was begging for attention. Shoot, he helped raise Donny and me."

Geraldine turned to Papaw. "I bet you're gonna miss him as much as me."

"I can't imagine life without him," Papaw replied. "Hardest worker and best friend I eva had."

"Donny, are you ready to visit Archie?" I was still standing, and Geraldine's conversation had given me the courage to walk over to the casket. Donny nodded and we walked to the front, holding onto each other, carefully placing our steps around the crowded room.

"He doesn't look much different than the morning we found him, Mama."

"See his pipe, Donny? I asked them to put it in his hands. And there's an apple in that casket going to heaven with him."

Donny scrunched up his face. "Why'd you do that?"

I shrugged my shoulders. "I can't tell you why, Donny, I just did. Maybe when he gets to Heaven, Jesus will see that apple and give him his very own apple orchard to enjoy."

🦋 🦋 🦋

I braced for the next day and prepared for an emotional rollercoaster.

"Papaw, you want me to get a wheelchair from the clinic for the funeral service? It's gonna be a long day."

"I don't need no dang wheelchair," he snapped. "Just get me there, I'll be fine."

Like an old lion he roared at my impertinence. I had hurt his male pride and felt bad about that. We would just have to take the day as it came.

The congregation and Archie's daughter, Ester, decided the church graveyard would be Archie's resting place. They thanked us for our kindness but felt the Barker farm was his place of work and, contrary to that, this town was his home. Geraldine and the Barkers could visit and tidy up on Decoration Day, so it seemed like a good fit for everyone. Especially Archie. I had hoped Ester would make her way north to Archie's service, but I don't think she was motivated to go out of her way. He was more of a friend than a father, and parenting had been an afterthought for him. Just like the rest of us, as the years collect and begin taunting our late-night thoughts, it likely occurred to him that he had missed something important. Archie was little more than a blank page in a book Ester didn't care to open. My promise to her was to get him a headstone. For now, the church would put up a white cross and nameplate. That satisfied her if she cared at all. I wondered if she'd ever return to his old home to collect any mementos from the father she never knew. For her sake, I hoped she did. Regrets like that can sneak up like an old dog and nip you on the ass.

Normally, most homegoings included a big procession from the funeral home to the church, but Archie had rested at the church since his wake, so he had nowhere to get to. Once the church filled, Reverend Williamson started in with a booming voice that darn near made my ears ache. Those folks were used to it though, and pretty soon they joined in.

"Brothers and sisters, we come here today in praise to God with his infinite love," he paused there, "and to thank him for taking our dear friend, Archie Jackson, back home."

Then all of heaven and hell broke loose starting with Geraldine.

"Oh Lord, oh Lord!" she wailed. "Jesus, take him to your side."

"Give him rest, Lord."

"Hold him tight, Jesus, I pray."

It spread through the church like they were speaking in tongues, except it was in English. Then came the Bible verses, the uplifted arms swaying through the crowd, and the sobbing. I couldn't tell if it was cultural, a sincere effort at grieving, or both.

I looked down the pew past Mamaw to Papaw and Donny. Donny looked my way as if to ask, *Mama, what is going on here?* Papaw sat like a pillar of salt, and only God knew what was crawling through his mind. For a brief moment, I had a flashback of Etta Mae and my younger self when we had been conducting a funeral for Mamaw's chicken, Henny

Penny. Mama found us wailing and crying over a dead chicken and got so upset she fainted. How was I to know she was holding the telegram that said my daddy had died in the war?

I do want to say the singing was angelic. The entire choir, dressed in shiny white robes, sang every old-time hymn I ever knew. Their voices were rich and harmonized, full of passion and depth. And, like I always do at funerals, that's the time I start crying. There was one hymn Archie always used to sing when he was whittling, and that's the one that pierced my heart. Mamaw handed me a hanky, but this time I was prepared with a handful of tissues so I brushed her offer aside. Pretty soon, I was quivering and shaking just like the rest of them. In time, I decided that sobbing and wailing was a purge of sorts, to let the grief seep out and start the heart's healing. It made perfect sense to me.

They insisted on giving Archie a parade, so after services, the pallbearers escorted him to the big white hearse that had taken him from our farm back to his community. We all lined up to walk him home. Three young women took the flowers from the church and draped them over his casket. They each carried a flower arrangement, walking with the pallbearers while providing physical support to some of the older women. The procession left the church, heading east, where they would walk past Archie's house, circle around, and return to the church graveyard.

"Would it be alright if Donny and I represent our family, Papaw?" I believe he was relieved not to be a part of the parade and, surely, he would not have made it full circle.

"I'll sit with Papaw," Mamaw added. "You can join us graveside."

I wasn't sure how Donny was taking all of this. He wasn't even in school when his father had died, just about the same age I was when I lost my daddy. Now he was closing in on ten years. He knew his great Papaw was sick and death spared no one. There was no way to tell if this would weaken him or reveal his strength.

Through my watery vision, I watched the white casket disappear into a dark earthen hole. It was what separated the living from the dead and signaled no turning back.

Archie got a sunshine-filled day, just the kind he found pleasurable, no matter the time of year. If not linked by blood, this community truly was his family, and that put both our souls at peace.

Chapter 15

They're Coming

The passage of time sees to it that there are moments we can't escape. Know they're coming.

🦋 🦋 🦋

After Archie died, something deep inside Papaw shifted. The fire and fight that kept him pushing at my back nearly all my life seemed to walk out the front door and slam it shut. Each day, he distanced himself further from the rest of us. Fear rose inside me that he was ready to join Archie. I reminded him we still needed each other and had a farm to run.

"You don't need me meddlin' in your work," he responded.

He sat under the trees, in one of the two chairs he and Archie had filled. I took the empty seat next to him. His lightweight flannel shirt and grey sweatshirt weren't enough to keep him warm on a breezy February day. His face was turned into the wind, like he was viewing the decades rushing past him.

"It hurts," he volunteered, "watching your friends die. Some go fast and sudden, others, like me, just fall apart little by little." He shook his head and stared down at the ground like it would swallow him whole.

I'd never seen him so serious, and it scared me down to the bone. It sounded like goodbye.

"Papaw, some of your sadness is about Archie, and I understand that, but you still have so much to give. Why, I ask you something about running this farm almost every day."

He held his stare at our Carolina dirt. "We're okay, aren't we, Leandra? I mean, I did right by you and little Donny? I tried to take good care of Mamaw. I got everything in order for you to take over the farm."

"Don't you worry a thing about that. Those ten years I was without you and living in Perth Amboy were the hardest years of my life. But when life got difficult, I always fell back on what you and Mamaw taught me. I hope to do the same with Donny. Papaw, that's what family does."

"You got enough help for this summer? Spring planting is a couple of months away."

"Yes, sir. Most every one of those boys who helped build the apple barn want to come back this summer. Leroy wants to bring his girlfriend. She's interested in farming too, so I thought I'd introduce her to Jake and John Sr. at the Angus farm. I could use a good mechanic, but one will turn up. And the clinic is busting at the seams. We need to take a look at that acre across the road and figure out how we're going to build a free-standing community clinic. Hope you like company."

"You need a companion." He blurted that out like he was saying it was a nice day to take a walk.

"You mean a man? Why do I need more trouble in my life?"

"What about that nice boy from New Jersey?"

"Well first of all, he's not a boy. He's a full-grown man with problems of his own. Namely a wife and kids. The other nice boy was a priest. That doesn't leave me much."

"Ain't there no good men in town?" His interest picked up. "I hear there's a new man down at the co-op, 'bout your age, newly hired."

"Men like that don't come without baggage. And can I have a breather for a while? I'm looking forward to a quiet, productive year when I don't have to worry about anyone else but my family and my farm."

Looking back, I found it odd I had picked those exact words about needing a breather. I remember that distinctly. Life was giving me a heads-up and I paid it no mind.

🦋 🦋 🦋

Not but a week later, I popped downstairs, still buttoning my flannel shirt over my long underwear. Winter was not going to let go without a battle and I was anxious to get down to whatever it was in the kitchen that smelled like cinnamon. Mamaw stood over a bubbling pot of cinnamon oatmeal made with our own rich milk, one of Papaw's favorite breakfasts. I expected to find him sitting at the table.

"Papaw already eat?"

"Why yes," she replied. "Wait. Well, I think he already ate. Why, I can't remember." She let out a snicker.

"Looks like a full pot to me. I'll check upstairs to see if he's in bed."

While I went up, I passed Donny on the stairs going down.

"Papaw wants to see you," he said. "He called out from the bedroom when I walked by. He didn't sound so good."

I didn't take the time to ask what he meant so I kept heading in the same direction.

"Papaw? Can I come in?" I found him sitting up in bed. His breaths were shallow and fast. "Not doing so good?" I sat on the edge of the bed and went through all my mommy moves: checking for a hot forehead, looking for pale skin, a fast pulse. "You looked pretty good yesterday."

"I know." He could barely get those two words out. "Maybe I got...too much...cold air when we was out there talkin'."

"Papaw, that was over a week ago. And we know that cold air or wet hair won't make you sick. Still, it's cold and flu season. You stay in bed. I'll call the clinic, but I bet they're gonna make us come in."

"Leandra?"

"Hmm, what?" I turned around. That's when I saw the fear in his eyes.

"I'm having...trouble...catching my breath." Every couple words was punctuated by a deep inhalation.

I looked at my wristwatch. The clinic wouldn't open for another two hours. "I'm calling Dr. Yoder. I'll have Mamaw come up here to help you dress."

My oatmeal would have to wait. I shooed Mamaw upstairs and poured a cup of coffee while waiting for someone to pick up the phone. Finally, a woman answered. I didn't know her name, but I introduced myself and she seemed to know me by reputation.

"Yes, ma'am, my papaw is having a hard time breathing." I did all my explaining. "He may need oxygen. We need a doctor to look at him."

"Well, hold on a minute while I talk with Dr. Yoder."

In the meantime, I yelled at Donny to get out to the curb to catch the school bus. I hated it when my day started like this. "Hurry up, child! If you miss that bus, you miss school."

"I can't, Mama. I have a test today."

"Then move your butt faster, no second chances."

"Ms. Tucker?"

"Oh, not you, ma'am. I'm talking to my son." I sounded like white trash.

"I understand," she replied. "I'm raising three boys. They never listen. Then they grow up into men that don't listen to their wives."

Well, we had bonded.

"What did the doctor say?"

"He said since he's already at the office, it would be faster if you drove him here. Is he strong enough to do that? We have oxygen tanks here for emergencies."

"Yes'm. We'll be there shortly. Ma'am? Remind Dr. Yoder he has farmer's lung."

I dug a spoon into Mamaw's oatmeal and shoved it in my mouth before running upstairs.

"How you coming?" I knocked on the bedroom door. "Can I come in?" I pushed open the door to see them struggling with his robe. He had on pants and shoes but was still wearing his pajama top.

"No matter about your dress, right, Papaw? Finish with your robe and we'll throw on a heavy jacket and a car blanket. You'll be fine."

"I tried tellin' her I wasn't dressed." He paused for his speaking to catch up with his breathing. "But she scoffed at me."

Mamaw ignored us, focused on tying the robe. I expected she was pretty scared herself.

"Let's help him down to the car," I told Mamaw.

We maneuvered down the stairs with me in front in case I needed to break his fall. Or hers. I had started my car to warm the motor and melt the windshield ice. We maneuvered him in the front seat. When I turned around, Mamaw climbed into the back.

"Mamaw, go back in and get a coat." She was wearing a paisley cotton blouse and corduroy skirt. Not much against the cold.

"Oh, mercy, didn't even notice."

She threw open the car door, stumbled over the back stairs, recovered her stance, and raced inside. *That's all I need*, I thought, *another senior needing medical care.*

I followed her into the kitchen. "I don't know how long this will take," I told her. "I'll get him back soon."

She must have been terrified 'cause all she could do was nod and agree.

Once we arrived at the clinic, Dr. Yoder stabilized Papaw, but we still ended up driving to Asheville. That resulted in a five-day hospital stay, while those medical experts figured out what to do with him. They didn't like us living on the fringe of a small town without a hospital and they wanted to put him in a care home in Asheville. I basically told them to go ahead and kill him right now, because that's what would happen if they took him from his farm. They reconsidered and backed down after that.

I acted sassy and ungrateful because I didn't think they understood our reasoning. I knew the risk and so did my family. I wanted to ask them, "What is the value of life if you're living in misery?" Why not spend the end of your time with the ones you love, in a home you love? I'd sacrifice a few extra days or weeks for that and Papaw would too. Still, I shared their offer with Papaw while we waited for permission to leave the hospital.

"You trust me?" I asked. "They want to send you to a nursing home."

"Tell *them* to go live there," he snarled. "I tried to tell that fancy social worker woman, but she wouldn't listen." He paused to adjust the oxygen tube gripping his nostrils. "This dang thing is gonna make me crazy."

"I think Mamaw, Donny, and I can take care of you at home. What do you think?"

"I think I'll be a bother, but home is what I want."

"Then that's what we'll do. It's not like you'll be living in a house of idiots. We'll figure it out as we go. Shoot, every one of us have been caring for living things all our lives. Why should you be any different?"

I started packing his belongings and observed as a peace settled over Papaw. I tried to make light of what was coming down the pipes, praying that when the time came, we would know the right thing to do.

※ ※ ※

It was at least a forty-five-minute drive from Asheville to home. More if the weather was bad. I situated Papaw in the front seat with his new best friend, a portable oxygen tank. His life was forever changed, as was mine, but we would adapt. I stopped short of asking the doctor how long my papaw would live. How would that doctor know when his soul would decide to turn home? I would leave that up to God. Papaw settled into a nice nap, mouth open and snoring like it was the most sleep he'd had all week.

Mamaw was sitting outside with Donny and a school friend when we pulled into the back. Relief washed over me, knowing I would have some help getting him in the house.

"They just delivered his medical bed," Mamaw advised. "A fancy thing that moves his head and legs up and down so he can breathe easier. It's a wonderful gadget."

"That will make our lives a lot easier," I replied. "Using that downstairs room will mean we don't have to struggle getting him upstairs to bed and he'll have access to the kitchen and television."

"You girls got this all figured out, do you?"

He'd found his smart mouth again, so I made sure to find mine. That was my reassurance that he felt better now, as he was home and able to mouth back to me in full sentences.

"Yes, sir, but don't expect us to be waiting on you hand and foot like you're someone special."

"Well, too late, darlin'. I already feel special."

All I could do was smile back at him. For sure we made the right decision. "Mamaw, let's get our patient to his new room."

Mamaw had already made the bed and found a cozy quilt to cover it. To the far side, the delivery men had set up the oxygen box that would pull extra oxygen out of the air and concentrate it for Papaw to use. All we had to do was make sure we didn't step on the hundred feet or so of plastic tubing that was literally his lifeline.

Donny's friend, Abe, picked up the tubing to examine it. "There's oxygen in here?" he asked.

"Yep, it squeezes the oxygen out of the air and sends it through the tube, so Papaw gets more than we do," I explained.

"Don't we need it too?" Donny asked.

"Of course, we do. But he needs more of it because his lungs aren't working as well as yours. This way he gets to stay home with us while he…" I paused. What crossed my mind was, *waits to die.* I wanted to say, *gets better,* but that wasn't going to happen. So, I settled on, "Gets stronger." That would be my fondest hope.

The days of our lives slipped by, just like that sappy soap opera by the same name that Mamaw and Papaw took to watching every afternoon. It amused me that two old folks who worked so hard all their lives, still found pleasure just keeping company. I had doubts that would ever happen to me. I thought back on Papaw wanting to marry me off to someone, but forty years was about to latch on and I wasn't sure I wanted any more challenges.

Late one afternoon, I was outside studying the garden plot to design the layout for the spring vegetables when I heard a large truck coming up the road. When you live in the country, you can hear an engine whining half a mile away. I looked up and saw the propane tanker pulling into our drive.

"Our tank getting low?" I asked no one in particular.

Two delivery men climbed out of the truck. I recognized Harry, who had been with the company since fire was discovered, but not the new guy.

"Nah, just your scheduled delivery," Harry replied. "But, with this winter, I'm shocked you didn't call us with an empty tank."

While he hooked up the delivery hose, I walked over to the new man, removed my garden glove, and offered my handshake. Harry wasn't much on formalities.

"I'm Leandra." I smiled and stuck out my hand. "And this is my piece of heaven."

He accepted my hand and looked around. "Nate Farr. I'm the new guy."

"Nate's going to be my new supervisor," Harry replied offhandedly. "Soon as I teach him his new job."

I raised my eyebrows to meet Nate's eyes, immediately distracted by their turquoise color. *Oh, mercy no!* This had to be the divorcé Papaw talked about. He was a fine-looking man with sand-colored hair smudged with grey on the sides. His arms were strong, and he looked to be close to my age—nothing objectionable. Damnit. I hadn't planned on him being so attractive.

Donny called out to me. "Mama, you better get in here." He stood at the kitchen door like he was afraid to leave the house. That could mean anything: a plugged toilet or busted pipe, an unwanted critter like a snake, something wrong with Papaw, a phone call. It all ran through my head like a lightning bolt. But I wasn't prepared for what I saw.

Chapter 16

Life Goes Sideways

After a certain age, you learn an important lesson. You get up in the morning with a list of things you expect to accomplish in an ordinary day. Then the day takes a different direction, and nothing is ever the same.

On that unexpected day I headed in two different directions at the same time. As one person came into my life, another one turned around and walked away.

🦋 🦋 🦋

"What is she doing?" Donny asked. "She can't get those logs in the oven."

I motioned for him to be still. We stood back to watch and listen while she muttered to herself.

"I can't get supper made if I can't get this oven lit. Now why can't I get this wood in the stove? Who in tarnation split this wood? Evan? Evan, did you do this?"

"Who's Evan?" Donny whispered to me.

"Her younger brother. She never talks about him. He died in his early twenties."

I reached up to wipe my wet face, laying witness to something I never expected, watching Mamaw continue her futile effort to heat a propane stove with logs for the fireplace.

There came a knock at the door. Nate pulled open the door without an answer from me. When I turned around, he got one look at my face and the propane receipt he had prepared to give to me dropped from his hand. He glanced at the logs and dirt scattered on the kitchen linoleum.

"What's going on? Can I help?"

I replied in my softest voice. "My mamaw's just lost her mind."

He stepped in and moved me slightly to the left. "What's her name?"

"Opal," I replied in a shell-shocked tone of voice.

"Opal," he called to her. "Opal, let me help you with that wood. I can take these logs outside and find some smaller ones."

"This is takin' too long," she argued. "I'm nevah gonna get suppa made." Her accent sounded heavy, like she was exhausted.

"Look, Donny is going to help. You remember Donny, don't you, Opal? Your grandson?" She gave Donny a blank stare. "While Donny and I take care of the logs, Leandra is going to help you get comfortable and I bet she can make a nice dinner for your family in no time. You don't have to worry about a thing."

Donny followed his cue. "Mamaw, we can fix this. Don't worry."

I looked to Nate, biting my lower lip to keep more tears from spilling. "Thank you," my voice croaked.

I directed Mamaw upstairs, reiterating that everything was going to be fine and a nap before dinner would refresh her. Barely breathing myself, I unbuttoned her house dress and let her rest in her bra and slip. I tucked her under her blankets and winter bedspread.

"I'm just gonna have me a little rest," she reassured me.

As I made my way downstairs, I clung to the handrail like a drowning man. My legs shook and could barely support my weight. Nate and Donny met me at the bottom of the stairs.

Nate took me by the arm. "Harry went on to complete his deliveries. Donny helped me put on some coffee, so I'm going to stay a while if that's okay. I think you could use some company."

I sat down at the same kitchen table, dated from the 1940s, where Mamaw and Papaw had served me coffee for forty years.

"I'm losing both of them." I covered my face with my hands, sobbing. "I don't know what to do."

Donny wrapped his arms around me.

"I know what to do," Nate replied. "I've walked the same road and not too long ago." I grabbed a napkin off the kitchen table to wipe my face while he continued. "My grandmother too." He filled my coffee cup, pausing to study me. "Cream, no sugar, right?" I nodded yes. He smiled at me. "Just a lucky guess." He poured himself a cup of coffee and sat down with me.

"One day, Grandma was there, the next day she wasn't. She just checked out. I missed all the signs. After her diagnosis, I started putting things together. I'd caught her talking to dead relatives like they were sitting on the porch having a conversation. She tried cooking with baby powder instead of cornstarch. We get so busy with our own lives. It's easy to miss those signals."

"Well, this signal wasn't somethin' I could miss. But how will I handle two of them, run the farm, and take care of my son?"

"There's no one else to help?"

"I'm a widow," I replied. "Trying to run a farm as a single mother is hard enough."

"Then you won't. It's worth it to hire help. You'll find a way."

I thought back to a time when Ana, my New York Mamaw, had told me the very same thing when I didn't have any money to get Raymond's body home to bury him by the butterfly bush. Help showed up out of nowhere to give me the wherewithal to get my brother home.

Nate looked at his wristwatch. "Harry's going to swing by here soon and pick me up, I hope. Here's my phone number. I've seen it all and lived through it. You call me if there's something you can't figure out."

Papaw's hacking cough came from down the hall, my signal he was up from his nap.

"I do need to get dinner ready." I was thinking out loud. "Might end up being soup and sandwiches, but they won't go hungry."

Donny and I walked Nate to the front door where he could meet Harry's tanker on his way back to the co-op. I was damn lucky Nate showed up when he did. I waved goodbye. My son put his arms around my waist and we walked back into the house not knowing what was going to happen from one minute to the next.

🦋 🦋 🦋

I had no clue how to break the news to Papaw that Mamaw was out of her mind. But, before that, I needed to get a diagnosis. Dr. Yoder stopped by for a visit and I explained what happened the day before.

"How old you say she is?"

"If she's tellin' the truth, she should be eighty. But I've never seen a birth certificate."

"And no other symptoms before this?"

I had thought overnight about what Nate had said. There was that day when she couldn't remember if Papaw had eaten breakfast or how to help him belt his robe. I wrote that off to a stressful day and a lot of worry.

"There may have been a few times when her thinking wasn't right. But it was nothing like this. She could have blown us to Kingdom Come if she turned on the propane for the oven."

"She might have nothing more than a bladder infection. Sometimes that throws older folks off. We can get a urine sample while we're there. I might as well give both of them a goin' over while I'm visiting."

That was an enormous comfort to me and Donny, especially when I saw Doc Sylvan standing at the front door with Dr. Yoder. It was like old times, and I nearly knocked Doc over with a big hug.

"I brought a friend," Dr. Yoder said with a kind smile. "Doc here knows your grandparents pretty well, so he agreed to a social visit."

"They're right here in the living room," I pointed to the couch. "Life might be going to hell but they'd never miss *Days of Our Lives*."

They brightened up when they saw Doc Sylvan. Papaw remembered Dr. Yoder, but Mamaw didn't have a clue to his identity.

Doc tried to reassure me. "If this is dementia, often they can remember their distant past, but the recent past is lost. That's why she remembers me, but not him."

I thought I'd better explain to the senior love birds how we rated for a visit. "Papaw, Mamaw, the doctors dropped by for a health check. Wasn't that nice of them?"

Mamaw stood up. "I'll put on some coffee, and I bet I have some cookies," she volunteered.

"I already started some coffee," I lied. "Mamaw, why don't you go first."

"I'm not sick," she replied. "Papaw's the one with farmer's lung." I was surprised she remembered his lung condition.

Doc Sylvan jumped into the discussion. He started sneaking in questions, experienced as he was with dealing with old farm folks past their prime. By the time he got done, Donny had been rechristened David and it was Tuesday, not Friday.

Doc Sylvan kept going. "What do you think of our president? What's his name again?"

"What's wrong with you, Doc? It's the same one that makes the cars. You know that Ford fella."

"So, it's not that guy that grows peanuts? I think his name is Carter."

"The hell you say, you crazy ol' fool. Pick up a newspaper once in a while."

That was not my mamaw talking. I didn't know who it was, but I hoped we would have some moments in between where I could talk to her again. I still had so much to ask her. She still had so much to share.

Dr. Yoder finished examining Papaw. His lungs were much the same and his blood pressure was good. He had lost some weight, but that was expected with all the work it took to breathe. Dr. Yoder didn't find any surprises.

Doc Sylvan had a few comments about Mamaw. "Leandra, I'm pretty sure it's dementia and it's well on its way. She may have had a stroke and you're lucky she didn't fall." He handed me what looked like a plastic bowl. "Slip this toilet hat into her commode when she's not looking. Take the urine sample to Dr. Yoder and we'll check her for a bladder infection. But Leandra, I'm bettin' it's her brain, not her bladder."

🦋 🦋 🦋

My first order of business was figuring out how to keep going. I had to think of Donny first and safety next, fretting over what kind of trouble my two grandparents could cause. Papaw was the least of my troubles, but after he found out his sweetheart was suffering, it was difficult to console him.

"Papaw, she doesn't know she's sick. The world she lives in is different from ours, but we can still find a middle point, call up a happy memory. They say food can do that. Maybe she can help me make some biscuits or cornbread this week."

"I never wanted to bring this on you. It isn't fair. You're too young for these kind of burdens."

"I'll get some help. These first few weeks or months will be a struggle. You can help by being my eyes and ears and get me if she needs redirection. That will be a big help. Look at me." He turned his eyes up to meet mine. Once they had been a bright blue. Now they were pale and empty, edged by a white ring common to old folks. "Day by day, Papaw. The answers will come day by day."

On the morning my former mother-in-law, Ruby, showed up at my front door, I had been wondering what it would be like to walk away from the farm. It had rained daily for almost a week. I called off planting twice, knowing I'd be pulling equipment out of the mud and worrying my hired help would leave me to find work elsewhere. How easy would life be in the Asheville suburbs? No animals to care for, no trees to trim and manage, no fields to fret over, and medical help at my fingertips. Donny could enroll in the best schools. I sipped at my fourth cup of coffee, contemplating what time I would make it to bed that night.

I almost teared up when I saw Ruby. "I am so happy to see you."

My shoulders dropped and I took a deep breath. If only for a couple of hours, I was rescued.

"Why darlin', I've missed you too."

I pushed open the screen door, and standing next to Ruby was a wide-eyed girl, petite, thin, and timid.

"Come on in, both of you." I smiled at the small girl, trying to figure out her age. She had bosoms, but no hips to mention. I guessed she was close to fifteen or sixteen years old. "It's so nice to have a couple of women to talk to. I have to get back to the kitchen. I left Mamaw in there sitting at the table by herself and I need to keep an eye on her."

I pushed open the kitchen door and, thank God, Mamaw was still mixing the same bowl of flour I left her with five minutes earlier.

"I brought cobbler," Ruby said, and handed me a delicious pan of sweet-smelling peaches and cake. "Last two jars I canned back in July." It was still warm from the oven. "Hi thar, Opal."

Mamaw looked up, smiled, and went right back to her bowl of flour.

"Nobody's home," I said to Ruby. "I try and keep her busy with things that are familiar."

"Where's Zachary?"

"He's out back getting some sunshine. Just follow the oxygen tubing if you want to find him."

Ruby peeked out the screen door.

"I know you like tea, Ruby. I'll start a kettle of water and grab some cold milk." I turned to the young girl. "What's your name?"

"Land-sakes, my manners!" Ruby nearly shouted. "This is Bethene Wetzel. I wanted you two to meet."

I had no idea what Ruby was up to but, without a doubt, there was something scheming in her busy little mind.

"Do I call you Beth?"

"Yes ma'am. If it suits you."

"You prefer Bethene?"

"It doesn't matter."

Oh no, I thought, *it always matters.* Either this girl had not been given a choice of her preferred name or lacked the self-confidence to declare her identity.

Ruby walked over to the cabinet and took down some cups, saucers, and plates for cobbler.

"Opal, we're gonna have some fruit cobbler. Would you like to join us?"

Mamaw sat and watched Ruby dish out the cobbler and motioned for Beth to sit down next to my grandma. Beth picked up one of the forks, put it down, and grabbed a spoon to hand to Mamaw, making sure she could feed herself.

"How are Jake and John? Is Ann still having babies?" I poured steaming water into the three teacups and a small glass of milk for Mamaw. Beth wiped up a blob of cobbler Mamaw dripped on the table.

"Ann's youngest is four now, and she claims to be done birthing. By the way, we wondered if Donny could spend some time at the farm this summer—unless you need him helping you with your grandparents."

"Ruby, I don't know what will unfold by summer, but if you and Donny want to spend time together, I wouldn't dare hold him back. This situation has got to be as discouraging for him as it is for me."

"Oh no!" My hand flew to my mouth. "I didn't get out to feed the animals this morning. They must be ready to eat each other. I took Mamaw out with me to milk the cow and never went back."

A little voice spoke up. "I can do that, ma'am."

"You know about farm animals, Beth?"

"She sure does," Ruby responded. "Bethene loves animals."

"Beth, I have some mud boots out by the back door. It's likely to still be a little messy out there from all the rain. There's a few chickens that need their feeder filled, a goat, a black pig and, if you see them, a few barn cats." I pulled a bag of vegetable scraps from the refrigerator and handed them to her. "All the feed's out there in the same corner of the barn. Thank you so much."

Once I heard Beth leave the porch, I turned to Ruby. "Okay, Ruby, what's goin' on?"

Ruby bobbed her teabag up and down in the hot water. I heard her sigh. "She's a runaway. Came from a bad situation and won't say much about it. She wandered into church one day and we been movin' her around home-to-home eva since. She's a grateful little thing. Simply happy to have a roof over her head, a few clothes, and hot food."

"And you brought her here because…"

"Look, Leandra, you need help and she needs help. She'd be good company and anotha pair of hands."

"Is she expectin'?"

"No, nothin' like that. This has been goin' on for a couple of months and I don't see no little belly poppin' up. Shoot, I don't know where she puts it, never gains a pound. Looks like a little pixie with that short haircut. We can keep shuffling her around, but it would be a good fit for the two of you."

"How old?"

"She says seventeen, but I wouldn't put her a day past sixteen."

"She know what you're up to, Ruby?"

"I told her about you and John and Donny, that you were a kind woman who needed someone to help out, and maybe she could exchange room and board for helping you."

I thought back to Ana and William and how they took me in when I had been with child. I remembered how I found Crystal on the street in the heat of July, and now she had a home and family of her own, and still found time to volunteer at the clinic. Then there was old Mrs. Pitterly who never would have survived or saved her farm if it hadn't been for Crystal moving in. I glanced at Mamaw feverishly polishing my stainless-steel spoon with her apron.

I pushed out my chin and raised an eyebrow. "Well, let's see what she says when she gets back in here after dealing with those animals." It wasn't long before we heard her chatting with Papaw and found her helping him up the stairs, careful to avoid stomping his oxygen tubing. "She seems to have some knowledge about dealing with the feeble."

"I noticed that," Ruby replied. "I sure enough don't know her past, but she has skills that will help you, Leandra. That's why I thought of you."

"If it hadn't been for this pretty girl, I'da never known there was cobbler in this kitchen." Papaw rarely missed an opportunity to scold me.

"We see you've met Beth," I replied. The girl settled Papaw at the table with Mamaw. "Ruby, can you sit a spell with Opal and Zachary, while Beth and I talk?"

Ruby winked at me. "Happy to," she replied, and dished up a plate of cobbler for an old man.

🦋 🦋 🦋

I took the saggy sofa while Beth sat in the faded chair next to me. "Ruby has told me about your situation. Can you tell me a little more?"

"Not much to tell," she started. "I had to go out on my own. I worked odd jobs. Sometimes I slept on the streets or in an empty barn or building. One day, I wandered into Ruby's church. I didn't know what I was looking for that day, but that big white steeple called to me. And they took me in like a sister."

"Ruby seems to think you might like it here. I'm not sure why, with a frazzled middle-aged woman minding two old people. On top of that, I have those scraggly animals and a young son."

"I'm not lookin' for much, ma'am. And your animals are sweet." She smiled. "Your barn cats came right up to me."

"How are you with your schooling? Did you graduate high school?"

"No." I watched her drop her head. "But I'd like to finish. Maybe get my GED."

"Graduating high school will be a stipulation if you choose to stay here. You can work on your studies in your free time, and Donny and I can help. Beth, you won't get anywhere without a high school diploma. Will that plan work for you?"

She nodded in agreement.

"I'll give you room and board and pay in cash on a weekly basis. We have to get your belongings and you can move in when you're ready. Where are your clothes and such?"

"In a paper sack in the back of Ruby's car."

I shook my head. I should have known. But that night, I slept a little easier knowing someone else would help bear my burden.

Chapter 17

A Helping Hand

How do we ever know when it's the right time to step in and help another person? Even if you think you're doing the right thing, you're still forcing your values on someone else. I'm pretty sure when I agreed to take Bethene into my home, it was the act of a desperate woman, not a Christian woman. I was mostly helping myself, but hoped that somewhere in our situation, I would discover my honorable deed.

🦋 🦋 🦋

Having Beth in my life changed everything. True, I let a complete stranger move into my home, but I hoped Ruby's Baptist church had instilled some moral values into that young woman. There was no reason to doubt this, but I was just paranoid enough to lock up anything important like our financial records, jewelry, and guns. I had mostly done that anyway with two crazy people living in my home. I had one short on oxygen and one short on brain cells so, doing the math, I calculated lots could go wrong.

Beth was accustomed to serving others, both a blessing and a talent. I could smell the morning coffee brewing, just like the old days when Mamaw made it for our family. These days, I laid out Mamaw's clothes the night before, and once she got a whiff of that coffee, she'd dress and make her way downstairs. Still, sometimes she'd get confused and walk out in her undies. One time, she marched downstairs dressed only from the waist down, and proclaimed, "What is this confounded thing?" while waving her brassiere like a banner for Christ. That memory, I will carry to my grave, and I will remain grateful Donny failed to witness her frustration and my shock.

I greeted Beth as cheerfully as I could, thanked her for the coffee, and poured myself a steaming mug. "If you go upstairs and make sure Mamaw is dressing, I'll whip up some eggs and toast. And, Beth, if she's still sleepin', leave her be. Papaw usually sleeps in a little later, but today the healthcare aide will visit to help with his bath and bring supplies, so he may be up a little earlier."

Goodness, if nothing else, it felt good to talk to another adult.

My life started working again. One by one, everyone was fed, including the animals. I let Mamaw wander out with Beth to milk the cow, knowing that would hold her attention, while I spoke with the nursing aide. I didn't know where Beth came from or where she was going, but it was certain she took to farm life. When she wasn't taking care of someone or something, she was cleaning or cooking. I had to remind her to call the high school about night classes.

"I can't drive," she replied.

"No matter. Donny will be home and he can keep an eye on them for the few minutes it will take for me to drive you to school." She was looking for excuses and I wasn't going to give her any way to wiggle out of it. "I want to see that diploma in your hand."

All I got back was, "Yes, ma'am," as her eyes drifted to the floor. She wasn't used to attention being laid on her.

"Look at me, Beth." Her sad little face turned up. "A woman needs an education, especially an independent woman like yourself. What you really need is to work your way through college or get a scholarship. Make it happen." I picked up our skinny phone book and handed it to her. "Only one high school in Mountain Grove. Look up the number and call."

🦋 🦋 🦋

I stood in the field, south of the farmhouse, surveying the beginning of planting season. The farming machines kept getting bigger and bigger, and so sophisticated they practically ran by themselves. I must have had Carolina dirt running in my veins as I still found it exciting to see the tractors and planting machines rumble down the road and lumber into the fields to drop their seed and bring life to the soil.

I had leased out fifty acres to a local farmer to grow his animal feed but, at Papaw's insistence, held back another fifty for tobacco. I dreaded planting another tobacco crop, the spraying, harvesting, drying—there was nothing I liked about it. I expected this to be Papaw's last crop of tobacco so I couldn't deny him the glory of sending one last crop to market.

Who should see me standing out there on the road but Nate. When he pulled up in his green and white pickup, my heart went to pounding. I put on my best smile and walked over to his open window.

"Good day for planting," he commented. "Your crop?"

"No, leased it out when we downsized. Got another fifty back there for tobacco." I rolled my eyes. "Not my choice, but Papaw wants it."

"Hear you got some help with your grandparents."

"Word travels fast 'round these acres. Yes, Beth is a joy to have around the house. Not sure she's pleased with me making her finish school while she's taking care of us, but if she wants her independence…"

"So that means you have some time on your hands."

I gave him a quizzical look. "What makes you think I have spare time running a farm, a nonprofit clinic, and taking care of the young and old?"

"Well, you gotta eat. Thought you might join me for dinner sometime. There's a new steakhouse opening in the next town over."

"I should be taking you to dinner after you rescued me from Mamaw."

"She doing okay now?"

"The question is, am I doing okay? And yes, we are all managing better with Beth's help."

"Good. Talk to Beth and figure out a good time when you can get away and join me for dinner. I'll call in a couple of days."

I didn't know how to respond. My eyes shifted to the dirt under my feet. I hadn't even considered dating since John's death. I blinked hard, prepared to meet his gaze to excuse myself from a stressful situation.

He interrupted. "Leandra, it's just dinner. For once in your life, let someone do something for you."

I agreed—reluctantly. I got a wink in return, and he drove down the road.

He was right. I needed some time off the farm. But why was I on the verge of tears? I turned back to face the field and wondered if Papaw had put him up to this. A pity date. But Papaw could hardly catch his breath and hated using the phone. No, this could be a sincere request. I was too old for this kind of social pressure and second guessing.

Beth and I talked the situation over like a couple of teenage girls. Mamaw and Papaw were in the sitting room fretting over the news while we conspired in my bedroom.

"Saturday is usually date night," Beth advised. "Maybe you should make it on a Friday night after work. Unless you want it to be a date…"

"No! That's not what I want him to think. I could give him two choices, like Thursday or Friday."

"That could work. You wouldn't appear to be needy and take up his weekend. Just something casual."

"Needy? Do I appear needy?"

Beth surprised me. "Miss Leandra, you need to calm down or you're gonna bust a gasket and I'm gonna have four people to look after."

"Okay. But help me pick something out to wear."

"Go shopping, Leandra. Get something new."

"You've seen my wardrobe? Is it that bad?"

"They were stylish ten years ago."

"Well, all I need are my Levi's and T-shirts. Maybe some flannel shirts in the winter."

"Listen, if I ever fill out like you, I'm gonna make the best of my figure. Even if you don't want to wear a dress, they have some cute polyester pant suits downtown at Tilly's Dress Shop. Everyone's wearing them and it will get you out of your blue jeans."

Lately, everyone was telling me what to do. Either I had let my life go to hell, or not given it a second thought in a long time. When Nate called, he accepted my offer for Friday night. That gave me most of the week to pull my nerves together and find something to wear. Fifteen years had gone by since I had a date as a single woman. I was out of touch with social norms and felt like I was starting from scratch. As a young woman, it was hard enough, but here I was, middle aged and learning it all over again.

🦋 🦋 🦋

Tilly's Dress Shop had opened two years before but, up until now, I had no good reason to go there.

The owner was about my age. Her real name was Matilda, but she refused to answer to it as a child, so they called her Tilly in exchange for her attention. She claimed her sandy-brown hair hung down to her waist but had pinned it up in a cascade of curls, feeling like that day was a good day to dress up. I got all this from her in the first five minutes we met.

She was all over me like a hornworm on a tomato plant. "I have several styles of pantsuits with jackets. I'll go collect a couple for you and 'long as you're in the dressing room, pick out a couple of dresses you might like. You never know what will strike your fancy."

The silver bell on the door jingled. Two women walked in and she called to them by name. I found a couple of cute knit dresses that would convince Beth I could still show off my curves. Next thing I knew, Tilly whipped by and took the dresses to hang in my changing room.

"Nice choices," she shouted and turned back to the other women.

Was I just depressed or exhausted, or was there another good reason I didn't have her energy? Maybe I needed to get excited about life. In no time at all, she had all three of us in the dressing rooms. I pulled back my curtain to find her sitting in an easy chair drinking a glass of white wine.

"Come on out here," she coaxed me. "Let's see what you got." She handed me a glass of wine and did the same to the other women when they emerged from their cocoons, dressed in new colors like spring butterflies. Maybe Tilly's goal was to get us plastered so we'd believe everything looked amazing on us. Truthfully, I didn't care. I was enjoying myself and couldn't remember the last time I drank a glass of wine in the middle of the day with a bunch of women.

"Everything on you looks gorgeous," the other shopper said to me.

She was a plump woman, about half a foot shorter than me and ten years my senior.

"She's right," Tilly said. "I'm not trying to push my clothes off on you, but you're a perfect size eight. Is this a special occasion or are you adding to your wardrobe? I haven't seen you in here before."

Wine glass in hand, I launched into my dilemma to all three women. They listened intently.

"You mean you have a date with Nate Farr? That cute little thing from the co-op? My neighbor has her eye on him."

"Not a date. It's just dinner."

"Oh honey, it's never 'just dinner.'"

I plopped down into a folding chair, still wearing Tilly's dress and clinging to my wine glass, now nearly empty. "I'm so scared," I confessed. "I'm afraid I'll do or say the wrong thing and embarrass myself."

Tilly refilled my glass. "I can catch you up with all that," she said confidently. "I been runnin' the circuit for five years now. Haven't found my man, but I know the ins and outs. Meet me back here after six tonight, and we'll have dinner at the coffeeshop."

I called Beth to make sure she could handle the family while Tilly updated my social skills. She assured me dinner was no problem and added, "You needed this, no two ways about it."

I returned to the dressing area where the women were making their final choices. I held out my glass to Tilly and we toasted to ourselves. "It's a date," I said. "I'll meet you at six."

I walked out of there with three new outfits, one new friend, and stopped at the grocery store for two bottles of wine.

🦋 🦋 🦋

Kate's Coffee House was almost empty by the time Tilly and I arrived for my dating life update. I pointed to a table in the far corner where no one could listen in on my pathetic dilemma. Kate's didn't have any spirits, and it was just as well I keep my head clear.

In the few hours that had passed since our first meeting, I started feeling awkward about spilling my guts to Tilly. It was a small town. I mean, she was nice and all, but I think it had been the wine and female companionship that gave me a loose tongue.

"How'd you end up in Mountain Grove, Tilly? It's not exactly a destination hot spot."

Tilly laughed, broad and full. I loved her hearty laugh, and it reminded me of my Atlanta Grandma, long since passed, who always had a confident sense of humor. I noticed her cleavage backed up to her neck as she practically rested her breasts on the table. I had heard some women were getting artificial ones and wondered if Tilly had made that choice.

Just then the waitress showed up to collect our drink orders. I knew she was within earshot of us, but I didn't recognize her as someone who ran in my circle. I couldn't be sure what was going to come out of Tilly's mouth and didn't want the waitress, a mere youngster, all up in my business.

"I'll have a coffee with cream," I replied.

"You want that flavored?"

I saw Tilly's eyes widen with excitement. I swear that girl could find something rousing in everything she came across. Again, I wondered if she was over the top or I was subdued by my natural behavior and upbringing.

"We got flavors?" Tilly probed.

"We have vanilla, hazelnut, and mocha. It's all new and the boss is trying it out."

"I'll take a hazelnut," Tilly said. When the girl walked away, she looked at me. "Wish they had a bourbon flavor." She slammed her hand down on the table. "Now, you were asking about my arrival in Mountain Grove. I made the mistake of marrying a local boy. My father was a chemical salesman and we lived in South Carolina. He wandered around to all the farms, across several Midwest states. Daddy was trainin' some cute thing fresh out of high school and would bring him home for dinner sometimes. You know the rest. We got married after a few months of dating and bought a farm we couldn't afford. Had a few bad years, said a few bad things, *did* a few bad things, and it all fell apart. So did we."

"So, you're not from around here. What's your last name?"

"Hartwick."

"You related to the Hartwick family?"

"Well, in an ex-husband sorta way. My uncle's wife's aunt lived out here and after my divorce I was more than anxious to get out of South Carolina and find a new family to latch onto. I was happy living with Aunt Sue, but my hormones got the best of me and I stupidly married again, that time to a Hartwick. That didn't work either. Got a son and a daughter from each ex-husband, so it wasn't all bad."

"The Hartwicks are one of the biggest families in the area. You must have done okay." I couldn't believe my boldness, but I wasn't stopping now. "I think I went to school with a couple of them."

"Yeah, there's a whole pack of them. You can't swing a cat without hitting a Hartwick. Lenny gave me the farmhouse so I had a home to raise the kids. We're on good terms and the kids all visit with their grandparents and cousins and shirt-tail relatives. I started running low on money when the kids moved out, so that's when I opened Tilly's."

That caught me up to the present. She took a deep breath and I followed, squirming in my seat.

"I need to clarify something," she said. "I assume you missed the sexual revolution."

"There was a revolution?" I asked, tongue in cheek. "You mean the bra burning, and women's lib?"

"No honey," she replied seriously. "I'm talking about sex."

And then, like clockwork, our waitress stood table-side with our coffees. I watched the waitress turn toward Tilly, her mouth agape, while two steaming cups of coffee slid off her tray. She managed to save mine, but the hazelnut variety splashed everywhere on the bench, table, and floor, barely missing Tilly's lap. My new friend pushed herself into a corner to avoid the dribbles. Another waitress ran over, or maybe it was the dishwasher, to help while the young waitress, nearly in tears, made us switch tables while she mopped up the mess. She promised Tilly a fresh cup of coffee. At this rate, it was unlikely we would ever eat or finish the conversation.

It's worth mentioning, we just didn't talk about such things back then. We hardly used the word "sex" unless it was in a hushed whisper with someone blood-related or nearly that. But that didn't slow down Tilly. She just sucked in more air and kept going as soon as we seated ourselves at our dry table.

"When 'the pill' came out and women didn't have to worry about getting pregnant—well almost didn't worry—a lot of gals saw that as a green light and didn't think twice about who shared their bed. It was a dang free-for-all for a while there. You probably remember that."

"Oh, I read about it in the papers," I replied. "I remember our church being up in arms over how promiscuous women were becoming and how it destroyed the family. But, by then, I was married to John. My mamaw would have beat me black and blue if I'd done any of that."

"That's okay," she waved her hand dismissively. "You didn't miss much. In some ways, it complicated things. Some men came to expect you to sleep with them, just 'cause they bought you dinner. It's a little different now. And, honey, you still have a choice to pick and choose. If he's too wound up and can't wait until you're good and ready, then send him on his way."

I cleared my throat and picked up a menu. "Let's order," I suggested. I noticed the waitress keeping her distance. I motioned for her to approach our table to take the order. I waited for her to escape earshot before we continued the conversation.

"Let me get this straight." I held up my fingers to count off my new knowledge. "Number one, they still pay for the date, but sometimes they expect sex for that. Number two, I can always refuse sex. Number three, I can change my mind if they can be patient. And how do I know if they have a disease I could catch? This is all very confusing."

"That's the tricky part. Always has been. I'd say make sure he uses a rubber until you know him damn good and well. Tell him you just started the pill and want to make sure you don't make him a daddy. That should scare him enough to listen to you."

From the corner of my eye, I saw our little waitress approaching us very slowly. Obviously, she wanted to give us due warning that dinner was served, and she had no desire to hear anything else from two middle-aged women trying to figure out sex in the seventies. I smiled at her, acknowledging her gesture. I think Tilly scared her.

"One meatloaf special," she placed a plate in front of Tilly. "And one Reuben with fries. Anything else?"

"I could use some more coffee," I said, laying my napkin on my lap.

She hesitated and glanced at Tilly, avoiding eye contact.

"Just a glass of water for me."

A wave of relief flowed over the girl's body.

"And I'll bring your check when I return."

She indicated she had no intention of offering us dessert and exposing herself to more vulgar talk. I could only imagine what she told the fry cook back in the kitchen.

"So, after this dinner…" I began.

"Oh right, it's just dinner. What are we worried about?"

I stopped stirring the cream into my coffee and looked up at her. She was grinning like she'd won a prize at the county fair ring toss.

"I'm going to assume it is only dinner 'cause that's what he said in the first place. You can think whatever you want."

"You'll know after a few dates. If he doesn't call, or the next time you see him is when you need propane then, yes, it was only dinner. Are you wearin' that cute, checkered dress you bought? Maybe with a string of pearls?"

"I don't need him thinkin' he's eating with the queen of England. I'm sure I have somethin' in my jewelry box. And what about after dinner? Do they still walk you to the door? Should I invite him in?"

"You could. I bet he'd appreciate dessert once you get back to the house. That would take the pressure off you. No foolin' around with the family around, know what I mean?"

"That's a good idea." I took a bite out of my sandwich. "And then he wouldn't have to spend a fortune on me, 'just for dinner.' Wait, oh Lord, will he expect a kiss? How will I know? What if I think he wants a kiss and I just make a fool o' myself?"

"If you like him, you kiss him," Tilly instructed. "If not, you be the first to offer him your hand. Nothin' wrong with a handshake since it's 'just dinner.'"

"Right. That way I control the situation." I nodded to myself, sure I had hit on the perfect ending.

Tilly put her fork and knife down on her plate and wiped her mouth with the napkin from her lap. "Leandra, you know there is a chance you might want that good night kiss at the end of the evening." She cleared her throat. "In which case, I don't care if it's midnight, you call me and report on your event."

I picked up the check on the table. "I got this," I said. "Payment for services rendered. And, so you know, I'm not one to kiss and tell. But I might make an exception for my dating coach."

🦋 🦋 🦋

It was not to my liking that Friday night rolled in faster than a Carolina thunderstorm. I told Beth it would take at least three hours for me to dress for dinner by the time I got done with all my manicuring, plucking, polishing, rolling, and styling. I was hoping the chilled chardonnay would put me in the right frame of mind and calm my nerves. More than once, I wondered again if this was worth the effort. Thinking about John and how easily we fell into place, made this feel like work. My high school boyfriend, Greg, was more of a battle with his hateful mother, yet all of that in my twenties had to be easier than this. By our forties, most women have accumulated pain, distrust, and regret. Yes, I had experienced love, but it was hit and miss. It could be I was bored with life and disappointed I wasn't living happily ever after. I wished I could talk to Mamaw about it, but I couldn't pull on her wisdom anymore. Then, for some stupid reason, I went to the phone and called Mama.

The phone only rang once before she picked it up.

"Mama? You must have been standing in the kitchen when the phone rang."

"Why, Leandra, is that you?"

"Yes, Mama. I just wanted to check in and see how you are doing."

"Roger got me an extension line, so I don't have to run into the kitchen. I kept getting my feet tangled and falling. I guess he was afraid I'd break something. Like his television! So now I have a phone right in the parlor."

"Are you having trouble walking, Mama?"

"Oh, you know me. Never did have much balance."

I wanted to say that usually happens when you're drunk all the time, but I held my tongue.

"Roger's been in and out of the doctor himself. Problems with his stomach and his prostate. Whateva that is."

I really didn't care about Roger's health. As far as I was concerned, he could have parts falling off left and right and I wouldn't say so much as God bless you. I changed the subject.

"Mama, I'm going out to dinner tonight with a man from the co-op."

"Oh? Is that right? He's not one of those old farmers, is he?"

"No, Mama. He's my age, but really it's just dinner. He helped me with Mamaw when we found her shovin' wood in the propane stove. I'm lucky he was here filling the outside tank."

"How are your grandparents? Any change?"

"I have a young woman helping me now. I pay her a little each week and she trades care for room and board. It's sure been nice. They're both gettin' by, but I can see Papaw growing weaker. Beth frees up some time for me so I can be with Donny."

"And is my grandson well?"

I felt like she didn't have a right to call him her grandson, but that kind of thinking was selfish. She didn't even send him birthday cards anymore.

"He's wonderful, Mama. Just like John. Caring and loving, and his grades are excellent. He's taken to Little League Baseball. His Uncle Jake coaches, so he sees his cousins and kin on that side of the family."

The conversation grew quiet and uncomfortable, and I figured it was time to hang up. "Well, I'd better go now, Mama. You take care, hear?"

"Leandra. Wait. There's one more thing." I grew uneasy. Damn. I knew I shouldn't have called. "I didn't want to worry you. They, the doctor, found a lump in my bosom. They're not too happy about it and they want a biopsy next week."

My words caught in my throat and I felt like I would gag. As much as Mama annoyed me, she was still my mama. Back in the day I prayed I would inherit her beauty. I had looked upon her as an icon until she started boozing. We had our differences now but say the word "lump" or "tumor" and relate that to breast cancer and anyone would quake in their boots.

"Is it big?" That's all I could get out.

"Like a good-sized walnut." I made a circle with my fingers trying to imagine it's size. "They are telling me if it's cancer, they'll need to take my entire breast."

"Oh, Mama."

My eyes burned with tears. What do you say to a woman when she tells you that? And to top it off, Mama was the first woman I'd ever known to have breast cancer.

"Well, we don't know anything yet, so let's wait and see. Will you remember to call me when the report comes back? I'm so sorry."

"The doctor thinks my smokin' might have something to do with it. And she sure doesn't like me taking a nip now and then. Well, like you said, we have to see."

We ended the conversation, but I could hear terror between her words. Likely, her fear raged more from losing her breast than from the cancer and her possible death. I don't think I had ever talked to my mama when something good was happening in her life.

My thoughts returned to Nate and I was glad to have a distraction. I glanced at my wine glass next to the phone. It was still half full, and I downed it like a man dying from thirst. Upstairs in my room, I opened my jewelry box. Sparkling trinkets collected over the years glistened, then my fingers reached out for a silver butterfly pendant, trimmed in shiny marcasite jewels. My first gift from John always brought a smile to my face. It would go nicely with my black-and-white dress and strappy sandals. I was sure John would have approved.

Chapter 18

Counterfeit

*W*hen you're a young'un, and you make a new friend, what you see and *hear is what you get. Kids are like that. They're unpretentious and real to the bone.*

On the other hand, adults go out of their way to make a good impression. Then you find out they're one step up from a bootlegger and good liquor isn't going to make it any better. I think at one time or another, all of us have come off as counterfeit beings to someone else. What matters is if we can match the person they think we are, with the person we really are, and even the edges when the pieces are stitched together.

🦋 🦋 🦋

Nate was late. Not five or ten minutes, but half an hour late. By the time he arrived, I took it personal, as if I wasn't important enough for him to arrive on time. He appeared to take his bad manners in stride.

"You still want to go out with me?"

I stuck out my chin and made a face. I intended to give him a hard time. "I'm not sure."

"Wouldn't blame you. This is not my style. One of our delivery trucks broke down and set me back. Had to make a delivery myself."

"Hmmm. You sure you aren't delivering a lot of hot air now?"

He smiled and shook his head. "That's what I like about you, Leandra. You call it like you see it. Second chance? I'll be extra charming."

His shirt was clean and pressed and he smelled like a pine forest after a rain. I had nothing to lose. I stared into those blue eyes that captured my attention several months before and shouted over my shoulder to Beth. "I'm leaving now."

She pushed open the swinging door from the kitchen. "Have a good time, don't worry about a thing. I'll call the restaurant if anything comes up with Mamaw and Papaw."

We walked in silence to the truck. He opened the passenger door and I climbed in. When he plopped in the driver's seat and started the truck, he said, "It's hard to leave them, isn't it?"

He was perceptive, that was for sure.

"I haven't been away from them since all this started. I'm sure I'll get the hang of it, but right now I am picturing every wrong scenario that two old people and one child can create."

"You can only try your best. What happens after that is fate. The steakhouse is about thirty minutes east of here. By the time we get there, you'll be fine."

From the outside, the steakhouse looked like someone took an old Appalachian cabin, pulled it from each corner, and made it enormous. But, inside, it was very modern with knotty pine walls, dark-red hobnail seating, and glossy pine tables. Wine glasses, giant steak knives, and white napkins rounded out each place setting. This felt more expensive than a simple meal between friends.

The waiter, dressed head to toe in black, arrived to introduce himself and offer cocktails. Nate looked expectantly at me. I tried to be sophisticated and ordered a glass of rosé wine.

Nate turned toward the waiter. "I won't be needing the wine glass. I'll have a club soda."

"Very well, sir."

"I have to drink alone?" I asked.

He smiled. "I don't want the date to go any worse than it already has."

I was more concerned that he used the word "date" than the fact that he wasn't drinking. Still, I was suspicious and expected a story.

"Well, Papaw is going to think the world of you. Did I ever tell you about him being a Baptist preacher?"

Nate laughed. "I'm going to give you an explanation. Then you can make up your own mind if you want to be my friend."

Our discussion paused when the waiter returned with our drinks.

"Some time back, I couldn't get a grip on my drinking. Mostly it was beer, but on a really bad day I would graduate to the hard stuff as the night wore on. I had been drinking since I was a young teen. It seemed to run in the family and I'm positive my parents divorced because of my father's drinking."

I took a sip of my wine when Nate paused to wet his mouth with his club soda. I'm sure every time he shared this it was difficult.

"My wife was at the end of her rope. She knew I liked to drink when she married me, but as time passed, I liked myself less and less, and finishing off a bottle was how I coped. We tried to have kids for years. Then we found out it was my fault. She wanted to adopt a kid, but I refused, saying I didn't want to take on some kid who already had problems. I was a real jerk."

I picked up my glass of wine and savored a long sip, already sorry I agreed to this dinner. My picture of who this man was went from being a beautiful picture to a chalk drawing in the rain with the colors washing away. So many times, our heart tells us what we want to believe. And, because we are human, we peel away the old layers to discover a different picture hiding underneath. My disappointment deepened and my attention was drifting. I didn't want to hear any more, but he continued.

"One night, we were fighting, and I had been drinking since the early afternoon. It was a rainy Saturday and I stormed out of the house with my car keys and ended up at my local hangout. Three hours later, I left. I still remember how blurry my vision was and how I struggled to find my car. At some point, I must have fallen asleep at the wheel. I woke up when our two vehicles crashed head on. I had hit a van with four kids and their parents. Ironically, me, a man who couldn't produce children left four kids without parents. I killed the parents and orphaned all those children."

"Nate, you don't have to tell me any more of your story."

"No, no. I do."

The waiter returned to take our order. My appetite was gone for the steak dinner as well as any notions I might have had about Nate Farr. I could hardly think straight, just staring at the printed words on the menu. In the background I heard Nate asking about the different cuts of steak.

"Do you mind if I order for you?"

Normally I would not have agreed to that, but it was unlikely I would find anything appealing on the menu. I don't know what I was expecting from this night, but none of it fell under the heading of "dream date."

He looked at me and smiled. "You doing okay?"

"Yes, sure, go ahead and order for both of us." My chest was so tight I could hardly breathe, and realized I was periodically holding my breath.

The waiter left. I took a deep breath. "How did you live with yourself after that?"

"I couldn't. My prison sentence couldn't remove the guilt and pain my heart held."

"Prison?"

"Yes, there are consequences to poor judgment, and that's where I found my forgiveness. For myself."

"Nate, I need a moment. I'll be right back."

He stood as I left the table. I could feel his gaze as I strode away.

I stood at the bathroom sink, staring at my weary face that wore his pain. Maybe it was Mama's pain I wore, thinking back to how her drinking had destroyed our family. I wondered what it would take for Mama to get her wakeup call.

When I returned to our table, Nate stood again and waited for me to be seated. "I was wondering if you'd return," he said lightly. I saw our salads on the table. Grateful for a distraction, I pushed the greens around the plate, yet couldn't lift the fork to my mouth.

I looked straight at him, bit my lower lip, and dropped my eyes. I could hardly look at him. Nate tightened his jaw, and I became uncomfortable with the silence.

"You feel bad for me," he said.

"That's a terrible thing to have gone through."

"I won't say it's been easy but I'm alive. It took something that horrific to get me to open my eyes. I destroyed an entire family. Not a day goes by that I don't ask for their forgiveness and the pain I caused."

"And you told me this because…"

"This is me, who I am. These days I go out of my way to help anyone I can in the name of the family I destroyed. I saw you needed help and I reached out. Where we go from here is entirely up to you."

I took a bite of my salad. Damn, if he didn't get the right dressing.

Nate paused to sip his soda water. "There's a country band coming out later. How's your two-step?"

"John wasn't much of a dancer, and I don't frequent the dance halls around here."

"I hear the Y has dance lessons on Thursday nights."

"I don't know. I barely had enough nerve to leave them tonight with Beth."

"I'm safe, Leandra. And you can't hurt me. I've survived hell."

"I'm sure we'll figure it out in time," I replied. "Long as you're not fixin' on marrying me anytime soon."

He shivered. "You just feel a chill in the room?"

I looked up at him and smiled. My salad was starting to taste delicious. "I'll make you a deal. I'll go dancing with you on Thursdays if you come to church with us on Sunday."

"Does that include a chicken dinner after Sunday meetin'?"

I looked up and studied his face. I couldn't be sure if he was making fun of my country upbringing or if he was serious.

"Someone told me your grandmother used to lay out a Sunday spread fit for Jesus and all the disciples."

"I'm not the cook Mamaw was, but I can find her recipes. It's high time to learn."

"Then you got a deal," he replied.

By the time our steaks arrived the band wandered out, and the rest of the evening smoothed out like a rumpled cotton skirt meeting a hot iron.

Sometimes when I look back on Nate's confession, I think this whole world would turn out better if we all got our guilt out in the open. Still, it was as hard for him to say as it was for me to hear.

🦋 🦋 🦋

I invited him home for dessert just like Tilly had suggested, mostly because I didn't want him to think I hated him after his confession. I'll admit, I was on shaky ground at that point, and I mean that in a literal sense. I could feel my knees knocking and my hands shaking on the drive home.

It wasn't that late, and it was Mamaw's TV night, when we let her stay up to watch Johnny Carson's *Tonight Show* for a spell. As we pulled into my drive, he turned off the headlights.

"What'd you do that for?" I asked.

"Good manners," he replied. "I don't want to blind them with my lights."

I bought the whole story.

We entered through the back door to the kitchen, me leading the way. I didn't even think twice about him quietly closing the door behind him, stealthily like a thief getting ready to take something that didn't belong to him.

"Leandra." His hands reached around my waist, he turned me to face him, and kissed me full on the lips.

I pulled back, stunned. "Nate! Why did you do that?"

According to Tilly, it wasn't supposed to happen this way. In my own kitchen?

"I had to. We needed to get that out of the way."

I opened my mouth to reply and Beth came through the kitchen door.

"You're home," she stated. "Mamaw told me she heard voices and I assumed they were in her head. What'd do you know, she was right!"

"We came home for dessert," Nate answered, trying to distract me from his bad behavior.

"Nate, why don't you go visit with Mamaw and Papaw so Beth and I can put on some coffee and get out the cookies?"

That devil just smiled at me and walked into the parlor. Nothing about him was turning out the way I expected. But that had been happening my whole life.

🦋 🦋 🦋

The next day, I shared my story with Tilly.

"Well, my stars," Tilly exclaimed.

"I'm fairly sure he's not making up some sob story to win me over. It's a wonder he didn't go back to his drinking." I shook my head. "And then kissing me in my own kitchen with my kin in the next room! When I walked him to his truck, I reminded him not to read anything into me letting him steal a kiss and that it was only dinner."

Tilly agreed. "He's not waiting for no one."

"I'll admit, it did take away some of the mounting tension, but what if I didn't *want* to kiss him?"

"Then he would have gotten smacked across the teeth, and you would have sent him home. He took a calculated risk. Now what? Will you go out with him again?"

"I agreed to dance lessons if he goes to church with us. He didn't seem too miffed about it. I don't want to discount him because he has a past. Besides, at our age who doesn't? Shoot, I'm a widow with a young child and two sick grandparents. I'd call that some heavy baggage."

"Does your son like him?"

"Don't get ahead of yourself, Tilly. Donny doesn't even know him. I have a farm and a family to think about. A date now and then is fine."

"There's plenty of women who would like a crack at him," she replied. "You might want to stake your claim first and worry about it later."

"Do you take me for a fool? When he walks into church with us this week, how long do you think it will be before it gets around town that he's spending Sundays with my family?"

Tilly nodded, deep in thought. "I may go to church just to see the show. You better ask God's forgiveness for crushing so many souls and making the entire female congregation cry."

Chapter 19

Predictions

A time comes when you start to see patterns repeated in your life. The seasons turn without fail while the same crops are rotated year after year. New babies, graduations, marriages, divorces, school events, and the death of loved ones fill the years. There are political elections and broken promises, the football team that never wins, and natural disasters. And how can I forget the last ten pounds I can never lose? It sticks to me and thickens, but never thins.

We can only hope the joy, happiness, and success repeats while sadness, despair, and failure stalls. Predictability is comforting, be it good or bad. But that is only human nature.

I'd been thinking about Sal a lot. I suspect being in circulation again and dating Nate started it all. I wondered how his love life was going and hoped he chose to stay with his wife and family. Those things in life are so precious, but Sal was a loose cannon, and anything could happen.

One evening, I thought I might have enough nerve to call him. I poured myself a second glass of rosé wine and waited for him to pick up the phone. I eyed what was left in the bottle, thinking of Mama and Nate and all the problems liquor could cause. Maybe I was doing the same.

"The number you have dialed is no longer in service," stated the cold robotic voice. Annoyed, I wasn't deterred. Maybe he had given up and divorced. I decided to call his childhood home and see if his mama had a new number.

I heard a familiar voice on the other end. "Mrs. Donatello, this is Leandra Barker. I used to live across the street. I went to school with Sal."

"Yes, what is it you want?"

I had expected a warmer greeting. I had been a fixture in the Donatello home for four years or more, always visiting Sal with my latest childhood crisis. I tried out my Southern manner.

"Well, ma'am, I gave Sal a call, we haven't spoken in a while. I got a recording that his phone number wasn't good anymore. Would you have his new phone number?"

"Whatchu need to speak to Sal about? He's a married man."

"Mrs. Donatello, I don't mean to be intrusive. Sal came by my farm for a visit a few years ago with Artie. I just wanted to see how he was doing."

"Sal is doing just fine. So are his kids and his wife. He doesn't need to speak to you. I'll tell him you called."

The line clicked and our connection severed.

Well, I never. Flying saucers would sooner land on Papaw's tobacco field than she would tell Sal I called looking for him. I slammed down the phone, boiling mad. Did she think I was some kind of hussy? I hated it when people lied to me. More determined than ever, I was going to find his phone number. I called my mama.

Roger answered the phone. That fool was the last person I wanted to talk to, but something was up. Roger wasn't one to run and pick up the phone.

"Roger, I'm lookin' for Mama. Is she around? I need a phone number for a high school friend."

"She's nappin' now. Got some bad news yesterday."

"You mean about her breast lump? Wha'd the doctor say?"

"I ain't gettin' into that."

"Roger! What did they tell her?"

Silence loomed on the other end. He was debating the consequences of telling me what was going on versus weathering a verbal assault.

He sighed. "They said they'd have to remove her breast, but they'd rather remove both."

My breath caught in my windpipe. "Is the cancer that advanced? Is she going to get another opinion?"

"See, that's what I mean. I knew you'd be askin' me all kinds of questions that I don't know nothin' about."

"Well, weren't you there? You must have heard the conversation."

More silence. "No. I didn't go. She dropped me at the plant and took the car."

He was such a pig. I wanted to forgive him for what he had done to Mama, to our family, but when he did selfish cold things like this, old hate and anger festered in my gullet. There just wasn't any good reason to forgive Roger for marrying Mama and ruining our lives as a cover to be with his boyfriend, Dave.

"Roger, a long time ago I warned you, you needed to take better care of Mama, or I would make your life miserable. Do you remember that?"

"Leandra, I don't give a rat's ass what you do. You already made my life miserable." The phone slammed down on the receiver.

Roger seemed genuinely hurt. For a long time, I hadn't thought of him as a human being with feelings. I suppose I did make his life miserable when I discovered his true identity. But look what he had done to us. No matter what way you sliced it, he had destroyed our lives. I waited a couple of days and called Mama again, knowing this time Roger was at work.

"Mama? It's Leandra."

"Oh, hey, Leandra." Her voice sounded like she'd been dragged through a swamp by her heels.

"How, you doin', Mama? Roger told me about your doctor visit."

"It doesn't look good, Leandra. They want to take both my breasts!" With that she started sobbing.

Have you ever had someone burst into tears and all you want to do is fix it? Without even thinking, I told her to come home to Mountain Grove. There wasn't much between me and Mama anymore, but I certainly didn't want her to suffer alone.

"Mama, they got good doctors in Asheville. You know Roger won't take care of you even if you do decide to have surgery there. Mama, what's keepin' you there in New Jersey?"

"Well, my husband, Leandra."

"You know he hasn't been much of a husband to you."

I heard a big sigh on the other end of the phone. "Let me think about it, Leandra. I'll call you in a couple o' days. I'm so tired now I can't put thoughts together. I'll talk to my doctor too. Now, Roger said there somethin' else you wanted."

"Oh, that's right. I was wondering if you could look up Sal's number in the phone book?"

I heard her put down the receiver and thumb through the fragile pages. While she did that, I tried to imagine what my life would be like if Mama died soon. Then I thought about what life would be like with her underfoot. What was I getting myself into?

"Let's see, it was Dona-something, right? I can't remember shit these days."

"Mama, did you just cuss?"

"Stop it, Leandra. I don't have any reason not to. Here it is, Salvatore Donatello. Hmm, he doesn't live too far away."

After we said our goodbyes, I told her I'd call back in three days. Giving Mama a deadline always helped her remember the task at hand. After all, she didn't have the money for a long-distance call and apparently, couldn't remember shit. I looked at the phone number I wrote on the chalkboard and lost my courage to call Sal. Maybe another day.

🦋 🦋 🦋

While Mama was deliberating her move to come live with us, I drove into town to determine what cancer connections I might have with the medical community. As usual, the clinic was packed, so I took a seat to wait my turn.

"Mrs. Tucker, it's nice to meet you." The young doctor extended his hand, and I noted his long skinny fingers. Mamaw's mama told her long skinny fingers were a sign of intelligence and paying attention to detail, so I was betting this man was going to be a fine doctor. "I hear you are the community member who started this clinic."

I wasn't comfortable with a lot of praise. "I didn't do it alone," I replied. "There's a lot of folks that keep this place going."

"I'm not sure how much longer we can stay here. We're busting at the seams."

"I always talked about settin' aside an acre of land and building our own clinic, but that takes time and money. Maybe we need a committee to work on that. Truthfully, I have two sick family members to take care of and I might get a third."

I explained Mama's situation.

"I'm sure we can refer you to a cancer specialist in Asheville," he replied. "Fact is, I have a good friend who works in that field. Just have your mother bring copies of what tests she's already had, or we can contact her doctor in New Jersey to open her case. Let me make a few phone calls and I'll call you later this week."

"I appreciate this," I replied. "Sometimes I get into things before I

174

stop to think. I do have some help at home, but it will still be a handful and I have a farm to run."

I walked away feeling a little more settled, but still wondering how this was all going to mesh. Right at that moment, it struck me that if I replaced Donny with my sweet brother, Ray, now gone for almost twenty years, my family was right back where it had been when I was a kid with all of us living under one roof. I felt a little tug on my heart. An orange and black butterfly, called a Monarch, returns to the same home on the same mountain for generations. Maybe my family had the same notion, and we were never gonna leave this farm or Mountain Grove.

🦋 🦋 🦋

I decided it was high time to consider that clinic expansion. Once Mama got here, her care would occupy time I didn't have, so I went around town to scrounge up community members and coerce them into volunteering for a special committee.

I planned to start by calling Nate to see if he was serious about helping people or if he was just making himself look good.

"Well, I know you started the clinic, but now what are you up to?" he asked. "Isn't one clinic enough?"

"It would replace the small, donated building from the Catholics. The committee will have the job of assessing our present situation to determine if and how we can build our own independent structure. I planned to donate an acre, maybe near the tobacco field. Can I sign you up?"

"You doin' this just to get me out of your hair?"

"No, you're bait. Once the single women in town find out you're on the committee, I'm sure I won't have any problem getting volunteers."

"We have a date tomorrow night. You promised."

"I didn't forget, and I won't break my promise. Dancing is exactly what I want to do after being on my feet all day taking care of a farm and family."

"Could be, you might enjoy yourself."

I think he was waiting for me to agree, but I pursued my stubborn streak and refused to admit I might enjoy dancing. "I'll see you at six-thirty tomorrow night. I'll be sure to scrape the mud off my boots for our first lesson."

After Nate, I drove into town and started in on the biggest business owners I could find. They were the ones who always contributed to the town parade and fireworks, sponsored the high school sports teams, advertised on the paper, and invested in their hometown. In general, these folks were incapable of saying no to any good cause. People always think that little towns are boring and nothing exciting ever happens. True, it wasn't Hollywood and we weren't movie stars. But when something happened, good or bad, and we read about it or heard it from a friend, we likely knew exactly who it was and how we could help. I was counting on the same. In a week's time, I had six additional members to begin their research, including Tilly. I figured she'd be able to keep an eye on Nate— because I wasn't stupid—but I also had plans to make him the chairman.

When that week passed, I called Mama back for her decision.

"Mama, I've already made up my mind that I will accept whatever you decide to do. It's your life and you should be the one to determine your care."

"Roger's here with me, Leandra. I have talked with my doctor and talked with Roger. We all feel that, if I am planning a move, it should be before the surgery."

I offered my piece. "I talked with the clinic doctor, Mama. He's given me the names of several doctors he considers to be experts in cancer care. One of them works out of Charlotte. That's a drive, but not too far away."

I waited for her response while both our lives balanced in time.

"I'm gonna accept your offer, Leandra. Roger's got his own health problems, and he wants to hold onto his job until he can retire. He'll get a better pension that way. Besides, he wouldn't make much of a nurse. This is really a female issue."

I was a jumble of mixed feelings. "I'll tell you what, give me a few days to figure this out and I'll drive there to pick you up. You start packing what's important to you and I'm sure we can load it up in my big sedan. Beth can watch the family. It's nearing the end of the school year, so I might bring Donny along."

I knew she'd be better cared for and much happier with me. Roger would be excited to finally have Mama and me out of his hair so he could live the life he wanted. The truth was that Mama would never return to New Jersey. I was no doctor or nurse, but I could see how this story would end.

✳ ✳ ✳

I bustled about the parlor, lining up two small suitcases and a jug of drinking water. I needed as much room as possible in the old Pontiac for Mama's belongings, even if it was unlikely it would amount to much. I figured Donny and I would stop for our meals along the way at McDonald's or some local burger place. It had been decades since I drove to and from New Jersey and I had designed it that way. The last time I drove away from there was to bury my brother, Ray, and my baby daughter, Autumn.

"Donny, let's go!" He bounced down the stairs wearing a pair of cheap dark-green sunglasses and a Farmall tractor cap. His dark-gold T-shirt was tucked into brand new Levi's, topped with a Western belt and an oversized buckle. He was country, head to toe, and would look so out of place in Jersey I wanted to laugh. I didn't have the heart to break his, though. Beth grabbed one of the suitcases and walked me out the kitchen door.

"Now don't leave those two alone too long," I cautioned. "Mamaw can get into all kinds of trouble and Papaw can run out of air at any time. Push food on him. He's gettin' skinny as a sick dog. The aide comes on Tuesdays and Fridays, so you'll need to wash them yourself on Sunday night."

"I know all this, Leandra." Beth stared at me like I was a crazy woman. "And I'll find time to do my homework."

"This is Mama's phone number in case you need me." I handed her a slip of paper. "And I'll call every night after we stop at…"

"You'd better hit the road," she interrupted. "I'm gonna start Mamaw on a new crochet project today while I study for my American history test, and you're wasting my time."

Beth always had her way to put my feet back on the ground.

Donny climbed in the front to ride shotgun.

"So, this'll be your first visit to Grandma's house," I stated. "It's not very big. We'll stay long enough to get her packed up, maybe one or two nights and then get out of there."

"That Roger guy, is he still there?"

"He's her husband. I would imagine so."

"He was your stepdad, right?"

"I don't think of him that way, Donny. Roger and I..." I stopped to think about what I wanted Donny to know about his grandmother. "Roger offered Mama a different life away from the farm. She was more of a city girl when she married my daddy. Roger and Ray and I—well—we tolerated each other for Mama's sake." Enough for now. I changed directions.

"Now, there's a family that lives upstairs." I hadn't thought about Mr. Scuderi in years and wondered how old he must be now. His sweet wife had been gone for more than ten years. I explained all this to Donny. "Wait until you see his garden. You won't believe how many vegetables he can grow in the city."

This was a new adventure for my little boy, now approaching puberty. The world I was about to show him was unlike anything he had ever known. Donny was close to the same age as me when I left Mountain Grove. I wondered what kind of questions he would have for me and his grandmother on this trip to another world.

My whole life was repeating itself, only this time I knew where it was going.

Chapter 20

Healing Old Wounds

When a wound is deep enough, a scar remains behind. While the pain and redness fades, running your finger over that fine white line brings the pain right back to the surface. Of course, there's another way to think about it. Could be that scar and the pain it brings are there to remind you, that you survived and moved on to a better place.

🦋 🦋 🦋

When we turned onto Mama's street, a cold chill ran up my neck bones. My heart pounded and I related it to the anxiety those Vietnam veterans felt on returning home after the war. I must have been going through something similar. I mean, it did feel like a foreign country, and I lived in fear most of the time I was there. I couldn't let Donny or Mama see me like this. Just like any war, you get in, do your business, and get out.

"The houses are all scrunched together," Donny observed, "Why'd you park back here? Where's the house?" He was so curious about this new city. "Roger rents this garage, and we're walking to the house yonder." I pointed toward the flat roofed two-story that seemed so much smaller than when I was a kid. I parked the car near the old garage. The garage door with its flaking paint stood open, and I peeked inside. There sat Mr. Scuderi's old Cadillac like a big black barge, long since grounded. I hoped to God he still wasn't driving. By the layer of dust and cobwebs coating it, it hadn't been moved in years.

We walked toward Mama's house and approached the old concrete garden.

"This is his garden?" Donny asked. The garden that thrived during my youth was overgrown and scraggly. I saw a few plants by the walkway, but it was obvious it rarely saw love and care. I tossed out a brief answer. "It was a lot greener in my time." Struck with such sadness, I almost dissolved into tears.

The door was unlocked so I pulled it open and called out. "Mama, you home? We're here."

Shuffling sounded deep in the house and we waited, me not wanting to catch Roger in his boxers and those nasty undershirts he had always worn.

"That you, Leandra? You bring Donny?"

She shuffled into the kitchen, looking worse than I expected. Her mottled grey hair was mostly white, and she wore an old cotton bathrobe with food stains on the front.

I put on my best face. "Yes, he's here," I boasted. "He's grown some."

Donny gave her a sheepish smile. I had coached him to hug her when he got there. I wasn't close enough to smell if she'd been drinking, but the day was young.

"Hi, Grandma."

He finished his hugging and immediately backed away. I'd hear about the encounter later.

"My goodness, farm life agrees with the both of you."

"This is your house, Grandma?"

"We rent it, from the man upstairs. I'll show you around."

I was curious too. I walked around with them into the parlor and out to the foyer. It still smelled like old cedar and the banister wood was polished shiny. I was told Mr. Scuderi had someone taking care of the place. I peeked out the front door window to gaze at Sal's house but did not plan to walk over there to visit after Mrs. Donatello's tongue lashing.

"And here's my bedroom, and the bathroom, and you can sleep in your mama's room in back. She and your Uncle Ray shared that room together."

I glanced in the old pantry and the shelves were practically bare. No wonder she was so skinny. I wanted to ask her how she was eating, but keeping my mouth shut was the wiser choice.

"Donny and I will run out to get some groceries and I can cook for you while we're here. Is Pathmark still down the road?"

Mama laughed. "It's barely standing. There are better stores nearby."

"A home cooked meal will do you good. We'll be back in about an hour. Those your boxes in the corner of the bedroom?"

She turned to look over her shoulder. "Yes, what I could do by myself. We can deal with the rest tomorrow."

Donny and I bought enough food to last us two days, because I had plans to leave on day three. Old memories crawled under my skin like vermin, and I didn't like the feeling. We bought a cut-up chicken, a bag of potatoes, and half a dozen ears of sweet corn. The greens didn't look appetizing, so we opted for frozen spinach. Donny ran off to get some breakfast foods and met me at the checkout.

"Tomorrow, we'll make time to go to the bakery downtown, assuming it's still there," I told him. "I have to show you all this stuff now 'cause, likely, we won't ever be back."

Donny loaded the last sack of groceries in the car. "Won't Grandma want to go home after she gets better?"

I faced my child. "Grandma isn't going to get better, Donny. She's goin' home with us so we can take care of her."

"So, she's dying. I never really knew her."

"I know, darlin.' I never knew my other grandmother either. But at least we both got to know one Mamaw." He nodded in acceptance of his fate. "You be sure to ask her lots of questions any time you get the notion. Once our Mamaws leave us, that time has passed."

Donny knew his way around a kitchen so, in no time, we unpacked the car and made a fine supper. Mama seemed to have an appetite but no place to put food. I had to work on this problem. The thought made it evident I had turned into a full-blown Mamaw myself.

Roger didn't say much during dinner. He looked like shit, as I expected: grey, fat, and doughy as usual. I'm sure he couldn't wait until we left. Maybe then he'd take some pride in his appearance and start his life over.

I heard voices outside in the concrete garden.

Donny stood by the back door looking out. "That Mr. Scuderi?"

I walked to the screen door. A small man leaning on a cane stood with a younger man, surveying the straggly tomato and pepper plants.

"It sure is," I told him. "C'mon, let's say hello."

He didn't know me at first, staring like he'd seen a ghost. I guess he expected to see my mama when the screen door slammed.

"Hey, Mr. Scuderi. It's Leandra. This is my son, Donny."

"Leandra!" He steadied himself on his cane. "Why, I didn't know who I was lookin' at. And, for a minute, I thought that young man was Raymond."

"No, sir, he's my son. Handsome thing, isn't he?"

"He looks a lot like your brother, rest his soul." He crossed himself. Mr. Scuderi always pretended to be religious but never went to church. "This is my nephew, Rodney."

"Nice to meet you," I replied. "Donny and I drove from North Carolina to take Mama back to the farm."

"She told me yesterday," Mr. Scuderi said. "Nice lady. She doesn't deserve to be sick. You know my Mary had cancer. She went so fast. Maybe you can get your mother some good care."

In my mind, I saw Mrs. Scuderi, finding me crying on the porch bench, a desperate sixteen-year-old trying to figure out her life. She took me upstairs and after a sandwich and sweet tea, her words of encouragement got me through another crisis. I still thought of her as my godmother.

I leaned in close to Mr. Scudari. "Mama needs a little more meat on her bones. I plan to fatten her up starting right now." I winked. "And how are you doing?"

"My younger brother helps out. He's upstairs watching his favorite TV show." He looked the old house over, top to bottom. "I guess he'll get this place after I'm gone."

I touched him on the shoulder. "I hope that's not for a long, long time."

🦋 🦋 🦋

Sleeping in my old bedroom was fitful that night. Donny was fast asleep, covered in Ray's old Amish quilt, and all I could recall was how Ray and I shared this bedroom, sometimes the two of us talking until deep in the night. We'd struggle not to listen to the two of them fighting, Ray with his head under the pillow. Sometimes he'd jump in bed with me, and we'd hold onto each other until one of us fell asleep and the terror passed.

Tears streamed down the side of my temples and puddled in my ears. What scars were left behind? How many more were waiting to resurface? I let them pass through me like syrup through cheesecloth at jelly-making time. The big chunks would remain there, and maybe most of the hurt could pass, be bottled up, sealed, and stored away in a dark place.

I was still on farm time, up early and making coffee. It was Saturday so, while the rest of the household was asleep, I woke Donny and told him we were going to the bakery downtown. Mesmerized by the brick buildings and quiet streets, most of the activity was limited to the area near the bakery. I was pleased to see Parnes had survived. We were hit with delicious, sweet smells when we opened the door. Donny and I picked out a dozen items, and I couldn't pass up buying one farfalla, just like the one Sal brought me once, decades before.

"See, it looks like a butterfly," I showed Donny the sponge cake wings. "Here, take a bite." I shoved it at him and laughed at his cream covered face.

"Well, *you* try eatin' this thing without making a mess," he wailed.

I ended up doing the same. We walked toward the car and passed the storefront where the old candy shop had been.

"What is it, Mama?"

I was staring into the corner where Sal and I had sat when I first met his family and friends.

"I spent a lot of time here, Donny."

"But they sell televisions here."

"Back then, it was a place where all the kids hung out on the weekends, kinda like the roller rink in town. They had food, and it was a safe place to meet and be seen." I turned away, feeling my eyes burn.

"Lots of memories, huh, Mama?"

"Some good and some bad. I was so young then. I had a lot ahead of me, and I struggled every day to get there."

🦋 🦋 🦋

There was a parking space on Mama's street, so we parked my car in front of the house. I figured it would be easier to load Mama's belongings while we packed that day. I grabbed the box of sweets and walked around to the front porch, until I heard my name. I turned around and there was Sal, crossing the street to meet me. My heart dislodged from my chest and leaped to my throat.

I handed the pastries to Donny. "Here, take these into Grandma and Roger. I'll be right in."

I gave Sal a big hug, in spite of his female kinfolk probably watching out the window with poison darts pointed my way.

"I don't believe it," he said, shaking his head. "Why didn't you tell me you were comin'?"

"It was sort of a last-minute thing. Donny and I are taking Mama back to the farm so I can care for her. She has breast cancer."

"God, Leandra, I didn't know. I'm so sorry. Did she just find out?"

"I'm not sure how long it's been. They want to take both her breasts. You know Roger won't take care of her. I already got Papaw and Mamaw with their own health problems, so I thought I'd add Mama to the mix." I worked up my courage. "Besides, I tried to call you, but your number changed. Your mama said she'd tell you I called."

"No, she didn't say anything. I'm shocked to see you here."

I was getting worried someone would run out of his house at any minute to chase me. I started making excuses to get away.

"I need to help Mama pack today, so I'd better get to it. It's good to see you again."

I was so short of breath. That happens when your heart beats so fast your lungs don't keep up.

"Wait, when do you leave?"

"Tomorrow, I suspect. Depends on what happens today."

"Meet me tonight."

I looked into those dark-brown eyes, now edged on either side with crow's feet, just like me. His temples were getting greyer, and he had put on about ten pounds, but Lordy, that boy still held a place in my heart.

"Your family will kill me."

"Not if they don't see us. No one knows your car. Let's go for a drive around eight or nine and we can catch up."

"Nothin' crazy, okay? Just talk. I have a new boyfriend."

"Really? That's great. I have my old wife and kids!"

I smiled. "I'm glad to hear that, Sal. Okay, we'll meet, but your family can never know."

"I'll call you later and tell you where and when."

🦋 🦋 🦋

Mama's packing only took a few hours. The most valuable thing she owned was her little jewelry box with costume pieces and a string of pearls her mama gave her on her first wedding day. She refused to part with her white, black, and brown gloves that no one wore anymore. She did sacrifice some old hats and stockings, and we left them at the house though she knew someday they'd be thrown in the trash.

I made supper early so I could free up time to meet Sal later that night. When the phone rang, I was just finishing the dishes.

"Let's meet at the Jesus Love Baptist Church parking lot. No one will look for us there."

I scribbled down the address. "Okay, sounds good. See you soon."

I found Donny and Mama in the parlor. As usual, Roger was nowhere to be found.

"Ya'll, I'm gonna meet a few old high school friends. We don't have to leave real early, but let's plan on leaving tomorrow."

Jesus Love Baptist Church was a small white clapboard church that looked more like you'd buy fish and chips there, instead of praying for your soul. The only giveaway that it was a church was the black cross on the door and the sign showing the scheduled church meetings. I parked my car under a row of large oak trees toward the back of the parking lot. Sal was already waiting. He leaned against his car and exhaled several smoke rings. Still showing off. He dropped his cigarette, ground it into the gravel, and moved in my direction.

I hugged that boy like I'd never get a second chance. Probably I wouldn't.

"God, Leandra, you been workin' out? I'm gonna stop breathin' here."

I pulled back and straightened out the collar on his plaid shirt.

"It's all the hay bales I been liftin'."

"You look good. Healthy." He walked around me, his eyes roaming up and down like our high school days. I patted his little belly. "Looks like that wife of yours feeds you well."

"Pasta," he justified. "And a lack of exercise." He reached into his car. "I brought a cold six-pack."

"Not very classy, but you'd make a good Appalachian hillbilly."

"C'mon," he directed. "Get in my car. I got a better place for us to talk."

"Where you taking me?" I pried.

"You'll see. It's someplace you been before."

When we pulled up in front of Perth Amboy High, nausea hit my stomach like a sledgehammer. That scared little teenage girl was still haunting the campus. "Here? You taking me back to high school?"

"Calm down, I found a special place for us." He opened the trunk and took out an old blanket, grabbed his six-pack from the front seat and said, "Follow me."

Nervous as I was, I kept flipping my head around to make sure no one was watching us. He moved toward the football field. The fence gate on the side of the schoolyard was chained, but he squeezed through the opening and gave me his hand, pulling me through to the other side. Two adults in their forties shouldn't be doing this, but a thrill of excitement came over me.

"I feel like a criminal, Sal." He spread the blanket over the soft grass under the bleachers making us invisible to outsiders. Once settled, he collapsed on the blanket, popped a Schlitz, and extended his hand for me to join him. I sat down facing him.

He handed me an icy cold can wet with the moisture in the coastal air. "You know, beer or not, I never thought of you as a hillbilly, Leandra. I always thought of you as a good girl, the kind I needed to stay away from."

"Maybe that's what your family is thinking. When did your Mama start hating me?" I gulped my beer.

"My damn sister Francine stirred the pot. She told Ma I was running off to North Carolina to have an affair with you. That's why Artie was in tow. They sent him to chaperone me. What does Francine know about my marriage to Gina? But she had to put in her two cents."

"Sal, we almost did have an affair. Or did you forget what happened in the barn?"

"I didn't forget. I think about it a lot." He gave me one of those devilish smiles from days gone by and brushed my hair behind my shoulder. "So, tell me about this boyfriend. Where'd you meet him?"

"He works for the co-op company in the propane division. Nate was the new bachelor in town. When Mamaw lost her mind…"

"Wait, your grandmother went nuts? She still alive?"

"Yep. Mamaw was always my rock. And Papaw's not much better. His lungs are failing and he's on oxygen. Maybe God knew what was comin' and sent me Nate to help out." I finished my beer and threw the empty aside. "But, get this, he's a recovering alcoholic."

"Oh God, after your motha and her drinkin'? You serious about this guy?"

"No, we're just getting started. I haven't made up my mind about anything. He's movin' a little too fast for me. When Mama got sick, that was a good excuse to put my life on hold."

Sal handed me another beer. "Don't put your life on hold. You been doin' that since you were a kid. Trust me. You turn around and twenty years go by."

My awareness turned to the summer wind blowing through the leaves with the cicadas chorus blending with the chirping crickets. They amplified our silence. Sal rolled onto his back and I joined him. I gazed at the stars poking through the bleacher benches.

"What happened to all our dreams, Sal? We never became famous or rich like we thought we would. Graduation was supposed to set us free."

"Maybe we didn't want it bad enough?" He sighed heavily and the conversation paused.

"What were your dreams, Sal? Did your life turn out the way you wanted?"

He shook his head in denial. "Dreams? I didn't have the money or education for dreams. I figured after the Coast Guard I'd get a job, marry some Italian girl, have some Italian kids, and scrape by. That's what my family always did. Except for ol' Artie. Father Artie's got it made. The Catholic church will take care of him until they give him up to God." He motioned dramatically with upward reaching arms, one still clutching his beer, which he promptly finished off and tossed to the side. Abruptly he changed the subject. "Hey, that Greg guy you dated, he's running for state senate."

I held up my half-drained beer in a mocking salute. "Well, then his mama should be incredibly happy. My white trash family would have interfered with his political career. On prom night, he said we'd all be rich and famous. Guess he was wrong about me, and his mama was right." It was my turn to toss my empty can.

"Cut it out, Leandra. You own a damn farm, started a community clinic, and take care of four other people. I'd say you've lived a life that's worthwhile." He popped open a fresh beer. "What are you going to do with your mama when you get home? You know it's all gonna fall on you."

"They have cancer clinics in Asheville and Charlotte. Donny pitches in, and I have a girl livin' with me who's helping out. She's watching the two of them now. I told her she could live under my roof if she promised to get her high school degree and look after the old folks and animals."

Sal laughed, sat up, and propped his head on one arm. He ran a fingernail along the length of my arm causing goosebumps to chase across my body.

"You always take in strays, Leandra. Always savin' someone or something, starting with your mama and Ray."

I pushed myself up to meet his gaze. "And I failed with both of them. Maybe I can succeed with Beth." I checked my wristwatch. "I should probably get back to Mama."

"We still have beers left."

"I can't drink any more. I'm dating an alcoholic and taking one back home. I have to keep my guard up in case somethin' rubs off on me."

"Wait, stay just a little longer." He put his hand over mine.

The darkness had deepened with the intermittent clouds and the leaves on ancient trees quivered in the breeze. I was close to tears, unsure if I sensed relief or a profound loss.

I looked into his eyes. "I don't think I'll ever return to Jersey." I popped one more beer and stared at the moon, lost in thought. "Mama was my last tie to this place. This could be goodbye."

"What about our fiftieth reunion? You said you'd come back to Jersey for the reunion if we sold the T-bird. We did."

Whether it was the beers or a return to my youth, I stretched across his chest and kissed him. It was supposed to be a farewell kiss. Instead, his arms reached around me and pulled me in like gravity. Damn. I knew I shouldn't have worn a skirt tonight.

It was just too easy. Before I knew it, I unbuckled his belt, shimmied out of my panties, and bounced on that boy like I was riding a John Deere tractor. Every lingering emotion between us exploded all at once. At one point, he covered my mouth to silence me so the neighborhood dogs would stop barking.

Exhausted, I fell off him, same as a lumberjack rolls off a log. I turned to look at him and we both broke out laughing. I don't think either one of us believed what happened. That was some farewell.

After we stopped panting, I insisted on an end to the evening. "You better just leave this blanket here," I warned him. "A woman knows." I shook my head. "She just knows."

He stared at it from where we sat. "Yeah, you're right." He grabbed the empty beer cans and the two remaining beers. "I'll drive you back to church."

"Well, that's good. Maybe before I leave the parking lot I can ask God for forgiveness for having sex with a married man."

He smoothed my rumpled hair. "It's okay, Leandra. This was going to happen one way or another." His arms pulled me into him once again and he kissed me gently on the lips.

If I had been a sparrow in his hands, my heart couldn't have pounded any faster. To this day, it was the best goodbye I ever had.

Back at Love's Baptist Church parking lot, I lingered in my car and watched him pull away. He made a U-turn, paused at the doorstep of the church, and deposited the remaining beers still connected to their plastic ring. Oh Sal. I chuckled to myself. I'm sure that's exactly what the Baptist church wanted. I only wished I could see the preacher's face tomorrow morning when he discovered what Satan donated.

🦋 🦋 🦋

Mama was slapping mayonnaise on bologna and salami sandwiches when I woke up the next morning. A paper sack sat on the counter with a bag of potato chips, Lorna Doone cookies, a can of salted peanuts, and Cheez-It crackers.

"Mama, you don't need to do all this," I said. I poured a cup of coffee. "It's nice of you to pack snacks and sandwiches, but we can get something along the road." She plopped down in the kitchen chair, clearly exhausted.

"I know, but I wanted to finish up the food you bought and do something for the trip." She stood again and loaded a six-pack of cola in a small Styrofoam ice chest, then dumped half a bag of ice over the sodas. Mama studied the empty plastic bag. "Oh well," she mused, "no ice left for Roger."

She crammed the bag into the trash can with a smirk on her face.

Donny and I each downed a bowl of Cheerios and finished the last of the coffee. Mama washed her coffee pot and took a good look at it. "Leandra, we got room for this? I believe I want to take my percolator with me. I've had this thing twenty years and Roger can make instant coffee if he wants some."

"Sure, Mama. We could fit a tugboat in that car." Happiness washed over me as I witnessed her confidence that everyone was going to be happier with this arrangement.

I called out, "Donny, grab those two quilts on the beds in there. Fold 'em nice and put them in the car."

I planned to take a little piece of my childhood with me. I would always think of Ray when I wrapped myself in his quilt.

Donny returned and I handed him the ice chest and sack of food. "Carry this out to the car and climb in the backseat. You all ready?"

"Yes, ma'am. Did Grandma say her goodbyes to that Roger guy this mornin'?"

"Sure did. All we got left to do is drive away."

He walked out the front door. Mama and I were the only living souls left in the house.

It was still as death. I almost felt like I couldn't breathe. Yesterday we said our goodbyes to Mr. Scuderi, never to see him again. I looked around the kitchen one last time and walked into the parlor. Mama was sitting on the edge of her saggy stained sofa staring into space.

I sat down next to her. The smell of stale beer and smoke clung to the walls, setting a picture in my head of yellow swirling smoke.

"A lot happened here," I said.

"Sure did," she replied. "Mostly bad. Not enough good."

"You'll feel better at the farm. I know you didn't like it there, but you don't have to work in the garden or do housework. You just have to get well."

Her gaze dropped to the floor. "Leandra, you know I'm not gonna get well."

"Okay," I said, "let's just get you feeling better. I know it won't be an easy fight, but I can get you good care. You're gonna love Beth, you'll get to spend time with Donny, and you'll get to meet my new beau."

"That's right, Leandra, you have someone in your life."

"Well, he's got one foot in the door. I'm not sure if he's gettin' in yet."

That made her smile. "Let's go make some new memories," she said.

I helped her up from the sofa, and we walked out arm in arm. The door to Perth Amboy shut forever.

Or so I thought.

Chapter 21

A Call to Order

I hate it when my life is disorganized. I can juggle almost anything when I know what to do and what direction I'm headed. But soon as things start scattering, I don't know where to start. Really, starting is the hardest part, and once you hike your heel over that first fence rail, the rest is easy going. Just make sure some mean old bull isn't waiting for you on the other side.

🦋 🦋 🦋

Mama slept for most of the trip driving home, although she repeatedly told me it was the most exciting thing she had done since we went to New York City some twenty-five years earlier.

My mind flashed to another New York visit I made, against Ana's wishes, after the loss of Autumn. As a peace offering, I'd given Ana a Rockefeller Center snow globe when I returned home. I think I still had that old dried-out snow globe somewhere. It represented my once beautiful, idealistic, but crushed dream of making a home in New York.

I found Mama's comment sad, making my ordinary life now seem thrilling in comparison.

When we arrived at the farm, everyone came spilling out the door to greet us, and I started making introductions.

"Mama, this is Beth. She's the best thing that could happen to a lady farmer and two old people."

"How do, Mrs. Atwood. Leandra said you'll be needing some help, so you just ask for anything you want."

"Then stop calling me Mrs. Atwood," Mama replied. "You call me Lilly. I understand you are working on your high school diploma so you let me know if I can help you study."

Mama turned to Mamaw. "How are you, Opal?"

"Have we met?" Mamaw asked.

Donny snickered as he walked by with one of Mama's boxes, and I wacked him on his behind.

"Yes, you have," I answered.

"Mamaw, this is Lilly, you remember her from a long time ago?"

Even a demented southern grandma can fake a polite response. I could see the lights weren't on, but Mamaw replied with a nod. "Yes, yes, I believe it was at the parade last year. That's right. It was the Veteran's Day Parade. I complimented you on a lovely wool sweater you were wearin'."

Mama grabbed Mamaw's hand, and they climbed the old wooden steps to the back door. I wasn't sure who was holding up who.

Papaw stumbled out from his room, his red suspenders still hanging from his pants. "That you, Lilly?"

Mama marched over to Papaw and hugged the stuffing out of him. She studied his face. "I'm sorry I haven't kept in touch. It never was my strong suit. How have you been doin'?"

"Still here. What about you?"

"The same. Some days are harder than others."

"That's the truth, isn't it?"

They were talking like two old cronies catching up with what ailed them. I hoped they could let bygones be bygones.

"Y'all know each otha?" Mamaw asked.

That got us to laughing. For just a moment, we forgot our worries.

I could smell a big pot of something delicious cooking on the back burner. Beth was gathering the silverware and dishes to set the table when a timer buzzed, and she paused to pull a sheet of biscuits from the oven. I walked over to the sweet-smelling bread, a welcome sight after eating fast food for three days.

Beth leaned into me. "Doctor from the clinic called today. He wanted to know when to schedule the surgeon appointment."

I glanced at Mama. Exhaustion etched her face.

"I'll give him a call tomorrow, Beth. I'm gonna settle Mama in upstairs. Donny's brought in all her boxes. You give us a shout when you're ready to serve supper. I guess, from here on out, this group will be back to eating at the big dining room table."

I gave Mama the small bedroom upstairs, adjacent to my room. I think at one time it had been sleeping quarters for one or more of the small children who grew up in the house and graduated to a shared room.

"This should suit you." I began unpacking her things.

"I can get that, Leandra. I'm not dead yet."

That hit a nerve. I'd been babying Mama since I first laid eyes on her and now, I needed to back off. I wasn't aiming to make her helpless.

"Of course, I'm sorry. I'll go down and help Beth."

"Leandra," she called out. I turned and Mama cupped my old face in her hands like I was a small child. "I am so grateful for you. I never said that enough."

I smiled, acknowledging her gratitude, and headed downstairs. Maybe there was hope for me to forgive her someday.

🦋 🦋 🦋

It took Mama a couple of days to recover from our New Jersey drive. With Beth's help in the kitchen, I was determined to fatten her up before surgery. Once well rested and in good care, Mama stopped sleeping late in exchange for a hot breakfast right off the griddle. If not, we prepared her a plate she could reheat in one of those newfangled microwave ovens.

I wasn't sure I trusted what microwaves did to food but, without question, it amazed Mama. She'd zero in on her food plate, pop it in the microwave, and in two minutes have a piping hot meal.

Mamaw, on the other hand, didn't take to the new apparatus. She got it in her head she could cook a whole egg in the microwave, shell and all. I walked into the kitchen just in time to witness the explosion and watch Mamaw open the microwave and point to what remained of her egg.

"Girl, how am I gonna eat this egg?"

She had taken to calling Beth "girl" when she couldn't remember her name. Beth peeked into the microwave and stared in disbelief.

"Look at all the itty-bitty pieces!" Mamaw exclaimed. "Can you hand me a spoon?"

Beth turned away with a smile, unable to get mad at her.

"Mamaw, I'm gonna make you another egg. Then I can clean the oven while you eat your new egg. Scrambled or fried? You want buttered toast with that?"

Beth pulled out a chair and directed Mamaw to the table. We were certain Mamaw was going to keep trying to cook until death forced her out of her kitchen.

I poured a cup of coffee and checked on Mamaw's coffee, cooling it with some cold milk. "Mama and I are going to the clinic today so she can meet the doctor and some of the volunteers."

"Here's your coffee, Mamaw." I joined her at the table.

"Is the girl making you an egg too?"

"Sure, why not? *Beth.*" I emphasized her name. "Beth, would you please make me an egg too? And better scramble one for Mama."

"That's three eggs, Beth," Mamaw quipped.

Beth and I looked at each other, shocked. Sometimes Mamaw was like Old Faithful, spouting off when we least expected it. She was a handful, but very entertaining.

After thirty minutes of microwave cleaning, we decided to hide the eggs in a covered bowl in the back of the refrigerator.

After breakfast, we drove into town. I was anxious to see what the new building committee had determined since I departed more than a week ago. It was the middle of the week and nearly noon when we arrived in town.

Road work in North Carolina is a continuous event. About the time they finish one leg of repairs, two more start up. Mama and I were stuck behind three or four cars, paused at one of five stoplights in town while we waited for our turn to pass. I looked up into the clear blue sky and saw what appeared to be a red-tailed hawk, distinctive by the red cast to its tail as the sun broke through the fanned feathers. A fresh kill dangled from its talons. It crossed in front of my car and, next thing I knew, I heard a thump. Mama and I both jumped, fixed on the dead dove lying on the hood of the car.

Carolina Appalachian people are born suspicious. I looked at Mama and she shook her head.

"Now don't go to readin' anything into that, Leandra. That hawk just dropped his lunch, nothin' more."

"Mama, in all my born days, I have never had a dead creature dropped on my car. This can't be good."

"Certainly not good for that poor hawk," she replied.

"I'm not kiddin', Mama. I have to get that dead dove off my car."

The traffic started moving and, instead of rolling off my car, it pitched forward, landing on its side and staring at me with a bloody eye, the grey head twisted abnormally to the side. Transfixed, I nearly hit the car in front of me.

"No, ma'am." I stated. "I can't disrespect the dead."

I pulled over to the side near a cornfield and put the car in park. I wanted to bury the bird, but without the right tools I couldn't. I spied an old mulberry tree, gently lifted the bird off the hood of my car and laid him to rest.

When I got in the car, Mama had her own opinion. "You have always had an abnormal interest in death. Rememba when you were little and I found you having a funeral for that chicken?"

"Of course, I buried that chicken. It was Mamaw's favorite hen. I was just a little kid. That was the same day we found out Daddy was killed in the war."

Mama stared out the car window. "Yes, I rememba," she said softly. "Leandra, you think I'll see him again? I mean when the cancer takes me?"

"Mama, please stop that kinda talk. You're not ready to die. I don't know what that hawk is telling me, but it isn't the first time one has brought a message. I just have to think on it."

We pulled into the clinic parking lot and my hands were shaking from that dead bird.

A new volunteer sat at the desk. "Honey, I can see you're not feelin' well. You're pale as a sheet. Come sit ova here."

"I'm not the patient," I told her. "I'm just a little rattled—I almost had an accident coming over here." I glanced sideways at Mama to see if she'd play along.

"Oh, I see." She turned to Mama. "Are you the patient?"

"We're expected," I butted in. "We have an appointment with the doctor for Mrs. Atwood."

"That's fine, darlin'. I'm going to give you some papers to fill out while you're seated."

She passed me a clipboard and pen and I relayed them to Mama. With my free hand, I handed the volunteer Mama's medical folder. It was about half an inch thick.

"This is a little something extra," I advised. "Can you make sure the nurse or doctor gets it?"

We worked through the forms together, finally getting to the bottom where they wanted to know her real age, if she smoked, drank alcohol, or used drugs.

"You don't have to answer these questions in front of me, Mama."

"Leandra, I'm too old and sick to care about family secrets anymore."

The way she said that felt like there was a hidden meaning tied up in her statement. She was saying I knew all there was to know and she was well-aware of what I was privy to.

"Well then," I smiled, "let's start with your age. I'm forty-two so that means you are…"

"Sixty-one."

"Why you're a youngster." She gave me a dirty look.

"Smoking?" I asked.

"You see me smoke?"

"No, ma'am. I'm hopin' you're not sneaking around behind the barn."

"What? So, I can start a fire and burn down the barn like your brother?"

I laughed at that one, remembering one of Ray's more stupid life events.

"And alcohol? You got a stash somewhere?"

"I'll admit to a nip now and then. And when they informed me I was full of cancer, wouldn't *you* take to drinkin'?"

I had to agree I would have needed something to steady my nerves.

If anyone had seen us sitting in the corner laughing over Mama's vices, they would have never known she was getting ready to remove her breasts. I considered the heavy burden my Mama was bearing and, for the first time ever, thought she was the bravest woman in the world.

My life seemed to be in perfect order. I reunited my family and developed a support system, rid Mama and myself of Roger, started dating again, the clinic expansion was moving forward, and the farm was financially sound. All my ducks were in a row—with the exception of one dead dove.

🦋 🦋 🦋

Nate's truck had appeared in the driveway while we were gone. I wasn't quite sure how to introduce him, but I assumed nature would run its course. More than likely, he would do the introducing.

Before I closed the driver's side door, he was shaking hands with Mama. "You must be Leandra's mom from New Jersey. Pleased to meet you."

Mama was her usual polite southern self.

"I see I'm too late to make introductions," I announced. "Why don't you come in for some cold tea?"

The house was still. Beth was studying for another exam and the old folks were napping. Somehow, as we humans age, we manage to revert to our infancy, taking naps and peeing our pants. Luckily, Mamaw and Papaw hadn't quite reached that point. Donny was spending a few days at the Angus farm with his daddy's side of the family. We smiled at Beth on the way in and quietly made our way to the kitchen.

"We're just comin' back from the clinic," I told Nate. "Any updates on the new building?"

"They're talking about a new fundraiser where everyone buys a board, like a two-by-four, and we have an old-fashioned barn raising. We can prebuild the sides and, on a given day, put up the walls and nail on the roof."

Mama took a long sip of her tea. "Why that's what the Amish folks do."

"Yes, something like that. It would take some coordination, but I think we could do it." Nate talked faster than usual, implying he was excited about my little project. "We could get a restaurant to sponsor dinner for the volunteers, and then folks can bring side dishes like any other town event. I bet four-hour shifts would be just about right."

"I don't know," I challenged. "People today are more interested in writing a check instead of working with their neighbors. But I do think the buy-a-board idea is kinda cute."

"That was my idea," Nate said. "Guess that makes me kinda cute."

"You're lyin'," I replied.

"Check the minutes from the meeting if you don't believe me." Nate studied my eyes with a steady gaze.

Past him, Mama's eyelids rested at half mast, evidence she needed her own nap. It had been a long emotional day for both of us.

"Mama, why don't you lay down before dinner? It would do you some good."

She nodded. "I think I will, Leandra. You call me when supper is ready."

We watched her push her way out the swinging kitchen door to the parlor and I waited until footsteps creaked on the stairs.

"You look tuckered out too," Nate said.

"To the bone. The news wasn't good. So far, the city doctor and the country doctor agree she needs a double mastectomy." I mindlessly played with the water drips running down my tea glass. "It's so mutilating. You'd think there was a better way."

"Will she need chemotherapy?"

"Without a doubt. She waited too long. They say she'll lose her hair. That will destroy Mama. The nurse suggested she get some wigs before they start treatments."

Nate reached out and touched my hand, still wet with water droplets. Pretty soon, my face was the same way.

"Even if you don't want us to be more than friends, I'm here."

"I know." I sniffled so loud he stood up to grab the tissue box. My shoulders shook with my sobbing. "I never really had her, you know what I mean? Then cancer brings us together. If that isn't a kick in the ass. I finally get a real mama and now she's dying."

"You don't know she's dying. Maybe she'll live for years on end."

"No, Nate. I saw a sign." I could see by his expression I had confused him. "We were driving to the clinic to talk to the doctor and some clumsy hawk drops a dead bird on my car right in front of us. Nate, that hawk brought a warning."

He shifted his chair closer to me and grabbed both my hands to fold in his. "That's an old superstition." His voice sounded low and soft. "You and I, we've been through so much. You know better than to get ahead of yourself. All the planning and organizing in the world isn't going to change what life has in store for us. One foot in front of the other, right?"

Snotty wet tissues lay crumpled on the kitchen table. My tears had dried up and I was tired of crying. I looked up at him.

"You are a good man," I reminded him.

"And kinda cute, don't you think?" He winked with a broad grin which made his turquoise eyes twinkle.

"Nate, I can't take any more disappointment right now. You get me?"

He turned serious. "I get it. You have a rough road ahead of you. I'll try and smooth out some of the bumps."

He kissed my hands and I almost started crying again. I wanted so badly to trust him with my heart but I wasn't sure I was ready to be vulnerable again.

We heard Mamaw arguing with Beth on the other side of the door. Fussy as a bumblebee, she burst through the kitchen and eyed my soggy tissues covering the table with the empty glasses pushed to the side.

"Land sakes, Leandra. You don't have to cry over spilt milk. We'll get it cleaned up." She marched off to find the mop.

Maybe Nate couldn't snap me out of my gloom, but Mamaw had her own healing ways. I was so grateful for her presence even if all of her wasn't there.

🦋 🦋 🦋

Mama's surgery was scheduled in Asheville two weeks from the coming Tuesday. That gave me about twenty days to set my house in order. I didn't expect her to be in the hospital more than a week, then I'd be watching her from home. But the really exciting news came at the consultation with the surgeon.

"You mean we can make her new breasts? How is that possible?"

Mama looked confused. "Why didn't they say anything about that in New Jersey?"

"There are promising advances in breast reconstruction. It gives women hope and contributes to their recovery. The chemo and radiation are problematic in and of themselves, but to give women back their breasts, well we are very hopeful about the advances we are making."

"How long do I have to wait for the second surgery?"

"We're trying to do it when we remove the cancer. Saves time, money, less pain, less trauma."

"Mama, what do you have to lose?"

"It's not without risk," the doctor warned us. "Things can happen that would require another surgery. And it means she is under anesthesia longer. Go home and take some time to think about this."

But Mama didn't want to wait. On the way home her mind was already set. "If I hav'ta think about any of this, Leandra, I won't do it. I'll just sit around and wait to die."

"That's not an option for me, Mama."

"Then we'll call tomorrow and tell her I want new boobies."

Mama was organizing our lives around her hope for the future. I don't think that woman had hope or plans in twenty years. She might outrun death after all.

Chapter 22

Dark Night to New Light

I have heard tell there is something called "the dark night of the soul."
In Appalachian terms, I guess it's akin to a come-to-Jesus moment when
you turn it all over to a higher calling and patiently wade through what
life has thrown at you. I'm pretty sure every faith has its own twist on the
situation and how God figures into the dilemma. In the end, it's all on us
to move forward with our lives or just give up and blow away.

🦋 🦋 🦋

After the surgery, Mama grew into a stronger woman pulling on a mysterious power from within. I didn't think it had anything to do with her will to live. I believe her spirit was set free like a helium balloon cut from its string. Roger always had his own motives and most didn't include Mama. No longer burdened by his rejection and neglect, she made her own decisions to define her life. I tried to stay in the background and provide support, but only when she asked for it. As I well knew, learning to ask for help was a lesson in and of itself.

One morning, I placed her steaming mug of hot coffee on the end table next to her bottle of pain pills. Her eyes fluttered and she shifted under the covers.

"Brought your coffee," I said. "How was last night?"

"Well, I won't be sleeping on my stomach anytime soon."

"Mama, you never were a belly sleeper. You said it would give you wrinkles. Why start now?"

She patted her chest and what she called her mounds. "You're right. I wouldn't want to damage these after the doctor worked so hard to rebuild me."

I helped her to the bathroom with a chorus of moans and groans. I couldn't imagine her pain, yet she kept her complaining to a minimum. We continued our conversation while she sat on the commode, me turning my back for her privacy.

"I bet you're ready for another pain pill."

"I'm getting there. My last one was at three this mornin'." I heard another groan and knew she had stood up from the commode.

"Let me bring you breakfast, then you can take your medication. Afterwards, would you be up for a stroll to the porch?"

"I think some fresh air would be good for me. Leandra, did Roger call?"

Ashamed, I looked down. "No, Mama. Maybe he just got his days mixed up and didn't know you were home."

"He did call once when I was at the hospital. Maybe he just needed to know I pulled through."

I debated about throwing Roger under the bus. It was hard for me to let that opportunity slip by but I didn't want to make her feel worse.

I softened my voice. "Mama, you know Roger never had concerns for anyone but himself."

She nodded in agreement, and that was one of the last times Mama ever mentioned Roger.

🦋 🦋 🦋

In no time, our home was filled with people I hadn't seen in ten years. Small-town Southern hospitality is hard to beat. The usual kin and neighbors dropped in to visit like Nate, Ruby and her husband John, and Mrs. Akins from the farm next door. Then came the pastor, the clinic doctor, and some of Donny's friends who had never met his other Mamaw. A lot brought covered dishes or desserts. Just the same, I asked Beth to bake up a batch of cookies in case we ran out of sweets.

I'd swear that all those folks had something to do with Mama's healing. Isn't it so that a happy spirit can lift you like no other? Human love is certainly the best medicine. The struggle would get real once she started those cancer drugs but, right then, I allowed our family to wallow in kindness.

Nate acted like my dang husband, being Mr. Attentive. Soon, I expected him to start wanting what a husband needed. I wasn't ready for that with all the people around me who needed care. But, I will admit, I was feeling some of those urges myself. I wondered when the bubble would burst and he would grow bored with me and all my family antics.

Another week passed and we returned to Asheville for Mama's follow-up visit with the surgeon. I was as nervous as a new mother cat guarding her litter. After a short time, she emerged and motioned for me to join her in the doctor's office.

"Her healing is remarkable," she started. "But now it's time to begin chemotherapy. We found multiple lymph nodes with cancer cells and had to remove them."

"And that means it's more advanced?"

"Yes, it's spread. But this isn't news to you. It's going to be a battle for quite a while."

"When should she start chemotherapy and how long will it take?"

"As soon as we can arrange for treatment. Plan on being around for half a day, every two to three weeks. We have to see how she bounces back."

"We've talked about the side effects," Mama added. "I'd like to look for a couple of wigs while we're in town."

"Maybe you won't need them," I suggested.

"And maybe I will. I want to be prepared."

"The nurse will give you a list of wig stores that support women with breast cancer. When you come in, we can get you some prescriptions that might help with the other side effects."

I squeezed mama's hand tighter and made eye contact with the doctor. "Like…"

Mama answered, "Nausea, anemia, fatigue, diarrhea, mouth sores. Oh, and maybe rashes. Doesn't that sound lovely?"

The doctor reached out and grabbed mama's other hand. "Everyone is different. We might not win every battle. Winning the war is more important."

I don't know about Mama, but my knee almost buckled when I walked out of that doctor's office. I hadn't planned to take this to heart. I meant to just help her along. Instead, I found myself fighting just like her.

We walked to the car, each lost in our own thoughts. Around us, the robins called to each other and my eye caught half of a blue eggshell resting on the ground. Life was going on around us like nothing was different. But, in fact, everything had changed.

She sat in the front seat and slammed the door shut. I followed her in, turning the ignition.

"I hate the fact that they are putting poison in my body," she said.

"I know, I know." I tried soothing her. "But that poison might save your life."

"Am I worth it, Leandra? I haven't been much of a mother."

"Maybe you will fight harder knowing you can make up for it with Donny. And, once Mamaw passes, I'm going to struggle without other womenfolk at the farm."

"You got Beth."

"Sure. For a while. But Beth ain't kin. And soon she'll run off with a young man and start the life she deserves. I wouldn't mind havin' you around the farm to keep me company."

She nodded in agreement. At least it gave her something to think about.

���

We had barely stepped into the house when Beth came running up to me. "Papaw isn't doin' so good. His color is awful and he's breathin' short and fast. He was out in the orchard wanderin' around, looking at the apple crop. I bet he overdid it."

"Is he out of oxygen?" That was the first thing that came to mind.

"Already checked. He's got plenty of volume. If I put it any higher, it'll blow his nose off. I called the clinic, but I don't think it can wait. Should we take him into the hospital?"

"My stars, I just got back from Asheville. Let me look at him."

Papaw's color was bluish grey. If he went into the hospital, he'd never make it back home. He saw me walk into his room and gave me a feeble smile. A wrinkled hand reached out. I grabbed onto him, clinging to our two lives joined since the day I arrived in the world.

"What happened, Papaw? I was only gone a few hours."

He could hardly get a word out. "Time," he said. "It's time."

Tears spilled everywhere on his face and mine. I panicked. Thoughts clouded with what my life would be without him. "What do you want me to do?" I begged. "We never talked about that."

"Mamaw," was all I heard.

"Get Mamaw?"

He nodded.

I raced across the parlor, wiping my face as I went.

"Doctor's on his way over," Beth said. "He told me he might have somethin' that can ease up on his struggle to breathe."

"Leandra, what can I do?" Mama looked so pathetic sitting on the sofa absorbed in the confusion.

I gave her instructions. "Call Ruby at the Angus farm, her phone number is in the drawer by the phone. Tell her to drive Donny over, that Papaw is failing."

"Beth, Papaw wants to see Mamaw. Let's get her to his room."

Mamaw sat in front of the television, mesmerized by her game show. Each of us grabbed an arm and launched her up from the chair.

"Here now, what's this about?"

"Papaw wants to visit a spell," Beth reassured her.

"Oh, well I'm always happy to visit with him. That's Zachary, right?"

"Yes, ma'am," I answered. "He's your husband."

"I'm married?"

By then we had her in his tiny room.

"Why, Zachary, it's so nice to see you." The oxygen machine muffled her voice.

Papaw nodded at us and motioned for her to sit next to him. "I don't think she can get into any trouble here," Beth said. "I've moved his medications out of sight." He reached for her hand and, as their fingers intertwined, I could swear I saw his breathing ease and he filled his lungs with a big sigh.

"Let's leave them be," Beth said. "She's his best medicine."

Cars rumbled into our gravel drive, first Donny and Ruby, then the doctor. The room was too small for all of us, so we took turns getting out of each other's way.

"I put some coffee on," Mama said. "It's gonna be a long night."

"Mama, you need to sit down," I cautioned. "You're doin' so well, I don't want you to backslide."

"I'm fine, Leandra. I sent Ruby to the store to get some cold cuts for sandwiches in case anyone gets hungry. I'm not sure what the doctor's doing in there, but he sure doesn't need us underfoot."

Donny emerged from Papaw's room, sobbing, shoulders shaking violently. He leaned against the stairway banister, shielding his eyes with his hands. I ran to steady him, but instead we mourned together.

"He was always so good to me," Donny cried. "When Daddy died, he just stepped right in, taught me all he could about being a good person. What will I do now?"

I couldn't answer. I heard a truck pull into the front drive. Maybe it was John senior. Nate burst through the front door.

"How did you…"

"Beth called. Figured you might need me." We all crumpled on the sofa and waited for the doctor to come out of Papaw's room. Part of me was afraid to go in there. I didn't want to watch him struggle.

The doctor's face was grim. "I tried to give him a breathing treatment. It didn't help much." He brightened a little. "But I did give him a little morphine to help him relax some. You all need to know this decline is serious."

"Can we take him to the hospital?" Donny asked. "Will they be able to help?"

"They can't do much more than what we're doing," he replied. "The ride would be hard on him. He could die in route. No matter how much oxygen we put into his lungs, it won't get into his blood. The air sacs are shot. I can already see discoloration in his extremities."

I could see Donny didn't understand doctor talk. "His legs and arms, Donny. His body doesn't have enough air to keep his body going. Papaw is at the end of his time."

The doctor continued speaking. My attention faded in and out. The room was filled with family and friends who had been in or around the Barker family for decades. We listened, longing for some sign of hope, but one by one, we faced the truth. An emptiness filled my chest.

The doctor continued. "I asked him if he wanted to go to the hospital. He struggled for every word and breath, but he made it clear he wants to die at home. I told him that would be his decision. Tonight, I'll stay as long as I can. And, Leandra, I'll give you some medication drops that will comfort him."

"Doctor, how long does he have?" Ruby asked. She was holding tight to Donny like she was squeezing out his pain.

"Hard to say with these things," he replied. "Could be tonight, tomorrow, or the next day. He might go unconscious, but still keep breathing. Toward the end, his respirations will get irregular."

The young doctor took a deep breath. I wondered how many times he had seen death in the face of the dying. "I'm going to give you folks some time to talk among yourselves while I go check on Zachary. Let me know if you have more questions."

"Leandra, let me get you a chair," Nate said. "For now, rest here." He positioned me on the arm of the sofa and left to grab a dining room chair.

"Thank you." I turned to Ruby, the senior in the group of long faces, and likely the one with the most life experience. "Should I call the mortuary now?" I asked. "It seems morbid."

"Yes, you probably should," she advised. "You won't be thinking clearly when the time comes."

"I'm not thinking clearly now. I'm losing my Papaw and my best friend. He was probably worried about those apples as we're getting ready to pick 'em. I wish he'd had the sense to rest. He'll miss this year's apple season."

Donny started sobbing again and turned his head into Ruby's shoulder. I was so grateful to have another Mamaw who could help with my family's care.

"Leandra, he was doing what he loved," Ruby said. "You know that's the best death we can all hope for."

Nate called out to Beth. "Let's make a plate for the doctor. Leandra, let me know when you get off the phone. I'm going to call off tomorrow so I can return in the morning."

For once in my life, I didn't try to argue. I accepted the help, too weak in spirit to fight this battle on my own. Maybe I was getting old. Or could be, facing Papaw's mortality allowed me to discover my own. Nate's take-charge know-how was exactly what I needed.

🦋 🦋 🦋

I shooed the doctor home at six-thirty that night. It was late, and he had a family of his own. "Call me when he passes," he advised. "Take your time and let your family say their goodbyes. I hope you'll consider getting some rest for yourself."

"I'll do my best," I promised. "Thank you for your help."

I stood on the porch and watched him drive away. After, I gazed upward looking for answers I'd never find in the darkening sky.

Momentarily, panic washed over me again but I took a deep breath and considered. I could do no harm helping an old man pass into his next life. I had heard, when you died, you see whoever you believed was your God and saving grace. Maybe your loved ones would suddenly appear, youthful again, to take your hand and walk you to your place of rest. No pain or worries, just pure joy. That's what I wanted for my Papaw.

Ruby stayed until I showered. I had no need for food, but I didn't know when I'd get to bathe next. The hot water spilled down my body and I imagined it washing the pain down the drain. If only it were so. I threw on some drawstring shorts and a tee shirt, knowing I would probably be sleeping in the same clothes. I heard Beth and Ruby ready Mamaw for bed. She insisted on saying goodnight to me, so Beth and Ruby maneuvered her to the back bedroom where Papaw and I sat holding hands.

She stood in the doorway and took a good long look at us. "How is the old man doing?"

Mamaw was the ice breaker these days. I almost cracked a smile. "He's very tired," I replied. "I want to stay with him in case he needs anything." I rose from my station and walked toward her.

"You look tired, child. You should get some rest."

I kissed her on the cheek. "I will, Mamaw. One of these days I'll get some rest. I have these fine, strong women to help me."

I thanked Ruby again and watched them steer her down the hall to her room. Mamaw had taken on an eerie calmness. I'd swear she was trying to be on her best behavior and realized the gravity of the situation. You might say these folks with dementia are crazy, but somehow she understood what was at stake.

Beth returned to me. "Leandra, I'm going to sleep a few hours and then take over for you. He won't ever be alone."

"That's not something I can do, but I thank you Beth. It's enough that you are helping with Mamaw. I can't leave him now."

"Excuse me." Donny pushed his way into Papaw's room, lugging an old cot. Without saying another word, he pushed Papaw's small dresser against the bed making a cozy corner just big enough to fit the cot against the long wall. "I found this in one of the closets and knew you wouldn't leave the room tonight, but maybe you'll lay down for a while. I'll be back with some clean sheets and a pillow."

I stared at him as he left the room. Love spilled from my heart, puddling on the floor at my feet. Where was the little boy who had been mine all these years? In his place was a young man taking on far more than his age allotted. I knew farm kids grew up faster than city children, but it wasn't fair that he had to bear so much more at his young age. In the two months he had been working at the cattle farm, I had been so busy I didn't notice how fast my little boy had moved toward adulthood.

Papaw's breathing settled into a familiar cadence, his chest rising and falling in a predictable rhythm. My ears told me his lungs were wet and filling with fluid. I looked at my watch calculating the time for his next dose of medication that would ease his struggle.

There was still so much I had to say, so much I needed to know. How had I wasted almost fifty years not knowing this time would come? I studied the veins bulging from his thin-skinned hands that rested on top of the bedsheet, hands that had worked so hard all his life. He certainly deserved a more glorious death than this.

"I'm not ready, Papaw!" I sobbed. "I can't do this alone."

I saw his eyelids flutter, but they remained closed. His breathing quickened. I knew he had heard me. I felt bad for laying that on him while the poor man was trying to die.

I cleared my throat. "I apologize," I said. "I don't want you leavin' me, but you taught me well. You stood by me when Daddy died, and again when my husband died. Despite Mama and Roger, you kept me standing when my brother Ray died. You saw that I had the sense to get an education and figure things out for myself." I swallowed hard. "I can do this Papaw. I'll take care of Mamaw, Mama, and Donny. You just be sure to look over us and the farm. And say hello to Archie for all of us."

I had said my piece and, like Mamaw, a calmness came over me. I made my bed on the cot and opened the window to let the late summer air drift into the stuffy room. Even though the drone of the oxygen machine was relentless, I focused on his breathing, growing increasingly harsh with each passing hour.

I woke every hour to check him. The last time I woke with a start, my heart pounding in my chest. I had dreamed I was a young girl again and Raymond was a toddler. We were helping Papaw in the tobacco field. That damn tobacco that had destroyed his lungs with the pesticides and poisons to kill the weeds, and the smoke and dust from the drying barn. At one point, Ray and I grabbed him by his hands, pulling him away from the field. I looked up to see Papaw and baby Ray in a rowboat drifting away from me. They were smiling and waving goodbye while I stood in the big tobacco field, confused and alone.

His breathing was a gurgle now with spacings of long intervals. It was early morning and no one else stirred. I stood over him wondering how to help. The oxygen seemed pointless now, so I unhooked the claws from Papaw's nostrils, gently lifted the loops off his ears and turned off the machine. The motor went dead and the room was still. I watched for a while, wondering if he would stop breathing altogether and finally be free. But he didn't and the struggle continued.

He was overdue for medication, and I was overdue for fresh coffee. I left the room and turned the corner to the kitchen. Light was just breaking. In a past time, Papaw would be getting out of bed for chores. We would be sharing morning coffee together.

I started toward his bedroom, coffee in hand, but when I turned the corner again, I heard nothing. I stood in the doorway, shoes fixed to the floor, unable to move. Again, I heard nothing.

"No," I told him. "You chose to die without me? Alone? Are you still trying to protect me?"

I saw him take his last breath. He lay still and silent, and I knew.

Steadying my gait, I proceeded into the room and sat down next to him. Gently, I draped my torso over his body and wished we could still hold each other. Sorrow gushed out of me with such force I felt like I was choking. This went on for about a minute until the window curtains fluttering in the cool morning air drew my attention.

On the windowsill sat the most perfect pale-blue butterfly stretching its wings in the light of day as it prepared for flight. It looked like an angel. Enchanted by its beauty, I rose from my chair and walked toward it. When my outstretched hand reached his sticky feet, he climbed aboard without hesitation.

Time stood still. My heart told me God sent this angelic butterfly to escort my Papaw to Heaven. No sooner did that thought escape my weary mind, than the butterfly lifted away, climbing upward into the sky. I watched him fight against a gentle breeze before he turned eastward toward the rising sun and the butterfly bush.

Since the family would need to say their goodbyes, I made Papaw presentable by combing his hair, washing his face, and straightening his covers. I left and shut the door behind me so others would know he had moved on. It was nearly seven and folks would be waking soon. I took in a lung full of air, grateful to be doing so, and prepared to meet a difficult day.

✄ ✄ ✄

The air had turned cool overnight. It was almost like Papaw took summer with him. Forced to get on with life while I was dealing with death, I didn't know if I was coming or going. The mortuary was due to arrive to pick up Papaw. I wandered across the road to the tobacco field, now barren and empty after harvest. If the crop had remained standing, I likely would have taken the tractor and plowed through it in anger, knowing it had contributed to thousands of sick people, including my Papaw. The rich-smelling leaves were curing in the barn, surely to be our last crop.

"I'm gonna make this right," I said out loud, and chucked a rock at the field.

A voice replied. "How are you going to do that?"

I jumped out of my skin, wondering for a split second if Papaw was standing behind me. It was only Nate. He had likely driven into the back while I slipped out the front door.

I was too tired to sass him and ignored his ribbing. "I'm taking every penny from this crop and putting it toward the new clinic. And I'm carving out a chunk of this field and it will be where the clinic will stand. This damn tobacco is going to pay back the sick, the dying, and the dead."

He put his hands around my waist, gazing out over the land with me. "I hear he passed a couple hours ago. Sorry I wasn't here."

"No need to apologize. We had our private moment to say goodbye. A good death if there can be such a thing."

"Of course, there can. A lot of us won't be that lucky."

I noticed the mortuary van coming up the road.

"Stay with me today," I requested. "I have to make arrangements for Papaw's funeral and Mama's treatments, and I don't trust my mind to figure all this out."

"I can do that. You know there's people standing by to help you share the load."

He gave me a loving smile and kissed the top of my head and we turned to follow the mortuary men into what was now my farmhouse, the fourth generation of the Barker Family Farm.

🦋 🦋 🦋

Beth had food prepared and family wandered in and out of the kitchen, picking at whatever filled their bellies. I saw Donny meander out to the barn, refusing all food. I don't know why, but somehow a barn could be the most comforting place on a farm. Nestling up in a pile of fresh hay with a warm animal was sometimes the most healing move a human could make. They wouldn't judge your tears or pain, but they would be a reminder of life. Rufus the pig was a given to provide comfort while begging for a handout. He always brought a smile to Donny's face with his cold wet nose and, since he had been a piglet, that spotted porker had taken to following him around.

"I have to make arrangements for Mama's treatments," I told Nate. "I want to take care of her needs first. Can you go check on Donny? I saw him wander off to the barn. Tell him I sent you to check on the animals. Don't let him know I'm frettin' over him."

"Happy to," he replied, and walked out the door.

I turned to Beth. "I'm counting on you to keep close tabs on Mamaw. All this is going to add to her confusion—and mine."

"She was already asking about the big black shiny car out front," Beth said. "But she didn't see them take him away."

"Just be truthful with her. I doubt she'll remember from one minute to the next, but you never know. I'm grateful she wasn't in her right mind to see him pass. The pain would have been overwhelming."

Mama and I sat down with the telephone, the calendar, and the hospital cancer department to mark out her chemotherapy treatment appointments. Once Papaw was laid to rest, her chemotherapy would be the controlling factor in our lives. I outlined the days on the calendar with a big red marker to signify our trips to Asheville. Even looking at the calendar filled me with exhaustion.

By then, it was old hat for me to prepare a funeral and burial. First, there had been Autumn and Ray, then Aunt Addie, my husband John,

Archie, and now Papaw. Each time, I told myself it would get easier during the next round. But it never did. Each death was unique and had its own special needs. Each life gave me pause and reflection, and blessings that made me who I was.

When the day came to climb the hill to the butterfly bush and I listened to the preacher's words, my eyes wandered to where I would lie and who would be here to say goodbye. Mamaw sat beside me. Donny and Nate had taken it upon themselves to set up chairs for us women folk and, for that, I was grateful. The air was gentle and warm, just like Papaw's life had been.

Mamaw tugged at my sleeve. "It's that nice man, isn't it?" she asked. "I was married to him, wasn't I?"

My puffy, wet eyes met hers as I blew my nose. "Yes." My chin trembled. "He was your husband and my Papaw. He treated both of us really well."

"I'm going to miss talking with him." She fought to blink away the tears.

I pulled out a black handkerchief I saved especially for funerals and handed it to her.

"That's exactly what I needed," she said. "Usually, I have one handy."

I smiled, remembering a time when Mamaw was always ready with a clean pressed handkerchief for all my emotional needs. Now it was my turn.

I watched them lower Papaw's glossy casket into the ground he had loved and toiled over all his life. The preacher signaled it was time to stand and throw our customary handful of dirt on the casket. There wasn't a soul there who failed to grab a fistful of dirt, the dirt that fed our families, fed our souls, fed the country, and then some. My moist dirt hit Papaw's casket and, silently, I told him while the farm was mine, I would nurture it exactly how he had taught me, or better.

🦋 🦋 🦋

When the luncheon was over and the guests gone, I finally let my guard down. The family gathered on the front porch telling stories and lingering through the early evening. I had found an old bottle of Papaw's "tonic" in the basement and brought it up to share. Nate refused so much as a teaspoon taste.

"No thank you. Your family can enjoy that in the coming years," he said, eyeing the dark jug. "It'll get better with age, just like the rest of us."

He was the eternal optimist. Not the case so many years ago.

I walked him to his truck. "Maybe sometime soon we can get together for something fun," I offered.

"Take all the time you need. Like I said before, you still need to eat. Maybe we can get together for a meal sometime."

"I think our dance lessons will have to go on hold for a bit. If you need to get another partner, feel free."

"I think I can survive without dancing for a while." Fast as a lightening bug, he placed a kiss on my cheek and climbed into his truck.

While I watched him pull away, I considered how different he was from Sal. He was as sweet as Sal was wily. I had avoided thinking much on what happened between me, Sal, and his wife. I should have felt guilty but I didn't. Maybe Sal and I were just acting on what should have happened in high school. The deed was done and I wasn't sorry. There was nothing any thinking on it could change, but would I ever find that kind of fire with another man? That answer would have to wait.

Chapter 23

Boyfriends and Girlfriends

Relationships are difficult. It doesn't matter if they are old or new, good or bad, or bring you heartache or joy. It's something you have to work at.

❋ ❋ ❋

Apple time was upon us again. With all due respect to Papaw's memory, we plunged into our duty. This was our second season, yet our first one without Papaw and Archie. It amazed me how much had changed in a year's time.

"Mama? You okay? Ready to call it a day?" I looked up to see Donny standing at the entrance of the apple barn.

"I'll be right there. Just makin' one final check."

He walked toward me, hands tucked in his tight jean pockets. "Not the same without Papaw, is it?"

I gave a great sigh. "I can't stop time," I replied. "Someday you might be doing this without me. It's just the cycle of life. But, yes, this will never be the same without him or Archie. I keep thinking back to my younger days when they would start picking. We knew in a short time we'd have money in our pockets and time to spend it. I had a great childhood on this farm."

"Me too," he said.

My mouth turned down and started to quiver. "Really?" I asked. "Donny, that couldn't make me any happier."

"I know some big city kids might think I'm missing out on life, living on this farm in the middle of nowhere, but I don't see it that way. I get to do things they don't. I saw that firsthand in New Jersey. I don't know how they don't get bored out of their minds."

I laughed out loud. "Ha! I thought the same thing when I moved there. I feel like tomorrow will be a turning point for us. God help us, let's hope our family is on the uphill swing." I looped my arm around my son's muscular arm and we walked back to the kitchen. I could smell Beth's cookies baking before we even opened the back door. Maybe before the end of apple season, I'd figure out how to replicate Mamaw's apple butter to add to our inventory.

For the time being, hired help replaced family. A couple of Donny's friends wanted to earn spending money, so they pitched in. Beth kept close tabs on Mamaw, while Donny minded the farm animals and the petting zoo. Nate helped too, refusing pay, and mostly taking care of me.

He handed me a cup of hot cider. "This should warm you up." He waved at someone across the yard.

"I think you are genuinely having a good time," I noted. "That's a pretty woman. Friend of yours?"

"I *am* having a good time and that's my barber. She keeps me looking good."

"Well, please express my appreciation. And can you take over the register for me? I need a bathroom break."

I raced into the house, not wanting to abandon my station for long. Immediately, I heard retching on the other side of the downstairs bathroom door.

"Hello? Do you need help?" I pushed my way into the bathroom.

There was Mama on her hands and knees, holding onto the bathroom bowl. Her wig was skewed to the side, and she was pale as the toilet.

"Just me, Leandra. Makin' love to the Porcelain God."

"Oh, Mama! Can I help? How can you bring humor into this horrible condition you're experiencing?" I ran to wet a cold washcloth and handed it to her.

"If I don't endure with humor, what do I have left? Here, hold this." She yanked off her wig and handed it to me. I stared at it, not fully grasping the stupidity of the situation. She started laughing. "Child, I wish you could see your face."

"You are so brave," I replied. "I'm so proud of you."

"Leandra, that's just about the nicest, most honorable thing you have eva said to me." She stood on wobbly legs, wiping the cold cloth across her mouth.

"Let me help you to bed," I offered.

"Hell no. You think I'm going to miss my soap opera? You take me to the sittin' room. I promised Mr. Markus I would keep up with the story so I could relay it to him at my next appointment."

"Mr. Markus?"

"Yes, he's the volunteer on our floor who brings around goodies while they put that poison in our veins. I've taken a liking to him."

"Why, Mama! You sweet on him?"

"I am. So is his wife."

"You little hussy," I teased.

"I'm not opposed to a threesome."

By then she was seated in front of the television.

"I can't listen to this smut," I told her. "Remember, you'll have to atone for your sins."

"Honey, bring me a cola and go back to your apples. I'll worry about my sins, you worry about yours."

I ran back to the apple barn floating on a cloud. She was in her sixties but finally coming into her own. But I debated which one of my personal sins she was speaking to.

🦋 🦋 🦋

Beth sailed through her classes and exams and, right before Christmas, we threw her a fine graduation party. I invited the entire Baptist church, the congregation members being the ones who took her off the streets prior to me shoving education down her throat.

I toasted her success and everyone applauded. "Now what?" I asked.

"Not rightly sure," she answered. "My boyfriend thinks…"

"Whoa! Boyfriend?"

Oohs and aahs erupted from the audience.

She cleared her throat. "I said," and she looked sideways at me, "my boyfriend, Tom, thinks I should continue with college."

"I think we might like this Tom," I answered.

"I'd like to see Tom at services," Pastor shouted out.

Everyone laughed. It had been a long time since our home was filled with joy. I sent out a prayer it would continue.

Beth approached me after the party dispersed and laid a half-eaten bowl of onion dip on the counter. "Let's leave this clean-up for tomorrow," I suggested.

"Leandra." I paused from packing leftovers in our refrigerator. Turning, I saw tears filled her eyes. "This was the nicest thing anyone has ever done for me."

My heart ached for her. She had become one of my own. "Oh, Beth. I could not have managed without you. All that has gone on in my life? What would I have done without you? It was my honor to recognize your hard work and dedication. You belong to this family now."

"I don't want to overstay my welcome."

"You have got to be kidding. Overstay? You thinking of getting hitched to this Tom?"

"Mercy no. It could come to that, but we're not ready."

"You think I'm gonna throw you out just because you're educated now?" She smiled when I said that. "See, even *you* know that's foolishness."

"I can support myself. I know I can take care of my own needs."

"I can't. I need you. If you want to move out, I respect that. But I still need your help."

"I just wanted to make sure I know where I stand with the Barkers."

"You stand on solid ground, just like the rest of us. Never doubt your value for a minute."

She nodded in confirmation. "Well then—I'm worried about Mamaw. She's declinin' fast. 'Specially since Papaw died. She keeps asking where he is. Yesterday, I found her cryin' in his room. It took me an hour to settle her down."

I shook my head. "I was afraid of that. A couple of times I've caught her wandering around at night. I probably need to let the doctor know what's goin' on."

"Maybe they can give her something to help with sleep," she offered.

"Well, don't you worry. You need to move forward with your life. I'll make sure we get Mamaw some help. If you just pitch in when you can, I would appreciate that."

🦋 🦋 🦋

Life plundered through. The fall leaves were a disappointment going from green to brown, skipping over their pretty colors. It had been a dry year and the trees had grown weary seeking water.

In the early weeks after Papaw's funeral, I routinely visited his grave to have myself a good cry. I missed him dearly. Up there one day, the wind whipped up and over the cemetery hill while my icy tears soaked the front of my clothes. No one knew I was hiding in the cemetery behind the butterfly bush so by the time I moped back to the house, Beth had left to visit Tom.

A note sat on the kitchen table:

Don't know where you are. Clinic called at 1:15 requesting you stop by. Problem with a patient and his family. They sounded worried and wondered if we should call the sheriff.

Sweet Jesus. This was the last thing I needed. I glanced at my watch. Seven minutes had passed. Tearing down a country road was natural for me, but this time I rolled. My wheels spewed gravel everywhere as I turned into the parking lot where only a few cars remained. About half a dozen people stood in small clusters on the clinic porch, some smoking cigarettes, talking among themselves and looking back at the front door.

I slammed the car door and took the steps two at a time until I reached the front door. Loud, tense voices boomed on the other side, and I yanked it open without hesitation.

"See here, woman. This is my child. I decide what's right and wrong for her."

I could see the terror in the face of the Asheville doctor. A beast of a man looked down on her, towering like a grizzly. Chances were, he was kin to one. Thankfully, the reception desk sat between them with the receptionist huddled behind the doctor. He was a hard man to look at with his wild frizzled hair, and pockmarks scattered across both cheeks covered by at least a week's scraggly beard. He smelled like his mouth was ready to drop a few teeth.

Cowering to the side stood a wisp of a woman looking to be my age. She clung to a frail girl in her early teens. It looked to me like the blood had drained from both of their bodies. I gently shifted them away from him, and we shuffled to stand behind the desk with the doctor. As I did, two men who had remained in the waiting room moved to stand with us. One was Big Bob, a male nursing student I had met previously. He was hard to forget. Word around town was he worked as a bar bouncer before his acceptance into nursing school. It was unusual to see a male nurse at that time, but I was delighted he was on shift today. If things escalated, I was betting it would take most of us to subdue the threatening man.

I summoned my bravery. "Can someone tell me what's going on here?"

"This ain't none of yo' business," the man hissed at me.

"I think it is," I replied. "This is my community clinic and I am in charge of operations."

That was a bold face lie, but no one was going to argue the fact.

"Theys tellin' me I cain't decide what kind of doctorin' this girl needs." He pointed with a dirty fingernail toward the child.

She flattened herself away from him, trying to disappear.

"She's pregnant." The doctor scowled at him. "He wants to terminate the pregnancy."

"'Cause it's his own!" the woman shouted. "He done it to her. His own daughter. She told me so. He's fearin' the law will find a way to lay claim to him if she keeps the baby."

He advanced on us. His hairy hand flew out and slapped the daughter's face so hard she fell to the floor. "Whore!" he screamed.

The mother ran to protect the child, throwing her body over the girl. She turned back to him. "You are nothing but trash, Leon!" she screamed.

His elbow came back and punched her in the face in an apparently automatic response. At that point, I may have peed myself a little knowing he could have snapped my neck with one quick twist.

The door burst open to reveal two deputy sheriffs, one with his hand on his revolver. I recognized their faces but was too scared to recall their names. I swear both wore a set of wings on their shoulders. The older deputy took a moment to survey the situation. He backed out the front door never taking eyes off the situation in front of him.

"Y'all clear off this porch now," he ordered the lookie-loo patients. "I don't want anyone else gettin' hurt if this goes further south. Time to go home. You can come back to the clinic tomorrow."

The younger deputy took a step forward. "Sir, step away from the desk."

Leon ignored him, and the younger man moved in front of him to gain his attention. It didn't work.

He pulled out his handcuffs. "Sir, I repeat, step back from the desk."

Big Bob and I reached for the bleeding women on the floor to pull them to their feet. I started shuffling backward and motioned for our cowardly little group to move through the kitchen galley toward the back door.

"Hands behind your back." Still fixed on his womenfolk, Leon put his hands behind his back, giving them a resisting shake before being shackled. He had done this before.

He called out to her as we stepped outside. "This ain't over, Mae. You're gonna pay for this. I'm comin' after you. You and that whore child of yours. I seen her charmin' the boys…"

I tuned out his ranting while the deputies marched him out to their car for what the deputy called "a little talk."

Mother and daughter sat at a rickety picnic table under one of the pine trees. I turned to the doctor.

"Let's send Big Bob and the other patients home, while we have our own little talk."

We thanked them for standing by to defend us, and they left.

"Stay with the girls," I told Dr. Benning. "I'm gonna get us some cold drinks and a couple of ice packs for their swollen faces. I'll be right back."

Dr. Benning began examining their injuries.

Once inside the kitchen, I heard the front door open. I froze. My impulse was to turn and run.

"Ms. Tucker?" It was the deputy's voice.

"In here," I called out, nearly choking on my own words.

He came around the corner and laid the truck keys on the counter. "Give these to those ladies. He's going to jail for a while so he can cool down and we can check his records. But, ma'am, he's a dangerous one. You need to get those women out of here so he can't find them. And I'd lay low for a while. He may come looking for you too."

"Thank you for your help."

Damn, I thought. *What have I gotten into?*

Back at the table, I passed out cold drinks. Dr. Benning made the introductions. "This is Mae and Deanne Wilson. This is Leandra Tucker. Leandra started the clinic."

"Pleased to meet both of you."

"I doubt that," Mae snickered. "All the trouble we caused. You don't remember me, do you?"

I studied her face. There was something so familiar about her. "It's Mae with an E, M-A-E. Last time I saw you, we was six years old."

My lower jaw dropped open like a bass chasing a fishing lure. It couldn't be. "Etta Mae?"

She shrugged her shoulders and nodded. I walked around to her side of the table and hugged her while Dr. Benning and Deanne looked on. We were full-on crying. It had been thirty years plus since her no-good father had hauled all of them off to California after they were kicked off their tenant farm for cheating the landowner.

"Last time I saw you your two front teeth had fallen out." I smiled at her. "I see they've grown back in."

"Yeah, well I've lost a few others in the back. Can't afford no dentist."

"Etta Mae, when I was getting those drinks, the deputy came in and gave me the truck keys." I laid them on the table. "They're jailing your husband. This is your chance to start over again."

"Deanne's about eight weeks along." Dr. Benning added. "Is that right, Deanne? She needs prenatal care if she wants to keep this baby."

"Yes," Deanne replied. "That's about when he got to me."

"I'm so sorry you went through that," I said to her.

What words could comfort a child after something like that?

"That pig got drunk and didn't know me from Deanne," Etta explained. "It all happened when I wasn't home. We was gettin' ready to move again and leavin' Oklahoma. Behind in rent as usual." She patted her daughter's hand. "I guess we can live in the truck for a while, Deanne." I handed her a tissue from the box I had grabbed in the kitchen. "He made me leave my other three kids with my sister. I want them back." She swabbed up the tears on her face, shaking her head. "I don't know how to get out of this marriage or away from him."

I turned to Deanne. "How'd your mama find out you were pregnant?"

"Mama caught me throwin' up with the baby sickness."

"I had no idea he did that to her." She reached out and stroked her daughter's light-brown hair. "Guess she was tryin' to protect me."

"I'd like to help," I said without hesitation. "How about coming home with me for the night. I'll make some calls tomorrow and find you shelter. You can't stay any longer than overnight. The deputy said he might come looking for me too, and I'm not hard to find."

Etta and Deanne were exhausted and, after I sent them off to bed, I curled up on the sofa with a cup of honeyed hot tea. Before I knew it, I was rolled up into a tiny ball, crying myself sick. In the quiet of my old farmhouse, my heart took me back to a scared little girl trying to make sense of the belt bruises on her backside and wondering why she had to go away. Here, thirty and more years had passed, and sweet Etta Mae was in the same place she had started. I looked at her and saw her mama, a beaten-down woman. I couldn't let that happen to Deanne. I wanted to help her keep her baby—or her sister—or whoever that was she was carrying inside of her.

My little baby Autumn's face rose before me. No one here, except me, even knew she had existed. Her ashes were buried by the butterfly bush, a ghost of a life that never started. I sobbed until I could hardly breathe anymore and pulled myself up the stairs to bury my pain under my quilts.

🦋 🦋 🦋

My former brother-in-law, Jake, was more than agreeable. "Well, I have farm hands livin' in that house where you and John used to live, but way back in the woods, we have an old ramshackle cabin that might be useful. Dad's grandpa built it in the thirties, but it's got an inside toilet and electricity. It needs a good clean out, but it will do for a short while."

"That sounds great. Keep this quiet, Jake. The fewer people that know, the better."

"Sure, Leandra. I'll drop wood off for the fireplace. It's gettin' a little chilly at night."

I gathered up the girls that afternoon and took them to the cabin. I had a trunk full of groceries, blankets, and cleaning supplies. The cabin was little more than a hard-shell tent but would provide shelter until she could escape him. By the time the sun was ready to go behind the mountain, they had a cozy little hideaway.

I faced the two women. "Soon as it's dark, I'll store your truck in Jake's equipment barn so Leon won't see it. Stay away from him, you hear?" I pointed toward the west. "The big house is over that hill so, if you have to, run head that direction. I'll check in every couple of days or so."

"What do we do all day?" Deanne asked.

I smiled at the young girl, clearly not prepared for this responsibility. "You have a new life coming into your family and a duty to protect that baby. You and your mama need to figure out where to go after this. But you need to get out of here before he's released from jail."

"How long you figure we got?" Etta Mae asked.

"I'm hoping for two weeks, but it could be shorter. What skills do you have? Can you get a job to support the two of you?"

"I can find work. I know how to clean houses, do laundry, and cook. So does Deanne."

On my way out the door, Deanne ran up to me, wrapping her arms around me like a little child. "Thank you, Ms. Tucker. You're saving me and my sister-baby." She pulled back and I stared into her small, wet face.

Sister-baby?

I shuddered.

"I want you to climb out of this, Deanne. You have a chance to make a new life for yourself. Now get inside where you can't be seen. You have a lot of work ahead of you."

She nodded and turned, and I watched her disappear into safety. I hoped they had the sense to stay in hiding until we figured out what to do next.

🦋 🦋 🦋

"You're not gonna like this." I found Beth pushed into the corner of the kitchen. She had just run her fingers through her short thick hair, something she often did when stressed or afraid.

Alarmed, I asked, "What won't I like?"

"I found Mamaw trying to start Papaw's old truck in the barn. She must have remembered where he hid the keys. The battery clicked, but it wouldn't start. When I asked her to get out of the car and hand me the keys, she said she was taking a casserole to Ruby. Said John told her to run it over. She had last night's leftover casserole on the seat next to her."

I shivered head to toes. So, John told her? Which John? Ruby's live husband or my dead one?

"This is gettin' real, isn't it? I'm not sure what to do with her. I wanted to talk to the doctor but then I got distracted with the trouble at the clinic.

Here it is in my face again. Where is she now?"

"I offered to make her some toast and apple butter to get her back in the house. She was exhausted from her little journey to the barn and fell asleep on the sofa. I'm afraid she's gonna run off to these woods and get lost."

"I need better locks on these doors. Maybe I can get Nate to help me and Donny to put in dead bolts."

"What about changing her medications?"

"I'll call the clinic today. I don't want to load her up on drugs, but maybe we can reduce some of this wandering."

🦋 🦋 🦋

I picked up the phone and called Nate. "I need help," I blurted out.

"I'm still at work. Is it urgent?"

"No, but Beth caught Mamaw trying to drive today. Can you help put deadbolts on the doors to keep her contained? The sooner the better."

"My truck is in the shop, and I can't do anything until the weekend. Come by for breakfast Saturday morning and, afterwards, we can buy some locks in town while I pick up my truck. That will solve at least two problems."

"Good. I'd like to get them in before I drive Mama into Asheville for her chemo treatment on Monday."

"I heard about what happened at the clinic. They're not stayin' with you, are they?"

"No, I hid them away. I'm not sayin' where, but it's nowhere near me. That man's a menace."

"Smart move. Soon as he gets out of jail, he's going to go looking for her. You better be prepared in case he shows up at your door. You know how to use a shotgun?"

"Nate, I'm a farm girl, 'course I know how to use a shotgun. But I got a senile woman underfoot and you want me to stash a shotgun at the front door? I'll have to hope the deadbolts keep Mamaw in and Leon Wilson out."

Saturday morning when I showed up at Nate's, the aroma of crisp bacon and fresh coffee oozed out the front door and hit me in the face. When I saw Nate, that hit me too. If he had premeditated our encounter, I had to credit him for his efforts. He was still in his blue-plaid bath robe, mostly open, showing a lightly-haired bare chest and coordinating pajama bottoms.

For a second, I forgot about breakfast and imagined myself waking up to him every morning. Folks were doin' that nowadays. Just "shackin' up," as Mamaw would have said. That railed against my Baptist upbringing, but I wouldn't mind having a test run before I considered taking in another man.

After I came to my senses I asked if I was early.

"No, I just got out of the shower and wasn't dressed when the doorbell rang."

"That's not entirely bad."

He grinned and planted a kiss on my lips. "I did get a shave in."

"Yes, I noticed." I stroked his jaw and got a whiff of his arousing aftershave. I forced myself in the direction of the coffee to ignore his allure. "Can I help with anything?"

He put me to work beating the eggs for the French toast. That was the perfect job to distract a woman with raging hormones. I hadn't planned on getting horny before breakfast.

He was standing next to me when he dipped his finger in the syrup pitcher and licked it off. "I can't tell if this is hot enough," he said deep in thought. "Taste this."

When I turned around, a warm sticky maple-syrup finger was lathering up my tongue. I don't know if the syrup was hot, but I was.

That was my first maple syrup kiss, right there in his kitchen. He took my hand and slowly walked me to the bedroom. Since he was mostly undressed, he lent a hand with getting me out of my jeans. Clothes flew everywhere and we wrestled on his unmade bed for almost an hour. It was nothing like my sordid tryst with Sal. Nate was an incredible tease. I was ready to burst into flames, but he kept finding new ways to make me squirm.

We were ravenous after our exercise and most of the morning was gone when we finally cleared the breakfast dishes.

"I could get used to this, you know?" I finished drying the skillet and laid it on the stovetop.

"It *was* a nice way to start the weekend."

"Could be we should be having more of these weekends."

He opened his kitchen drawer and pulled out a house key hanging from one of those cheesy-yellow smiley faces. He was reading me, staring into my eyes while he reached for my hand and dropped the key in my open palm. "Been saving this for someone special."

Handing someone a house key says so much more than unlocking a door. I trust you. I'm yours. Come over anytime. This is a safe place. I'm here for you.

I was ready and needed that key. Right there in front of him I put the key on my key ring. I smiled back at its smiley face. Figures he would choose that key chain. My eternal optimist. It would make me grin every time I looked at it.

🦋 🦋 🦋

Most old farmhouses have only two doors: one front, one back. It took us a little over two hours to put both locks in, considering the old farmhouse wood in the door frame was nearly petrified. I started handing out keys.

"Mama, Donny, Beth. Every time you plan to leave her alone for more than three minutes lock her in and take the key. Better yet, take her with you. And don't leave the key layin' around where she can get her hands on it."

"Where's my key?" Mamaw asked. I handed her a key. "It's so shiny." She turned the brass key over and over in her hand.

"No way," Donny spoke up. "You can't give her a key. What's the point of the new locks?"

"Your mama is as sneaky as an old possum," I answered. "I can give her a key if it's a blank. In two days, she'll forget all about it and wonder what the key is doing on her dresser."

Donny shook his head in disbelief. "I'm going to remember that trick when you're a crazy old woman."

I gently patted his cheek. "Let's hope I make it that far, sweetheart."

I walked Nate to his newly repaired truck. "It's been quite an afternoon," I said.

"It started off with a bang." He smiled his boyish grin and climbed into his truck.

I reached through the open window. "This is for you." I handed him his own key to my new locks.

Chapter24

Remember or Forget

There are moments in our life we can never unsee. Age and experience rob us of the mind's ability to procure mental spaces that in a better time, were filled with childhood wonders. Eventually, joyful memories compete with memories of pain. No wonder old people are so confused all the time. We don't know if we should remember or forget.

🦋 🦋 🦋

On a stunning windless winter morning in December, Leon Wilson came looking for me. The sun warmed my face as I crossed the yard to the spring house and the sky was the perfect combination of clouds and blue yonder. That all went to hell in a heartbeat when I stepped inside the back door only to hear pounding at my front door. Beth came running down the stairs as I deadbolted the back door.

"What the Sam Hill?" she asked.

"It's not Sam. It's Etta Mae's devil man. Don't answer the door!"

"Open up!" he thundered. "Where is she?"

"We're calling the sheriff, Leon. She isn't here. Get off my property!"

I had a whole list of descriptive adjectives I wanted to lay on him, but you don't provoke an angry animal. He was slurring his words so, likely, there was alcohol in his system and no way to anticipate his next move. We peeked out from behind the curtains like two scared mice.

"I can't figure where he got that car," I told Beth. "He probably hotwired the darn thing and stole it."

"Is he holding a gun?"

"I doubt that since he just got out of jail."

"Where's Mamaw and Mama?"

"Left them upstairs. Told them to stay put until I got back up there."

"Go ahead and finish dressing Mamaw in case this fool breaks down our door and we have to run. Try to distract her 'cause I don't want her gettin' scared."

His fist slammed my door again. I thanked God the locks were holding when he tried the doorknob, twisting it back and forth with violent force.

I called the sheriff but knew it could be a while before anyone arrived.

"Leon! I don't know where she went. She lit out of here right after they arrested you, so get on out of here!" I kept a keen eye on the front door. "Don't make me use my shotgun!"

I called Nate. No answer.

"Beth, what's your boyfriend Tommy's number?" *Where's a man when you need one?*

She didn't answer. I walked over to the coat closet and grabbed the 20-gauge hidden in the back. The soup tureen in the dinette brimmed with ammunition hidden from Mamaw, so I grabbed a handful of shells, loaded the gun, and threw the rest in my coat pocket.

My next call was going to be to Tilly. I didn't want to risk dragging Jake into this as it could lead him back to Leon's women folk. I knew Tilly could handle a gun and wouldn't hesitate to use it.

I stayed out of sight. Heavy footsteps clomped down my porch steps and I heard a car start. I sucked in a lungful of air. That dumbass was finally giving up. Out of the corner of my eye, I saw Beth standing at the top of the stairs with Mamaw and Mama.

"He's gone!" I hollered up.

Mamaw wore a bright-blue jogging suit and looked like she was ready to run a marathon. I took a moment to laugh at the situation and motioned for her to come down. I discreetly emptied the shotgun and returned it to the closet, keeping the ammunition in my pocket.

"Here are today's ground rules. No one goes outside unless someone else is with them. Until we get rid of this demon, we have to keep our guard up."

The sheriff department vehicle pulled into our driveway.

"Well, how nice," Mamaw said. "We're gettin' company."

"C'mon, Mamaw," Beth urged. "Let's go in the kitchen and blow up some eggs in the microwave oven."

I struggled out to greet the deputies with knees knocking, gripping the porch rail to help steady me.

🦋 🦋 🦋

I needed to travel out to the cabin to warn Etta and Deanne but had dealt with enough drama for one day. For all I knew that maniac might be in the trees across the street watching us. Nate finally called back, insisting he'd spend the night on my sofa cradling his shotgun. I didn't say no and he showed up later that evening.

"I'm gonna sneak back there tomorrow and check up on the women," I told him. "I called Ruby earlier today and she said she hadn't heard any yelling or screaming, so I assume he doesn't know they're back in the woods."

"What have you got yourself into?" he asked.

I confessed what Etta Mae had meant to me back when we were kids. She had suffered at the hands of her angry drunk bootlegging father before he whisked her out of my life. Given my empathy for Deanne's condition, I stopped short of telling Nate about my baby Autumn and how an unexpected baby can be a blessing from heaven. He seemed to understand and didn't judge my ignorance for helping them.

I had wanted to tell the deputies about our situation. But country law had its own set of rules. Sometimes it isn't until the body is lying in the driveway and the house is burning down before the law gets involved. Some of it comes down to folks who have lived and married in the same county for so long, there's no one you can't think of as family. Then there are those who show up unannounced and are considered strangers and potential problems. The best thing for them is to pass through and be on their way. Etta Mae fell into that category. Not only that, but her family had an ugly history in these parts.

The next day, I approached the back door to the cabin, knocked, and asked Etta Mae to let me in. Deanne answered the door instead.

"Etta Mae's not here? What do you mean she's been calling her sister and driving around town?"

"Mama ain't come home for a day. She said we needed groceries, then she was gonna call Aunt Jessie to see how the otha kids are doin'— the three we left behind. Probably she needed cigarettes too."

Deanne paused to open a can of pork and beans.

My gut tightened. I had to find her before he did.

"You stay in this cabin, you understand? Yesterday, he came to my house looking for you two and he was none too happy. Don't even start a fire in the hearth. If he sees smoke comin' out of your chimney, he'll bust down the door to get to you. Stay under blankets to keep warm. I'll send word when I find your mama."

The truth was my hands were tied. I could do nothing until Etta Mae came to me.

Beth had just put Mamaw down for a nap. The house was quiet except for the steady hum of Beth's sewing machine running in the parlor. I heard a car door slam. I reached for the shotgun and went to the back door to check the lock.

It was Etta Mae. She looked like shit and didn't smell far from the same.

I hurried her into the kitchen. "Where have you been? I was worried sick about you. Leon's already out of jail and he's been here looking for you."

She ignored my question. "I need to show you somethin.' Can you come with me for a while?"

"He's out there, Etta Mae. You need to pack up and leave these parts."

"Please, just come with me for a couple hours. I gotta put this to rest. We can take my truck."

I grabbed a jacket and told Beth and Mama we'd be back in a few hours, reminding them to be cautious outside. "Mrs. Blake is droppin' off Donny after basketball practice. Beth, if you go outside to feed the animals, take Donny and the shotgun with you." She nodded to acknowledge, licking blood off her pinpricked finger.

I climbed in the cab with Etta Mae. The seat was shredded and grimy, and I had to push an empty chip bag off the bench. "Where we headed?" I asked.

"Near my old farm," she replied. "Remember that nasty swamp toward the back field?"

I laughed. "How could I forget? We used to say it was filled with haints from the Civil War. I'm pretty sure we had your younger brother convinced we were chased by a real ghost."

"Could be there's a real haint there now."

I studied her face but she gave no hint of what she meant.

She parked the truck, opened the door, and threw the keys on the seat. The woods had thickened since her family left. We passed her old shack of a house, collapsed under years of snow, ice, and neglect. I walked to the other side of the truck. Fresh footprints marked the damp ground, big footprints, and smaller ones that likely were hers. We walked about twenty feet from the truck.

"*Shh*," I hissed. "I hear an animal whining. Sounds like it's hurt."

"It's an animal all right."

We kept walking, approaching a hole in the ground. It was long and not perfectly square. It sent a shiver up my spine. My neck stretched to see inside the hole Etta Mae stood over.

I was speechless.

"I didn't worry none 'cause I had the truck and the shotgun Leon always kept behind the seat. But he seen the truck in the store parkin' lot. He waited on the other side of the truck until I got back. He was on a bender and forced me in the truck, holdin' the gun on me. He brought me out here."

She paused to shake her head and wipe a dribble of snot from her nose with the sleeve of her stained coat. She took a big mouth breath.

"He said he wanted to see the old homestead where I'd grown up. I drove until he made me stop and we ended up here. Then he tied my hands and feet and sat me down under that tree." She pointed to a stately maple. "He started diggin' a hole. Said he wanted me to watch him dig my grave. He always kept an old shovel alongside the shotgun in case he got stuck in the mud or snow."

She shook her head. "I spent hours watching that drunk fool dig. I watched him shovel while I worked my ropes off. He got about four feet down, finished off his jug, and passed out."

"Well, what's he doin' in the hole? And who duct taped his mouth?"

"That was my doin'," she replied. "He keeps all kinds of shit in this truck. Let me finish."

I was scared now and not about to make her mad.

"See that tree yonder?" She pointed toward a large elder tree. "He passed out there from all his diggin' and alcohol. Since my hand ropes were loose, I untied my feet and found the biggest rock I could lift. He rolled to his side, so I aimed for the soft spot on the side of his thick skull."

I shook my head back and forth in disbelief.

She answered my action. "I had to, Leandra. I knew he meant good by his promise to bury me."

At that point, Leon came to and saw us standing over him. He squinted and moaned, thrashing wildly in his earthen bed.

"Shut the hell up, you pig," she scolded. "You was gonna do this to me. Now I'm doin' it to you." She paused to snicker at him. "See, he done pissed himself, Leandra. Guess he knows he's gonna meet the devil."

I could not have imagined this situation in my life. I had been dumbstruck more than once with ugly surprises but never saw this one coming.

The man grew still again.

"I crushed his skull, hopin' I could kill him. I used all the hate on him he had for me. It didn't work. He came to a little, tried to come for me, but fell even closer to the grave. That suited me fine. He passed out again and I hog-tied him with his own ropes, taped his ugly mouth shut, and rolled him into the grave. I was gonna tape his eyes shut but I want him to see what's happenin'. He managed to squirm face-up."

"You were out here all night?"

"Yes'm. I stayed in the truck to keep warm. I thought he'd be dead by mornin' an' I could finish buryin' him, collect Deanne, and be on my way. But, damn, he's still alive. I didn't know what to do so I came and got you."

Calmly, she walked toward the tree and picked up the large rock, still marked with blood from his head. She stood at the edge, aimed carefully, and dropped the rock on his groin. Leon's eyes flew open, shuddering with the new pain. He screamed as well as any man could without the use of his mouth.

"Hurts, don't it? Rememba when you kicked me between the legs? That's what it feels like."

I didn't know who this person was. The loving child I grew up with was long gone, suffering her own death at the hands of poverty and abuse.

"Someday, I'll have to face my sins," she said. "I needed someone to know he was here."

"Well, what are you going to do now? Etta Mae, I can be a witness to your sufferin' and his threats, but you have to call the sheriff and get some help."

"They'll put me away." Her thoughts drifted out to the woods like wisps of smoke. Black, cold eyes looked to the distance and past the old swamp. "Then where will my children be? Who'll care for them? No. I need to be done with him."

I watched in silence as, without warning, she threw the rusted shovel in the grave with Leon, climbed in after it, and straddled his body with her two tiny feet.

He started thrashing, wide-eyed and frantic.

Horrified, I watched her take hold of the shovel with both hands and bring the blade down with all her hate, anger, and strength. She cut him across the throat, his blood splattering her bare legs.

All of it happened so fast and yet it moved in slow motion. What was I to do anyway? I was witness to a murder. And, in truth, I was frightened for my own well-being. Blood pumped from a severed artery as he struggled, unable to scream. I had seen John kill snakes that same way. A shovel imbedded into the body just under the head would keep a poisonous snake from biting and killing again.

He stopped moving before the blood stopped pumping. The last thing I focused on was one bloody eye staring back at me. It was the same bloody eye I saw on the grey dove that had stared into my heart when it fell from the claws of death. Now death had its grip on Leon Wilson.

"Gimme a hand up," she ordered.

My legs were tingling and felt unsteady. In a state of shock, I got down on my belly and reached into the grave. Etta Mae was still light as a bird and practically walked her way up the side of the grave. She had been a survivor all her life and would do whatever it took to stay alive and protect her children. I could feel heat coming off the dead man's body. One final bubble of blood and air burst as the remaining wind in his lungs exited his black soul.

"Help me fill the hole. You take this shovel. I'll see what otha tools he's stashed behind the cab."

By then, the sun looked to be an hour or two away from passing behind the west mountains. At least two hours had passed. I couldn't think straight, but knew I had to do something. Beth was going to think I forgot to come home, or worse, would call the sheriff, assuming Leon had come after me. I started pushing dirt into the grave. My life, my farm, and my family depended on me working fast to bury this evidence forever. Etta Mae returned with a handpick and a short-handled hoe.

"Do you know what you've gotten me into?" My anger rose like swamp gas. "You take off and I have to live here knowing what I've seen! Always wondering if someone is going to find out."

"It's not your property," she countered. "Who'd think to blame you?

Why you're thought of as an angel of mercy 'round these parts."

"Stop it, Etta Mae! You're simple-minded if you think we're going to get away with this. Someone is going to look for that old cuss—a buddy, a sibling, his old landlord."

"We'll be dead and gone by the time they find his broken bones." She would have no part of my guilt and fear. I believe she was so relieved to be rid of the old bastard that nothing else mattered.

Two hours later, I stood back to watch her scatter branches and leaves over the fresh dirt. She stomped the fresh grave over and over. The air started to turn cold.

"Rain's comin' tomorra," she said. "I can feel it in my hips. That'll pack down the dirt and make it look like nothin' happened here." She picked her way across the fall leaves not to disturb more of the grounds. When she could go no farther, she chucked the shovel, hoe, and pick into the swamp.

"Hate to throw out good tools," she commented, "but I can't be found with these and they've served their usefulness."

Inside the cab, we sat in silence, our clothes and shoes covered in mud and blood, my soul covered with a black shroud.

"We have to burn our clothes," I told her. I hardly recognized my own voice. "Throw yours in the fireplace tonight. Then take the ashes and get rid of that too. But not on the Angus farm. I'll hide mine at the bottom of the burn barrel tonight and light the slash tomorrow. I've been needin' to do that anyway this fall. Get me to the main road and I'll get out and walk the rest of the way." I pointed to the north. "There's a spring off the main road, about a mile down. Get yourself washed up before you go home and change. Stop at the filling station down there too. Get gassed up and you be gone tonight. I'll clean and bleach the cabin tomorrow."

"I didn't mean to do you this way, Leandra." She hung her head. "I loved you when we was kids. You nevah judged me for being white trash. I tried to pretend what it would be like being your sister and livin' in you fine farmhouse. I was so filled with hate when we left. When the beatin's kept coming, all I could do was hope to escape. Leon was a lot more handsome in his younger days and promised me the moon. Mostly, all I got was bruises and four more mouths to feed."

"I can't ever see you again," I answered. "I have to live with this sin. I'm glad you're free, but now I'm a prisoner."

We drove through the woods that smothered me with their darkness. When we hit the pavement, she stopped. I grabbed a rag from the floor and reached for the door handle to pry it open. Then I rubbed it down hard.

"Wipe this truck down for prints as soon as you can," I advised. I threw her two twenties and a ten from my wallet. "Take it to a carwash. Goodbye, Etta Mae. I'll hold onto our childhood memories and do my best to forget this ever happened."

I didn't even look back. I ran across the road and ducked into the woods, stopping to vomit bitter green bile. My head pounded and my body ached. I supposed fear could do that.

It was nearly dark when I snuck around the back of the barn and worked my way up the front steps. Everyone was in the parlor watching television. In my stocking feet, I carried my shoes in hand, wanting to act as nonchalant as possible. Mamaw was the only one who turned around.

"Well, that was sudden," she commented.

I had no idea what she was talking about and had no interest in making conversation. I started up the stairs to the shower.

"Got some leftovers," Mama said, never taking her eyes off the television.

"You get what you needed, done?" Beth asked.

"Yes," I reassured her. "I'm just gonna take a quick shower before I get a bite to eat."

I located a trash bag to hold my murder clothes. I couldn't get them off me fast enough and threw the plastic sack in the back of my closet. Somehow, I had to sneak my belongings downstairs and out to the burn barrel early tomorrow morning. I scrubbed my skin until it was red and hot. Crying, I crumpled to the shower floor. No amount of hot water could wash this away. Another damn secret to hide in the folds of my soul.

Afterward, I called Nate on the upstairs extension line. It took me ten minutes to convince him I wasn't afraid of Leon Wilson anymore.

"You sure?" he asked repeatedly. "It's no bother for me to stand guard another night."

I wanted to say I watched Leon suffer and die. I threw dirt on his face and helped tamp down the soil that covered him. It would have been a lot faster and easier than explaining my certainty that I was safe, but some things you carry to your own grave.

Chapter 25

Mamaw

W hat a gift we are given with grandparents. Back in my time, extended families were a necessity. Grandparents provided helping hands, knowledge, family history, wisdom, and comfort. I pity those who have never known that kind of love.

🦋 🦋 🦋

Half a week passed, and I was relieved when the time came to drive Mama to Asheville for her chemotherapy. I knew her sickness would follow, but I was grateful to escape what lurked across the road in the woods. The nightmares came hard and fast and, many a night, I wandered through the house like a spirit, seeking rest, but unable to sleep. On those nights, I woke in a cold sweat, sometimes screaming out loud and not knowing why. I swear Leon was haunting me.

"Mama, you ready to leave?"

I stood at the door with our provisions for the day: a car blanket, a jug of water with two cups, crackers, sliced cheese, dried fruit—anything that might settle her stomach. The door pushed open.

"Here I am. Ready to go."

"You alright? You look a little pale."

She slid into her coat. "Oh, you know. Another day of poking and prodding and stealing my blood. I get a little squeamish thinking about it."

"At the end of the day, you'll be halfway through your treatments. We should start planning a celebration for when you finish."

We returned feeling like battle-scarred soldiers. Mama was ready to sleep so I told her I'd make some hot chocolate and bring it upstairs. I was expecting to put on some warm pajamas and slippers and call it a night. Then I pushed through the kitchen door and got a look at Mamaw.

"Mamaw, your face!" I took my hand and placed it alongside her bruised cheekbone. She looked like a prize fighter who had lost the match.

This time she didn't mouth off to me. She appeared dazed, like she didn't know me, sitting in the kitchen chair and hardly moving.

"I found her in Papaw's room," Donny said. "She must have fallen or tripped. The chair was laying on its side and her forehead was bleeding. Beth and I cleaned her up and bandaged the cut. Her house dress was covered with blood."

"I got it soakin' in cold water," Beth continued. "We're afraid to leave her alone."

"Mamaw, what happened?"

She sat very still with a shit-eating smile on her face, the proverbial cat that swallowed the canary.

"She told me she was looking for the nice old man," Donny said. "She missed him. She called him by name."

That officially tore my heart in two.

Her fall marked the beginning of a rapid downward spiral. It was like we were sledding down an icy slope with no way to stop.

"What's happening?" I asked the doctor as he examined her bruised face and arms.

"The dementia is taking over," he replied. "Eventually, her brain function is so diminished, she can't walk, swallow food or water, or manage in any way. The brain runs the show. The good news is she will have very little discomfort."

On the way home from the clinic, she turned to me, lucid as she could be. "Leandra." She paused. She had not called me Leandra in months. "I can't take care of myself anymore."

"I know, Mamaw, but we're here to take care of you."

She didn't reply. She stared out the car window, studying the empty fields. Covered in snow, corn stalk stubs sticking up through the hard ground marked what had once been full of life. She would not be around to help plant the spring garden.

🦋 🦋 🦋

"She won't get out of bed," Beth said. "I tried everything to get her up and dressed, but she said she can't. I'm pretty sure she's messed herself."

"I have some adult diapers in the basement. I bought a box a few weeks back. I have some bed pads too. Let's get her changed."

She fought us like a badger using every bad name she could recall but never used before. At one point, she tried to bite me. Rage can bring out the fight in nearly everyone.

"Mamaw," I struggled to be patient, "we just want to get you clean. You just lie there and let us do the work." Finally, we wore her out and she quit squirming, content to moan, groan, and grunt. "Now, let me get you something to eat."

I swear her eyes looked right through me like she never saw me before. "Get away from me," she hissed. "You hurt me."

"Beth, I'll stay with her. There's some oatmeal on the back of the stove. Heat it up in the microwave with a little butter and sugar. And sprinkle on cinnamon. She'll like that."

The oatmeal stayed in the bowl. She clamped her mouth shut like it was glued that way.

"We gotta move her downstairs to Papaw's old room," Beth said. "If she falls out of bed that's one thing, but if she falls down the stairs, it's all over."

I concurred with Beth, and we immediately started the transition.

Mamaw started her own transition. She ate nothing that day which drove me crazy. Mamaw had never missed a meal in her life. Beth talked her into a chocolate milkshake, one of her favorite treats, but even with that she had to be spoon fed. Trying to get her to drink water or juice only resulted in sputtering and choking.

She caught her breath, and I wiped the spittle from her chin and straightened her bedding.

A big grin crossed her face. "You see them?" she asked me.

"See who, Mamaw?"

"Those blessed angels," she answered. "They come and see me almost every day now." She pointed at the foot of her bed. "Sometimes Zachary is with them." She took a deep breath.

My hand flew over my mouth, and I looked toward the footboard like I was going to see spirits. An act of faith. I wanted to believe her. In reaction, I backed out of the room, blinking back my tears.

Beth sat on the parlor sofa, holding her forehead in her hands. I sat down next to her to stop the shaking.

"I feel so helpless," she said. "There's nothing we can do but comfort her. She has done made up her mind that it's time to pass. I sure am gonna miss her sense of humor."

"She just told me she has angels visiting every day. Sometimes Zachary is with them."

Beth stared into my face while the tears flowed. I pulled her into my shoulder, and we cried together until Mama heard us and joined in, bringing her box of tissues.

Mamaw was moving on. Soon she would be with her Zachary again.

🦋 🦋 🦋

During the week that Mamaw was failing, Mama muddled through her sickness on her own. We had struggled through her hair loss, and I was glad we had those wigs on hand. One day, I looked up and her head was shaved clean. She had moseyed out the back door to meet me as I came back from the barn. It took me a minute to register what I was seeing. I almost dropped my basket of eggs.

"I always wondered what I would look like as one of them military boys." She stroked the bristles on her head. Wordless, I found myself unable to breathe. "Now, Leandra, you knew this was comin'. I was tired of seein' a dead rat in my sink ev'ry mornin'."

She was referring to the pile of hair clinging to her comb.

"Does your head hurt?"

"In fact, it feels much better. Think how cool this'll be in the summer."

"Has Donny seen you?"

"Why, yes he has. He's taking this much better than you. He's already given me one of his prized knit caps to wear around the house. Think how much better my wigs will fit." And that was her conclusion. After all my mama had endured, she finally hit bottom and, like a rubber ball, was bouncing right back up.

It was Mama who suggested we call the pastor for Mamaw. Each day brought further decline. We gave up pushing nourishment on her and she refused to drink. She slept constantly, apparently catching up after a lifetime of hard work.

"You gave your grandparents a good life," Pastor Dave reminded me.

"It was me she gave life to," I replied. "She picked up pieces of me all her life. I never would have made it without her." From her deathbed, Mamaw mumbled to herself and smiled. "I think she's talking to her angels," I told Pastor Dave. "Heaven's getting a good woman."

My foundation, previously cracked, crumbled to pieces without acknowledging I still stood on top. I was losing my biggest fan.

Mamaw passed on a Sunday morning. The four of us surrounded her, taking turns saying our goodbyes. I promised to keep the farm going for as many generations as I could. Beth thanked her for shelter and her entertaining humor. Donny told her she and Grandma Ruby were the two best Mamaw's in the county. And Mama said she wished she had paid more attention to her cooking lessons because nothing had sunk in.

I asked Beth to call the mortuary while I crossed the road and climbed the hill to the butterfly bush to pick out Mamaw's special place. I knew we'd put her next to Papaw, but I had to see it for myself and confirm this was really happening. I did give some thought to Leon, buried in the south woods, turning around to look in his direction. He was an awful man, but he didn't deserve to be in an unmarked grave like he never existed.

I was on the downhill side of forty sliding into fifty, head-first. I had figured out how to keep the farm going but, for sure, we were dirt rich and cash poor. The new clinic plans were underway, and I was certain the next decade or so would mark a critical turn in my life. I wondered what to do with Nate, how long I would have my mama, when Donny would find the woman of his dreams, and who would be here for me when my time came.

Chapter 26

Carousel

W̲hen I was a little girl at the county fairs, I'd usually get to ride the carousel. It starts off real slow but then builds to a dizzying spin. Pretty soon, life becomes blurry and you can't see shapes or forms, just a blur of colors.

There have been times when I felt like my life ran in a big circle. Sometimes it would spin wildly out of control and, at any moment, I expected to lose my grip and go flying off the wheel like a burning star. Other times, it was a lovely ride full of magic and expectations.

🦋 🦋 🦋

Somehow, we managed to time it so the new clinic opened the same weekend as my fiftieth birthday. Chrysalis Free Clinic had become a well-known fixture in our parts, although most folks knew it as the Mountain Grove Health Clinic. The county health clinics continued to expand in North Carolina, eventually serving the younger folks in town, while the old timers chose to find their healing in the home-like atmosphere of our humble clinic. On occasion, I would stand at the window to watch the cars and trucks come and go, knowing that one acre of land was far more productive than the other forty-nine we leased to grow corn or beans.

Once Mamaw passed, Beth chose to move out and move on. Before I knew it, she was engaged to be married. She planned to let me walk her down the aisle and give her away to Tommy. Though a little unusual at that time, I was her family, her mama, and her lifeline. She brought the same to me, as much a daughter as a friend.

Nate hosted my surprise birthday party at his house—the first time I ever had a birthday celebration in my honor. Mama had always been too busy or too drunk, and Mamaw didn't believe in such frivolous things. So, the years rolled by, me paying little mind to how they accumulated. Just like menopause, it kind of snuck up on me.

Halfway through the party, I pulled Nate aside. "Did you invite the entire town?" I asked. "And what do you mean telling everyone to wear black?"

He laughed, proud of his antics. "They're all having a good time, aren't they?"

"You fit into this community like a puzzle piece. I could understand the women taking to you, but the men like you too."

"C'mon, let's gather everyone and open some of your presents."

Country folks can be quite creative. One woman made me a pretty shower cap and threw in a bag of Epson salts for soaking my tired bones. Sandy Davis gave me a pair of knitting needles and promised free lessons to knit myself a pair of warm booties. The most amusing gift was from Abe Hatch, one of our neighboring farmers and my grade-school friend. He handed me an official looking certificate for my burial plot in one of his fields.

"Abe!" I scolded. "You know I'm gonna get buried with all the other Tuckers and Barkers in the family plot."

"I wanted to give you an opportunity to change your mind," he replied straight-faced. "It's getting crowded up on that hill and you could have acres and acres to enjoy all by yourself. You want to be laid to rest in beans or corn? Why, I'd even bring you flowers."

"You old coot!" I shouted. "You're older than me. How you gonna bring me flowers if I expect you to die before me?"

I had been running around these hills for half a century, but those early days seemed like they were only yesterday.

🦋 🦋 🦋

Donny returned from college to attend my birthday party, bringing with him his most recent girlfriend, Kathleen. They had met in an animal husbandry class, and this relationship had lasted the longest during his college career. As Donny planned to work with Jake running the family Angus business, I figured it was a celestial pairing and Kathleen could be here to stay. I was not prepared for any of it, as Nate had chosen to surprise me with the party.

My son brought me another surprise too.

We returned home after the celebration, and Donny pulled me aside.

"Which room should we take?"

I turned to look at Mama and raised an eyebrow. "What do yo mean 'we?'"

Mama just smiled, grinning like she just got a new set of dentures.

"We got plenty of rooms here, Donny. No need for you to bunk up."

"C'mon, Mama, you must know…"

"No, I don't want to know. You keep yourself out of trouble, Donny. You're almost a graduate, both you and Kathleen. You don't need someone else to worry about."

"I understand." He lowered his voice. "But, Mama, I think this is the one. I may ask Kathleen to marry me."

"That's fine, honey. I like her a lot. You can both breed cows 'til the cows come home. Just don't go breeding yourself until you can give her a home and take care of her."

"Mama, Kathleen doesn't need takin' care of. She's tough as nails, ambitious, hard-working. Fact is, she reminds me a lot of you."

"You poor child." I turned to Mama. "I think he's got it bad, wouldn't you say, Grandma? Maybe we're getting another woman in the family."

I gave in to Donny's sleeping arrangements There I was, carrying on with Nate, so who was I to say my son should be any different from me. Anyway, they had their own lessons to learn.

🦋 🦋 🦋

Mama had been cancer free for almost a year. I could see chemotherapy had taken a toll on her general health in the process of saving her life, but she was still with us and holding her own. She packed on some pounds, including a few she didn't need. The doctor thought that was what caused her gallbladder problems. His answer was to remove it, which they did promptly. She appeared to be doing fine.

She still wasn't any good at cooking, so she assigned herself light dusting and folding laundry to make herself useful.

Shortly after her surgery, I noticed a change. She was coming in from the clothesline with the clean sheets, short of breath and winded. That didn't make any sense since the clothesline was three steps from the back steps.

"Gimme that basket," I said, grabbing it from her hands. "Sit down here." I pulled out the kitchen chair. "What's going on?"

"I got the worse back pain I have eva had." She reached around to her right back. "I been puttin' Bengay cream on it, but I must have pulled a muscle when I moved the chest-o-drawers a couple days ago."

"Why'd you do a fool thing like that? I wouldn't call that light dusting."

"I know, it was stupid. It was a struggle to get the dust bunnies out with the duster, so I made a little room and pulled it out from the wall. I've nevah been the same since."

"We're a couple of old women," I reminded her. "If you want furniture moved, we got two young'uns running around here this weekend."

"I wanted it clean for when they visited," she justified. "Like a little homecoming."

"Once they return to school, I'm calling your doctor. It's been a while since you've had a check-up."

"I'm sure it's nothing," she replied. "But suit yourself. I'm gonna go lay down for a while."

The fact that Mama didn't fight me was a good reason for concern.

When I woke in the middle of the night, I wasn't sure what it was that stirred me. I was getting a drink of water when I heard it again and this time there was no mistake. I ran into Mama's room.

"What's wrong?" I blurted out. "That you moaning?"

"My back, Leandra. It hurts so bad I can hardly take a deep breath."

"I'm calling your surgeon. It's on the same side as your gallbladder. Something must be wrong."

In another time, I would have called Doc Sylvan and he would have answered the phone at his house and immediately known what to do with Mama. The first thing I had to do was find the dang doctor. I got the answering service, who called the doctor, who called me back. He was so wigged out with Mama's colorful medical history, he told me to call for an ambulance.

"You're kidding," I replied. "It's three in the morning. Call an ambulance for a pulled muscle?"

"We can't be sure that's what it is. If she's not breathing right, she needs to be seen. I'll call it in, you get her ready."

I went in to wake Donny and Kathleen. "An ambulance is on the way to take Mama to Asheville. You two are on your own."

He bolted up in bed. "What's wrong? Can't we drive her in?"

"She's having severe back pain, can't breathe right. I got no time to talk. I need to get ready. Maybe you can stay with her while I do that."

The ambulance drivers didn't like her color. They were what they call paramedics. The concept was something new to me. They had medical training and put her on oxygen for the ride to the hospital. I was grateful when they gave her something to ease her pain.

That was the longest ride of my life, even with their lights flashing and siren running. Crazy thoughts can run through your mind when you're riding in the back of an ambulance. My memories returned to Mama's last ambulance ride, and me as a scared six year old standing in the driveway with Etta Mae while my newborn baby brother, Mama, and Aunt Addie, drove away in a long white cab to who-knows-where. She survived that ride. I had to believe she would survive this one.

I released my hand from hers just as they whisked her away to the emergency department. They swarmed her like a pack of hornets, pushing me away from the door that separated us, into the room with bright lights and equipment that could ease her pain. She lifted her head and smiled at me, then was gone from sight.

Minutes crept by, turning into hours. The room where I waited in the quiet was suddenly pierced by her painful scream. I knew it was her. I ran to the desk.

"Can't I see my mother?" I begged. "I know that's her screaming. Please!"

The lady was kind but couldn't help me. I moved toward the door. "Ma'am, I'll have to call security if you go in there. I can let the staff know your concerns."

There was no one for me to turn to. I wished Nate were there to hold me. He could make me believe the world was right even if it was caving in on me. I wasn't as strong as I used to be. When we're young, most everyone has the notion we can't be defeated. I slumped in my seat, beaten down.

I must have dozed off. I heard my name being called. When my eyes focused, I saw a man dressed in green standing before me. He sat down next to me. I rubbed my eyes trying to focus. Then I read his face and knew Mama was dead. It was the same look the doctors gave me when my brother Raymond was dying.

"Mrs. Tucker, your mother didn't make it. We believe she had a blood clot. Her pain moved to her chest and her heart stopped beating. We tried to get her back but we couldn't."

"But she had a pulled muscle," I whimpered. "No one dies from that." He stood and grabbed a box of tissues from the counter, handing one to me. He tried to explain. "There may have been more than one clot, or it could have moved to her heart. The only way to tell is if we do an autopsy."

"Cut her open?" It seemed barbaric.

"That's the only way we can be sure."

"No," I shook my head. "No one's cutting into my mama."

"I understand," he said. "Would you like to see her?"

I nodded my agreement. "I didn't say goodbye." I chewed at my upper lip to keep my eyes from running. "I thought I would be taking her home."

"Give us a few minutes, then you can go in to be with her."

I called Donny. "I'm sorry," I apologized. "This isn't a very happy homecoming."

"I'm glad I am here for you, Mama. We'll be there shortly."

I hung up the phone and turned to the woman at the counter.

"I need to make another call. I have to take my mama home."

"Sure," she replied cheerfully. "Has she been discharged? Does she need a wheelchair?"

"I need to call the mortuary," I replied flatly.

It took the wind right out of that poor woman's sail, but I didn't have the strength to put on airs.

🦋 🦋 🦋

Mama was laid to rest to the far right of Daddy's hickory tree. Donny had suggested a space closer to Great Papaw Jonas, but that would have been on top of Autumn's ashes. He had no way of knowing his sister was buried there or why I insisted Mama's grave be moved west, but I made the excuse that it would destroy the flowers I planted twenty-five years ago, and Mama was always taken by the sunsets so that's where she belonged.

We had a small affair. Donny and Kathleen's teachers let them extend their visit to stay for the funeral. One instructor didn't believe him, so I got on the phone and gave him my say-so. I'm not sure the man's hearing was the same when I finished.

In another week's time, I stood by Donny's old pickup to say my goodbyes. Nate stood with me.

"You're gonna be all alone now, Mama, rambling around in this drafty old farm."

I turned toward Nate and grinned. "No, I won't. Nate's moving in to keep me company."

Donny got a big smile on his face. "You two are getting hitched?"

"No, we're not getting married," I answered. "We're gonna live in sin."

He appeared dumbfounded. "Mama! What will the neighbors say? And Pastor Dave?"

"Who cares? I'm just a modern woman keeping up with the trends."

I never bothered to call Roger. I had managed to get my mama back and hold onto her for another eight years. The best years were at the end of her life. I was happy I could make that happen.

That was the first night I had ever been alone in the farmhouse. Family had always kept it alive with laughter, tears, frustrations, new faces, and old tired ones. It was just like a big old carousel. Round and round we go. Some left, some stayed. More would come.

Chapter 27

Comin's and Goin's

Getting old doesn't give you the right to assume the hard part is behind you. No one can say for sure that another lesson isn't around the corner. And, who knows, maybe somewhere in that challenge, a blessing is waiting to appear.

🦋 🦋 🦋

For a bachelor, Nate had more belongings than I ever imagined. Some were left boxed and stored in Papaw's old room. He promised to do his sorting sometime later when he recovered from his move. His landlady was sorry he left, saying he was one of the cleanest men she had every rented to, and "downright handy" when it came to fixing things. Then he was mine and fell into working the farm like he'd done it all his life.

I finally gave into trusting someone again. It was such a load off my shoulders just knowing I didn't have to bear all the family weight. Now and then, Tilly would call up, wanting to go on one of her adventures.

"Hilton Head? What's that?" I asked.

"It's a resort spot on a little island near South Carolina. Maybe we could check out Savannah or Charlestown too. Don't be makin' no excuses, Leandra. I got a new car and you got someone to watch the farm. I'm gettin' the wanderlust."

"You're lookin' for a new boyfriend," I told her. "You can't fool me."

"Then you need to go along to keep me out of trouble. I might get pregnant."

"My God, Tilly! It just never ends with you. I'll talk to Nate. How long you planning to be on this adventure?"

"Not sure, couple of weeks?"

Turns out, Tilly not only found a boyfriend, but she also found a husband. I ended up flying home alone but returned later for their wedding.

Donny kept his word and asked Kathleen to marry him. She was from a small town outside of Raleigh and had a peck of sisters, so there wasn't much for me to do but show up and have a mother-son dance with the groom. It was a tad nicer than my wedding reception in the machine house on the Angus farm. But you always expect your child to do better than you.

Before I knew it, I had a granddaughter. Three more followed, including a set of twins.

For fifteen years, Nate and I watched each other turn grey while making fun of one another's aches and pains. We finally had time for those dance lessons. Like always, I looked forward to apple season and opening up the stand, but the farm animals were long since gone. We let the FFA students bring their animals for the petting zoo to interact with the younger children. All the fields were leased to nearby farms so the land could continue to sustain us. Nate was nearing retirement about the time I was nearing my fifty-year reunion at Perth Amboy High. Sure enough, one day the worrisome invitation arrived.

For a long while, I stood by the mailbox, clutching the afternoon mail and staring at the envelope postmarked from New Jersey. Fifty years had passed since I graduated high school, and I wondered why I would want to dig up those four miserable years. I promised Sal I would go, but now that it was here, it hurt my insides just thinking about it.

Did I really want to know who had survived and, if they had, how they were holding up? What if they had some horrible disease and showed up with an oxygen tank and a wheelchair? I bet I couldn't recognize half of them. I stood there so long holding the mail that Nate came out to find me.

"What's wrong?" he asked. "You look as white as that envelope your holding. Any magazines?"

I inhaled a big gulp of mountain air. "It's my reunion invitation."

"Which one? You going?" He snatched the envelope from my hand. "You haven't even opened it."

I didn't expect Nate to understand my anxiety. That part of my past was safely tucked away, kept in a dark closet, and only brought to light when absolutely necessary.

"It wasn't a good time for me," I explained. "There were struggles. It brings up a lot of buried bones."

"It's a privilege to attend. I bet a lot of your classmates won't be there."

"And that's what's bothering me. I'm not sure I want to know what happened to them. Right now, in my mind, they will always be young and invincible. If I go…" I shook my head.

His voice softened. "Sometimes the past comes looking for us whether we want it or not. That's happened to me more than once. There's always a reason."

"I made a promise," I told him. "Sal made me swear I would go. It seemed like a better idea thirty years ago."

He smiled. "You're not one to break a promise. I'll leave you to open it when you're ready. Just give me my *Popular Mechanics* magazine and I'll be on my way."

I gave myself two days to decide if I would attend. In that time, I could discover any pro or con that might sway my decision one way or the other. Besides, I couldn't go more than two days without sleep.

On the third day, I got up to make coffee, sat down at the kitchen table, and marked my RSVP. Still wearing my robe, I walked out into the chilly morning, shoved the envelope in the mailbox, and flipped up the red flag so the mailman would whisk it away. I wanted that invitation out of sight so I couldn't change my mind. I needed something more than coffee to settle my nerves, but it was a little too early for whiskey.

Nate came downstairs as I came in the house.

"So?" he asked. "What was the decision?"

"I don't know what you're talking about, old man. I went out to get the newspaper."

"Quit lyin', Leandra. You're no good at it."

I tossed the paper on the table. "You're gonna need a new suit," I advised. "Time to show off my prize bull."

"I'm not sure how I feel about you comparing me to a hunk of meat but, yes, I will accompany you to your reunion. Someone has to hold you up while your knees are shaking." He turned me away from my coffee mug and gave me a hard kiss. "It's going to be fine," he reassured me. "Everything happens for a reason."

This one time, I had to believe he was right. He didn't know how close he was to the truth. My greatest fear was that Greg would be there with his wife and that's why Nate would need to hold me up.

With a mess of shopping to get done, I wasn't waiting until the last minute. Beth agreed to shop with us and see that we looked appropriate for those Yankees. She picked out a smart brown suit for Nate and some casual clothes that didn't include Levi's or flannel shirts. I bought a dress in royal blue that went nicely with my peppered hair, and we found a comfortable pair of heels. Nate and I planned to get some serious use out of those dance lessons. We brought up the old suitcases from the cellar.

We hadn't decided how to introduce ourselves at the reunion. I liked the idea that he was my boyfriend, but on more than on occasion he had expressed an interest in becoming my husband.

"We could fake it," I suggested. "Let's just wear wedding bands and no one will be the wiser."

"I can't do that," he whined. "I'll mess it up somewhere and make us look foolish." The disagreement hung in the air for weeks. One day, I had my head stuck in the refrigerator, pulling out things with an offensive smell and questionable identity. I heard him call my name and backed out, shutting the door.

"We need to talk." Nate had never said that to me. We operated on an instinctive basis, usually knowing that something wasn't quite right and getting it out in the open. I had seen a change in him over the last week, but nothing I considered weighty.

Oh God, I thought, *he's sick. Please, God, don't take him from me.* My throat tightened up. "Let's sit down at the table."

He pulled an envelope from his back pocket and removed a letter. "I got this about a week ago."

I couldn't read his voice. Was he ready to cry? I certainly was.

"I have a daughter. I didn't know I had a daughter. She's known for the last ten years. She didn't want to bother me, but now she needs me."

"I don't understand," I replied. "You said you couldn't have children. How can this be?"

"I remember her mother. It was a fling, lasted about a month. She was a little unstable, but then so was I. I guess she got pregnant and never told me. Believe me, Leandra, I didn't know."

"You're sure she's yours?"

"The DNA doesn't lie. You know, they can do that these days. It's a fairly new thing, but it's fully accurate. I called the company that filled out the report and ran my own test. My DNA matched up with hers."

He sucked in air and blew it out like he'd been holding his breath for a week. "Her husband just divorced her. Her mother has been dead for years. She was in a bad car accident a month ago and still can't work. She's behind on the mortgage. I'm all they got. Her daughter is ten years old. My granddaughter goes by Mandy. My daughter's name is Sharla."

I was trying to sort out everything he said but it wasn't coming together. Selfishly, I stated, "You're not going to the reunion."

"I'm packing up some things. I'll be leaving in a couple days."

"Well, Nate, you always did like a good rescue."

I stood up to go back to cleaning the refrigerator. I was furious but wouldn't give him the satisfaction of seeing me like that.

He gently grabbed me and turned me around. "I'm giving up something so precious," he said, hugging me to his chest. "How am I supposed to choose between my daughter and the woman I love? Someone I made my life with?"

My tears soaked the front of his shirt. "Where does she live?"

"California. But I still want you to go to the reunion. They're expecting to see you."

"I'm not making that decision now."

"You know, it might not be permanent. Maybe I just get her off the cliff and then come back."

"You can't make that decision now either." I pulled away. "I need some time alone."

I made my way out to the barn. It was still the best place to go when you needed time to think.

Chapter 28

The Reunion

It's never good to live in the past. I've known several people my age, and every time you talk to them they bring up something that happened decades ago: their ex-husband, a winning touchdown, an unkind word that sticks in their craw, or a love lost to time. Keep living in the past and you'll miss the present, the most precious moment of all.

🦋 🦋 🦋

I couldn't stand by and watch Nate drive out of my life. I was losing him and had convinced myself I would never see him again. If I did, it would be nearly impossible to get back to where we were. I needed him now and until the end, not whenever Sharla was done with him. I hated this girl and I didn't even know her. Mamaw would have told me to be grateful for the time Nate and I did have together. But all I could think of was the time we were missing.

"I'm saying my goodbye from this living room," I told him. "Is that your last box?"

"Yes, the rest is all in the truck."

"Then here is your goodbye kiss." I took the box from his hands and put it on the end table. Then I grabbed his face and kissed him like there was no tomorrow, immediately breaking down in sobs. For certain, he felt bad about choosing her over me. He was crying when he walked out the door. I expect he was anticipating the same outcome.

I made up my mind I was going to stay busy from the time he walked out the door, until I left for the reunion. I told no one about my grief. I didn't need any sympathy or empathy that would start me to crying all over again. Could be something good was waiting in New Jersey—although that would be a first.

Once I landed at LaGuardia Airport, it felt like one big ant hill. Everyone appeared to be in a race headed in different directions. Since the tragedy at the Twin Towers, flying was a complete pain in the ass. I couldn't wait to rent my car and get out of there. It sure felt different from the time I explored New York as a young woman. Back then, I was thrilled to be there and now I couldn't leave fast enough. Without Nate, half of my confidence was missing.

The reunion committee had recommended a hotel in Woodbridge, about five miles from Amboy. I hadn't bothered to find out who else was coming. The whole thing with Nate left me with hollow insides. Still, I had to eat.

I handed the desk clerk my credit card. "How far am I from the Reo Diner?"

"You could walk there," she replied, "but I wouldn't recommend it. At night, it would be safer to catch a cab or drive there yourself. You got a car?"

"Yes, a rental from the airport. I'm in town for my high school reunion. We hung out at the Reo a lot, back in my days."

"Oh yeah, there's a few other people here for the reunion who rented rooms. I can't give out their names, but maybe you'll recognize them."

My heart was breaking. I didn't care about anyone else. I had never felt so alone.

I dropped my bags in my room and drove to the diner. The smells and sounds were all the same. I sat down alone in one of the booths, looking out on the street, thinking about our after-prom dinner at Reo, three couples saying goodbye. I smiled, remembering my fear that my boyfriend Greg was going to park in some remote woods, jump my bones in the back of a sedan, and thereby insure my virginity was a lost cause. That never happened.

"Can I get ya somethin' to drink?" I looked up to see a young waitress standing beside my table. She deposited a menu.

"A cola will be fine."

"Have you been here before? We have some specials tonight."

"Do you still have a meatloaf platter?" I asked. "I need comfort food."

"Shua we do. I'll put in the order and get your drink."

It was like going back in time except for the extra wrinkles and pounds I carried.

I finished my drink and prepared to pay my bill when a woman walked toward me. I didn't pay attention until we made eye contact. She smiled and paused at my table.

"My name is Betty," she said. "You're Leandra, aren't you?"

I covered my mouth to keep from gasping. I wouldn't have recognized her if we bumped bosoms on the street. Her hair was short and grey, her face puckered, lined, and framed by glasses. She had to have put on fifty pounds. The girl who had been so fast, craved older men, and claimed to be a professional at "backseat bingo" was on level ground with the rest of us old ladies.

"Sit down," I offered. "I was just getting ready to leave, but we could catch up over coffee. Last I heard, you were leaving for California."

"Are you alone?" she asked.

"Yes, my boyfriend had a family emergency."

"Well, I don't even have a good excuse for bein' alone. I'm just tired of men."

We had a good laugh while the pretentious walls of high school crumbled. No more competition remained, just reflection. Hours passed. Her high school marriage and pregnancy ended in divorce with husband number one. Then there were two and three. She held up fingers, counting off men.

"I gave up after numba three, certain I didn't have a knack for picking a good man. Hey, what happened to your boyfriend, Greg?"

There would be a lot of questions about Greg. The kids saw us as one of those happily-ever-after couples. "We broke up right after he left for college. His parents hated me. His mother bribed me to break up with him. Said I was the wrong woman for him. I took the bribe. I knew I wouldn't win."

"Think he'll be there tomorrow night?"

"Probably. With his wife. I hear he's in politics now, just like Mommy wanted. Hey, you wanna be my date at the reunion?"

"Shua! We can hold each other up out on the dance floor! 'Course, if some otha hunk comes along, I'll be off and runnin'!"

There was the old Betty I remembered. She just needed a little help coming out. Maybe it was true that high school never ends.

🦋 🦋 🦋

I was so nervous on the day of the dinner-dance, I could hardly think for myself. I decided a walk downtown might distract me. I wanted to kick myself for even coming. All the places I knew and loved looked as worn out as I felt. When I had brought Donny to pick up Mama a decade or so earlier, it was lookin' sad then. How could I expect it to be any different?

I had to see my old home. I couldn't help myself. I was the moth, and my history the flame. I parked my car at the end of the street and started walking over the bridge where the railroad tracks below reminded me of my veiny hands. I wanted to wander down under the bridge where Sal and I first met, but the area had changed, and I was a little uneasy. Either that, or I had changed.

I walked past the house where Roger lived. If he had been out front, I would have stopped, but he wasn't, so I didn't. A new face stared out the window from Mrs. Scuderi's old upstairs apartment. I bet she had been dead for twenty years.

Two dark-haired teenaged girls sat on the porch steps at Sal's house. I stopped. "You live here?" I asked.

They eyed me suspiciously.

"Yeah," one answered.

The other just glared.

"Either of you related to Sal?"

"Who's that?" the dominant one asked.

"Never mind," I answered. "I used to have a friend who lived here, about the time I was your age."

They looked at each other, surprised.

"I know, that was ancient history."

There was one last look at Sal's house, then Penrose Avenue, and I walked back to my car. Driving away, I turned toward the park near the bay. The Tottenville Ferry was long since gone, a relic after a new bridge made it obsolete. I stood on the green grass, remembering the time Greg's mother had bribed me to leave him, how Greg and I took the ferry to Long Island for a "pie," and Evy's majestic house and graduation party.

All of it was gone. I needed to let it go.

Betty was waiting when I arrived at the dance. She waved at me to get my attention. My defenses down, we embraced, and I gave her a kiss on the cheek.

"I'm so glad you found me," I said. "I don't know if I could have done this alone."

"I have seats for us," she bragged. Then she made introductions to the couples at our table, none of which I knew. "You don't have a name tag. C'mon, we gotta get you a label so everyone can find you."

Little by little, conversations started. People could hardly believe I ran a farm in North Carolina. A 1954 yearbook sat on the registration table. I couldn't even remember what I did with mine. I lingered over the book, eyeing the young hopeful faces. In a photo of our student council, Greg's smile reached across the years. I touched it lightly as if to awaken him. My chest burned with regret. I looked up to scan the crowd for his aged face. Nothing.

The music played from our window in time. Couples danced. Someone came up behind me and started speaking close to me.

"I would ask you to dance," he said, and came around to face me, "but my cane would probably trip us up!"

It was Sal. His brother, Father Artie, stood next to him.

I reached out to both of them. "We were late," Artie justified. "I had to absolve him of all his sins before he would come to his own reunion."

"Eh-h. Reunions are for old people, right, Leandra?"

I looked around. "Where is Mrs. Sal?"

Artie and Sal glanced sideways at each other.

"Divorced?" I asked.

"Nah. Deceased. She gave it a good fight. Lung cancer. She liked her cigarettes."

"He was a good nurse," Artie added. "He was with her when she passed."

"I'm glad you two stuck it out," I replied. Referring to the cane, I asked, "Who pushed you down the stairs?"

He didn't answer my question. "Hey, at least it isn't a walker. So how long you in town? Wait, is that guy with you?"

"Nate had a family emergency and couldn't come." I resisted sharing all the details about me and Nate. I wanted closed doors to remain that way. "I'm leaving early tomorrow evening, but I may try to get an earlier flight."

"What for? You got nothin' back at the farm."

"My life's at the farm, Sal. Truth is, I got nothing here."

Betty walked up to us. "Hey, Father, you wanna be my date? Looks like these two got somethin' goin' on."

"My child, you need a drink," Artie said. "Let me buy you one."

We walked to the bar, the four of us old cronies. Betty was having the time of her life, but I was melancholy and feeling like it was time to go home. I was about ready to tell her that when a younger man walked toward me. I stared. Hard. My peripheral vision pulled away from me, blurring like I was in a tunnel.

"Leandra Barker Tucker," he said, staring at my name tag. He didn't have one. "I'm Greg Humes, Jr."

The resemblance was uncanny. Even as I stared at him, I saw Greg's face: the same hair, eyes, lips, and height. He held out an envelope with a card inside. "This is my address. I hope you can meet me tomorrow. Will you still be in town? It was my father's dying wish that we speak."

The air caught in my throat, weighted and heavy. "Greg has passed?"

"It was fast," he said. "Pancreatic cancer. He desperately wanted to attend his reunion, but it became clear he wasn't going to make it."

"I'm so sorry. Greg meant a lot to me." My voice shook. "My plane leaves LaGuardia at five tomorrow evening."

"If you can join me late morning, I'm sure that will give you time to get to the airport. It was the last thing he asked me to do."

I had been terrified to confront Greg and his wife, but this was so unexpected. Greg Jr. left as mysteriously as he had appeared. When he disappeared into the crowd, I looked at the drink in my hand and wondered what was in it.

Betty took hold of my arm. "Holy crap! I saw that too. It was real. I wonder what he wants." I remained silent. "Hey, hon, you look a little pale."

"Let's go sit down," Artie suggested.

We found an empty table. "You both know the story," I began. "His mother paid me to walk away from him. I never spoke to him after that."

"You think he knew?" Sal asked. "What his mother did?"

"I promised to never tell him," I said. "If he knew, someone else spilled it."

I drove back to the hotel in a daze. I expected Nate to call tomorrow and see how the reunion went. I didn't want to talk to him. Losing Greg and then losing John, also Nate, and losing Greg again—it was all too much for one woman to take.

🦋 🦋 🦋

Attempting to sleep was pointless. I cried as much as possible, grieving for a man who was never mine. I fell asleep watching TV, woke around three, took two ibuprofens for my throbbing head, and turned off the television. Still on farm time, I woke again at seven. The life I had known only two weeks ago was turned upside down. I grabbed a cup of coffee from the lobby and started packing. I planned to drive to the airport right after Greg Jr. and I met. I needed my little farm now more than ever.

Greg Humes, Jr. lived in Morganville, fairly close to Perth Amboy. It was an area of sprawling front lawns, long driveways, and two-story homes. I checked the address five times before I drove up to the house. Greg saw me coming and came out to greet me.

In the light of day, I had a better perspective. I was still terrified, but his warmth, like his father's, prevailed. He took both of my hands in his and, in a flash, I was back in the schoolroom when my Greg had done the same, asking me out for our first date.

"I'm delighted you came. Please come in."

I stood in the open foyer, trying not to stare. He shut the door and three dark-haired children came from nowhere in a full gallop, laughing at the top of their lungs.

Greg threw his hands in the air. "Angel, can you come get these guys?" Struggling to speak over them was futile.

"I'm sorry, honey," she replied. "They escaped!"

"Wait," I stopped them. "These are Greg's grandchildren." The mother smiled knowingly. "What are your names?"

"Gregory three!" the youngest and only male shouted. He held up three fingers.

"I'm Patty Ann Humes," the next one said enthusiastically.

"Jillian," the oldest replied, still out of breath.

"And my wife, Angelina," Greg said.

"It is so very nice to meet all of you," I replied.

"Please sit," Angelina said. "I'll bring some coffee and cake to the sitting room so you can talk."

I walked into the spacious room, bright with a wall of windows that looked out on the front lawn. Photo albums lay stacked on the coffee table.

"I don't know where to start," he began. "I just know that Dad wanted you to know the whole story. After Mom and Dad divorced, about twenty years ago, he told me about a woman he used to know who he loved, and still loved until his dying day. You were the one who got away."

Thickness rose up in my chest again. I tried to be objective as I listened to this ancient history. I pictured a bucket of Legos thrown on the floor that I was expected to put together.

"Dad kept a box of letters and mementos he would look over all the time. Toward the end, we moved him into our house. One day after work, I went into his room and asked him about the box sitting on his lap. That's when he told me what my grandmother did to separate you two. He told me he loved my mother, and she was good to him, but he could never forget you. Could be, Aunt Julia told him in one of her fits, how you were paid to leave him."

Tears chased memories down my face. I dug in my purse for a tissue, fully prepared for crying when I got there.

"I never forgave myself," I whimpered. "But I knew she would win. Why not take the money? I couldn't tell him his own mother put a dollar amount on his feelings and what we meant to each other."

I realized what I had just said to him and my hand came to my mouth. "I'm sorry, I don't mean to talk badly about your grandmother."

"She was a witch," Greg replied. "So was Aunt Julia. Julia couldn't stay married to one man more than a year. She was a lot to take and enjoyed her cocktails. Grandmother became a bitter woman surrounded by her money. I don't see Julia anymore."

"Did Greg do well in politics? That had been his family's wish."

"Twice, he ran for office, but his heart wasn't in it. I think he gave up to spite Grandmother when he found out why she divided the two of you." Greg Jr. reached to pick up an envelope from a table nearby. "He asked me for two things toward the end of his life. One, he wanted you to have this letter from him."

He handed me the sealed envelope. I recognized Greg's handwriting.

"Two, he wanted me to go through his photo album with you. He said, even though she isn't in the pictures with me, she was always there in my heart."

I spent the next hour wiping tears off his photo album. I saw his college graduation and when he completed law school. There was his marriage, his first home, the birth of his two children, Greg junior and a little girl. I saw his first office, the holiday celebrations, and watched him age into mid-life. He was divorced by the time the first grandchild came along.

When I gushed over the picture of him holding the baby girl, Greg pulled it off the page and handed it to me.

"Here," he said, "take this. This was the happiest I think I ever saw him. You should have it."

Hours had passed. I still needed to drive to the airport, drop the car, and find my gate. For three days, I had walked back in time, but only then did I come to an understanding of what my life could have been. I had walked through one door and glanced back at another. How lucky was I? Greg and his entire family knew how much we had loved each other.

He saw me to the door though I could hardly speak.

"Come see us any time you are in town," he said. "You're always welcome here."

Chapter 29

When the Pieces Fit

When is an ending a new beginning? Always.

🦋 🦋 🦋

You know how it is when you try to move faster and faster, and all it does is slow you down? When I reached the back steps to the farm, I heard the phone ringing. I dropped my keys twice, fiddling with the lock, while I struggled to get in before the caller gave up in disgust and disconnected. My suitcase remained on the back steps and I ran as fast as an old lady could to grab the receiver. I had yet to give in to one of those new mobile phones. Knowing me, I'd never be able to keep track of where I left it, and I was too old to be running from room to room looking for the dang thing.

I didn't even get to say hello.

"You left without saying goodbye? Is that what you think of me?" It was Sal.

"I'm sorry, I didn't plan to run out on you," I said. "I just got home. I was going to call you tonight."

"I wanted to visit with you." His voice had softened like a sad little boy. "You know, catch up over a plate of pasta and a glass of vino."

"It was a very emotional trip, Sal. I couldn't take much more."

"You see Greg's son? I bet that was tough. You find out what he wanted?"

I paused to collect my emotional strength. "He wanted to share his father's life with me. It was beautiful, Sal. It hurt something awful but it was beautiful. And they all knew what Greg's mother did to us. Greg wrote a letter to me before he died. I'll open it later when I stop crying."

"I miss you, Leandra. We always had such good times. Do you ever think 'o comin' back here to New Jersey? It's really lonely since my wife died."

"We could take turns visiting," I suggested. "You'd love it here in the spring."

"Eh-h, traveling is hard for me now."

I assumed he was referring to his cane.

"What about a cruise?" I asked. "I could take a bus or train to New York, and we could cruise along the East Coast or…"

"Money is tight. Medical care ate up our savings."

"Then pick up a phone." My voice was probably too stern. "You have always talked me off whatever cliff I perched on. We can still help each other."

I told him what I was going through with Nate. Could be, this was Sal's way of reeling me in one more time. Without warning, my heart ached for him, and I regretted not visiting before I left. Once, we had been young kids, surviving on our own and taking care of each other. When had we weakened and become so vulnerable? Is this what aging did to you? Maybe he sensed my emptiness as he reflected on his own.

It was a silly notion, but it strengthened my resolve to carry on. Not saying goodbye reassured me our friendship would never end. Until the day one of us died, I could keep pretending we were always there for each other, hundreds of miles apart but still together. I promised to call every month, measuring out our moments together like spoonfuls of the sweetest sugar. There would never be another Sal.

The next day I was ready to talk to Nate.

"Well, it's about time," he scolded. "Do you know how many times I called? I didn't think I would ever hear your voice again."

"You old fool. It's only been a week."

"Doesn't matter," he said. "I was worried. I knew the reunion was going to be hard."

"It actually turned out very nice." I tried to sound cheerful. "I got to have some closure. Isn't that what the kids say nowadays?"

"Sharla and Mandy want to meet you."

I paused, a little confused. Did he do a complete one-eighty on me? Guess that was all the sympathy he was dishing out for me today. But I wasn't done.

"Nate, I'm not sure I want to get into this. I've had enough heartbreak to last the rest of my life. I can't leave the farm. This is where I feel safe."

"And I can't leave my family."

That was a stab to my heart. I thought I was his family. "Are you happy?" I asked.

"I feel complete. But I did think we'd grow old together. I'm a younger man by a couple of years but I can make an exception for a handsome older woman."

I laughed out loud. "Well, thank you. But how are we going to stay together on opposite sides of the continent?"

"I have a plan," he said. I caught myself rolling my eyes. "But first come out to California and meet my family."

Nate was absolutely joyful. I couldn't take that away from him. The last thing I wanted to do was hop on another plane and visit a bunch of strangers.

Later, I sought counseling from my dear friend. Tilly, always brutally honest, was convinced I had no choice.

"Just go, damnit!" Her shout made me pull the receiver away from my ear. "What harm will it do to get off your old farm for a while? It's getting cold. Livin's a lot better in California."

I agreed I could visit, but the farm would still be home. I noted how married life on the Carolina coast had not softened Tilly in the least.

My sweet daughter-in-law, Kathleen, was a little more restrained. "Mom, quit fussing. You won't know until you try."

🦋 🦋 🦋

Days later, I stood on the airport curb, saying my goodbyes. "I don't like missing Thanksgiving with the family."

Donny didn't bother to respond. "Have a nice time," he said smiling. "We'll call on Thanksgiving Day and you can talk to all the kids."

He left me standing there like a dog without a home. I tucked my tail and went inside the terminal to check my luggage.

For just a moment, I paused to soak in my surroundings. I dropped into a chair, elbow to elbow with a massive crowd of humanity. Some were laughing, babies cried, you could sense the energy and excitement. I felt like I couldn't breathe.

But it was time to put on my shiny face and remember I was going to see the man I loved. I wondered what kind of foods they served for Thanksgiving in Los Angeles. I pictured all our favorite foods, and I had doubts there were any farms near Nate's home. So, who knew where their city food came from? Never mind food, this trip could change my entire life forever. The event at the reunion had weakened me, and sacrificing another man just might send me over the edge. What if I had to spend the rest of my life alone?

They called my seat number and I boarded the plane, still clinging to my sorry-me thoughts. Three hours later the inflight movie ended, and we prepared to land. In minutes, I would meet the family that stole the love of my life. Seems like some part of some family was always laying claim to the man I loved.

Once the plane stopped, the pushing and shoving commenced. I couldn't remember people ever being so rude and impatient and, East or West Coast, it didn't make any difference. The herd shuffled out the chute and into a large lobby, me bringing up the rear.

I saw Nate immediately and he was absolutely glowing. If I didn't know better, I'd say he was pregnant. But maybe that's what it's like when you suddenly discover a grown child. Sharla and her daughter, Mandy, stood with him, little Mandy looking like a miniature of her mama. Both were petite with delicate features and blonde hair. I secretly wondered what Nate's girlfriend had looked like, probably a version of the same in her younger days.

We hugged and I said my how-dos to the blonde pair. Once we all piled into Sharla's car, Mandy tapped me on the arm. I looked down to her tiny face.

"What's your name?" she asked. For a minute I wondered if the child was hard of hearing. "I mean, what should I call you?"

"Back home, all the young'uns call me Miss Lee."

She nodded to show her understanding.

I went back to sightseeing. Seconds later there came another tap on my arm. "What exactly is a yung-um?"

I didn't want to laugh and make her feel foolish, so I went on to explain how "young'un," was a shorter and faster version of "young one," and because Southerners talked so slow, we had to make up for that time somewhere else.

That was followed with a, "Thank you, Miss Lee."

I started to think she was the cutest thing ever and we might be good company for one another.

The car pulled into the driveway of a modest block home, painted sky blue and trimmed in white. It looked like the ocean. I noted Sharla still walked with a limp from the accident.

"It's my ankle that hurts worse than the other injuries," she explained. "It just tires out faster."

Truly she tried her best, but I could see she needed help, so I quit acting like a guest and started acting like a Mamaw. I had mastered my mamaw identity with Donny's babies and imagined it transferred cross-continent.

Turns out, Sharla was a good cook. I didn't have much of an appetite, but what I tasted was delicious. Nate cooked the turkey outside on the barbeque, something we'd never do in North Carolina. Sharla whipped up potatoes, broccoli, and carrots, and Nate requested my special cornbread dressing. We sat together, our blended family, at a beautifully set table with decorations Mandy had made in school. Sharla gave the blessing, nearly bringing me to tears, expressing her gratitude that we were together to share the holiday.

To me, Thanksgiving wasn't the same without cold air warmed by a roaring fire, sweaters, crunchy fall leaves, and the scurrying of animals preparing for winter. I'm not sure I could ever get used to this much sunshine and warm air.

On the last day of my visit, I sat on the back porch—well, they called it a patio—basking in the sun and still amazed that it was nearly seventy degrees in late November. I was avoiding Nate, certain he wasn't coming home with me.

He spied me sitting outside. "There you are," he said, as if he discovered a long-lost treasure. "I'd like to talk to you about my plan."

I put my book down. "You don't have to tell me. I can see how happy you are here. I won't take that away from you."

I hardly believed my own words. I was giving up without a fight.

"That's not what I want to do," he interrupted. He sat down on the cushioned wrought-iron chair next to me and took my hand. "I don't want to leave you, or Sharla, and I don't have to." I decided to shut up and listen to his genius plan. "What if we, you and I, lived in both places? I would buy a small house here and we winter in California. Then, soon as North Carolina defrosts, we spend the summer at the farm. Right after you close the apple stand, we come on back over here. We could make this work, Leandra."

I'll admit, I was a little taken back. His plan almost made sense. Tilly was always saying I never got off the farm. Well, here was my chance.

"You're not saying anything," he stated. "Is that a yes or a no?"

"Do I have to fly back and forth?" I was thinking how much I hated those planes.

"Don't see why. We could drive and see some of the country."

"I've been thinking about getting a dog."

"So, get a dog. The dog will go with us. Mandy loves animals."

For the time being, I was plumb out of excuses. "I'll think about it. I need to talk to Donny and Kathleen."

"There's no hurry. Even if you want to do it in a year or two, it's an open invitation."

He never asked about the reunion. I suppose he had moved on to something else and a new world had opened up. Maybe that was something I needed to do too.

🦋 🦋 🦋

Back home, I told Donny and Kathleen about Nate's suggestion. My oldest grandchild interrupted. "You mean you're movin', Grandma? You can't leave us."

"I could never leave you, Blake. Come here." I wrapped my arms around him, remembering how reassuring it was when Mamaw did the same for me. "I would just take long vacations."

"Can I come?" the littlest asked. "I've never seen Calforna."

Donny held up his hand to halt the feedback. "I can't get a word in edgewise, Mama, but if it makes a difference, I think it would work."

Kathleen hadn't said a thing.

"What do you think, Kathleen?"

She smiled and I saw tears in her eyes. "I'm so happy for you, Mom. It sounds like a perfect life."

Chapter 30

God's Moment

The years have caught up with me. Today I feel like a ragged butterfly, tattered wings, worn out from too much living. I am no different than one of God's creatures who has journeyed a lifetime to reach her destination. I never got my God-moment, my private miracle, but I haven't given up hope. Maybe it will come soon.

🦋 🦋 🦋

I finally accepted Nate's offer to spend our winters on the West Coast. I got to see more of the ocean than I ever did in New Jersey. Mandy became another granddaughter, and Sharla, bless her heart, found a good man to love her. If it hadn't been for Nate, I'm not sure she would have made it over the hump to a better life.

We traveled for years until one morning when I woke to find Nate had passed peacefully in his sleep, just like old Archie. His soul deserved that kindness. Donny helped me find a place for him near the butterfly bush where I planned to join him later.

Decades passed before I opened Greg's letter. Every year I pulled it out and held it in my hands, not finding the courage to open it. I was afraid I'd break the feel-good spell I had known when I spent the afternoon with Greg's son. When I finally peeled open the envelope, now tattered and dog-eared, I felt like I was reaching out to the dead. I imagined him sitting on a heavenly bench somewhere, surrounded by misty clouds, pleased that I was reading his final words.

> *My dear Leandra,*
>
> *I am so happy you are getting to read my letter. I never knew if you read the other ones I sent when you were forced to break up with me. Although the years have gone by, you never stopped being the great love of my life.*

I know what my mother did to you. I know she broke our hearts. We should have been together. I pray someday we will.

Your love forever, Greg

Still clutching his letter to my chest, I rested on my daybed trying to catch my breath. Breathing was difficult with a broken heart. It had patched itself, but the scar was still visible.

I gazed out the window while the red maple tree danced in the wind. The same summer breeze reached in to cool my bedroom while the steady tick, tick, tick of my old brass clock marked the passing seconds.

My eyes grew heavy and I closed them easily. In my mind, I pictured myself climbing the hill to the butterfly bush. Others would carry me to join my kin. I would rest with my daddy's spirit and the two men who had loved me in spite of my wily ways. There were the crushed bones of Mama, brother Ray, my daughter Autumn's ashes, Mamaw, Papaw, Aunt Addie, and my great Mamaw and Papaw who made the land our home. I had wanted to do something great with my life, but I never did. Still, I would leave behind my only son and a mess of grandkids. At least I saved the Barker farm for two more generations. I had given all I could to the land. Now, it was her turn to give to me.

I held far too many secrets in my heart: my sweet baby girl; a lost love; and a lost soul, unmarked for eternity, buried deep in the woods. Some of my secrets I had been forced to swallow whole. That was a choice I made, yet now, they could be set free. And, to my family, if I could say something to them upon my death, it would be one thing: remember us. Remember what the family stood for, the love we gave to the land, and the love it gave to us.

I wondered if my purposefulness would mean nothing and if, in a generation, I would not even be a memory. I had to believe it wasn't so. That somehow, I would leave behind a special skill I had taught an Appalachian child, a story about the old farm and how we completed our days, or a recipe that filled a home with remembering.

Remnants of me were all over these hills. One summer, I had gathered wildflower seeds from the meadow and scattered them up on the ridge. To this day, wildflowers still bloom up there. I thought about my initials carved into the trunk of that old hemlock tree by the barn. What remained of my treehouse was now home to some critters in the woods. Yes, I would remain behind.

Perhaps my soul will merge with that old butterfly bush and nourish the roots it drives into the land. Maybe that was the butterfly's secret. To arrive without expectations, make the world beautiful, pass life to the next generation, and leave behind body and soul. Each year, we will bloom again and again, forever a part of these mountains that will never die.

Epilogue

Lee's Secrets

D ad, we think we found something."

Logan and Noah struggled to move a large carboard box up and out of the narrow basement staircase to the parlor where Donny sat on the sofa.

"Kathleen, I'm overwhelmed. Do you know there's enough canning jars in the basement to fill a grocery store?"

Kathleen laughed out loud. "They're probably from three generations of Mamaws. That shouldn't be a surprise."

The boys dropped the box at Donny's feet. It made a loud thud and they rubbed their dusty hands on their jeans. Without another word, Donny opened the box. The first thing they saw were two shoe boxes. Donny handed one to Kathleen marked, "Letters." He passed the other one to the twins. In the bottom of the brittle box, lay a thick stack of yellowing papers, typed and bound with string.

"That has to be her life's story," Donny said, eyeing the papers. "'Find the box. It will tell my story.' Those were her exact words."

"Why don't I get a grandma box to look through?" Andrea complained in a sad voice. She stomped her foot. "Daddy, that's not fair."

Donny's worries passed over the little girl.

"Come help me, Andrea," Kathleen said. "Let's look at these letters." Kathleen read the outside of the envelopes. "These are all from the 1940s, Andrea. I bet these are letters from your great grandfather when he was in WWII. Here's a telegram. This is how they talked to each other back then."

"They didn't have phones, Mommy?"

"Probably all they had was a radio. No television, computers, tablets…"

"Wha'd the heck they do all day?" Noah asked, digging through the box. He carefully displayed his discoveries on the end table.

Kathleen handed the telegram to Donny. "This is when he was shot down."

Donny took the brittle telegram from her hand, reading the ugly words. He tried to imagine how his grandmother must have felt that day.

"This her?" Logan asked. He handed his father a faded picture of a young girl holding a baby.

"Looks like her younger self," Donny said. "I don't know whose baby that is. It's dated Autumn 1960. Must have been taken in the fall. Couldn't have been hers, she wasn't even married then."

"Here's another baby picture with an old man," Noah said. "It says, 'Grandpa Greg.' Who's that? We didn't have a grandpa named Greg."

"Daddy, what is this?" Andrea shook an empty snow globe.

He took it from her hand.

"Now why would she save this?" he asked out loud. "Normally it has water in it, Andrea. See the sparkles? They would have floated in the water around the statue. This gold man is named Prometheus. He's the mythical god of fire. That's a famous statue in New York."

"When did she go to New York?" Kathleen asked. "Did she go with Nate? She was happy with Nate, wasn't she?"

"I always felt like something was missing," Donny said. "Sometimes I'd catch her looking off in the distance, wiping tears off her face." He shook his head. "She accomplished so much. She was the first family member to graduate college. She started that free clinic and kept the farm in the family. And that was without my dad. She lost him early in her life. Same with her own father. Maybe that's where she hid the heartbreak."

Donny returned to the box. He untied the ream, scanned the first page, then stared at the historical papers in his hands. "Good God. My mama wrote down her whole life's story."

"Cool! Can I read it?" Andrea asked.

Kathleen tousled Andrea's hair. "Dad gets first dibs, but you can read it next, my little bookworm."

Donny retied the strings, holding the papers in his lap, then pulled the last item from the box. A notecard came out of its gold envelope, and he read a chain of numbers.

"This is a map position, a longitude and latitude." He grabbed his cell phone and searched Google Maps. "I'll be. It's the woods across the street by that crumbled homestead. Her childhood friend lived there. I bet those kids buried something in the woods. Could be we'll learn the secret from her story."

Questions for Discussion

1. Prior to President Johnson's health care reform in the 1960s, many rural Appalachian families relied on folk medicine and spiritual practices for healing. Begin a discussion on some of these practices. Hint: Research the *Foxfire* books.

2. Why were so many college campuses the location of protests against the Vietnam war?

3. Name some of the historical events in the United States that led to the expansion of female operated farms. How do the statistics of today compare to the 1970s?

4. What is green tobacco sickness, who is most at risk, and how are symptoms managed?

5. Who was your favorite female/male character and why?

6. How have corporate farms influenced family farms today?

7. Did Leandra have a favorite Southern quote that spoke to you, and would you use it today?

8. What were some of the emotional responses generated by the media during the civil rights protests? Were they positive or negative?

9. Who or what initiated the development of the Appalachian Trail?

10. Did you or would you ever attend your 50th high school reunion and why or why not?

11. Leandra believes she has discovered the butterflies' secret to a fulfilling life. Do you agree with her theory?

12. Butterflies are often thought of as representing the cycle of life. Why is this?

Acknowledgments

There are so many wonderful people that bring an author's story to life. I am blessed to have such a talented team.

Andrea Davis and Jan Hanson, once again, thank you my two fellow beta readers, my judge and jury, that stuck with me to the epilogue. I will always respect your guidance.

Ann Videan, my editor for both books in the *Butterfly Series*, you corrected my words with knowledge and grace.

Traci Osborn, I hear you call your artwork therapeutic, but to me it's divine creation. Both my book covers are stunning.

Amy Albright, your graphic designs bring out my books' personality and entice my readers to take a chance on me. Thank you for that.

Thea Rademacher, my publisher and friend for life, you wrapped it up and tied it with a ribbon to share with the world. Past and present, you leave me speechless. Often.

To Joe Kennedy, the man that promised to live with me to the end of our days, not knowing an author would emerge someday, thank you for making space for that in our lives.

About the Author

Josephine DeFalco loves to tell a good tale. With three adult children and their children, a multitude of pets and wild things in her life, she finds ample material for her stories. As a registered dietitian, she worked in public health and wrote for *Arizona Woman Magazine* for ten years, before returning to college to become a registered nurse and EMT. She will rescue anything with fur, feathers, or skin as long as it promises not to bite.

Jo divides her time between an urban farm in Arizona and a rural farm in Wisconsin, growing much of the food her family eats. She has written two books on food preservation which support her drive to teach others food gardening, health, nutrition, and self-sufficiency.

Born and raised in Arizona, the desert Southwest inspired her first historical novel, *The Nightbird's Song*, reflecting on the hardships of the early desert settlers. Her latest novels, *The Butterfly Bush*, and *The Butterfly's Secret*, examine the sacrifice of the Appalachian people and a time when their way of life was destined to change forever.

Her Facebook page, BestLittleOrganicFarm, is filled with photos, stories, and information on gardening. Jo's website and author page can be found at JosephineDeFalco.com.

Printed in Dunstable, United Kingdom